Under the Sign
of Venus

Under the Sign of Venus

ENTHRALLED

MYSTIQUE

NO GENTLE POSSESSION

THREE COMPLETE NOVELS BY

Helen Mittermeyer

SMITHMARK

This edition published in 1993 by SMITHMARK Publishers, Inc., 16 East 32nd Street, New York, NY 10016.

SMITHMARK books are available for bulk purchase for sales promotion and premium use. For details write or call the manager of special sales, SMITHMARK Publishers, Inc., 16 East 32nd Street, New York, NY 10016; (212) 532-6600.

Library of Congress Cataloging-in-Publication Data

Mittermeyer, Helen.
    Under the sign of Venus : three complete novels / by Helen Mittermeyer.
        p.   cm.
    Contents: Enthralled—Mystique—No gentle possession.
    ISBN 0-8317-9066-0 : $9.98
    1. Man-woman relationships—Fiction.   2. Love stories, American.
I. Title.
PS3563.I86A6   1993
813'.54—dc20   93-2064
                                                                    CIP

Printed in the United States of America

10   9   8   7   6   5   4   3   2   1

*This collection is dedicated to women everywhere,
who are a never ending source of joy,
amazement, and pride to me.*

Introduction

―――――――――❀―――――――――

Dear Readers,

This is an exciting time for me. I am returning some of my treasures to you. Why should that be exciting? Easy. Everything I've written and published from Day One is as valid and meaningful to me now as it was then. And I'm delighted that my works are coming into your homes again. Even after having six million books on the market throughout the world, the golden joy has not dwindled to dross. I find myself more eager, more enthusiastic with each book.

I was born under the sign of Venus, Goddess of Love. I don't know if that led me to read, then write romances, but I can't discount my placement in Fate's plan. Love is the great equalizer, the compassion giver, the onset of understanding. How could I possibly count it out of my life!

From the moment I wrote my first romance novel, I knew I was doing what I'd be happy with, what I was fashioned to do, and I've never changed my mind about that. And when I turn to other patterns of writing, I know that my experience with romance writing will give me the discipline, the stamina, and the writing tools I'll need.

Writing about women—their lives, relationships, pleasures, and pains—is an ongoing challenge, and to see my books come to life again gives me great joy and a satisfaction hard to equal. I wish you the same joy in reading these books as I have had in writing them, and I hope the associations and relationships I've always had with you, my readers, will continue to grow and deepen in the days ahead.

I also wish you joy in living, and in giving—love, I'm sure, is the only map you'll need.

Sincerely,

Helen M. Mittermeyer

Enthralled

- 1 -

TEEL LAY FACE-DOWN on the hot, moist earth. Ants and other insects began to crawl over her cheeks, stinging her, and she knew she had to move, though her body screamed in protest. Sweat dribbled into her burning eyes. The buzz of flies was loud in the fetid heat. Groaning, she pushed herself to a sitting position. Cross-legged, swiping at the flies that swarmed over her the moment she was still, she tried to take stock of her situation. She refused to accept the thought that she could, indeed, be utterly lost.

Somehow she had to retrace her steps to the mission and Aunt Tessa. For the hundredth time she cursed the folly of having given in to her aunt's pleas and journeyed with her to the mission outpost in Central America that was run by Aunt Tessa's friend, Sister Mary Mark. When the formidable sister had informed them that they should

3

don nuns' habits as a safety precaution against the unwanted advances of patrolling soldiers, she should have insisted that they leave at once.

Teel's forehead burned with fever. Her lips were cracked and sore from lack of water. Still, she was determined to get herself out of this—this stupid situation.

She had only gone a short distance outside the mission area, in order to give Aunt Tessa a chance to talk alone with her old school friend. She had not meant to wander beyond the perimeter. Now she cursed her stupidity and the density of the jungle that had made her take a wrong turn, away from the mission instead of back toward it.

She stood up slowly, swaying in the heat. "You're going to get out of here, Teel Barrett," she said aloud, the sound of her hoarse voice startling some birds into flight. She blinked at an orange and blue parrot and wished she had its vantage point. She slapped at a mosquito on her cheek. "I never thought I would find a nun's habit useful" she muttered, "but it sure is a buffer against you." She blinked at the dead mosquito in her hand, then took her bearings as best she could and began walking.

An hour later she knew she was weakening from the effects of the stifling heat. She no longer spoke out loud to herself. It took too much energy.

She squinted up through the thick curtain of trees to the cloudless blue sky, listened to the cawing and squalling of the jungle creatures, and wondered if she had really heard the sound of the surf or if it was just another jungle noise.

Barely able to push the light branches aside, Teel staggered through the underbrush toward the sound, then stared mouth agape at the sand and sea in front of her. The Pacific Ocean! It had to be the Pacific. She knew that the beaches on the Pacific side of Central America often consisted of black sand like this one. She felt a shaky sense of triumph. She didn't know exactly where she was, but she did know she was facing the Pacific Ocean. She reeled out onto the beach, trying to shade her eyes from the blinding sun, seeing nothing but beach and ocean shimmering under its flaming disc. Then, suddenly overcome by heat and fatigue, she fell forward on her face and slept.

When she awoke it was dark and she was cold, the cold that comes to anyone who has had too much exposure to the sun. She shivered and looked around her, hungry and frightened.

Sometime later she saw lights moving on the water and stared at them in disbelief. "You're hallucinating, Teel," she told herself through cracked lips. But a small, motorized dinghy came ashore. She watched two men and a woman beach the craft and shine a flashlight across the sand in a great arc. "You're seeing things, Teel," she said firmly, not bothering to lower her voice because she knew figments of her own imagination would pay no attention to her.

But the man holding the flashlight jerked his head up and said, "Hey, I heard a voice. We better get out of here. Chazz will be madder than hell because we took the dinghy. He said the repairs would be finished in an hour and we were to stay on board." He swung the flashlight across the beach again, but the beam of light kept missing Teel.

"Come on, stop it, Zack," the woman said in a high, wheedling tone to the other man, who was nuzzling her. "I don't want Chazz mad at me. You know how he gets."

"Damn you, Elise, I thought you wanted a little beach party: a fire, a little wine..." The man called Zack lowered his voice to a seductive hiss as he moved closer to the woman.

Teel watched them, her arms and legs like lead, her voice a dry croak in her parched throat. She had to get their attention. They were her only hope.

"I don't want to stay now," Elise continued. "Jim said he heard someone talking. What if we run into revolutionaries?" She shuddered, her exaggerated shadow quivering in the beam of the flashlight.

"He didn't hear anything," Zack protested.

Just then a shout reached them from the direction of the lights on the water. Teel couldn't understand the words, but the tone was angry. She watched the three people scramble toward the dinghy. They were leaving her! Desperate, she forced herself up from her knees. Her body trembled with the effort. Slowly, erratically, using every last vestige of strength and will she had left, she shambled forward, watching in mute horror as they pushed the dinghy into the water. The woman was already in the boat. Then one of the men jumped aboard. As the second man prepared to follow, Teel's feet splashed into the water. The last man let out a startled shout, but she didn't stop. She headed straight for the dinghy.

"Who the hell are you?" the man called Zack demanded from his vantage point at the motor. "Where did you come from?"

Without answering, Teel just fell forward, clutching the gunwales. She heard a woman's shriek, a shouted oath, and then blackness closed over her head.

Teel awoke to turquoise. She wasn't surprised, but she hadn't expected the afterlife to be turquoise. Long ago she had stopped practicing the religion that was so sustaining to her aunt and her friends, but Teel had retained the idea of an afterlife. She had just never thought it would be turquoise.

"So you're awake." A man's face loomed over hers, with strong planes and amber eyes. Lion's eyes, Teel mused, thinking he looked rather stern for an angel. Did angels have firm mouths that appeared to have been whittled and cheeks faintly shadowed with a beard? Angels didn't have coal black hair, did they? Perhaps this was a devil, Teel thought, too tired to really care.

"Aren't you going to speak?" the voice asked.

"No." The one word made her dry lips feel as if they'd been split. She had no idea where her voice had come from, but it was like sandpaper on raw wood.

"Who are you?" the man asked her, leaning closer.

Teel flinched and tried to pull the sheet over her head, but her hands wouldn't do her bidding.

Irritation flashed across the man's austere features. "Listen, I have to know who you are."

Teel closed her eyes to make him disappear. Sleep came as a welcome gift.

She woke again to the same turquoise, but this time she was able to turn her head and see that she was in a bedroom. It hurt to move, but she forced herself to look as far as she was able. She was incapable of lifting herself but realized she was on a boat of some kind. A large window revealed a patch of blue sky, and she felt the motion of the ship under her body even though she could not see the water from where she lay.

The door opened, and she turned her eyes to see the man who'd spoken to her earlier—the one she thought of as the devil—and another man, who looked like a leprechaun and carried a tray with covered dishes. They stared down at her for a long time.

Every instinct told Teel to run, but she was thoroughly immobile. Every nerve ending stood at full alert. The hair on her arms prickled like tiny antennae receiving danger signals.

The larger man bent toward her and lifted her easily. All at once Teel realized that she was naked under the silk sheets. Her fingers moved futilely, unable to grasp the slipping material.

The devil held the sheet around her and lowered her to a cluster of pillows the other man had provided. "Darby, get her that robe from Clare's cabin, the short one with the long sleeves." He grinned at the smaller man, making dimples form on either side of his mouth.

The devil has dimples, Teel thought as she lay back against the pillows, completely exhausted. Her skin felt on fire from insect bites and the burning sun. Her face felt swollen and dry. She wanted to immerse herself in cold, cold milk.

"She'll have my eyes if I touch her precious clothes," the smaller man protested, frowning at Satan, his bushy brows bobbing up and down.

Satan's smile disappeared into granite. His teeth snapped together. "Tell her I want that jacket, and I don't want to have to come after it." He turned to Teel, then back to the older man, who was crossing to the cabin door. "And bring some lotion. I want good stuff. These dames spend enough of my money for the best, so I know there's some on board. I want it."

Teel struggled to shout that she didn't want the little man to leave, but all that came out was a groan.

"All right, darling, let's see if you can take some of this cold soup." Satan lifted her, his arm cradling her, but still she moaned. "This is cold cucumber soup, and my chef tells me it's just the thing for someone suffering from heat exposure such as yours."

Teel kept her eyes on him as he edged the spoon into her mouth and let the creamy mixture slide down her throat. The cooling sensation was immediate. So was hunger. She was eager for the second spoonful and the next and the next. Then she was tired. She closed her eyes and let sleep take her.

Teel realized vaguely that she slept off and on for a long time. In brief moments of lucidity she was aware that her swollen body was gradually returning to normal, the itching was disappearing, her appetite had increased, and her general soreness was beginning to fade. Strength returned slowly to her limbs, and she took more note of her surroundings.

The devil didn't return. After a doctor had examined her, she'd been left in the able care of the man called Darby. At last she felt strong enough to talk to him. "Darby, what happened to the other man?"

His mouth agape, Darby stared at her. "So you can talk, can you? For days all you've said is 'no'." He smiled at her, his sandy hair quivering on his head like tufts of wild grass. "That other man, as you call him, is gambling with his guests on the island of Alidad, where we've dropped anchor for a time. It was lucky for you we had engine trouble. What were you doing on that beach, anyway?"

Teel told him of losing her way in the jungle while on a visit to the mission in the jungle.

Darby shook his head and again commented on her good luck. "We didn't originally intend to land off the coast. Too much trouble in those banana republics. Chazz usually gives them a wide berth. But,"—he shrugged his thin shoulders—"bilge pumps aren't usually temperamental; so we put in for repairs."

His elfin grin made Teel smile. "You scared the bejabbers out o' those low-class friends of Chazz's," he went on. "It's a wonder they didn't throw you into the ocean. You should have heard them excusing themselves for bringin' you. I don't know why Chazz keeps them around—them and the rest of his 'guests'. They're not the kind of people he has business dealings with, I tell you." He pursed his thin lips as he set a tray on her knees with the ritual tonic and tea he usually gave her in the evening. The biscuits were light and flaky and running with butter.

"I often think he hangs with that bunch to somehow make up for his success. Ya see, Chazz was very poor when he was growing up. He worked his way through college, then began his own parcel service. From that he went to shipping, and now he has a fleet of planes, and—"

Teel smiled, feeling both mentally and physically comfortable for the first time. She was getting better. "I know about Chazz Herman," she said. "I read that article in *World* magazine about how he flew the flood relief plane into a remote area of the jungle after a volcano erupted. He plays polo with European royalty"—Teel ticked the facts off on her fingers—"he's a self-made millionaire, who rose from the slums of New York to become a member of the jet set . . ."

Darby wrinkled his nose. "Whatever that is!" He threw his thumb over his shoulder in the direction of what Teel surmised must be the guests' sleeping quarters. "Chazz is a good man," Darby explained, "but sometimes he crews around with the likes o' them." Darby looked at the glass Teel was holding, his bushy eyebrows quivering comically. "Drink all your tonic now. Tomorrow you're to go up on deck and get some air. But I won't let you go if you don't drink your tonic."

Teel made a face at him and drank the licorice-colored brew.

He smiled at her, set the tray on a table, and returned to sit on a chair next to her bed. "Now are you going to tell Darby who you are, Sister? We don't even know your name, and you haven't been strong enough for us to question you."

Teel stared at Darby in surprise. He'd called her "Sister." But of course! She had come aboard the *Deirdre*, as Darby called the yacht, wearing the torn habit. She opened her mouth to tell Darby she wasn't a nun when a warning sounded in her brain. It might be safer if she pretended to be a nun until she was safely back home in Selby, New York. After all, she really didn't know these people, and what she had read about Chazz Herman—he'd been written up in the tabloids as well as in *World* magazine—was not encouraging. She had refrained from mentioning his shadier reputation to Darby, even though she was sure the little man was aware of his employer's propensity for well-developed blondes. Even if half of what the yellow press said about Chazz Herman were true, he was an unmitigated and unrepentant womanizer. He went out with, and undoubtedly slept with, some of the world's most sophisticated women, and some of the most common. He dined with royalty and high-priced call girls, making little or no distinction between the two. From the many takeovers he had successfully manipulated, Teel knew he was a dangerous man in his business dealings. From the many scandal sheets that gave extensive and colorful coverage of his escapades with women—including his often tearful, usually indiscreet breakups with them—she knew he was ruthless in his personal life as well. She had read too much about Chazz Herman to trust him and wasn't ready to risk becoming his next sexual coup.

"Aren't you going to tell me your name?" Darby quizzed, his pale eyes gentle on her.

Teel swallowed in a throat that was desert dry. "I'm Terese Ellen Barrett, from New York."

"New York is a big place." Darby grinned at her. "And is your convent in Manhattan?"

"I'm in charge of a school for exceptional children in Selby, New York, about sixty miles northwest of the city," Teel told him truthfully. She had no intention of revealing that she was a *lay* director of the Mary Dempsey School for Exceptional Children, that she had once been a model during a summer break from college, or that she had once been seduced by a man named Ben Windom, a New York advertising executive. She shook her head, clearing it of dark memories.

"Is this a school for smart ones, then?" Darby leaned back in his chair and tapped a round-bowled pipe on the sole of his sneaker, catching the ashes in an ashtray he held under it.

Teel smiled. "No. Our children are mentally retarded and physically handicapped. For them it is a vocational school, a school in which they learn to read and write, understand signs and count money, and generally how to survive in a world designed for people of much higher intellectual ability. We deal with children up to the age of fifteen. A great number of our pupils are then sent on to a more advanced training school."

Darby stared at her wide-eyed. "And did you train for this, Sister, this special work?"

"Oh, yes. I did my undergraduate work at Nazareth College in Rochester, New York. I also took classes during the summer at Columbia University. I—er—I also worked there to help support myself. I did graduate work at Columbia in order to get my master's. Soon now I'll be finishing my doctoral dissertation," Teel concluded, her voice a whisper.

"Oh, it's 'doctor,' is it?" Darby's eyebrows danced up and down. "Well, I'm proud to know you, doctor."

"I'm not a doctor yet, but I will be in less than a year."

"Your parents must be proud of you," Darby said, obviously fishing for more information.

Teel smiled at him. "My parents are dead. They were killed in that plane accident in Washington a few years back." Teel felt the smile slip off her face. "My Aunt Tessa, who traveled with me to the mission, is my only relative now." Teel swallowed. "I must let her know that I'm all right. She'll be so worried."

"Shhh, now. Don't upset yourself," Darby soothed her.

"But . . . but she doesn't know where I am," Teel protested, feeling a weakness assail her. "I . . . I don't know if she's all right. I'm worried about her."

"There, there." Darby patted her shoulder awkwardly. "I realize you've been worrying. When you were so feverish with sun sickness you called out to her many times. A number of nights Chazz held you in his arms while you cried."

"What?" Tell rubbed her eyes and sat up quickly, experiencing a momentary dizziness that soon dissipated.

Darby looked surprised. "Don't you remember that either? Sure. Chazz heard you calling out. You're closer to his suite than any of the other rooms. He thought you would be disturbed less often here. The Turquoise Cabin is usually for, well . . ."

"His women," Teel supplied, feeling red run up her cheeks. "Well, I'm certainly well enough to be moved into another cabin now," she said coolly.

"Don't be silly, girl. This is the most comfortable cabin of them all except for Chazz's own suite." Darby rose to his feet. "You won't be moving, but you will be going to sleep."

"I'm not tired, really. Stay a bit longer."

"No." Darby grinned. "Chazz would kill me if you took a turn for the worse. He watches over you like a mother hen." Darby frowned, making his grizzled face look like a troll's. "But I'd like it better if he quit drinking and carousing with that bunch. Seems to me he's been drinking even more lately." Darby left the cabin, shaking his head.

Teel lay quite still thinking, wishing she could get the owner of the *Deirdre* off her mind. He was the kind of man she detested. Her one experience with Ben Windom had soured her on the sophisticated, womanizing type, and that was Chazz Herman in spades. Of course there were some differences between the two men. Ben Windom was a product of old money, the best schools, the most prestigious clubs. He traveled in exalted circles, yet Teel considered him an inferior person, more lacking in integrity than anyone else she had ever met.

She was sure Chazz Herman had a similar lack of morals. From now on she would try to avoid that class of men, she told her pillow, her eyes heavy with sleep.

A noise woke her hours later and she sensed immediately that it was very late. The bumping sound came again, and she sighed. Chazz Herman and his guests were staggering around outside her cabin, probably on their way to bed. Someone was saying, "Shush," but they made little attempt to lower their voices.

"Aw come on, Chazz honey, I can get you in the mood," came a woman's slurred voice. "I know you don't like us to come to your cabin, sooooo why not come to mine?" The thick voice had a familiar ring to Teel, who was suddenly wide awake as she strained to hear the conversation beyond her closed door.

"Dammit, Elise, I've had enough. Now go to bed or get off the Deirdre." Chazz's voice wasn't as slurred as Elise's, but he had obviously been drinking too. To Teel's senstitive ears he sounded like someone picking a fight.

She let her pent-up breath out in a *whush* when she heard Elise's retreating staccato steps. Her muttered expletives grew fainter and fainter.

Teel gasped as someone suddenly opened her cabin door. She slid down further under the silk sheets and closed her eyes, feigning sleep. Then she sensed Chazz standing over her, staring down at her, and knew his lion's eyes were fixed on her as though she were prey. They seemed to have the power to see through her subterfuge, to X-ray and catalogue her thoughts. Just when she was sure he would say something, or perhaps pull the sheet from her naked body, he turned and left the room. She heard a thud and a mumbled curse. He must have stumbled against the doorjamb.

For long moments she didn't move. Then, the sound of the lapping of the water on the hull that came through the large, open porthole was muffled by sounds from the larger cabin next to Teel's. Chazz seemed to prowl the cabin for hours, muttering to himself and slamming into furniture. Finally he fell quiet. For a long time the only sounds Teel heard were the creaking of the ship as it slid through the waves and the splashing of the water against the sides. She felt certain Chazz was asleep.

Teel willed the motion of the *Deirdre* to lull her to sleep. But, what seemed eons later, she was still wide awake. Suddenly she wanted to get up and move about. Though still weak, she was determined to find fresh air, to put her muscles into motion. She sat up and shrugged on a terry robe that lay on a chair next to the bed.

For a full minute after she rose, she was sure she couldn't take a step. But the stars and circles dancing in front of her eyes finally dissipated, and she was able to take a firm footing on the shifting floor. One step. Two steps. Three steps. She looked over her shoulder to see how far she had come from the big double bed. She was halfway to the door. Three more steps and she reached it. Taking a deep breath, she opened the door and stepped out into the passageway, which was wider than she had imagined. The staircase leading upward was as broad and twice as steep as any in a house. Would Chazz call it a ladder in nautical terms, Teel mused as she calculated the distance to the top, which seemed farther than the summit of Mount Everest, and determined to climb it. By the time she reached the last rung, she was breathless and reeling.

The boat seemed to sink and rise through massive swells. Teel knew she might have a rough time keeping her footing even with the full moon to guide her. In her weakened state she wasn't able to control the pull and thrusts of her body as the ship surged onward.

"You damn little fool!" Without warning two hands came round her, lifting her up and back against a man's hard chest. The fingers tightened under her breasts as Chazz sought to steady himself and hold her at the same time. "Are you trying to kill yourself? I couldn't believe it when I woke up to hear you moving around." He started to turn her away from the rail.

"No." Teel's hands flailed outward. "I want to breathe. I want to walk a little and breathe." Tears rolled down her cheeks and her head lolled on her neck. Chazz's hand loosened under her breast and came up to press her head back on a hard shoulder.

"All right." He sounded amused, and the slight slurring of earlier was gone. Chazz Herman had a hard head. He put her down but did not release his firm hold.

Teel reached out, wanting to hold onto something, her hands weak as she tried to grasp the smooth oak rail. She took deep, reviving breaths and closed her eyes in delight as she felt the salty sweep of air into her lungs. "Oh, the night is so wonderful." Teel wasn't aware that she had spoken aloud until the reedy sound was pushed back to her ears on the heels of the wind.

"It is beautiful," he agreed, his voice husky in her ear.

For a moment Teel stiffened, thinking she felt a light caress at her neck. Then she was sure she was mistaken. It was only the wind. But how strange to have her body tingle like that. She walked slow, precise steps across the undulating deck, relying on the arms around her for the support she needed. Although her legs wobbled a bit at the unaccustomed effort, she was elated when she

reached the stern area. But as she began her return journey, her knees buckled. At once she was swept high into
heavily muscled arms.

"Enough for you this evening, Sister Terese Ellen,"
Chazz murmured hoarsely. "Why the hell did you have
to be a nun?" he added, ending with a muttered curse as
Teel tucked her head into his broad shoulder and closed
her eyes against a sidden giddiness.

"Tired," she muttered into his neck.

"Are you, angel? I wish I were. You seem to have
the opposite effect on me." He buried his face in her
hair.

"Hair's a mess." Teel's lips were so dry that she had
to push the words through them.

"But I bet it's gorgeous when it's washed. That chestnut color must take fire." He took the stairs easily and
pushed open her cabin door with his shoulder, then lowered her to the bed, pushing the now sweat-soaked terry
robe away from her body.

The cool air made Teel shiver. She was hazily aware
that Chazz had left her for a moment and returned with
a fluffy towel. He dried her body with long, gentle strokes,
soothing her. When he leaned over to brush the damp
tendrils of hair from her forehead, she reached up two
limp arms and clung to his neck. His surprise at her move
aided her in pulling him down. It was he who held back
when Teel's mouth moved over his, her lips and tongue
an invitation.

"God," he groaned, lifting his head for a moment.
Then his mouth came down again, the penetrating pressure a revelation.

Teel enjoyed it for mere seconds before she fell asleep.

The next day, Teel remembered little of what had
happened the night before. She'd gone up on deck for
some fresh air, and then Chazz had appeared. She vaguely

recalled a sensation of having his strong arms around her, then nothing.

Darby told her cheerfully that she was allowed on deck. He had asked a crewman to carry her up to a chair. "Not that you aren't as slim as a reed and as light as a feather and that I couldn't do it myself," he said, "but—" he shrugged, giving her an owlish grin—"why should I strain myself?"

"Why indeed!" Teel's tone had an amused tartness.

"You're a tall one, that's for sure, and with your hair washed and a shower behind you, you look half decent. Not that *I* like leggy gals with hair the color of a bay horse, mind you."

"Thanks."

"But your skin isn't so bad, and you have a nice long neck like a filly should. Why them nuns let you keep your hair so long, I'll never know. I always thought nuns had short hair under them wimpoles." Darby turned away to reach for a sweater for her.

She was glad he couldn't see the blush burning her cheeks. She pressed her hands there to cool them before he turned to look at her again.

"Chazz has been trying to contact your aunt on the ship-to-shore radio," Darby informed her. "Once he does, Sister, you'll be on your way again." He held the sweater out to her.

"Oh? Ah—thank you. It's very nice. Where did you find all these clothes for me? So many of them are in my size too."

Darby shrugged, jerking his head in the direction of the guest cabins. "Them." He chortled. "Chazz just burst in and took what he wanted. Why not? He paid for most of them, that's for sure."

Teel was aghast. "I don't like taking other people's clothes," she exclaimed. "Especially if they don't choose to give them up."

"You have eyes like liquid jade when you're angry, Sister," Darby commented. "Sure and you must be Irish."

"I'm everything. A little Irish on my father's side, but I'm also Swedish, German, and Dutch. My father's grandmother was Spanish, and I had an uncle by marriage who was Armenian. He sold Oriental rugs in upstate New York. So, you see, I'm a real melting pot."

Darby looked momentarily disappointed, then his brows lifted. "But the best part of you is Irish," he declared. "I can feel it."

Teel's laughter rippled across the cabin just as the door opened. The sound died abruptly as she faced an indolent Chazz Herman, a thin black cigar held in his white teeth.

"You must be making her better, Darby," he said. "That's the first time I've heard the sister laugh." He pushed himself away from the door frame and extinguished the cigar in a convenient silver ashtray. His walk, more a lope than a stride, Teel decided, carried him to her bedside in an instant. He leaned over her, a muscle in the right side of his jaw working, and she had to struggle not to dive under the covers. His lips jerked upward in the semblance of a smile, as though he had read her thoughts and fears and already dismissed them. "I've come to carry you up on deck," he told her. "The sun is shining and the air is balmy. Before noon we'll be dropping anchor at a little island I know. You can swim if you feel well enough."

"I don't want to swim. I want to go home. My aunt will be worrying about me." She coughed to clear the dryness from her throat. "You don't have to wait," she added. "One of the crew is coming to carry me on deck." She knew her words were terse and impolite, but she felt smothered by him, threatened by Chazz Herman. It was an unbearable strain to be in his company.

Chazz's mouth closed shut as though he had just bitten

through bone. His eyes had a hard sheen to them as he looked down at her. She shivered under the cold heat of that look. "I'm the one who's carrying you on deck, Sister." He spat out the words, harsh mockery in his voice. Then he bent, stripped the silk sheet from her body, and stared down at her as she lay there clad in a light cotton shift.

"Now, Chazz—" Darby came forward with an outstretched hand.

"Quiet, Darby." The command ricocheted off the walls, seeming to turn the serene turquoise room an angry, metallic color. Chazz swooped down and swung Teel up into his arms, his gold eyes daring her to defy him.

She wanted to level him with insults, but she couldn't form her lips around the scathing words bursting inside her head.

"That's right, Sister, keep quiet." An alien fury seemed to emanate from him. His strong arms clasped her body.

She made a mental addendum to her previous thought. She felt not only threatened by him but downright menaced. What fuel burned him? she thought, caught between panic and anger. For some unknown reason she had roused as fierce an antipathy in him as he had in her. Perhaps anger responded to anger and grew.

Whatever the reasons, Teel knew she would never be comfortable with this man, that they could never be friends. She would be balanced precariously as if on the edge of a knife until she could escape the *Deirdre* and leave its owner behind forever.

- 2 -

THE DAYS THAT followed were golden, warm, and relaxing. The constant ministrations of the crew left Teel feeling thoroughly pampered aboard the *Deirdre*. After Chazz had first brought her up on deck, he had occupied himself elsewhere, which relieved her. If only she could talk with her aunt instead of getting second-hand messages through Darby, then everything would have been perfect. She knew Aunt Tessa was fine and on her way home to Albany, but Teel longed to reassure her personally of her own safety.

Often the *Deirdre* anchored at sand beaches on obscure islands whose names Teel forgot the moment she heard them. Otherwise they cruised through crystal-blue waters. Teel didn't much care where they went. Her most important concern was her returning health, her only unsettling worry that of seeing Chazz Herman. But since

21

days had gone by without his appearance, she was at least partly successful at putting him out of her mind.

"Darby"—Teel was resting in a lounge chair on deck— "that lunch was delicious. Would you tell the chef I love fish pan-broiled in lemon like that?"

"I hate to give him any more compliments," Darby retorted impishily. "Rowan will be getting above himself."

Teel laughed, delighting in the Irishman's company.

"We're going to anchor at Moon Bay today," he told her. "It's very beautiful there. Chazz wants to do some diving." Darby lifted the tray from Teel's lap. "You won't be able to dive, but you can sunbathe and swim."

"Darby," Teel groaned. "I must get back to work soon. My vacation will be up in a couple of days. Besides, I should get in touch with my school and let them know I'm all right."

"Not to worry. Chazz took care of that after he called your aunt. He says, among other things, that he discovered you have more vacation time coming to you. He wants you to have a nice rest on board the *Deirdre*."

Teel jerked upright, wondering what Chazz had said to the school and her aunt and angry at his high-handedness. "Who said he was in charge of my life?" she demanded. "I'm not one of his lackeys."

"Aww now, Sister, you've hardly been treated like a lackey." Darby grinned at her glowering face, then ambled off with her tray, whistling out of tune.

Teel gazed across the sapphire waters. "He still has a hell of a nerve," she whispered, clenching and unclenching her hands on the arm rests. "I'm not ungrateful for his care of me," she murmured to herself, "but I'm damned if I'll allow myself to be manipulated by a . . . a womanizer." She took a deep breath and lay back to rest. She would need all her strength to tell Chazz Herman just what she thought of his methods the next time she

saw him. Not that she wanted to see him. She did not.
She yawned, not wanting to think of him.

They anchored well off the beach at Moon Bay. The
crescent-shaped harbor with its swath of white sand leading to the clear blue water was a tropic jewel. As she
leaned over the rail, Teel could see almost to the bottom
of the bay. Fishing boats, sail boats, and power boats
with water skiers swaying behind them all decorated the
bay with creamy wakes.

Off to one side was a section delineated with orange
flags that Darby explained was for diving. Neither power
boats nor sailing vessels were allowed in this area. Only
a few craft designated as diving boats moved within it.

Darby helped Teel down the ship's ladder into the
dinghy, not even allowing her to carry the string bag that
held her personal belongings. He assured her that Rowan
had made a nice lunch for her.

Darby pointed to a cabana on the beach that several
crew members had set up for her. "It's there you can sit
when you come out of the water," he explained, scowling
at her. "And don't be forgetting that your skin is still
sensitive, so use the lotion and don't sit in the open too
long." He cocked his head. "But I will be saying that
your skin has a nice golden color. Ah, but it is your hair
that is the most beautiful, with them red and blond streaks
in it."

"You're a flatterer, Darby," Teel accused him, laughing.

He cleared his throat, embarassed. "Now, Sister, don't
you be shy about swimming. That's a nice one-piece you
have. No one will know you're a nun."

"Nuns swim, Darby." Teel smiled at him as he spread
out a blanket for her. She didn't tell him that she had
often posed in bikinis during her stint as a model because
the photographer thought her narrow-hipped, long-legged
look perfect for bathing-suit ads. Not even to Darby

would she reveal that she was not a nun. As long as she
was on Chazz Herman's yacht, she felt safer in the disguise.

Darby sat with her for a few more minutes, reminded
her of the suntan lotion, told her to swim near other
swimmers, and pointed out a crowd of people. "I'll be
back later in the afternoon, Sister," he told her.

Teel called to him as he turned away. "Is Chazz diving
with his other guests?"

Darby made a face at her and nodded, then left.

At first Teel just lay back on her elbows in the shade
of the cabana, watching the skiers and the swimmers.
She didn't want to look toward the orange-flagged area.
Several times she shaded her eyes and scanned the more
remote section of the beach, where several divers came
in and out of the water. Could the one in the orange
bikini be Clare? Was one of the other women Elise?

Finally, even with the cool breeze filtering through
the cabana, Teel felt too warm. Standing up, she lifted
her arms to coil her long hair on top of her head and
fixed it there with two bone pins. She looked down at
the almost transparent metallic green lycra suit stretched
over her body, noticing the prominent hip bone that emphasized her recent loss of weight. Her firm, round breasts
strained against the material, the nipples clearly visible.
No, Aunt Tessa would not think this an appropriate garment—not for her niece and certainly not for a nun. Teel
smiled to herself as she thought of Aunt Tessa, then lifted
the water goggles and placed them over her eyes just
before entering the water.

The ocean felt cold on her overheated skin, but refreshing nonetheless. She reveled in the gentle waves.
Wanting to avoid other swimmers, she headed diagonally
away from the cluster of people. At first she stroked
easily, content to get the exercise, but soon the colorful

underwater world drew her attention, and she dove repeatedly to get a closer look. She was searching the bottom for an unusual crustacean formation she had just glimpsed when a dark shape angled rapidly down toward her. A shark! Panic engulfed her as she twisted abruptly, kicking wildly upward. As her head broke the surface, she gasped for breath.

"Hey! What is it? Do you have a cramp?" Chazz held her arm easily and pushed back wet tendrils of hair that had fallen forward on her face.

"I thought you were a shark," Teel choked out, trying to control her breathing. She pushed at his shoulders, but her hands were shaking, and she had no strength.

Chazz smiled devilishly down at her, his hair as sleek and black as licorice as he treaded water beside her. "I've been called that by several people, but I'm really quite harmless."

"A likely story!" Teel retorted, still breathing hard.

He threw back his head and laughed. "My ego will never be in danger of over-inflating from the compliments you throw me, *Sister* Terese Ellen."

Teel's skin tingled with a sense of danger as she looked into his lion's eyes. She wanted to ask him why he had emphasized the word "Sister," but some instinct kept her quiet. "You don't have to worry about getting a big ego," she said. "You have one already. Now would you please release me. I'm a good swimmer and in no danger of drowning."

"You may not be, but I am."

"What did you say?"

"Nothing." He released her slowly. "How would you like to go snorkeling? Then you could really see the underwater life."

For a moment, in her distraction, Teel forgot to tread water. She sank like a lead weight. Immediately two strong arms brought her to the surface. But even when she was treading water once again, his hands remained at her waist, exploring it restlessly and moving upward. Teel pushed hard against Chazz, sending him backward but splashing water into her own mouth at the same time. "I told you I can swim," she gulped, coughing. Irritated, she slapped water at him, hoping he too would get a mouthful.

Chazz threw back his head, his dark hair glistening in the sunlight. "Playful?" he asked, "Good. I like to play games." He floated toward Teel, his teeth bared in a menacing grin. Years of training came to Teel's aid. Her body knifed through the water with a strong racing stroke. The surge of power surprised her, but she knew she couldn't keep up the fast pace. If only she could make the beach before she faltered.

Victory seemed a distinct possibility when she felt a sudden tug around her calf. Chazz had caught her! She stroked even harder, trying to kick her leg free, but all to no avail. She turned to face him, breathless from the unaccustomed exertion. "You—said—we—were—going—snorkeling." She put one hand on his shoulder to ward him off as he pulled her closer, his laugh a muted growl.

"And so we are." His grinning face came closer. "That was quite an exhibition, *Sister*. Do you coach swimming at this school of yours?"

Hearing the mocking inflection in his voice, Teel frowned. His glittering golden eyes dared her to question him.

She breast-stroked away from him. He swam ahead of her. She dove deep in the opposite direction—and surfaced inches from his bare chest. No matter which way she turned, he was there. She had no choice but to confront him. "Yes, you could say I teach swimming," she told him. "I help coach our children, who compete in the Special Olympics, not just in swimming but also in the broad jump and the fifty-yard dash. In the winter I coach them in cross-country skiing and snowshoeing." Teel touched bottom as she and Chazz entered shallower water. She felt his eyes on her as they emerged but refused to look at him.

When she leaned down for her towel, he took it from her hand. Before she could protest, he was drying her off. He turned her to face him, his grin irritating her but taking her breath away just as the swimming had. "I can't allow you to catch cold," he said. "Darby would kill me."

"Your concern is touching," she retorted sarcastically, trying to pull the towel from his hands. When he wouldn't release it, she glared up at him.

"At least now you're looking at me," Chazz said, his eyes narrowing on her as they moved over her from ankle to eyebrow. "Your eyes are like green fire," he mused. His eyes turned to liquid gold, his neck and shoulders tightening with some hidden strain.

Teel opened her mouth to make a willing retort and froze. Her eyes had a will of their own as they looked at his broad, muscled body. It didn't matter how many times she told herself she didn't like the kind of man Chazz Herman was. He still exerted a powerful hold on her. He was too tall. She didn't like looking up at men. She felt more comfortable if they were on eye level . . . or lower. She didn't try to analyze why Chazz had such an unsettling effect on her even when he wasn't in her company, but she knew her former peace of mind would not return until she had put him behind her for good. Why in heaven's name did he wear those silky briefs? They made his thighs look even more muscular than they were already. Teel turned her back on him on the pretext of drying her hair.

"Shall we go?" The gentle question was whispered

into her neck, making her stiffen.

"Ah—yes."

They crossed the beach in silence, the walk seeming even farther because of the shifting sand under Teel's feet.

"I should have gotten the dune buggy for you," Chazz said, giving her a long look.

"No. It feels good to do something as safe and sane as walking on a beach on a hot, sunny day." His arm went round her waist, an impersonal support. She watched many of the bikini-clad women stretched out on towels stare as Chazz walked past. They irritated Teel.

"Darby tells me you're quite a mixture and not the purebred Irish girl he took you for." Chazz chuckled.

"I'm not a girl at all, Mr. Herman," Teel replied. "I'm a twenty-seven-year-old woman with a very satisfying career."

"Sorry, *Sister,* I didn't mean to tread on your toes. I was just making conversation."

Teel shrugged. "I'm jumpy about my age, I guess. A few of the board members think I'm too young to handle the job adequately." She glanced at him. "I didn't mean to bark at you. I'm really very grateful for all you've done for me."

"The pleasure has been all mine." His deep, smooth voice made her skin tingle.

"Ah, you mentioned my background. Tell me about yours. What sort of name is Herman?"

"My father was Jewish—German Jew on his father's side, Sephardic Jew on his mother's side. My mother was of English descent. She and my father met at school in the Bronx. Father sold musical instruments. My Mother taught piano. They were killed in a fire at the store when I was seven. I stayed with an aunt who was kind to me but very poor. I grew up a little on the wild side, determined to be rich so that my aunt could have a few of the finer things. When things began to go well, she allowed me to move her into a brownstone, but she won't move again. She would rather I get married and have children than provide her with a fur coat, car, or any of the other luxuries she considers unimportant."

"She sounds nice." Teel smiled at Chazz and was surprised to see him suck in his breath.

"Here we are." His voice was ragged. He went over to a large tent and brought out some equipment.

"Do you think I could try scuba diving too?" Teel asked, staring at a man near them who was sorting through a pile of more sophisticated equipment.

"No," Chazz exclaimed, glowering at her. "Scuba diving requires special training and lots of practice. You're not to attempt it until I've had the chance to teach you. Maybe in two or three weeks, when you're much stronger."

"I won't be on the *Deirdre* that long," Teel pointed out, wary and uncertain in the face of his sudden anger.

"No?" Chazz snorted. "We'll see."

Teel was about to ask him what he meant by that remark when he scooped up a mask from the blanket and fitted it to her face. She gulped at the sudden lack of oxygen. But the ringing in her ears subsided as she realized that she was in no danger. She listened carefully as Chazz explained how to breathe and soon felt ready to enter the water, but Chazz restrained her, insisting that she repeat his instructions. She did as he told her, and at last he was satisfied. Then he motioned for her to sit on the blanket and proceeded to fit the fins to her feet.

"I can do it myself," she protested.

He smiled, slipping on his own fins with practiced ease, then waiting for her.

"Oh." Teel sank down on the blanket several times before she was able to rise to her feet. She scowled at Chazz when he laughed.

He seemed to have no trouble walking to the edge of the water. To Teel it was like trudging through miles of desert. Several times she staggered and almost fell. She cursed Chazz for not telling her it would have been easier to carry the flippers to the shore before putting them on.

In the water Teel followed Chazz's example by using a breaststroke. She was close behind him, and when he pointed downward, she nodded and dove with him, remembering to blow through the tube as he had shown her.

The sparkling sea world awed her so much that at first she almost forgot to surface partway to clear her breathing tube. Then the motions became automatic. She delighted in the aquatic panorama spread below her. She lost all sense of time passing as she cruised through the sea grass and past crustacean life.

When Chazz motioned that it was time to rest, she shook her head and turned away, but steel hands grabbed her waist, brooking no resistance.

As they waded ashore, Teel yanked the mask from her face and glared at Chazz, whose hand still gripped her.

"You've been ill. It isn't wise to exhaust yourself," he explained, his voice bland.

"I'm not tired," Teel declared, but she swayed dangerously and immediately his hand tightened at her waist. She clutched his shoulders as he removed her flippers.

"You're more tired than you know," he warned her. "That's the seduction of the water world. Haven't you heard of 'rapture of the deep,' the disorientation that deep divers suffer from the combination of water pressure, lack of oxygen, and, of course, the beauty of the ocean?

You can lose your inhibitions, your wariness, and all your good sense. Even while snorkeling a mild effect of that same phenomenon can overtake you. You're particularly susceptible, having been recently ill."

"I see," Teel answered, feeling chastened. "I didn't understand." She put her hands on Chazz's arm as he rose with both pairs of flippers in his hand. "Thank you for taking me," she added. "It was wonderful." She grinned. "And you're right, I do feel a little slow and sleepy."

She was taken aback when he wrenched his arm free of her hold and strode toward the tent without answering. Stunned, she pressed her lips together to keep from shouting that he was a capricious barracuda and she couldn't stand people who blew hot and cold. Teel watched him drag the gear into the tent. Hurt and angry, she kicked at the white sand.

"What are you doing here?"

The terse question made Teel spin around. Two women stood in front of her shedding scuba gear. Realizing that the voice was Elise's, Teel assumed that the other woman must be Clare.

"I was snorkeling," Teel explained, keeping her voice flat.

Their unfriendly stares raked her coldly. "Oh, is that where Chazz disappeared to?" Clare said. "I don't recall ever meeting a nun with such a good figure, honey. Or do I call you, Sister?" The two bikini-clad women laughed, then turned to share the joke with several men behind them.

Suddenly an arm snaked around Teel's waist. She stiffened under Chazz's tight fingers, knowing his touch and sensing his anger. When she looked up at him, she saw that his anger wasn't directed at her. Red streaks had appeared on his high cheekbones and his jaw was clenched as tight as a vise.

"Darby is arranging for a plane to pick you up later this afternoon," he told the others. "I suggest you get back to the *Deirdre* and get your gear together."

"But Chazz," Elise wailed, "we were going to gamble at the casino tonight. Did you forget? Besides, Clare and I wanted to shop for some clothes, and I wanted—"

"If you don't make the afternoon plane," he interrupted, "you'll be stranded here. If you don't pack your things, Darby will fling them overboard. Good-bye."

Teel felt almost sorry for the sulking women and the truculent men, but she couldn't help but be glad that she wouldn't have to see them again.

When Chazz took her arm and led her up the beach, Elise called after them, "Fooling around with a nun is playing with fire, Chazz—even for you." The high-pitched voice had a nasty ring to it, but when the others laughed and Chazz turned toward them, a snarl on his face, they fell silent.

Chazz and Teel traversed the beach in silence, but she had trouble controlling her breathing. Elise's rude words had injected a personal note that quivered between them like a live wire.

"Would you like to swim again?" Chazz's voice was harsh.

"No." Teel tried and failed to keep her voice steady. "I think I've had enough sun. I'd like to go back and lie down."

"Good idea. I'll get Darby to bring the dinghy."

"There's no need. I can swim to the yacht."

"No!" Chazz roared.

"Don't shout at me!" Teel burst out, her chin jutting up.

"Then don't talk like a damn fool."

Teel stamped her foot on the hot sand. "I was trying to save Darby the trouble."

"Don't bother. That's his job."

She opened and closed her mouth, struggling to think of something suitably scathing. "Ill be glad to leave this beach just to get away from you."

Chazz turned his back on her, his neck red, his shoulders stiff. He strode over to the cabana, reached inside for a two-way radio and spoke into it in terse sentences.

Chazz stayed with Teel, not speaking, until Darby came ashore, then he mumbled something incoherent and strode away up the beach.

Teel was seething, angry with both herself and Chazz. She blinked back tears. She wasn't crying because he was a boor, she told herself, but because she was still a little weak from too much sun. When she was stronger, she was going to tip him over the side of the *Deirdre* with an anchor chain around his neck.

Darby brought the still-full lunch basket back with them, shaking his head and muttering that the chef would be angry. He opened his mouth, studied Teel for a long moment and finally said nothing for the rest of the short trip to the *Deirdre*.

Teel went straight to her cabin and threw herself face-down on the bed. She only meant to rest a minute, then rise and shower, but her heavy eyelids closed and sleep took her away.

Teel's first thought as she struggled out of her deep sleep was that the yacht had hit rough weather. Her whole cabin seemed to be tilting in the storm. Then, fuzzily, she became aware that the rocking was only caused by Darby shaking her shoulder.

"Come along, Sister. It's time to get dressed."

"Dinner." Teel forced the word around the cotton wool in her mouth. "Hungry. Forgot lunch."

"Forgot? Baloney. No doubt you'd been tiffing with

himself and didn't eat 'cause you was miffed." Darby
ignored her glare. "Now come along. It will soon be
cocktail time.

"Dinner." Teel licked her dry lips.

"Argue with me, will ya?" Darby's half grin, half
growl made his bushy eyebrows go up and down. "Up
you get now," he badgered her before urging her into
the bathroom. "I'll lay out your clothes," he called to
her through the closed door. "Not to worry."

I'm not worried, Teel thought, rubbing her hair with
one of the exotic shampoos she had found in the stockpile
of emollients on board the *Deirdre*. She wasn't worried
about what to wear, but she was worried about how soon
she could eat. If that bear of a man hadn't made her so
mad, she would have eaten the lovely lunch that Rowan
had fixed for her. She ground her teeth together at the
thought of Chazz.

She was going to yell over the noise of the shower to
tell Darby to lay out jeans for her, then decided that he
wouldn't hear her anyway.

She padded out of the bathroom wrapped in a thick
bath sheet that hung almost to her toes and stopped dead,
her mouth falling open as she caught sight of the wisp
of a dress that Darby had draped across the bed. Beside
it were cobwebby undies and ultra-sheer stockings. Back-
less slippers in a sea-green color with medium-high heels
lay at the foot of the bed.

Teel looked around the room for her other clothes, or
anything else she might wear to tell Darby to find something for her. But there was nothing but her towel. She
balked at leaving her cabin wrapped in that, afraid she
might run into the owner of the *Deirdre*. She had no
wish to watch Chazz's lion's eyes laser over her, separating her bones from tendons, muscle and tissue, disas-
sembling her and putting her back together again. And

she didn't like the all-over tingle she felt at the mere thought of him.

She shrugged and decided to put on the dress. What difference did it make what she wore as long as she could eat?

It wasn't until she had slipped the sea green silk chiffon dress with the uneven hemline over her head that she noticed the jeweler's box on one side of the dresser. Curious, she opened it and gasped. Emeralds! Drop earrings of braided gold interspersed with emeralds and a matching thin necklace glinted up at her. The ring was a marquise-shaped emerald that fit perfectly.

Teel ooohed over the cache, chuckling to herself as she thought of Darby taking these from Chazz's safe. He had often described the safe in Chazz's bedroom, where he kept the valuables. She hoped the gremlinlike little man wouldn't get into trouble because he had tried to give Teel a chance to pretend to be a gem-laden lady.

She knew she couldn't wear the jewels and maintain her pose as a nun, but she laughed out loud to think what her fellow schoolteachers would say. They had never seen their director in anything so exotic. Teel laughed to herself as well as she twirled in front of the mirror. A sense of freedom and abandon made her feel lightheaded. She had no choice but to wear the clothes even though the cut of the dress precluded wearing a bra and the combination of silky panties and dress plus very sheer stockings gave a sensuous, naked feeling to her skin. She was surprised to see that the contrast of the sophisticated dress with her unmadeup, sunwarmed skin gave her a uniquely striking look.

She gripped the green clutch bag and left the cabin, feeling like the Queen of the *Deirdre,* not just a temporary, unwanted passenger. As she traversed the ship toward the dining area at the stern, she wondered idly what her host would be doing this evening.

She stopped, open-mouthed, when she saw him, dressed in evening clothes, leaning against the rail, the rich aroma of a Corona Colorado cigar wafting toward her. She would have turned and retraced her steps, but he whirled around, like a lion at the ready and flicked the cheroot into the water.

"Ah . . . so here you are. Come and sit down and have some appetizers. Darby tells me you're hungry. I hope you won't eat so many canapés that you can't enjoy Rowan's specialty this evening—*truite en colère.*"

Teel resisted the hand leading her to the round table laden with cold delicacies. A chafing dish bubbled nearby, and her palate was teased by the spicy aroma of deviled clams. "I don't want to intrude on your guests and your dinner," she began.

Chazz grinned at her and settled her gently into a chair. "Not much chance of that since you're my only guest."

"How come?" Teel asked, her composure deserting her.

Chazz laughed, throwing his head back in open enjoyment.

Teel stared at his exposed throat, which was strong and muscular like the rest of him, and felt her heart slip sideways. "I mean—don't you have—you must have—" She glared at him when he continued to look at her, his eyes glittering with amusement. "You know darned well what I mean," she finished lamely.

Chazz's black eyebrows rose high on his forehead. *"Sister,* I'm shocked.

"You bring out the worst in me," Teel murmured, uneasiness assailing her at the mockery in his tone. She reached for some of the gold caviar molded in ice, refusing to look at him and swallowing before she spoke. "Why do you say 'Sister' in that peculiar way?" She reached for another canapé without thinking, then felt embarrassed at her greediness. But when she hesitated, Chazz served her himself.

"Do I say 'Sister' in a peculiar way?" he asked, his voice like velvet on steel. "I wonder why that should bother you." His smile looked as threatening as a shark's.

Teel tried to hold his narrowed gaze with her own, but looked away first. She was relieved when Rowan announced dinner.

The food was a delight, not only to eat but also to look at. Teel had seen pictures of the trout dish with its tail in its mouth and the attendant vegetables, but she had never tasted it. Nor had she ever tried Dom Perignon champagne.

When she finally sighed and pushed back her plate, Darby appeared with a silver tray laden with French pastries. Teel briefly tried to resist the temptation, but gave in and selected an eclair.

"That's the size of the dinghy—dipped in chocolate," Chazz commented, then grinned at Teel's glowering look as he reached over to wipe a bit of chocolate from the corner of her mouth. Just then Rowan arrived on deck to urge her to try the Napoleons as well. She felt herself redden as the three men watched her finish the sweet with broad smiles on their faces.

"These are luscious, Rowan," Teel said admiringly, determined to keep her eyes on the chef when Chazz chuckled. She couldn't help smiling, though when she glanced at Darby's delighted, grinning leprechaun face. She laughed out loud. But when the others left carrying away the last of the dishes and she turned to Chazz, her smile faded. Chazz's features looked as if they'd been etched in stone. "What's wrong?" Teel asked in a strained voice.

"I have a consuming wish to see you laugh like that all the time, *Sister* Terese Ellen." Chazz ground out the words between clenched teeth. "It would be like Christmas and Chanukah for me to smother you in jewels and furs."

"I—I don't live like that." Teel felt her skin tighten with fear at the glitter in his eyes. "I don't *want* to live like that," she added.

"No?" he asked softly.

"No. What's the matter with you? I don't understand why you should question everything—"

"Do I do that, *Sister?*" he interrupted.

"There you go again with that sarcastic way you have of saying 'Sister.'" Teel failed to keep the shrillness from her voice. "Why are you doing that?" she demanded. *He knows, he knows,* her mind clamored. *He knows you're not a nun.*

Chazz took a sip of cognac after swirling the amber liquid in his snifter. He took a deep breath. "Come along. Darby will have brought the dinghy around to the platform."

"Where are we going?" Teel gulped. "I don't understand you."

"Oh, but you will." Taking her arm, he lifted her from the chair. "I'm going to have a flutter at the tables. I thought you might enjoy it."

"If you mean by flutter—gambling—I don't gamble—well, what I mean is, not as a rule."

"It wouldn't fit the role of a nun, hmmm?" His dry tone stopped her dead in her tracks.

"Now what do you mean?" She took a deep breath, bracing herself for his answer.

"Let's go." He spat out the words like bullets from a gun. His hands gripped hers like iron bands as they descended the steep stairs leading to the loading platform.

When Teel would have balked at the side of the dinghy, Chazz's golden eyes bore into her until she fell still. Then he jumped into the dinghy, clasped her round the waist, and lifted her into the boat.

"You're certainly arrogant," she gasped out.

He stared in harsh amusement as she attempted to straighten her dress. "I'm glad you decided to put on that stole," he said. "It's not much but it covers your charms more than that dress." He turned his back on her and eased the dinghy away from the *Deirdre*; the boat shot toward shore as he gave it full throttle, throwing Teel back against the cushions in an inelegant sprawl.

- *3* -

CASINO ROYALE WAS a revelation to Teel, even though Chazz assured her that casinos throughout the world were pretty much the same.

"There are probably three hundred Casino Royales in the world, differing only in the degree of opulence," he explained. "Many are frequented only by the jet set. Others are notorious tourist traps, but by and large they are much the same." The gold lighter in his hand flared under his cheroot, making Teel think at once of Rudolph Valentino. Her involuntary laugh brought his eyes to her.

"Tell me the joke."

"I don't think you'd like it."

"Try me."

"I was just thinking that if you were less tall and less muscular and your hair were slicked down, you would look just like Rudolph Valentino." She couldn't stop

41

chuckling as she said it and was unprepared for Chazz's answering laugh. She was flabbergasted by his dimples. They just didn't fit the man—but oh, how endearing they were! She felt a blush creep up her neck at the thought.

"So I'm the Great Lover, am I?" His voice was like velvet. "Perhaps I should act the part."

Teel looked abruptly away from him, feeling as though her heart had just stopped beating. She gazed around the room in desperation. "I guess this must be a jet setters' hangout," she commented tartly. She felt his golden eyes sweep over her.

"What makes you say that?" he asked, amused.

"You're here. After what I've read of your international escapades, I can't see you frequenting a second-rate casino."

Chazzed shrugged and took her arm, nodding once to the maître d' as they approached the game room. "One of the perks of having money. I like first class. Does that annoy you?"

"Yes, as a matter of fact it does. Why not try second class and give some of your money away?" She studied the huge room with its silk moirré walls and ceiling, and sparkling chandelier. She was astonished by the way the people's clothes seemed to match the room's gold and glitter.

"Don't be pompous, *Sister*." The icy voice at her ear seemed to carry a double meaning. "Perhaps we all hide . . . certain aspects of our life from other people." Teel's head whipped around to face him, but his eyes swept the room as he continued to speak. "Don't assume that because I live first class I have never cared for those less fortunate than myself."

She put her hand on his arm, making him face her. "I was out of line, but I still don't see you as the philanthropic type." She could have bitten her tongue at her choice of words. Everything she said came out sounding self-righteous. She was attacking him and enjoying it, she mused to herself, bewildered by her reactions to him. Why didn't she stop?

"I don't see you as a nun, *Sister Terese Ellen,*" he said, ignoring her startled gasp.

He took her arm without another word and led her to one of the gambling tables where he stopped and looked down at her, a muscle tensing in his jaw. "This is a baccarat table, *Sister.* I'm going to play. You may watch or wander—or play." He dropped a roll of bills in her hand, then sat down in one of the chairs.

A dozen questions crowded Teel's tongue, but there were too many people looking at her already. She didn't relish a verbal confrontation with Chazz in this posh public place.

She wandered away, the money clutched in her fist. Nothing interested her until she came to the black-jack table. She remembered playing twenty-one with her father when she was a child, but they had played for matches. She sat down at an empty place and plunked down a bill that the coupier changed immediately into chips. When he looked at her, his head inclined, she nodded. The fast deal mystified her. She was glad when she lost and could rise from the chair, shaking her head when the croupier gave her a questioning look.

She sighed and wandered aimlessly, startled when a glass of white wine was pushed under her nose. She looked up at a medium-tall man with thinning hair and shook her head.

"Are you sure?" he asked. "Well then, would you like to play roulette with me? You might bring me luck."

Teel shook her head, her smile cold. "No thank you. I'm with someone."

The balding man took her arm, his thin hands surprisingly strong. "Oh, come along and play," he insisted.

Suddenly Chazz loomed large at Teel's side.

"Walk while you still have two unbroken legs," he bit out, his smile grim. The balding man melted away.

Teel faced Chazz, the silver cast to his skin and the light in his amber eyes clues to his fury. Her own anger rose hot in her throat. "You didn't have to come on like the mob's leading hit man," she accused him.

"Should I have let that cheap shill strong-arm you to the roulette table?" He bit through the words as though he were chewing steel.

"I thought you only went to places that wouldn't have cheap shills," she pointed out, her chin thrust forward.

"*You* said that, I didn't." He took her arm, swallowed the contents of his glass and led her toward what seemed to be a night club with music for dancing and a small floor show. "I need a drink," he said.

"You just had one." Teel tried to pry his fingers from her arm as they followed a maître d' to a table.

"With you I seem to drink more." His mouth was close to her ear as he transferred his grip to her waist.

"Is that possible?" she countered. "When Elise and Clare and the others were aboard you were always blitzed," she said baldly.

"*Sister*, how you talk!" Chazz seated her and ordered a double Irish whiskey, raising his black brows when Teel insisted on Perrier and lime. The waiter informed her they were out of Perrier. Teel frowned as Chazz shot her a mocking grin.

"Then I'll have Gerolsteiner Sprudel please—with lime." She explained that it was a German charge water.

"Oh Lord." Chazz regarded her in exasperated amusement. "It wouldn't hurt you to have a drink, you know." He lit one of his ever-present cheroots.

"And it wouldn't hurt you *not* to have one." Teel looked away toward the comedy act that was just beginning on the stage. She had thought she had seen and heard bawdy material, but this show brought home to her with terrific force that she was just a babe in arms. In minutes her face was flushed with embarrassment.

She had no idea that Chazz had hitched his chair closer to hers until he spoke directly in her ear. "Forgive me. I was stupid to bring you here. Shall we leave? I forgot how bad these sometimes are."

The thought of walking through all those laughing people, perhaps drawing attention to herself, perhaps having one of the comedians spotlight her with a lewd remark, sapped her strength. She shook her head, but when Chazz's arm went round her shoulder, she was glad to sink back against him. Somehow the show didn't seem so bad that way. It surprised her to realize she was sorry when the act ended and the lights came up. She hadn't wanted to move away from Chazz. As it was, even when she straightened, they weren't far apart. Chazz kept his chair close to hers.

When the band began to play dancing music, Chazz lifted Teel from her chair and led her onto the floor. "Now don't tell me nuns don't dance," he said. "This is a unique situation and one dance won't hurt." A devilish light glimmered in his golden eyes, but Teel attributed it to the Irish whiskey he continued to tip down his throat.

Teel had always loved to dance and had taken ballet lessons when she was a child. It didn't surprise her that Chazz was a very good dancer. A man who moved as well as he did, not only walking but also swimming, had to be good on the dance floor.

"Well, well, Sister Terese Ellen has another talent," he commented wryly. "You continue to surprise me, or do you?" He swung her away from his body and Teel laughed out loud. She felt his intent gaze on her, but she was having too much fun to pay attention.

They danced slow, fast, and even waltzed. When the band played a polka, Teel moved to sit down but Chazz wouldn't let her. He whirled her expertly around the room, seeming to know all the nuances of the dance.

"Where did you learn that?" Teel gasped.

"You forget I was raised on the sidewalks of New York. We danced all the time. My father and mother and later my aunt had friends of all ethnic persuasions who encouraged me to take part." Chazz didn't seem as winded as Teel and had no trouble talking with her. That alone made her itch to get back at him somehow.

When they returned to the table, Teel reached for her seltzer water and drained the glass. Chazz had already finished his Irish whiskey, but he ordered another.

They danced again and then rested while the band took a short break. Teel was having fun, and if she had a niggling suspicion that Chazz was drinking more than even his hard head could handle, she pushed the thought aside. She was enjoying herself more than she had in years. She needed it.

Near the end of the evening the band played more slow tunes, and though they often returned to the table to quench their endless thirst, Chazz and Teel still managed to dance most of the time. When Chazz first put both arms around her, Teel stiffened, but when she pushed at his arms, he pulled her closer. She shrugged and relaxed. Everyone else in the room was embracing the same way.

They danced and danced. Other couples left and still they danced. Finally they were the last ones on the dance floor. The music was mellow and smooth and Teel became even more comfortable with her arms looped up around Chazz's neck. Their bodies seemed fused, as though the two worked as one. Teel had never felt so relaxed yet so tense with excitement. She could feel every sinew in his thighs. His arms seemed to cocoon her. His fingers seemed to touch every pore. When his mouth moved over her cheek, she began to draw back, but he

wouldn't let her. "Beautiful, beautiful," Chazz murmured, his lips teasing her ear. "You're not what you
seem, lady mine." His voice was thick.

"We'd better go now," Teel whispered. "You're being
foolish."

"Yes."

Chazz kept her close to him as they returned to the
table to retrieve Teel's wrap and clutch purse. He gulped
down the last of his drink, then signed the bill without
looking at it, his eyes never leaving Teel's face. She said
good night to the maître d'. Chazz still looked at her,
his fingers kneading the flesh at her waist.

The balmy night sky was filled with stars. When Teel
looked up, Chazz turned to face her. "I have to," he
murmured, "even if you hate me for it." And in the warm
darkness he pulled her into a tight embrace. His mouth
was open on hers, hers open as well—in surprise. Her
heart hammered in fear and excitement. She had known
Chazz was as aware of her as she was of him, but she
had felt safe in her guise as a nun. Now the barriers
between them had been broken and she was no longer
safe at all.

She struggled at first, her hands pulling at the fingers
that cupped her face, but Chazz took no notice. His
fingers tightened. His tongue soothed her lips, then invaded her mouth, searching, savoring.

A hot sword seemed to pierce Teel. No, it couldn't
be happening to her again. No man could scale her defenses. No man could touch her!

One warm hand left her face to trail down her neck
and over her shoulder, then lower to softly cover her
breast. "Darling," Chazz groaned.

"No . . . not like this . . . no . . ."

"You're right," Chazz whispered into her neck before
he swept her up into his arms. "You're so beautiful. Do
you know that?"

Teel stared at him, clutching his neck, a niggling snake of panic uncoiling in her stomach. "Where are you taking me?"

"To the *Deirdre*."

Teel let out a sigh of relief. "Good. I'm tired."

"Are you, darling?" Chazz's voice was slurred as she'd heard it once before. The whiskey was having its effect.

Teel was determined to head for her stateroom the moment she boarded the yacht. She watched intently as Chazz fired the dinghy, his movements less precise than usual. He really had drunk a great deal this evening. Thank God she was sober, Teel thought. How horrible it would be if she had drunk something. How vulnerable she'd be if he ever made any moves toward her. As it was, her senses seemed heightened by the evening she'd spent with Chazz. Even now as they sped across the water toward the *Deirdre*, she could almost feel the warm touch of his hands on her waist and back when they'd danced.

As Chazz tied the dinghy to the landing grid, Teel hurried up the ladder. She was halfway down the wide set of stairs leading to her cabin when a hand closed over her arm. She shivered as she turned. "I'm tired, Chazz. I'm going right to bed."

"Good, so am I. But I brought you something to help you sleep." He raised the bottle in his hand. "I told Darby to leave this in the lounge for us. Just one."

Teel shook her head. "I'm too tired to go back to the lounge. I'll just say good night here." She entered her cabin and turned to see that Chazz had followed her. She opened her mouth to argue, but the glitter in his eyes stopped her. "All right," she conceded. "Just a small one. Shall we go back to the lounge?"

"Nope." Chazz grinned, then brought his other hand from behind him. He held two glasses. He sat down on the bed and poured the cognac.

Teel sat on the edge of a bench, thinking that Chazz didn't need any more to drink and certainly not the generous portion of brandy he had poured into his glass. She looked at her own glass and knew that she wouldn't be able to finish it.

Chazz raised his snifter toward hers. "To us."

"Good luck," Teel said, and she sipped the aromatic liqueur, welcoming its hot bite as a sudden chill made her shiver. She had a sense of waiting, of not being able to move because a large invisible hand held her in place. She didn't believe in destiny or Kismet, she told herself. She should just get up and leave. But her body refused to do what her mind urged.

Chazz finished his cognac, came over to her, and lifted her from the bench. "Let me help you drink that," he said, taking the snifter from her hands and tipping the contents into his mouth.

"You've had enough," Teel said through dry lips.

"Have I, darling? Then you have some." He fitted the snifter gently to her lips and let some of the liquid trickle into her mouth, then turned the glass and let his own lips drink from the same spot, his eyes never leaving her face.

Teel felt as if she were falling backward through space. Chazz was standing so close that the hairs on their bodies might have been touching. A personal electricity generated between them seemed to have fused them together. Mesmerized, Teel felt Chazz outline her lips with one finger, delineate her jaw, smooth the line of her brow, and snake toward her ear. She cleared her throat and opened her mouth to speak, but suddenly his tongue was there, moistening her dry lips and entering her mouth like a brand. Against her will, her eyes fluttered shut. She felt hot, stinging bites on her neck that came lower and lower. Her skin caught fire, and her flesh seemed to curl in the heat. She tried to protest, tried to fight the heat, but all that came out was a groan. Instead of pushing Chazz away, her hands clasped his waist as his hands and mouth made sensual forays over her body.

A sudden feeling of being swung into space made sense when she opened her eyes to find Chazz lifting her in his arms and carrying her to the bed. She met his liquid gold gaze and tried to struggle away from him. "No."

"Yes." She felt rather than heard the throbbing answer as he lowered his body to hers. "Drop the disguise and admit you're mine," he mouthed almost inaudibly against her skin.

She felt the rasp of his beard and realized that her dress was down around her hips and that Chazz was nuzzling her breasts. A hazy memory of the pain that Ben Windom had inflicted on her, both mental and physical, flashed before her, and she began to squirm in panic.

Chazz lifted his head. "Let me, darling. Let me love you." His eyes were glazed, hot and wanting. He seemed to sense her panic. "I won't hurt you, love, I promise."

Teel wanted to shout at him, to yell the question at him. How did he know she wasn't a virgin? For she was now certain of what she had suspected several times— Chazz knew she wasn't a nun. *How?* she shouted at him, but only a moan came from her mouth. She was both repelled and attracted by him. It was as though her body wanted Chazz but her mind remembered Ben.

Instead of pummeling him with her fists, as one part of her screamed to do, her hands twined into his crisp black hair. His muffled groan of satisfaction sent a thrill through her as he began to caress her breasts again, his tongue making her nipples harden. His mouth stroked over her body as though to imprint himself on her flesh.

Then he raised himself slowly over her, his mouth coming back to hers, one leg separating her thighs. "Darling, I'll always be gentle with you," he murmured.

When she would have spoken, his mouth fastened to

hers once again, wet tongue meeting wet tongue. Teel's body arched as his manhood pressed against her. She felt suffused in new blood, burning with a vibrant, driving need. There was no turning back. She surrendered to him, her mouth sighing into his, their bodies melting together as if in a dream. She felt him moving over her in restless readiness, as though he could wait no longer. But he *would* wait.

"My God I've never wanted anyone like this," Chazz breathed, as if surprised. His hands skimmed over Teel again, heating and reheating her body wherever he touched. "It will be good for you, love. You'll see." His words slurred over her as his mouth moved down her body once again.

"It's good now," Teel moaned urging him closer.

"Love, oh love." His passion built and vibrated between them, yet still he controlled it. He seemed to sense she was ready for him, but he continued to minister to her, building the yearning in her to an intolerable level.

"Chazz," Teel groaned.

"Yes, darling."

She felt his penetration and welcomed it. And then the electricity between them burst into flames, and Chazz began a mounting rhythm that was like nothing Teel had ever imagined. They crested again and again, then spun away into a warm, dark well...

Teel felt as light as air. When she saw the confused look on Chazz's face as he leaned over her, she pulled his head to her again and began a velvet assault of her own. The tiny kisses over the stubble on his face stimulated her already overheated senses. She shocked herself by becoming the aggressor, her hand caressing him in excited possession.

Chazz seemed delighted to relinquish control, and his lazy grin was soon replaced with a deep groan as Teel found her way through the labyrinth of his feelings, exposing the core of the man and joining her inmost self with him.

Ecstasy took them both, and then they sank together, Chazz folding her close.

"You took me apart, beautiful lady, you took me apart." The words were barely out of his mouth when he was asleep, his hold binding her to him throughout the night.

Teel slept. When she awoke, it was still outside. Chazz's iron hands had loosened somewhat around her, but she was still within the protective circle of his arms. She turned her head on the pillow and looked at him long and hard. It brought a raw, sweet pang to realize that she loved him. God, what a mess! In love with a lecher who cruised the ports of the jet set seeking his prey. She sighed deeply, momentarily overcome by the hopelessness of her predicament. Still, without Chazz, Teel mused to herself, lifting one finger to gently trace his features, she would never have known what it meant to love. Her mouth lifted in a wry smile. Sweet irony.

As she lay there she had no sense of time passing. She knew only one thing. She was leaving the *Deirdre,* Chazz, and everything connected with his life on the next available flight back to New York—and reality. Running away wasn't usually her solution to difficult situations, but this time she was going to gallop. The idea of Chazz ever finding out what he meant to her threatened to tear her heart in two.

What a paradox! She had run to the *Deirdre* for succor, for surcease from fear, for rescue from her ordeal in the jungle. Now she was enmeshed in as frightening an ordeal as before. Oh, she was no longer in danger of dying of exposure or starvation, but her spirit was in danger of being destroyed by Chazz Herman. If she stayed here any longer, she wouldn't be able to leave. She would end up being his concubine. She swallowed a bitter

chuckle in the darkness. *You're a fool, Teel Barrett.*
Where in all of blue Hades did you find that word? She
chided herself, needing to punish herself for the weakness
that kept her in bed with Chazz Herman, as if chained
by love for him. How long did she think he would keep
her? she scolded herself as she cuddled against the warm,
hard form curved around her. He would sicken of her
just as he had the rest, an inner voice promised her, the
harsh thoughts freezing the blood in her veins. *Go back*
to your work, she told herself. Maybe after a few years
she'd forget him. Ha! She would never forget him. Maybe
that was true, she argued with the voice, but her work
was important and fulfilling. She would make it be enough
for her.

In the dawn silence she heard the ship come awake.
She knew Rowan would be in the galley, preparing breakfast, serving the crew. Teel edged out of bed, grateful
for Chazz's heavy breathing, aware by the sound that he
was in deep sleep. He would probably wake up with a
hangover. If she hurried and was lucky, she could be
well away before he even thought to ask for her.

She took a short, freezing-cold shower in an effort to
remind herself of hard reality, of unrelenting necessity,
while she ached for Chazz's touch.

Darby raised his eyebrows at her appearance on deck
and would have hurried off to get her breakfast, but Teel
forestalled him. "Didn't you tell me that Chazz had informed the State Department of my plight and that a new
passport had been issued to me?"

Darby nodded and explained that the new passport
was in Chazz's rolltop desk. He nodded slowly when she
asked him if he could get it for her. But when she asked
for transportation to the nearest port with an airport,
Darby frowned.

"Please." Teel placed an entreating hand on his sleeve
as he regarded her, open-mouthed. "I must return to my

school. I'm way overdue. I must go today." She tried to keep her voice from rising. "And I want to see my aunt. She must be so worried."

Darby stared at her for long moments, then nodded once. "I'll pack clothes for ya to take," he told her, "and don't waste your breath arguing 'cause you won't change my mind."

Just before noon Teel boarded the dinghy, which was manned by one of the crew. Tears filled her eyes as she waved good-bye to Darby, the captain, and Rowan, all of whom stood at the rail waving back at her.

The inhabitants of the bustling tourist town where she was let off paid scant attention to Teel. She went to the cable office and wired her aunt for money, then after picking it up at the local bank, she arranged to fly to Acapulco Airport. There she made connections to Mexico City and on to JFK Airport. In New York, tired and miserable, she booked a room at the Algonquin Hotel for one night. She knew she couldn't face even the short trip to Selby. She was exhausted.

Once in her hotel room, she dialed her friend and assistant, Nancy Weil. "Yes, Nancy, it's really me. Yes, I'm fine. Yes, of course I'll tell you all about it when I reach home." She tried not to cry when she thought of all the memories she wouldn't be able to share with Nancy. "What? No, of couse I haven't forgotten the Special Olympics tryouts here in New York next month. Are the children excited?"

"Excited isn't the word I'd use." Nancy's laugh came over the phone. "Hysterical is closer. I'd say we're in for a wild but wonderful time."

"I can't wait." Teel smiled as she thought of her children at the Mary Dempsey School and some of the desperate tiredness left her. "I'll be home tomorrow," she promised.

"Good," Nancy replied. "There is some bad news.

The sweats that came for the kids aren't the ones we picked out. How would you like to make a fuss while you're in New York? Would it be too much trouble to go to the Complaint Department of Acme Sporting Goods?"

Teel assured Nancy that she'd be happy to "make a fuss at Acme," but her nerves screamed that she wanted to jump down a manhole and pull the top over her.

The next day, feeling physically rested if not emotionally revived, Teel stood before the glass and chrome doors of Acme Sporting Goods and stared at the modern skyscraper. Who would listen to one school director at this cool, sophisticated establishment? As Teel entered the posh but sterile main lobby, she felt as if she just walked into a chrome museum. She stared at the long index of office names and suddenly the words ran together in a dizzy blur because the chrome scroll informed her that Acme Sporting Goods was a subsidiary of C. Herman Associates, Inc. She would have run away then and there if her trembling legs had obeyed the fuzzy command from her brain.

"May I help you, miss?" a uniformed attendant asked at her side.

Teel had to swallow twice before the words came out. "I would like to speak to someone at Acme Sporting Goods about an incorrect order."

Teel hardly heard the man, but she followed his pointing finger toward the third bank of elevators where she repeated her request. She knew the man was looking at her closely, but she couldn't help moving like an automaton. She was sure there was little chance that Chazz could be in the city, let alone in this building, still she was torn inside from wanting and loving him. She felt out of breath, as though her lungs and heart weren't functioning properly. Her legs and arms ached. Her head began to throb. She had to get over Chazz Herman. She

couldn't stand the agony just seeing his name provoked.
What would happen if she saw a picture of him with—
with one of his women?

She punched the elevator button with unnecessary force
and glared at the light that moved from floor to floor,
stopping at four.

The receptionist at Acme Sporting Goods was very
efficient and spoke to Teel as though she were a mental
incompetent. If Teel hadn't been so busy looking over
her shoulder in morbid expectation of seeing Chazz, she
would have straightened the woman out in a hurry.

"Now, I think we're all set, are we not, Mrs. Barrett?"
the receptionist, who had introduced herself as Mrs.
Eldred, asked her smoothly, handing her the amended
invoice that Teel was to include with the return order of
sweats.

"Ah, yes . . . I guess so . . ." Teel looked blankly at
the folded paper in her hand, then stuffed it into her
purse. "Ah . . . good-bye Mrs. Elfred." She peered through
the crack in the door out into the hallway. All clear.

"It's *Eldred,*" the woman called after her.

"What? Oh . . . whatever." Teel jerked her head toward the woman, then scurried out into the hall to the
elevator. She held her breath until the doors opened on
the next floor.

Two men entered, hardly pausing in their conversation. "I tell you, Bert, the Old Man has gone crazy. Max
was downtown this morning and overheard the brass
talking to him on a ship-to-shore. Max said he was raging
mad, that he chewed everybody's . . ." The man glanced
at Teel, who sensed his gaze though she kept her face
averted. ". . . tail about anything at all. Max heard Teller
say he'd never known the Old Man to have a *tantrum.* . . . That's what he said—tantrum."

"What happened on that damn cruise anyway?" the
other man replied. "He should have come back a happy

man. He took those two high-flying models with him, Clare Henry and Elise Burrell. He shouldn't be able to keep a smile off his face."

The first man laughed, throwing another quick glance at Teel. "How the hell do you know who was with him?"

"Hey, when Chazz Herman vacations on his yacht, the whole world knows who goes with him." The two men chortled.

Teel didn't hear the rest of the conversation for the roaring in her ears. She surged into the lobby when the elevator doors opened and practically ran into the street.

Teel was so confused that she plunged pell-mell through the door of a cab that had just disgorged its passengers in front of the building. She gave the driver the address of her hotel. It was just three blocks away.

- 4 -

THE MARY DEMPSEY School for Exceptional Children
was a beehive of activity. Teel found few calm moments
in her day as the time approached for the children to
leave for the finals preceding the Special Olympics.
Nevertheless, she welcomed the constant preoccupation
with work. She was only happy when she went home
reeling from fatigue and fell immediately into bed. Only
then could she avoid dreaming of Chazz. Only then could
she awaken without tears on her cheeks.

Her house had always given her a quiet joy and a
sense of peace. She'd decorated it with potted plants
against cream-colored walls and trim and cheerful blue,
red and cream braided rugs to compliment the stone fireplace. Now the place seemed a veritable torture chamber.
When she beat eggs to make an omelet for supper, she
saw Chazz's face in the swirling mixture. When she
watched dramas on TV, she saw him dashing through

the air with athletic ease to rescue the damsel in distress. It did no good to tell herself that the actor wasn't Chazz, that he wasn't kissing the full-breasted blonde. She still writhed with jealous anger. She considered talking to Alison James, the staff psychologist, but she couldn't face discussing Chazz with anyone. So she buried herself in work. It didn't solve the problem, but it helped.

Teel hadn't planned to accompany the children to New York, but two days before departure one of the coaches came down with the flu. Teel crossed her fingers that it wouldn't spread to other teachers or the children and said she'd help chaperon.

"I'm so glad you're going, Teel," Nancy Weil shouted over the heads of the noisy children she and Teel were shepherding onto the bus. "I couldn't believe how much you had gone through until that man from *Day* magazine came to interview you—Stop that, Timmy. No, get on the bus, the cat can't come—It must have been horrible for you."

"It was, but I hope you don't think you and I are going to rest in New York with this crew." Teel laughed.

Nancy screwed up her face. "I don't mind the kids at all, but sometimes the parents are tough going." She shrugged as she and Teel took their seats with the other moderators.

"When the children have reached this level in sports, we don't usually have much trouble," Teel soothed. "It's the parents whose children have never done much athletically who are the most fearful."

"Well, I'm not going to worry," Nancy said firmly. "I'll just watch you and do the same."

As Nancy took a cat nap, Teel watched the rolling hills of New York state, but she was barely conscious of the pine woods, the granite cliffs, or the mountains marked with ski runs. She hardly noticed the last-ditch skiers who were taking advantage of the late spring snows.

All Teel could see was Chazz's face. It was like having a constant toothache, she thought. It was like being caught in a trap. She shook her head, trying to force his image from her mind.

They arrived in New York with few mishaps. Their hotel, the Saratoga, was past its prime but had the advantages of being able to accommodate all the children competing and being located fairly close to Madison Square Garden. Even so, they would let none of the children walk there. Teel was adamant on that point. The bus would take them back and forth, not only for practice sessions that afternoon but also to the finals at the Garden the next day.

Nancy came puffing up to Teel as she got the children ready for the trip to the practice session. "I need two huggers," she explained. "Somehow they missed the bus. Where am I going to find two people to greet each child at the end of each event with a hug and tell them well done? It's so important that they all feel like winners."

"You and I will be huggers," Teel decided. "There are already enough coaches." She slapped the door of the bus and nodded to the driver, who pulled away from the curb.

"I have to change into sweats, then we can run over to the Garden." Teel smiled at Nancy as they strode across the lobby to the elevators.

"I hope you don't mean that literally." Nancy sagged against the wall of the elevator.

Teel laughed and headed for her small single room on the eighth floor. She had no desire to share a room with someone. Since her return from the *Deirdre* she had suffered chronic insomnia. There were many nights when she tossed and turned until dawn.

In minutes she had taken a quick shower and donned the emerald green sweats with the white stripe down the sides. She could almost hear Aunt Tessa's words of approval when she'd first seen them. "Teel, my dear, the color is perfect for...everyone." Tessa had given her niece an impish smile when Teel had laughed and called her Irish.

Teel's aunt had spent three days with her after her return from the *Deirdre*. Tessa had always been able to smooth Teel's rough edges, but this time the job had been too tough. Nothing seemed to take Teel's mind from Chazz Herman for long.

She sighed and tightened the laces on her pale green running shoes. They were as comfortable as slippers. She zipped her money and identification card into an inner pocket and took the elevator to the lobby.

As soon as Nancy joined her, they left the hotel. Despite Nancy's complaint about running to the Garden, she was an inveterate jogger, and the two women found a mutual rhythm to their running almost at once.

"I didn't believe all those stories about New York until now," Nancy huffed into Teel's ear as they jogged in place at a side street, pausing to let traffic pass.

"What do you mean?" Teel puffed back as they crossed with the light.

"A really gorgeous car has been following us for the last half block. Wouldn't it be wonderful to be accosted in a Ferrari?" Nancy quipped sarcastically.

Teel gave a breathless laugh but refrained from looking at the well-heeled stalker. "Don't pay any attention. Whoever it is probably gets his kicks from intimidating joggers. Just ignore him."

Madison Square Garden came into view. At the door the two women paused to identify themselves and were shown the door for the athletes and workers.

The next hours passed in a whirl. Both Nancy and Teel acted as huggers as well as go-fers for misplaced items. When a co-worker tapped Teel on the shoulder and told her he would spell her awhile, she sagged and gave him a relieved smile. She was starving. She hadn't been hungry for breakfast, and lunchtime had slipped away, but now she realized that the day's physical activity had made her hungrier than she had been since her return from the *Deirdre*.

She grimaced at the long line in front of the refreshment stand as she passed there on her way to the ladies' room. On her return the lines were no shorter. Resigning herself to a long wait, Teel took her place. When she felt the nudge at her back, she assumed it was someone behind her getting into line and didn't turn around.

"Damn you. Trying to convince me you were a nun, then running out on me. You must have taken me for thirty kinds of a fool, lady." The silky growl in Teel's ear made the hair on her arms and neck stand straight up and sent the blood draining from her limbs. A wave of dizziness swept over her.

She reeled in shock, and her legs wouldn't accept the command from her brain to run. Her shoes felt cemented to the floor.

"Turn around and face me, *Sister Terese Ellen.*" The voice had the jarring effect of a jackhammer breaking through concrete. Chazz lifted her out of line with an ease that panicked her. "So what do I call you now?" he asked in a menacing tone. "Terese Ellen? Or Teel, as your aunt and the authorities at your school call you?"

Teel licked dry lips, noting that his eyes followed the movement. "You've known since the beginning, haven't you?" she said.

"Almost. Yes. Why the hell didn't you tell me yourself? I gave you enough opportunity," Chazz exclaimed, apparently oblivious of the people thronging around them.

"Protection." Teel felt the curious stares of onlookers and tried to free herself but to no avail. "Will you let me go?" She forced the words out of her mouth, feeling shock waves course through her at his touch. "Many of the people here are parents of my students. I do not enjoy making a spectacle of myself in front of them."

"Damn you, you lied to me! By not telling me who you were." His teeth snapped shut like fangs.

"I told you all you needed to know about me," she retorted."My name is Terese Ellen Barrett, and that's what I told Darby. He assumed I was a nun." She glared up at Chazz. "Why are you complaining? Why didn't you just come out and tell me that you knew who I was? You're just as guilty of subterfuge as I am. Why weren't you honest with me?

"You began the charade. I just continued it."

"On board your yacht I thought it better to pretend to be a nun," Teel blurted out, trying not to shout yet struggling to free herself at the same time.

"As I recall, darling, your masquerade didn't work," Chazz drawled. Teel's neck and cheeks grew hot with embarrassment. "Shy, darling? It's a little late for that, isn't it?"

"You knew I wasn't a nun," Teel hissed. "You should have said something. Stop grinning, you...you bastard." She tried to kick him in the shin. She wanted to bury him up to his eyebrows in sand.

"Bastard, am I? After what you put me through in the last month, I ought to drag you out of here by your hair," Chazz snapped.

"Tough!" she threw back at him, fury overriding prudence.

He hauled her hard against his chest, knocking the breath from her body. She could only stare up at him, her eyes wide, mouth agape. His own mouth fastened on hers in a moving, searching caress that horrified her. Then his kiss blotted out all of her senses, blinding her, deafening her, drowning her in Chazz. There was no world but him. Her body betrayed her, and she moved closer to him just before he released her.

"You're mine," he gasped, his amber eyes leaping with liquid fire. "And I'm taking what is mine. You're coming with me to get something to eat now. You've been working too hard."

"I can't leave." Teel swayed, her voice unsteady.

"I'll have you back in a little while. I'll just make a call, then we'll go." He pulled her behind him, not looking left or right.

Teel was faintly aware of Nancy calling to her, but Chazz's rapid strides made it impossible for her to turn around. "Where are we going? I won't go." She struggled against his grip on her arm, but her efforts were useless. She sailed along behind him like the dinghy following the *Deirdre*.

Chazz kept Teel clamped to his side even as he dialed and spoke into the phone in terse sentences. She glanced over her shoulder and saw Nancy behind her, hands clasped anxiously.

"Should I get security?" Nancy mouthed, her throat working with concern as her eyes darted from Teel's face to Chazz's hand manacled to her wrist.

Teel had opened her mouth to say yes when she was suddenly whirled around, her back to the phone booth, Chazz at her side. "Who's this?" he growled, nodding toward Nancy.

Teel glowered up at him. "Don't you dare pull that Hitler act on Nancy," she panted, anger making her out of breath. "This isn't the deck of the *Deirdre*. You have no authority here."

"No?" he cooed, making Nancy jump.

"No!" Teel flung the words at him, using her free hand to try to pry the other from his grip. "You try your strong arm tactics here and I'll have you thrown into the slammer." She thrust out her jaw, itching to place a well-aimed running shoe into his midsection.

"Introduce your friend. Then we'll leave." Chazz

transferred his grip to the left hand and held out his right to Nancy, who leaped backward in alarm. "I'm Chazz Herman and I'm taking Miss Barrett to lunch. Any objections?" he snapped.

"From me?" Nancy replied. "Hell, no."

"Nancy!" Teel cried, grimacing at her friend and jerking her head toward the uniformed security guard who was passing fifty yards away through the press of people.

"Survival. That's the key word," Nancy muttered, giving Teel a weak smile, then beginning to edge away.

"Bright girl," Chazz pronounced, giving Teel a gentle smile that had all the sweetness of a barracuda on the prowl.

Teel sagged in defeat as Nancy disappeared into the crowd. She looked back at Chazz, whose expression was serene, and hauled in a deep breath. "Mussolini," she hissed.

Once again Chazz began pulling her after him, down a long tunnel and through double steel doors to the outside. He didn't stop until he reached a Ferrari parked in a loading zone.

Teel prayed he'd been ticketed and was incensed not to find a slip of paper under the windshield wiper. "Carpetbagger," she seethed as he pushed her into the passenger seat, then hopped around the car and under the wheel before she could figure out how to open the door.

"Don't bother, love. It's locked at the wheel." Chazz smiled wickedly at her and fired the engine.

"Bandit," she growled. Then something clicked in her head, and she flung herself around to face him. "Were you in the car Nancy saw following us this morning?"

He nodded. "Fasten your seat belt."

"Monster," she said. "You should be arrested. How dare you harass innocent women."

"I didn't harass you. I had to make an emergency trip to Singapore the week after you left the *Deirdre* and I

just got back last night. I realized that my best chance
of seeing you now was to hang around the Special Olympics tryouts. When I saw you and your friend jogging
toward the Garden, I couldn't believe my luck." He shot
her a quick glance as the Ferrari peeled through traffic.
"Don't you know how dangerous it is to jog alone in
New York?"

"I realize now that I could meet someone like you,"
Teel replied. "From now on I'll take an attack dog with
me."

"That's what I love about you, Teel. You're so af-
fectionate." Chazz chortled, then gave her another quick
look. "Teel. That's an unusual name."

"My father combined the first two letters of my name
Terese Ellen. The name stuck. I've never been called
anything but Teel," she answered in stilted tones, her
chin in the air.

"I like it."

"It is immaterial to me whether you like it or not."

"Ouch. That tone of voice would fast freeze a herd
of elephants."

She gave him a saccharine smile. "Suspicions confirmed. You have a thicker hide than an elephant: otherwise you would buzz off."

"Never, darling. I've decided you're not getting rid
of me."

"I'm not going to be one of your prostitutes." Her
voice echoed loudly in the car, the fear that he might
find out she loved him trembling through it.

"Wait until you're asked, love."

Teel felt as though she had suddenly swelled to twice
her size. She was about to explode in withering denun-
ciation of all things that made up Chazz Herman when
he made a sudden right turn, throwing her against her
seat belt. She watched open-mouthed as the Ferrari
dropped down into the darkness of an underground ga-

rage. They parked in a space marked Herman. Two other spaces were marked the same way. One held a Rolls-Royce. "Lousy capitalist," she hissed at him as he came around to open her door and released her from the seat belt that refused to separate under her own hands.

He followed her gaze toward the cocoa-brown Rolls. "Don't you like the Royce?" he asked blandly, helping her from the car, impervious to the hand that tried to pry his fingers from her arm.

"You're a selfish, egotistical, manic, pompous, less-than-human amoeba." Teel scraped her heels against the concrete as Chazz half-carried, half-dragged her to an elevator in the underground garage.

"Does that mean you don't like Rolls-Royces?" He gave her an interested glance.

"Don't patronize me!" Teel said, staring up at him ready to explode as his one arm clamped her to his side while the other hand punched the number board in the elevator.

"You mustn't get so excited. It will upset your lunch," he pointed out in soothing tones.

"Louse," Teel hissed as he pulled her out of the elevator into a foyer paneled in rich oak with a shiny oak floor. A round Kerman rug in cream, green, and pink formed the focal point of the circular room. Several doors led off from it and a stairway followed the curve of the room to an open balcony on the second floor.

Teel was staring at a cut-glass lamp suspended from the two-story ceiling when Chazz tugged on her arm, urging her toward one of the doors. "Where are we?" she demanded, digging in her heels and glowering up at him.

"Where do you think? My apartment. We're going to have lunch," he explained impatiently.

"I knew it," Teel cried. "You lured me here . . . you . . . lecher."

"Will you keep your voice down. My housekeeper will think you're crazy." He frowned at her, taking her arm again, then opening the door behind him and leading her into a beautiful room that appeared to be a lounge or library.

Teel glanced around her at the book-lined walls. "I'll bet you stole these books from the New York Public Library," she muttered, gazing at the large green Kerman rugs. The same green was repeated in silk-covered sofas that were placed at right angles to the Adam fireplace. A huge painting depicting the green sea and a storm-tossed whaling ship hung over the mantel. A ghostly white lighthouse seemed to waver in the background. "It's beautiful," Teel whispered, walking closer to check the name of the artist. "Tilda Charles," she read, turning to frown at Chazz. "Wouldn't you know you'd have an original Tilda Charles!" She sniffed. "Such ostentation. This is probably the largest canvas she has ever painted, and you have to have it over our mantel." Teel looked back at the painting, craning her neck to read the title— "'Saving the Whale Off Martha's Vineyard.' Wow. I wonder if she ever saw such a thing or if she just imagined it."

"Oh, she saw it." Chazz leaned down, grazing Teel's neck with his lips. "Don't you recognize the man standing in the bow with the hawser in his hands?" His breath sent tingles down her neck.

"I beg your pardon?" Teel struggled to keep her emotional and physical balance. It was an ordeal to be with Chazz. Her eyes didn't focus, her hearing faded, her muscles became limp, her backbone seemed to disappear. He gave her headaches and gas. God, Chazz Herman was a one-man torture chamber for Teel Barrett. She took deep breaths and kept her mind on the picture. She tilted her head as the high cheek bones, chiseled chin, hawklike nose, and dark hair of the young boy depicted in the painting all seeped into her consciousness. "You! What are you doing in a Tilda Charles painting?" she accused him, as if he had bought his place in the painting.

"She's my aunt."

"Oh!" Teel closed her eyes, then looked blankly from him to the painting, and from the painting to him.

Chazz put his arm around her waist. "She and I were staying at my place on Martha's Vineyard when a sperm whale beached itself. Some of the locals and I struggled for hours to get the animal into deeper water. It returned twice. The third time out we circled it until it seemed to orient itself and swim away. Of course we have no way of knowing if it beached itself someplace else, but I can't describe to you the exhilaration we felt when that whale began to move smoothly on its own. We celebrated all night. It was wonderful. Aunt Tilda stayed on the beach the whole day watching, and I suppose sketching too. The first I knew that she had painted the scene was when this"—he pointed upward—"was delivered to my door." He sighed. "The sea was just that color." He smiled down at Teel. "You and I will go there soon." He leaned down and pressed a hard kiss on her open mouth. "But for now, it's time you had lunch. I have to get you back. I've already volunteered my services for the afternoon, so I'll be with you for the rest of the day. Tonight, I'll take you to dinner and a show."

As Chazz spoke, he led her through double doors into a very large dining room that could easily seat thirty people. Teel looked up at him questioningly. Chazz laughed. "No, we're not going to eat here. We'll eat in the morning room. It's smaller and cozier. I think you'll like it."

"Does it matter?" Teel asked, feeling as though she were walking on air as Chazz carried her along at his side.

"Don't be testy. It isn't good for your digestion," he

soothed, leading her out into another hallway, then through more doors into a circular room with a glass wall that overlooked a large terrace with a swimming pool and garden. The view of New York City was breathtaking. Teel heaved a sigh of satisfaction. The round table in the middle of the room was set for two. The table and chairs were of rich rosewood, as was the paneling on the walls. On the floor was a round Chinese rug in deep blue and cream. Teel studied the room carefully, turning slowly. "I wonder what a psychiatrist would say about your penchant for round rooms," she mused. "It's probably your emperor complex surfacing."

"No doubt," Chazz agreed smoothly. "Won't you be seated, Empress?" He smiled at her, then turned to greet a portly woman who entered through swinging doors from the kitchen. She had salt-and-pepper hair and wore an apron that belled out around her form like a small circus tent. She clasped her hands in front of her and looked at Chazz expectantly. "Ah, Mrs. Pritchett," he said. "This is Miss Barrett. She is the lady I told you I was bringing for lunch."

"How do you do, Miss Barrett."

"It's nice to meet you, Mrs. Pritchett." Teel felt a sudden discomfiture at the assessing look the housekeeper gave her.

"I'll bring lunch right along sir. I made it light, as you ordered."

Mrs. Pritchett disappeared, but before Teel could say anything to Chazz, she was back with a tureen of soup. As the fragrance of the home-made mushroom broth reached her nostrils, she realized that she was ravenous. When she sat back a few minutes later, after finishing her bowl, Mrs. Pritchett seemed to answer some unheard signal. This time she appeared with two large bowls of julienne salad, which she placed with care in front of Teel and Chazz.

"I've added cubed chicken breasts and tuna steak instead of ham, sir. I think it makes the salad more piquant," Mrs. Pritchett announced proudly. She pointed to a cut-glass cruet. "That's my own celery seed dressing," she told Teel. "But of course, if you prefer, I also have commercial dressings."

"I would much prefer the homemade, Mrs. Pritchett. Thank you." Teel smiled as the older woman nodded once and her cheeks flushed. She looked at her employer.

"It's high time you were bringing one home. Your taste is better than I thought it would be." Mrs. Pritchett turned and left the dining room.

Teel looked at Chazz, unable to stop the laugh that bubbled up. "She's certainly an original."

He shrugged. "She worked for Aunt Tilda for years, then decided she wanted to work for me." He grinned. "I assure you I had little say in the decision. She just turned up one day and stayed. She runs the house like clockwork and handles the few parties I have here with aplomb, but she's quick to point out my faults."

"The woman must have a computer mind if she can remember them all." Teel smiled and sipped from her glass of chilled Riesling.

"Don't be nasty, love." Chazz's menacing smile appeared. "I'll have to paddle your lovely derrière." He seemed not to hear her gasp of anger as he steepled his hands and gazed toward the ceiling. "Now, let's see, where was I? Ah, yes, I was saying that Pritch is quick to point out my flaws. Did I mention that she dotes on me? That she is looking forward to being nanny to my many offspring when I marry? Interested in the job?"

"I'm interested in tipping you off the George Washington Bridge with a cement block fixed to your neck," Teel snapped, hoping to keep her face expressionless. She couldn't keep the thought of a gurgling baby with black curly hair and golden eyes from invading her mind.

Who would bear that child? The question was like an electric prod to her insides.

"I take it that means you won't marry me?" Chazz inquired, leaning forward to pour her a cup of coffee from the silver pot.

"How like you to poke fun about something as beautiful as marriage!" Teel took a mouthful of scalding coffee and tried to cool her burning tongue with a quick swallow of ice water. She coughed when the water went down the wrong way. Chazz rose to stand next to her and proceeded to slap her back with all the gentleness of a sledge hammer.

"Better?" he asked.

"Better?" Teel cried, wiping tears from her eyes. "Were you trying to break my back, slapping at me like that?" She took a deep, ragged breath, and sent him a murderous look when he sauntered back to his seat, took his chair, and smiled at her benignly.

When Mrs. Prictchett walked into the room with a cheese board and more coffee, Teel was still so furious that she could only shake her head when the housekeeper offered an alternate dessert of cheesecake.

"That will be all, Mrs. Pritchett," Chazz told her. "We have to leave shortly. Miss Barrett has children entered in the Special Olympics tryouts."

Mrs. Pritchett's interest seemed genuine, and as she left the room she told Teel that she must come again soon.

"You've made a hit with her," Chazz commented as he came around the table and held her chair.

Teel felt his breath on her neck, "I must get back," she choked.

"We still have a few minutes. Let me show you the terrace."

"No need," Teel said. "I've seen terraces before."

Chazz chuckled and led her down the hall to the room

with the beautiful seascape over the mantel. He motioned her through glass doors that opened outward onto the terrace.

"Nice," Teel managed. "Large."

"Nervous, darling?"

"No."

"Good." Chazz put his arm around her and led her around a corner toward the swimming pool. "Would you like to swim?" He pushed a tendril of hair from her forehead, then leaned down and pressed a feather-light kiss on her cheek.

"No time," Teel gasped, feeling his mouth continue down her neck. Heat curled in her lower abdomen as his lips forayed across her shoulder. Somehow the zipper on her sweat jeacket had come down, and Chazz had pushed the material away from her skin. "Too soon after eating," Teel protested through cardboard lips. "Getta cramp."

"I would save you, darling," Chazz crooned into her ear.

"Gotta go. Late," Teel gasped, trying to rally her defenses and free herself from the velvet heat of his hold.

"All right, love. We'll go this time. But you won't always get rid of me this easily." Chazz chuckled, letting his hand cruise down to the end of her spine, his palm making circles on her derrière, then patting it, not so gently. "This time you get away." His voice was like a liquid chain manacling her to him. "But not the next time."

Teel looked up at him, wanting to bite his nose off, wanting the words in her throat to scorch him. Instead a pain burned behind her eyes. Drat the man! He was giving her a headache. How would she ever survive the two days in New York if he was going to be everywhere. The man short-circuited her nervous system, interfered with her digestion and de-activated her antiperspirant. He affected her like poison ivy, like the bubonic plague.

"I can't go out with you tonight. We've all made plans to see a show. The tickets are already bought. Ten coaches and teachers will all be sitting together. No ticket for you," Teel finished woodenly, her eyes on his throat.

"What show are you seeing?" Chazz asked casually, steering her from the apartment into the elevator.

Since Teel's secretary had booked the show, paid for the tickets, and already given them to Teel, the answer should have been on the tip of her tongue. But her mind went blank. She struggled to remember. "Palace Theater," she managed.

"Very good show. You'll enjoy it." Chazz took her hand as they stepped from the bright elevator to the more dimly lit underground garage. When Teel turned left, he pulled her back. "No, this way, love. See, there's the car."

"Oh." Why wasn't he fighting her on going to the theater? On the circuitous trip back to the Garden, Teel agonized over what he was thinking.

Chazz parked the car, then led her into the chaotic din of screaming children, shouting coaches and applauding spectators. Cheers and general pandemonium surrounded them.

Teel didn't believe Chazz would want to help out until she saw him observe the activities for a few moments, then whisper to one of the moderators, and go over to where several youngsters were lined up for the fifty-yard dash. She watched in wonder as Chazz coached, instructed, hugged and encouraged the young people as they competed in this event.

Again he was defeating her on her own ground. Cold perspiration coursed down Teel's back as she tried to concentrate on the broad jump, the event she was moderating. Her forehead felt hot. Now he was making her feel as though she had the flu! What in heaven's name was she going to do about Chazz Herman?

- 5 -

THAT EVENING SHE and Nancy returned to the hotel hot, tired, and dirty. Instead of running, they were transported in the Ferrari.

Teel knew Nancy wanted to ask her about Chazz, but she forestalled her friend's questions by saying she needed a nap before they dressed for the theater.

What a relief to throw herself face down on the bed. She was asleep before the thought could surface that she wouldn't be able to sleep for thinking of Chazz.

She awoke to the ring of the telephone. "'Lo," she mumbled into the receiver, trying to unstick her eyelids.

"Were you sleeping, love? Ummm, how nice. I'd love to join you." Chazz's voice set her on fire and made her leap up in dismay, sending the lamp on the table next to the bed tottering on its base.

"Up. I'm up," Teel declared, standing at attention in her bare feet.

Chazz chuckled. "Look outside your door before you shower."

Even after the phone clicked to indicate that the connection was broken, Teel stood there holding the phone to her ear. She took a deep breath, replaced the receiver, and tiptoed to the door, opening it just a crack. A spray of white roses in a tall crystal vase was accompanied by a smaller florist's box and an even smaller parcel. Looking up and down the corridor and not seeing anyone, she reached out and pulled the items into her room one by one. "Who the hell does he think he is? Rockefeller?" she muttered as she pulled the card from the rose spray and read "Love, Chazz." She held the card with the tips of her thumb and index finger as though it carried typhoid. "I'll bet there are two dozen roses in that arrangement," she murmured, counting to herself. There were three dozen. "Plutocrat."

She opened the smaller florist box and discovered a wrist corsage of baby orchids with a thin gold bracelet lying underneath. The card read, "Love, Chazz." She unwrapped the smaller parcel slowly. The jeweler's box was marked Cartier's. Inside were drop earrings in filigreed gold interspersed with emeralds. A pendant in a similar design hung from a thin gold chain. Again the card said, "Love, Chazz." "Damned unoriginal," Teel moaned, backing away from the array of gifts. She felt as though she were in an arena with a wise and canny bull who was slowly backing her into a corner without her cape or sword.

She bolted for the bathroom and took a cold shower. After she had shampooed her head and finished with a hot shower, she felt better. She stepped back into the bedroom, feeling more confident. She would keep the vase of flowers. She loved flowers. But she wouldn't wear the corsage. Tomorrow she would arrange to return the jewelry by messenger.

After she had put on her silk slip, it suddenly struck her that she couldn't keep such valuable gems unprotected in a hotel room for the entire evening. When she called down to the desk, they assured her that, if she labeled the package, they would arrange to send it by messenger.

Relieved, Teel put on a hunter-green silk chiffon dress that was almost the same color as her eyes. It had tailored styling and looked much like a shirtwaist, but when she moved the inverted pleats belled full and drew attention to her long, well-shaped legs. The dress just touched her knees. With it she wore black *peau de soie* slings with a matching *peau de soie* clutch bag. Her only ornaments were a pair of jade earrings, the moon shape following the curve of her ear. Of course she wore her gold watch, which had been a college graduation gift from her parents. She shrugged at her image in the mirror and thought she didn't look half bad. Over her dress she wore her satiny raincoat in steely green that had a mandarin collar and was belted at the waist.

She almost forgot the jewelry Chazz had sent and went back to the room to retrieve it. She then counted it good luck that the elevator sped her right down to the lobby. She went directly to the desk and when she had attracted the clerk's attention, said, "I'm Miss Barrett. I called a short time—"

"Never mind, darling. Don't bother the man." Chazz took her arm, smiled at the clerk, and turned her toward one of the couches in the lobby. He was wearing an evening suit with a cream silk jacket that made his shoulders look even more powerful. The black silk trousers fit so perfectly that he might have been sewn into them.

"Go away," Teel said, taking a deep breath to calm herself. "I'm not keeping this." She held the jeweler's box out in front of her.

Chazz smiled, his eyes glinting dangerously. "You'll

keep them, or I will begin sending more jewelry every half hour until your room is filled." He pulled a cheroot from a gold case and flicked a lighter under it as he held it between his teeth. "I'm getting tired of indulging your foolish whims."

"Foolish whims! How dare you patronize me!" Teel sensed the interested gazes of several passersby and lowered her voice. "I'm not one of your kept women, and I am not going to keep these gems."

"Then throw them away!" Chazz snarled, tossing the partially smoked cheroot into a receptacle. "They belong to you. Either keep them or throw them away."

"Throw them away!" Teel was horrified. She looked down at the box in her hand. "I can't do that." Her voice sounded alien to her ears. She felt the web Chazz had cast about her on the *Deirdre* beginning to tighten once again. "You can't come with me tonight." She tried to struggle free of his invisible hold. "We're going to a show. You don't have a ticket."

"I called your friend Nancy and asked her for the numbers on the tickets," Chazz explained kindly. "I...ah...was able to procure one in the same row."

"I'll bet you bribed the mayor," Teel accused him, her voice throbbing.

"Don't be silly, darling." He looked past her shoulder. "Here come Nancy and some of the others." He took the jeweler's box from her hand and slipped it into the clutch bag he had taken from her limp fingers.

"They won't have evening clothes on," Teel muttered, not looking around at her approaching friends.

"Wrong again, my dove. The three men are wearing dark business suits. Perfectly acceptable for evening," he pronounced in sonorous tones, mocking her.

Without thinking, Teel lifted her foot and kicked him in the shin. It gave her great pleasure to see Chazz flinch.

He leaned down to graze her cheek with his mouth.

"Another one I owe you, darling."

Teel whirled away from him and fixed a smile on her face, ignoring the questioning look Nancy gave her. Rena Listman, another of the teachers at Mary Dempsey School, was eyeing Chazz with speculative interest. Teel felt a sudden aversion for the buxom woman. She introduced Chazz to Buz Denton, the vice principal, Clint Wills, the athletic director, and Dave Chess, the vocational director.

In minutes Chazz had explained his presence and informed everyone that he had booked a table for supper after the show at a club where the music was good to dance to.

Teel wanted to smack Nancy when she "Oooohed" right along with Rena. "We'll be too tired for that," Teel struggled to say.

"Come on, old girl, we only get to New York once in a while," Clint said, smiling down at her. He took her arm and lead her out to the street. To Teel's jaundiced eye, his face had a Machiavellian cast.

When she saw the chauffeur behind the wheel of the Rolls-Royce, she gritted her teeth. "There won't be enough room for all of us," she pointed out hopefully.

Chazz proceeded to show her the jump seats in the back. Buz and Dave were only too glad to ride up front with the driver.

Teel gave Chazz a sweet smile and wished with all her might that a piano would fall out a window when he alighted from the limousine. The thought mollified her, making her smile widen.

Chazz's eyes narrowed on her as he helped the others into the back seat. "Plotting my murder, are you?" he muttered.

Teel sniffed and turned her back on him to engage Clint in conversation. It was a tight squeeze in the Rolls but not uncomfortable for the short ride. She was annoyed when Rena spoke to Chazz and he responded readily.

They alighted in front of the theater, and the car seemed to melt away into the traffic.

Teel was very conscious of the feminine glances aimed at Chazz. Several people spoke to him. When they walked through the lobby, a uniformed attendant said, "Good evening, Mr. Herman."

Teel felt frown lines form on her forehead. When the woman usher came forward to show them their seats, she would have followed, but a strong hand gripped her elbow. "Let me go", she hissed.

Chazz smiled down at her but didn't release her arm until they were standing in the aisle the usher had indicated. "Of course, darling. Here you are. Your seat is right next to mine. Nice, huh?" Chazz purred, helping to remove her raincoat and folding it with his over the seat in front of him.

"The person who has that seat won't appreciate that you've thrown coats over the back of it," Teel said, her lips stiff.

"Relax, love. I bought that seat for the evening too," Chazz soothed.

"What?" Teel cried out, making heads turn toward them. Both Rena and Nancy leaned forward in their seats to look at her quizzically. She smiled weakly back at them, then turned to Chazz, her jaw clenched. "You— you philistine, you," she sputtered.

"No—no, love, you must have misunderstood. I'm Jewish, not Philistine." He took her hand, lifted it to his mouth, and pressed his lips to the palm.

For long seconds Teel just stared at him, horrified, while her body betrayed her by responding eagerly to his touch. She fought against falling into his arms. "Stop that. People can see," she hissed, trying to order the hand he held to free itself.

Chazz laughed, then pulled her arm through his just
as the lights dimmed and the overture began.

The show was good. Teel knew by the laughter that
penetrated the lavender fog enclosing her. When Nancy
leaned forward and stage-whispered, "Isn't this great?"
Teel whispered back, "Marvelous," but she really had
no idea whether it was marvelous or not.

At the intermission they all headed up the aisle for a
cool drink. Teel looked at the glass of white wine in her
hand and wondered how it had gotten there. She glanced
up to see Chazz watching her. He saluted her with his
glass and flashed a devastating smile that turned her knees
to jelly. She rubbed her hand along her cheek, which
ached from keeping her jaw clenched. She moved away
and glared from a distance at the cause of all her misery,
a man who seemed to hold in her in thrall much like a
fox with a rabbit.

"You're awfully quiet, Teel," Rena pointed out as
Teel joined her, not taking her eyes from Chazz. "Chazz
said you spent a great deal of time on his yacht—alone—
with him."

"Hardly alone!" Teel returned. "There was a full crew
with us as well as the captain and Darby, who took care
of me most of the time"

"Oh?" Rena's tone indicated that she didn't believe
Teel. "I'll tell you right now, I wouldn't care if the whole
world knew that I'd slept with Chazz Herman," she murmured softly, as if to herself.

"Slept with him!" Teel's sharp tone turned a few heads
in her direction, including Clint's and Buz's. Nancy was
busy talking with Chazz.

"You never used to be so...so noisy, Teel." Rena
glowered at her, coin-sized red spots appearing on each
cheek. "It's embarrassing."

"Tough." Teel lifted her chin and looked away from

the two puzzled men. She spent the rest of the short intermission pretending to be interested in the other theater-goers.

Sitting through the rest of the musical posed serious challenges for Teel as she tried to concentrate on the show, ignore Chazz, and keep her body from overheating at his nearness. She breathed a sigh of relief when the curtain fell and applause rose like a wave. She watched in sightless concentration as the actors came out for several curtain calls, then she stood like a robot so that Chazz could put on her coat before ushering her back up the aisle toward the exits.

It gave her a measure of satisfaction to see that the Rolls was not in front of the theater.

"I'd thought we would walk from here," Chazz explained. "The club isn't far." He smiled down into Teel's stiff face before taking her arm and adjusting his long strides to her shorter steps.

Despite her agitation, Teel began to feel better, able to push the lavender fog to one side. The animated crowds moving along the sidewalk lent it a festive air, as though the show had imbued them with new life. Teel became preoccupied with looking in the windows of shops that were shut tight with latticed steel gates.

When Chazz threaded his fingers through hers, she stiffened momentarily, then, seeing that he wasn't about to release her, she shrugged and relaxed.

The club was located down some steps from the sidewalk and, when the door opened, Teel heard muted laughter and music and the underlying sound of dishes rattling.

The maître d' appeared before Chazz could remove Teel's coat. "Mr. Herman, sir," he said, his face wreathed in smiles, "we were so happy to hear that you were joining us this evening. It's been too long."

"Good evening, Arthur. You have a table for us?"

"Of course, sir." Arthur bowed, his smile stretching wider.

"Fawning idiot," Teel muttered under her breath. Chazz's shout of laughter made her heart bump against her ribs.

Their table was oval and set in front of a curving leather banquette. As the others slid along the long bench, Chazz held one of the two chairs for Teel and sank into the one next to her.

The waiter described the entrees for the evening. "I hope you all know you are my guests tonight," Chazz announced, smiling around the table. "Teel and I are anxious to entertain all her friends." His grin widened at her gasp of outrage. He turned to her and kissed her lightly on the mouth. "Aren't we, darling?"

"I'm going to draw and quarter you and put you into a tank of piranha," Teel hissed.

"She says, of course, that's what we want to do," Chazz assured the others. "The sky's the limit," he added, holding both her hands in a tight grip as she clenched and unclenched her fists.

"Teel, you sneak." Nancy laughed, leaning forward to look past Clint. "You kept this surprise all to yourself."

"I'll bet it was his idea," Rena stage-whispered to Buz.

"You're correct there, Rena." Teel stretched her mouth in a semblance of a smile. "It was all Chazz's idea."

Buz looked at her wisely. "Ah, cut it out, Teel. We know you, how generous you are. You just wanted to surprise us."

"Surprise, surprise," Teel managed with false brightness, looking at the array of drinks that the waiter had set before them. Had she ordered something? She didn't remember. Drat the man! He was making her lose her mind. It wasn't bad enough that he caused her aches and pains. Now he was making her mentally incompetent. She could feel Chazz's web tightening around her.

"I hope you don't mind"—Chazz glanced at the others—" I took the liberty of telling Arthur we would all like to try 'Arthur's Star,' the specialty of the house, for the first round. Of course, you must order anything you like, no need to stick to this. I just thought you might enjoy sampling what Arthur considers his *pièce de résistance* of drinks." Chazz lifted his glass in a salute. The others did likewise, all except Teel, who frowned into her drink. When she noticed the others watching her and waiting, she raised her glass too. "Here's to—good relationships." Chazz clinked glasses with Teel and drank. "Try it," he urged.

Teel sipped and found that the drink had a piquant pineapple flavor. It was good. She took another swallow and blinked.

"Careful," Chazz warned, leaning toward her. "That's first-class rum."

"I was hoping yours was first-class hemlock." Teel tittered, then sat straighter in her chair. The sound coming out of her own mouth irritated her.

"Shall we dance?"

Teel was about to tell him no when he reached down and lifted her to her feet. "Don't you ever wait for an answer?" she hissed as he headed toward the dance floor. Several couples were already dancing, but it wasn't crowded.

The vigorous beguine rhythm seemed to seep into Teel's blood. Despite her determination to stay as stiff as a board in Chazz's arms, she soon found herself swaying to the music, caught up in the beguiling beat. Chazz was an excellent dancer. It was so satisfying to follow his movements, to twist and turn lightly and surely to the music.

Teel didn't know the dance they were doing by name, but the intricate steps challenged her. All at once her irritation fled and she whirled around Chazz, his hand holding hers high as she spun wildly. Glee bubbled up as she felt her body respond and answer the challenge. She forgot everything but the fast, swaying rhythm that curved her body away from him then back to fit perfectly to his form like pieces of a puzzle. Held close to him, with his face looking down into hers, she saw the laugh lines etched around his eyes and the dark flecks that rayed out from the center. She had the startling sensation that Chazz was sending her telepathic instructions, that her body had to obey.

"You are one beautiful lady, Teel Barrett." Chazz gazed down at her, his breath coming fast. "I think I could spend my whole life dancing with you." His voice held a hint of surprise and he continued to look at her, his eyes going from her nose to her mouth to her hair to her chin.

"Wonderful way to exercise," Teel said absently, her eyes steady on him.

"I can think of many ways to exercise with you that would be wonderful," Chazz growled softly.

"Pushups are good too."

"Exactly my thought, darling," Chazz crooned, twirling her around, then back into his embrace. This time both arms encircled her. He chuckled as her cheeks grew flushed. "You're lovely when you blush."

"Don't be silly. I don't blush."

Chazz leaned down and let his tongue graze her hot cheek."Then you have a most delightful sunburn, my angel."

"Stop doing that," Teel moaned, feeling as though she had just walked through fire.

"Doing what?" Chazz's arms clamped her close as the music changed and the room grew darker. Now his tongue was tracing her ear lobe.

"People will see," Teel protested, feeling her throat close and her heart begin to thud. "You have an awful effect on me," she whispered, trying to get enough strength into her hands to push him away. "Whenever I'm with you I feel as though I'm coming down with the flu." She tried to focus watery eyes on him. "I think I'm allergic to you," she finally pronounced solemnly.

Chuckling softly, he lowered his head to kiss her, and her knees seemed to turn liquid. She clung to him. "Stay with me. Live with me, Teel," he whispered.

"What? What did you say?" She struggled to focus on him despite the cold symptoms that seemed to be affecting all her senses.

"Live with me." He kissed a tendril of hair on her forehead. "If you still want to teach, we'll get a house near Selby. I can commute into New York every day."

Teel looked at him blankly. "Are you saying you want to come to Selby to live with me?"

"I also have a home out on Long Island if you'd prefer that."

"Or you could bring the *Deirdre* up the Hudson, park it in some secluded waterway, and we could fool around on that," Teel said hoarsely, her throat so dry and scratchy she could hardly get the words out. She needed a doctor! "And then what would I do when you tired of me in a few weeks? I might even last a few months. If I was very, very good. Then would you tie an anchor round my neck and drop me into the Hudson? No? Too dramatic?" Strength began returning to her arms—or was it that Chazz was pulling away from her, thus removing the source of her affliction? She bit her lip and stared up into his golden eyes, which were as dull and hard as freshly mined rock. "Perhaps I would just slip back into my old routine as though nothing had ever happened," Teel went on, "as though the bulldozer called Chazz Herman had never gouged through my life. Well, speak up. Tell me how to handle being dumped by a playboy."

"Stop it!" Chazz grated, shaking her, his fingers digging into her arms. "It wouldn't be like that with us," he exclaimed. "You know it wouldn't"

"No," Teel's voice wasn't loud, but her firm tone penetrated to a few of the dancers and several heads turned toward them. "I won't be your plaything," she said more quietly. She stepped away from him, turned on her heel, and headed back to the table. Her hand reached blindly for the drink at her seat, and she emptied it into her mouth before sitting down, desperation making her numb to the bite of the liquor.

"Would you like to dance, Teel?"

Teel looked blindly at Buz, noting the puzzlement that replaced his smile. Before he could say anything else, she gave him a stiff smile and rose.

Just then the waiter stopped at the table and set another round of drinks in front of each person.

Teel stared at the glass, then reached for hers, taking three big gulps before setting it back down and walking toward the dance floor.

"Hey, lady, take it easy on those things," Buz said just behind her. "I've never seen you drink before. Is this some new kick you're on?"

Teel turned to face him, holding out her arms. "You could say that, I guess." Her face hurt when she tried to smile, so she turned away and rested her cheek on his shoulder. She closed her eyes, but that made her dizzy, so she kept them open. This way she didn't have to talk, and Buz couldn't see her face, which she was sure reflected all her misery.

Chazz danced by with Rena, her eyes closed, a dreamy smile on her face. His gaze swept over Teel's face, making her sinuses contract.

Without thinking, she stuck out her tongue at him and was horrified when his eyebrows arched in amused inquiry. Quickly she closed her eyes again and was at once dizzy. What was the matter with her? She couldn't re-

member doing such a thing even as a child. She swallowed around her sore throat. The man was a menace.
She would make him pay all her doctor's bills, and that
included the psychiatrist! She would see a good lawyer,
too. She would sue him for taking away her good health,
her peace of mind. She would take him to the Supreme
Court!

When the dance with Buz ended, Teel felt much better. Deciding on a plan of attack against the enemy was
very salubrious, she concluded, arriving at her chair and
reaching for her drink at the same time.

"Don't you think you've had enough?" Chazz murmured into her ear.

"Stick it in your barracks bag, buddy." Teel sounded
out each syllable, looking him square in the eye.

"You're wifty now," Chazz told her, reaching to take
the glass from her hand.

"Monster," Teel countered, upending the glass carefully down the front of his silk shirt.

"You little witch," he whispered ominously, grabbing
for a napkin with one hand and her arm with the other.
After rubbing at the wet spot, he glanced around the
table. "I'm taking Teel home now," he told everyone.
"The rest of you stay. I'll arrange the bill, so eat, drink,
and whatever until closing." He managed to say the words
in a pleasant tone, but the hand holding Teel's was gripping her so hard that she was sure the circulation had
stopped. "I'll also arrange for the car to be waiting for
you so you'll have transportation back to the hotel or
any other place you might choose to go."

Teel squinted up at Chazz, trying to read behind his
tight smile. "Viper," she said, then gave a sigh of satisfaction—and was surprised when Nancy gasped.

"It's been very nice meeting all of you." Chazz added.
"I'll say good night again."

"Yes," Teel said, holding out her right hand. "And a

good night to you." She frowned, wishing he would release her left arm, shake her hand, and leave. She was most annoyed when he told her to say good night, then spun her around and escorted her through the supper club to the front entrance.

There he paused, said something to the maître d', and whirled her through the door and up the stairs to the sidewalk.

Teel inhaled great gulps of fresh air—and then wished she hadn't. The sidewalk began to undulate, making her dizzy. She squeezed her eyes shut, which helped a little. A firm hand in the small of her back propelled her forward.

Once in the car, Teel wanted to open her eyes, but they seemed stuck closed. She was about to argue with Chazz about several things. One, she had not wanted to leave her friends. Two, she did not want to be sitting there enclosed in his arms. But it was too much trouble to form the words, so she said nothing.

She didn't even open her eyes when Chazz guided her into the hotel. She heard him mumble something to the driver, but she didn't catch the words. She knew she should open her eyes to walk across the lobby, but they reached the elevator so quickly that it didn't seem worth the trouble. The elevator flew up—it must be going faster than before—but Teel still didn't open her eyes. She had no desire to experience the dizziness she had felt on leaving the supper club.

It annoyed her that she was so tired she had to lean on Chazz. She took a deep breath of relief when she heard the door close behind her. At last, she opened her eyes to tell Chazz to please leave her room, that she would be fine now, but her mouth dropped open. They were in the foyer of Chazz's apartment! She rounded on him at once and almost fell. When his arm reached out to anchor her, she shook it off furiously. "You tricked

me, you—you Svengali, you!" She took a deep breath
and reeled.

"You have the most amazing selection of archaic epithets in your vocabulary that I've ever heard." Chazz
shook his head, his voice mild.

Teel watched him unbutton his jacket, then begin on
his shirt. "What are you doing?" Her voice had a faraway
sound to her ears.

"Getting out of this sodden shirt, sweetheart. You
aimed so well." Chazz watched her closely, his golden
eyes glittering.

Teel squinted to keep in focus. "Well, you don't need
me here for that. I'm going home." Damn the man for
bringing her here! It was going to take so much effort
to hail a cab and get to her hotel.

"You *are* home, angel," Chazz crooned close to her
ear.

Teel's eyes opened wider. How had he managed to
get so close to her all at once? He was damned sneaky.
"You don't seem to understand me very well," she pronounced loftily, enunciating each syllable very carefully.
"I am not staying here."

"Yes, you are, my lovely. I wouldn't dream of letting
you out of my sight, especially considering the condition
you're in at present." He dropped his shirt and jacket on
the tile floor and bent to lift her into his arms.

It seemed very natural to place her arms around his
neck. She had to hang onto something. "I have to go,"
she mumbled into his chin, liking the velvet roughness
of his beard on her nose. "You have to shave twice a
day," she intoned solemnly.

"Yes." Chazz chuckled and held her more tightly.

"I have to get up early." Teel felt very sad at the
thought. She sniffed, trying to stem sudden tears. "Very
early. If I stay here I won't get up in time." The rush of

tears made her face wet." "I can't disappoint the children."

"You won't. I'll get you up in time," Chazz soothed, pushing open the door of a ballroom-sized bedroom with a circular bed in the center. The room was decorated in cream and blue with brown accents. A handwoven Indian carpet in blue, cream, and brown covered the entire floor and looked plush and inviting.

"Oh." Teel stared around her, momentarily diverted. "Is this where you do your womanizing when you're not on the *Deirdre?*" she asked *sotto voce*.

Chazz gave a hard laugh and squeezed her tight. "You do say the damndest things," he answered.

Teel smirked at him. "I'll bet you get dizzy on that silly bed." She widened her eyes at him. "Does it go round and round with a motor? Because if it does, you mustn't put me on it. I'll be sick," she promised.

"It doesn't have a motor," he said patiently, placing her on the bed and proceeding to take off her shoes.

Teel put her hand on his head and patted. "I do like thick hair on a man... thick black hair... thick black hair that's straight... thick black hair that's straight but with a little wave." She rubbed his hair. "But did you know that bald men are smarter?" When Chazz looked up at her and shook his head, she wagged her index finger in his face. "Grass doesn't grow on a busy street, you know." She nodded her head sagely, then stopped. It made her feel queasy to do that. "I think I'd like a shower," she told Chazz as he took off her dress and eased her panty hose down her legs. "I'm feeling just a tad under the weather." She swallowed and licked her lips. "Apple juice would be nice."

"Apple juice?" Chazz inquired, standing her up to remove the rest of her clothes.

"I'm thirsty." Teel felt sad again. "Of course you don't

have to get me any." She felt new tears on her cheeks. "I can drink water." She heaved a gusty sigh as he helped her to the bathroom. She felt very comfortable, naked in his arms.

"I'll get you something refreshing to drink." Chazz set her down in the tiled shower cubicle, then adjusted the water. "Will you be all right alone for a few moments? I have to call Sibley and tell him to get the drink. I don't like to waken Mrs. Pritchett at such a late hour."

Teel stood under the stream of warm water and nodded. She reached her index finger up to tap the side of her nose. "Very smart. Don't wake Mrs. Pritchett at such a late hour."

"Sibley won't mind," Chazz said, staring at her body, then swallowing hard.

"Sibley won't mind," Teel parroted, nodding again, forgetting for a moment that such an action made her dizzy. "Good man, Sibley." She closed her eyes and let the water massage her.

A little later, when Chazz stepped into the cubicle with her, it seemed sensible for him to be naked too. She took the drink from his hand without stepping out from under the spray of water.

"You're a kind man." This time her tears mixed with the shower water.

Chazz eased her out from under the water so that she could drink the lime and lemon mixture he held for her. "I'm sorry there was no apple juice."

Teel nodded, feeling magnanimous. "Don't worry. I'm sure you'll do better next time."

"Thank you." Chazz kissed her collar bone.

"Think nothing of it." She smiled at him, then drank the lemon-lime with gusto. She stared at the bottom of the empty glass. "Oh. I was going to offer you a sip." She hiccupped a sob.

"That's all right." His voice was unsteady as he pressed

her close to him and removed the cup from her hand. "I assure you, darling, that I want nothing more than to drink from your cup, but I'm afraid tonight is not the night to do it." He washed her body, then lifted her from the shower and wrapped her in a fluffy bath sheet.

"Tired." Teel yawned, her fingers fluttering to her mouth to cover the gap. She felt herself being lifted and placed between silk sheets. "Thank you," she murmured, then she snuggled closer to the warm body that curled up against her.

She was sure it must have been her imagination when she heard someone growl, "Tonight I'm going to go out of my mind."

- *6* -

TEEL STRUGGLED UP through a woolly world and forced her eyes open. Her teeth ached, her eyes burned, her head throbbed. "Chazz must be nearby," she muttered, then was sorry she had voiced the thought aloud. It hurt her throat to talk. Her eyes focused. She wasn't home in her carriage house in Selby or in the hotel where she had checked in with the rest of the staff. "Oh, God," she mumbled, hazy recollections beginning to intrude. She gritted her teeth and turned her head on the pillow, but what she saw made her temples thump and her teeth clench in horror. She closed her eyes again, hoping Chazz wouldn't be there when she looked again. He was. She tried to roll away from him but found she was immobilized by a heavy arm covered lightly with black hair that was draped over her breasts.

Chazz mumbled in his sleep, and the arm tightened.

Suddenly Teel realized that they were both naked. "Oh, no!" She massaged her throbbing forehead. She had slept with him last night! What was the matter with her? She was definitely going to have to see a psychiatrist. Going to bed with a womanizer, knowing full well what that would mean to Chazz: exactly nothing. She had slept with him twice. She must be mad!

When she tried again to free herself, Chazz opened his eyes.

"Good morning, darling," he crooned, folding her closer and kissing her nose, her cheeks, her hair.

"Now listen to me, Chazz—" Before Teel could tell him what she thought of him, his mouth had taken hold of hers. She felt her heart skip out of rhythm, then begin to race.

His mouth gently teased her lips open, his tongue flicking over them before penetrating into her mouth, heat building between them at once. His hands feathered over her body and came to rest on her breasts. "You have beautiful breasts, my love. My hands remember them. Since we made love, my mind has been filled with thoughts of your body." He murmured the words against her skin as his lips slid down her body.

"No, don't," Teel protested. "Have to get to the Garden. The children." But her hands betrayed her and clung to his shoulders.

"Not to worry, angel. I'll take you there," Chazz soothed, his hands exploring her body as though he were a blind man reading braille. His mouth took hold of one nipple, and her whole being snapped bow-like into his. "Oh yes, my angel, yes," Chazz breathed. "Kiss me, Teel. I need to have you kiss me, love me." Chazz's voice was as fevered as his touch.

Teel hesitated, looking up at him, her hands caught in his hair. Her heart thumped hard against her ribs as she studied his every pore. "Chazz—I—we—"

His arms convulsed around her, and he buried his face in her neck. "Teel, don't ask me to stop now. I need you so much. Tell me you want me too."

"I want you," she whispered without thinking, then swallowed hard. A picture of burning bridges flashed across her mind, the flames shooting high into the air. She moved restlessly beneath him, and he groaned her name.

"I am going to kiss every inch of your body, woman of mine," he crooned, not taking his mouth from her breasts.

Teel wanted to laugh at such a ridiculous idea, but she was too wrapped in her own pink world to make a sound. When she felt him caressing her instep with his mouth, then feathering each toe with his tongue, she gasped with delight. Slowly, ever so slowly, and with increasing passion, he worked himself up the other leg and over her body. Teel felt as though she were being sectioned with a hot, liquid blade. When at last he reached her face, his features looked carved from stone, blood throbbed at his temples, and his breath came hard, as though he had just run up a mountain. "Darling, I can't— do you feel—" Chazz's mouth crashed into hers, making her already heated body flame out of control.

"Chazz—Chazz—please—" Teel's head rolled wildly on the pillow, and she clasped his body fiercely as he lifted himself over her.

"I have never wanted anyone the way I want you," he panted into her neck.

Her body trembled like a volcano about to erupt, the need that filled her shocking her. She sensed Chazz holding back to pleasure her further and her body writhed against him, telegraphing her readiness to him.

Their coming together awed them both, passion blinding and guiding them to a fulfillment that encompassed only them, in a world that was only for them.

Sometime later Teel opened her eyes and cursed the weakness that had robbed her of the strength to say no to Chazz. At once her headache returned. Her eyes and teeth ached. She had to get away from this man before she began to age prematurely. Already she felt one hundred and nine years old.

Chazz nuzzled her ear. "Stop it," he told her. "You're looking around in that little narrow mind of yours for a reason to call our love-making wrong. You can't do it. It was perfect—for both us us."

"I have to get to Madison Square Garden." Teel pushed the words past wooden lips and tried to edge away from him on the round playing field he called a bed. "I must get back to the hotel. My sweats are there."

"Don't worry, precious. I had Sibley go down to Acme, open the store, and get you more team sweats." Chazz leaned up on one elbow, his index finger tracing ima-ginery circles around the tip of one breast. He watched the path his finger made as though mesmerized by the movement. "Of course there is plenty of underwear for you to try on in the bedroom connecting to this one. The room is stocked with clothes in your size," Chazz in-formed her, his voice vague, his eyes still fixed on her breast.

"What did you say?" Teel whispered.

"There are clothes in the connecting room in your size and—"

"That's what I thought you said," she gritted, lifting his arm from her body and shoving him backward.

Surprised, Chazz lay prone on his pillow and stared up at her as she jumped from the bed and turned to face him, her arms akimbo.

"And you thought I would just jump at the chance to wear clothes that belong to your—your women, did you? Well, let me tell you something, buster—"

"Teel, calm down. Come back to bed, angel."

"Don't you call me angel, you—you disgusting Don Juan." She took a deep breath. "And let me tell— What are you laughing at?" Her chin rose higher as her temper reached the boiling point. "Why are you looking like that?"

"Like what?" Chazz asked casually, sitting up and throwing the covers to one side before rising. He yawned and stretched.

"Must you flaunt yourself?" Teel yelped at him, wanting to look away from his beautiful body but unable to do so.

"No more than you, my angel." He chuckled, coming round the bed toward her.

"What?" Teel put up one arm as though to ward him off and looked at the long expanse of her uncovered limb. Her eyes dropped down the front of her. "Oh, no," she groaned, closing her eyes, then opening them at once and sprinting for the bathroom. "You bastard!" she shouted just before slamming the door shut. Even through the thick partition she could hear his laughter.

"I'll get you some fresh underwear, darling," he called out.

"Drop dead," she shouted, turning the gold-handled faucets in the shower on the full blast to drown out anything else he might say.

She stared at the floor-to-ceiling array of shampoos, washing aids, and soaps of every description.

Even after shampooing her hair twice and scrubbing her body until it glowed pink, she stayed under the steam of water as if to wash the previous evening from her mind. Lord, that man should be declared a disaster area by an act of Congress!

Teel would have taken longer drying her hair and lotioning her body, but she happened to look at her watch as she snapped it to her wrist. Eight o'clock! The workers were supposed to gather and be ready to go at nine o'clock sharp. And she had to call the hotel and talk to Nancy first. What she would tell her friend she had no idea, but she must talk to her.

Teel peeked around the door of the bathroom. Chazz wasn't there, but a note was pinned to a small pile of clothes on the vanity.

Teel, these clothes belong only to you. No one else has ever worn them. Love, Chazz.

"Bull." Teel fingered the silken, flesh-colored undies and was tempted to toss them in the trash can, but an aversion to waste instilled in her by her Scottish grandmother and an inordinate love of fine lingerie stayed her hand. "Does he think I was born yesterday?" Teel quizzed her mirror image as she fastened the bra, then sat down in the dresser chair to put on the athletic anklets she would wear with the all-leather running shoes, which she had always wanted and never been able to afford. The color of the sweats was right for the team, but the texture was finer than the outfits the team wore. The sweats fit like a glove and were as comfortable as anything Teel had ever worn.

She looked at her dress draped over a chair and shrugged. She would write it off as a part reckoning for her night of foolishness. What a jackass she was! She gritted her teeth and rubbed her aching temples.

When she opened the bedroom door, Chazz was standing there, wearing a dark blue suit that seemed to have the finest gold thread running through it, bringing out the color of his eyes. A gold chain lay across his vest and, as Teel looked, he pulled a watch from the pocket and studied it. He looked every inch the successful businessman.

"Very good, my love. We have time for breakfast. I

wish I could join you at the Garden today, but duty calls."
He put his hand on her arm and escorted her down the
stairs and through a series of doors to the morning room
where they had lunched the day before.

Mrs. Pritchett smiled at Teel and recited what she
would make for breakfast.

Teel didn't hear her. Embarrassment thrummed in her
ears, her headache grew worse, and her eyes stung. Chazz
must have ordered for her, because Mrs. Pritchett nodded
and left.

"Headache, darling?"

Teel glared at him. "Of course I have a headache,"
she snapped. "I always have a headache when you're
around. You make me ill—literally."

"I don't suppose it could be Arthur's Specials that did
that?"

"Are you implying that I have a hangover?" Teel lifted
her chin defiantly.

"Yes." Chazz smiled at her, then leaned over and
topped her cup with fresh coffee from the pot.

"You're a boor." Sunlight shone through the sparkling
clean windows, making Teel's eyes hurt.

"I dote on your archaic language, love." Chazz looked
up as Mrs. Pritchett entered from the kitchen balancing
a heavy tray, which she set down on the sideboard. When
she'd served them, Teel stared down at her scrambled
eggs in horror.

"I hope you like the centerpiece, ma'am," Mrs. Pritchett said. "Mr. Herman says you'll be doing most of the
flower arranging from now on." She smiled, but Teel
could hardly focus on her face.

"What? Flowers? Oh yes, I like flowers." Teel heaved
a sigh of relief when the housekeeper nodded and disappeared into the kitchen again. "I can't eat breakfast,"
Teel added weakly.

"Here, have some toast. I'll eat your eggs." Chazz pulled her plate toward him and set a plate of toast triangles in front of her.

"Thank you," Teel said faintly. She was sure she wouldn't be able to eat the toast either, but when she looked again, the plate was empty and she felt a little better. The aches and pains remained, but the queasiness was gone.

"More coffee?" Chazz offered, lifting the silver pot.

"No, thank you. I think I'd like more of that tomato juice, please." Teel ignored his smile as he refilled her glass. Just then something that Mrs. Pritchett had said penetrated Teel's foggy head. "What did Mrs. Pritchett mean about the flowers? Didn't she say something about me arranging them? What did she mean?"

"I told her we'd be getting married soon and that you had definite tastes on everything," Chazz explained, rising from his chair and coming around to help her up. "Time to go if you're not going to be late."

"All right," Teel replied. She was out of her chair when his words hit her. "You told her *what?*" she cried, turning to face him. Chazz took hold of her arm to steady her. She wrenched free. "What did you tell her? Did I hear right? Are you out of your mind? How dare you say such a thing?" Her voice rose with each question, becoming more and more shrill.

Mrs. Pritchett poked her head through the open door. "Is something wrong with the food, sir?"

"Not at all. Tell Mrs. Pritchett how good you thought it was, Teel darling."

"Good. Good, Mrs. Pritchett." Teel spoke through teeth clenched so tightly she was sure she would have lockjaw. The older woman disappeared, and Teel turned again to face Chazz. He was gone. "Where are you? You—you Svengali." She stormed out of the morning room and down the hall to the foyer, where Chazz stood with her sweat jacket over his arm.

"Ready, darling?"

"Don't you 'ready darling' me." Teel slipped one hand into the jacket sleeve that Chazz held out for her. "How dare you tell Mrs. Pritchett that we're getting married, you liar."

"We *are* getting married." He took hold of her arm and piloted her out the door. "And please don't call me a liar. I don't lie unless I have to, which isn't often. So don't call me a liar."

Teel faced him in the elevator as it took them to the underground garage. "I would never marry you. I'm not masochistic enough to tie myself to a womanizer."

"That's all behind me now. You can keep me happy in bed, just as you did this morning." His eyes roved from her head to her toes, sending a hot flush to her cheeks. "You have a lovely body, my angel, and I loved making love to it and to you."

"Stop that." Teel gasped, feeling her sinuses fill.

"Never. I'll be making love to you when I'm ninety." Chazz looked smug.

"Me—or a reasonable facsimile thereof," Teel snapped, fighting the insidious languor that seeped into her limbs. "There's no way I would spend my life with a dedicated ogler like you."

"Ogler?" Chazz looked pained as he gestured for her to precede him from the elevator.

"Yes—and worse." She thought of him chasing other women down a street, a white beard flowing over one shoulder. "No," she moaned, reaching for a tissue as her nose began to run. "I'm not a masochist. My life would be one long series of colds and flu, headaches and back-aches. No, I refuse to live like that. It would be an ordeal."

"It would be beautiful." He drove out of the under-ground garage into bright sunshine. New York looked magnificent on this beautiful spring morning.

But the sun hurt Teel's eyes, so she closed them and leaned back against the cushioned headrest. "No, no. Don't talk like that. I'll never marry you."

"You *will* marry me," Chazz promised.

"You're crazy." She made plans to escape to Kenya. He would never find her on the Serengeti Plain. No, Teel changed her mind, with her luck a lion would eat her— a lion with golden eyes.

"I'd like to have children. Would you?"

His question brought her up short. "No," she said out loud. *Of course. I would love your children,* she moaned inside. What a beautiful boy they would have—and maybe a little girl. No, she told herself. There she'd be, taking care of their beautiful children, who would be asking where Daddy was and she would have to tell them that he was out that evening with a busty blonde, or a curvaceous redhead, or a lissome brunette—or all three! "Never. I'll never be your wife," she murmured.

"Do you want a large wedding? I'd like a small one."

"Drop dead."

"A small wedding it is then, as long as I'm doing the planning." Chazz eased the car to the curb at a side entrance to the Garden and leaned across to open Teel's door. "I'll say good-bye now, love. I have a meeting in ten minutes. See you tonight."

"Go suck an egg." Teel poked her tongue out at him, then started to get our ot the car. Suddenly a muscular arm whipped her body backward and she was looking up into Chazz's face.

"I need to kiss my fiancée good-bye."

"Turn blue," Teel retorted, watching his face come closer until it blotted out the light. She groaned against his open mouth.

When he released her, her body seemed to slide forward out of the car. She almost landed in the gutter, she was so weak with longing, but Chazz's chuckle behind her stiffened her spine. She walked away without looking back.

"Wish the kids good luck for me, darling," he called; then she heard the Ferrari shoot away from the curb.

The day was chaotic, and Teel's headache didn't help. More than once her posting of the medal winners was wrong and, though it wasn't the end of the world to make a mistake, Teel felt Nancy and the others staring at her. She sensed the questions they were dying to ask and knew they could hardly contain their curiosity.

Nancy joined Teel for a lunch break. They sat on folding chairs in the crowded snack area, waving to friends between bites and speaking to acquaintances, officials, and parents. The dry-as-dust sandwich Teel was trying to eat seemed to match the way she felt inside.

"I don't think they can get one more person in here," Nancy said, grimacing as she shifted to a more comfortable position. She was about to take a sip from her milk carton when her eyes widened. "Good God, what's that? Did someone win the first race at Aqueduct?"

Teel turned to see what had astounded her friend and gasped at the huge spray of white roses coming toward them. It was impossible to see around the mountain of flowers, but Teel assumed someone was carrying them. A weak, grabbing sensation assailed her stomach.

A capped head poked around the spray. "One o' you Miss Barrett?" the redfaced carrier inquired. "Teel Barrett?"

Teel had the strongest desire to say she was Minnie Brown, but Nancy pointed to her without taking her eyes off the roses. "She's Miss Barrett. Those sure are beautiful flowers."

"Yep." The sweating attendant set them down and regarded them with pride. Then he whipped out a pad and pen and handed both to Teel. "Sign here, please."

"No," Teel whispered through dry lips.

"Lady." The attendant gave her a long-suffering look. "You can't have the flowers without signing. So sign."

"Give them to a hospital." Teel shook off Nancy's pinching hand.

"Now look, lady, I got a lotta deliveries to make and I don' wanna play games." He cocked his head and shifted his weight to the other hip.

Teel stared at him, then nodded and scrawled her name at the bottom where the x indicated.

"Open the card, Teel," Nancy hissed, trying to smile at the gathering crowd. "Just a little congratulations for the team," she improvised when a curious woman looked from the flowers to the card clutched in Teel's hand. "Open the damn thing, will you?" Nancy muttered out of the side of her mouth. "See who it's from."

"I know who it's from," Teel whispered back, ignoring a man who was trying to ask her about the flowers.

"Open the card or I will." Nancy snapped her teeth together over the last of her sandwich, then glared at a matronly woman who had begun to pull one of the roses from the spray. "Stop that!" Nancy stood up and grabbed the rose from the woman's hand. The woman sniffed and walked away.

Teel opened the small white envelope and looked at the card as though she had just drawn the black marble in a gladiator's arena.

Thank you, my darling, for a beautiful evening. Always yours. Chazz.

Teel's head thumped. "I'll kill him," she said as Nancy pulled the card from her lifeless fingers and read it.

"Wow!" Nancy looked at Teel, shock and envy warring in her eyes. "You're a dark horse on the field of love." Her exaggerated sigh penetrated Teel's haze.

"Give me that," she raged at her friend. "You had no business reading that drivel, those lies."

"You're a regular Jekyll and Hyde, ain't ya?" Nancy laughed and stepped out of range when Teel would have poked her in the arm.

"Nancy," Teel fumed, "if you want to continue to be my friend, you will say nothing more about this disgusting flower arrangement."

"It may be disgusting to you, but it's sexy to me." Nancy's face fell. "Why doesn't something like this ever happen to me?" She studied Teel, grim-faced. "I'm telling you right now, if I thought I could find someone like Chazz in a banana republic in Central America, I'd be on a plane in a minute."

"Be quiet," Teel pleaded, then rose and left the flowers where they were.

By the end of the day, everywhere Teel looked, she saw people with a white rose in their hair or pinned to their shirts. The sight made her ill.

That night when the other moderators gathered with Nancy and Teel in the hotel lobby, Teel kept looking over her shoulder expecting to see Chazz coming up behind her. She knew he had planned to pick her up at the Garden and would be angry when he arrived and found the place closed and Teel nowhere in sight. "Ah, listen group," she said, "I've decided to fly back to Selby tonight and not wait for the finals."

Everyone looked surprised. Nancy stepped close and whispered "Chicken." Teel ignored her.

"But why do you want to go back now?" Buz asked.

"There are a lot more helpers for the games than we figured," Teel explained, "so it's just as well that I get back and tackle some of the paper work that has been accumulating."

"But we were planning such a nice dinner at that French place Chazz told us about," Clint said. "Sure you won't change your mind?"

"Do change your mind," Nancy cooed.

Teel glared at her. "No, I think I'll see about getting an evening flight. I can eat at home."

"If you're sure you won't change your mind," Clint urged.

Teel shook her head, anxious to be gone. She hoped she had time to pack her belongings and leave before Chazz caught up with her. Once back in Selby on her own turf she would be able to rebuff the great Chazz Herman quite easily. The thought cheered her as she rode the elevator to her room. It sustained her during a call to the airline to ask for a reservation and then to the desk to say that she was checking out.

When she'd finished packing, she slung her garment bag over her shoulder, picked up her purse, and balanced a small bag in the other hand. All the time she was at the desk checking out she expected to feel a hand on her shoulder. Her back began to itch in anticipation. The desk clerk stared at her as she wiggled trying to alleviate the annoyance.

"I have an itch," she explained.

"Oh." The desk clerk looked suspicious.

Teel considered taking the Port Authority Bus to La Guardia but decided the walk to the terminal was too long. She didn't want to take a cab for such a short hop either, so she decided to take a cab directly to La Guardia instead.

She leaned back against the seat, feeling safe for the first time, until the ride began. Her breath caught in her throat as her driver caromed off the wall of the tunnel and zoomed up the ramp. Teel felt as though she were on a roller coaster ride.

"I don't like tunnels," the driver explained, chomping

on a big wad of bubble gum and grinning at her in his rear-view mirror. It seemed to Teel that he looked at her too much and at the road too little. She was about to mention this when he careened around a truck with much horn-blowing, yelling, and shaking of fists. "Some of these guys think they own the road," her driver informed her, blowing a huge bubble that Teel was sure obscured his vision. "Trying to quit smoking," he explained tersely.

"Admirable," Teel answered finally, when he continued to look at her expectantly.

"Yeah. The way I figure it, you gotta do something else close to smoking, so I chew bubble gum." Another bubble began forming on his lips.

"Marvelous."

During the rest of the ride the driver expounded at length on religion, politics, and his deep reverence for capital punishment. When Teel at last stepped out of the cab at La Guardia, she had to restrain an urge to kneel and kiss the cement. She tipped the driver ten dollars. "That's for flowers in case you have an accident."

"Thanks, lady. You sure have a weird sense of humor."

"So I'm told." Teel escaped into the airport lounge, glad that she had to wait only half an hour for her flight. Between watching the doors for Chazz's appearance and trying to fight the blues at leaving him, she was feeling a little sad by the time she boarded for the short trip to Selby.

She sipped a Coke the air flight attendant served her and gobbled down a small package of peanuts. Her stomach protested at not having had lunch or dinner, but after seeing the roses arrive at the Garden, she had been unable to finish her lunch. Right now the rest of her group would be sitting down to dinner.

Teel's thoughts of Chazz didn't stop even on that brief plane flight. She missed him as though he had been a

limb attached to her that someone had amputated. She
swallowed and blinked away the sting of tears. She would
just have to work hard and force herself not to think of
him. Sure, an inner voice chided, don't think of him—
for maybe fifteen minutes out of every twenty-four hours.
No, it wouldn't be like that, another inner voice insisted.
Time was a great leveler. Maybe she wouldn't forget
him altogether, but there would be long periods of con-
tentment in her life. Her work was satisfying mentally
and physically, and spiritually uplifting as well. She
couldn't be around her students long and still feel down;
they always buoyed her spirits. She took a deep breath.
She would be content with that.

It was raining when the small jet landed in Selby.
Teel stood at the empty cab stand and sighed. She would
have to wait. It was too long a walk to her house, and
she didn't want to disturb any of her friends during what
could be their dinner hour. Binny's was the only local
taxi service. No doubt Monica Binny would be the driver.
Teel settled down to wait in the dingy waiting room and
listlessly flipped the pages of some year-old, dogeared
magazines that had been flung on a rickety coffee table.
The cab arrived forty-five minutes later. She stowed her
bag in the trunk and got into the back seat to listen to
Monica Binny's long list of complaints.

"My bunions are killing me," Monica wailed. "All
the hard work I do." She glared in the rear-view mirror
as if daring Teel to disagree with her. "I'm going to
Florida for a vacation. Boy, do I need the rest. I'm going
to Disney World."

"Oh," Teel replied, wondering how Disney World
would help Monica's bunions.

Monica drove through the center of town and began
the circuitous climb up the narrow road that led to Teel's
house, the old stone carriage house on the Minder estate
just outside of town. The estate had been sold years ago.

The big stone mansion had been converted into the town historical museum and renamed the Selby Museum.

Just inside the stone walls—the iron gates had been removed many years before—stood the carriage house that Teel had purchased shortly after arriving in Selby. The town fathers had decided that the sale of the unused carriage house would bring revenues they could use on the mansion-museum.

Teel had been delighted with her purchase, despite the fact that it needed a thorough cleaning and lacked every modern convenience except electricity. With great enthusiasm, she had wangled a home-improvement loan from a local bank and proceeded to remodel the inside. She had hired a couple of college kids to paint and clean the stone work outside and had planted a small garden on the quarter acre of land that the town fathers had staked out as her property. It had taken Teel five years to refurbish the cottage. Though there was nothing fancy about it, she was happy there.

The downstairs consisted of one large room that served as a combined living room, dining room and kitchen. At the carpenter's suggestion, she had added a tiny but convenient powder room with a shower cubicle.

As Teel unlocked the front door, she looked around her and sighed with pleasure. Everything was just as she had left it. The round, braided rugs in red, cream and blue looked bright and colorful when she turned on the light. She glanced up the steep stairway that hugged one wall and smiled at the braided rug oblongs in the same red, cream, and blue colors on each step. She left her garment bag and suitcase at the foot of the stairs. She would carry them up when she was ready to go to bed.

She walked into the small kitchen, which was separated from the lounge area by a long counter topped in azuelos tile that her aunt's friend had sent her from Central America. She was leaning on the counter eating a peanut butter sandwich and drinking a glass of milk when the doorbell rang. She frowned as she walked across the room to answer it, wondering who it could be.

She threw the door wide open, not fearing intruders, and gasped when she saw who was standing there.

"Hello, darling. You have peanut butter on your mouth." Chazz stepped inside and pulled her into his arms, his mouth covering hers, his tongue licking the peanut butter from her lips.

Immediately Teel's head began to ache, and a sweet lassitude invaded her limbs. Chazz had found her!

- 7 -

THE KISS DEEPENED before Teel could rally her defenses and fend Chazz off. His tongue teased the inside of her mouth, lighting small fires wherever it touched.

Teel heard someone groan his name, then, as her arms came up to hold him, she realized it had been her own voice. Sanity returned in a cold wave, and she tried to thrust Chazz away. She succeeded in wedging only a centimeter of space between them.

"Stop that! Just where do you think you are?" she huffed, getting crosseyed from staring at him so closely.

Chazz nodded and swept Teel off her feet. "You're right. It's too cold here to make love. We'll close the door and do it inside."

"We will not!" she shouted at him, struggling to get free. It irritated her that he managed to hold her and close the door with his shoulder at the same time. "This is my

115

home . . . and . . . you . . . have no rights here." She continued to push at him even when he sank down onto the couch next to the fieldstone fireplace.

Chazz held Teel in his lap and looked around him. "This is very nice, Teel. I think we'll be very comfortable here."

She looked at him, mouth agape, anger pulsing through her. "You have a few slices missing in your loaf, man, if you think I'll let you stay here."

"I'm staying. You owe me for all those days and nights on the *Deirdre,* all those great meals Rowan cooked for you. Good chef, isn't he?"

"Yes." Teel tried to wriggle out of his lap.

"Darling, when you move like that you make me forget everything but how good we are together in bed." Chazz feathered her forehead with tiny kisses.

"Stop that," she hissed, glaring up at him, cursing her blood pressure that was steadily rising. "If I owe Rowan for those meals, then I'll pay *him.* Just make out a bill."

"I'm Rowan's employer. You owe *me.*"

"Then make out the bill," Teel repeated.

"You couldn't afford it. But since I'm a magnanimous—"

"Balderdash and twaddle," Teel interrupted, taking in deep breaths, trying to keep her fury in check. "You're a Sephardic rug merchant who intends to take me to the cleaners."

"You got it," Chazz agreed simply, kissing her under the chin.

"Stop that." Teel glowered. "I'll get a loan. I'll pay you back."

"You aren't listening, sweetheart. You couldn't afford it." Chazz leaned back on the couch, taking her with him, keeping her pinned to his chest. "Yes, it's nice here. I like it. And it's just a short flight from New York."

"Is that how you got here? There wasn't another flight before or after mine." Teel's eyes narrowed on him.

He chucked her under the chin and kept a firm grip on her. "I flew my own plane, love."

"Oh, no!" Teel closed her eyes. "You're disgusting."

"Love, I wish you wouldn't call me names. Think how upset our children will be."

"We're not having children."

"Of course we are. You're not the kind of woman who would want to be childless. But we won't discuss it right now, if you'd rather not." Chazz lifted her hand to his mouth and sucked on each of her fingers in turn. "You taste good, Teel."

She took advantage of his absorption and wrenched her body away from him. In her scramble to be free of him she almost tumbled to the floor, but finally she staggered to her feet. She stood in front of him, her fists on her hips. "If you think I'm going to listen to my children bewailing the absence of a father out gallivanting with assorted women, you're one brick short."

Chazz leaned back against the cushions, his arms folded across his chest, a smile lifting the corners of his mouth. "I love your expressions, angel. What did you do? Take a crash course in archaic English?"

"Don't mock me, you—you—international woman chaser, you." Teel sucked in a deep angry breath.

"Angel, did you know that your breasts look wonderful when you do that?" Chazz's voice held a soft promise.

Teel hunched forward, suddenly remembering that she was braless. "Don't change the subject."

"What was it?" Chazz took off his jacket and leaned down to slip the short tooled boots from his feet. "Ah, that's better. Courting you is exhausting. You'd think you'd take pity on a hard-working man and not hop all over the state."

"Take a walk," Teel said unfeelingly.

"I'd love to, but not tonight. I'm tired."

"Then get a motel," Teel said between gritted teeth.

"No. I'm staying here. I've already left orders for Sibley to pack more of my things. Darby will drive them up here once I phone and give him more specific directions." Chazz grimaced. "You might have given me a more detailed idea of my destination."

"Leave."

"No." He met her gaze without flinching. His voice was still bland, but a metallic glint shone in his golden eyes.

"I'll call the police." Teel fought down her growing panic. She had to get rid of him, she just had to.

"Go ahead. I'm not leaving. And if they try to take me forcefully, I'll call the newspapers and give my side of the story."

"Which is what?" Teel demanded, her voice hoarse.

"Only that you promised to be mine and now you're intent on dumping me. That I'm pining with a broken—"

"Stop that. Stop it right now." She tried another tack. "How can you want to stay where you're not wanted?"

"Oh, I'm wanted, love, and by you. Shall I show you just how much we want each other?"

"No!" Teel shouted. "You can't sleep in my bed."

Chazz shrugged. "I'll sleep in another room if you insist."

"I don't have another room," Teel said, triumphant. "You'll have to go to a motel."

"No." Chazz's voice was like steel rivets. "I'm staying here." He looked around. "If worse comes to worst, I'll sleep here, on this couch."

"You can't. You're too tall. You'll be cramped," Teel argued desperately.

Chazz pulled up the cushions. "This is one of those hide-a-bed things, isn't it?"

"Yes, but it's a regular size, not a king size. Your feet will hang off the end." She watched him. When he turned a speculative look on her, she hurried on. "My bed is queen size. It would be too short for you, too."

"But better than the double bed."

"I'm going to use my bed—alone." Teel prayed he wouldn't try to change her mind. She knew she would take very little coaxing, despite all her intentions.

"All right," Chazz conceded. "I'll take this bed." With that he was on his feet, making Teel jump backward like a scalded cat. He pulled the cushions from the couch and placed them neatly on a nearby chair. "Where are the sheets?"

Teel stood staring at him, her hands clasped into tight fists.

"Well?" Chazz asked.

"What? Sheets. Yes, I'll get them." She rushed up the narrow staircase, taking the steps as fast as she could.

At the top of the stairs she tried to catch her breath, feeling disoriented. *I'm going to marry that man*, she moaned silently. *I'm not going to resist him at all*, she groaned, her teeth coming together so hard that she wondered briefly if they'd cracked. *He's holding me in a velvet trap! The more I struggle and yell at him, the tighter the trap gets. Why don't I fight harder?* she grated to herself.

Because you want to marry him, her inner self pronounced like a death sentence. *You want him, no matter what the cost, despite the pain.*

I'll keep fighting, she moaned to the voice.

Save your strength for when you're married to him, crackled the unfeeling person deep inside her. *You'll need it.*

Teel plunged her hand willy-nilly into the shallow linen closet, grabbing whatever she found, tumbling several neatly folded sheets and towels onto the floor. "Damn,

damn, damn," she muttered. "He makes more work for
me. And he's ruining my health." She refolded the linens
that had fallen and returned them to their proper piles.
"Why should I put up with this? I'll hire a body guard.
No, a guard dog would be cheaper. I'll get a killer Doberman," she told the lace-edged pillow case that Aunt
Tessa had embroidered for her.

Teel ran gentle fingers over the beautifully worked
lace, remembering how her aunt had told her to save the
pillow cases and sheets that she had embroidered for her
own hope chest.

Teel blinked, then grabbed two sheets, two pillow
cases, and a blanket from the pile and started pell-mell
down the stairs.

Chazz's voice froze her in her tracks. "For God's sake,
Teel, be careful." He frowned up at her from the bottom
of the stairs. "Do you always come down the stairs in
that headlong fashion? You need me in more ways than
I realized." A smile spread slowly over his face. "Come
down the rest of the way. Don't just stand there."

Teel lifted her chin defiantly. "I'm just waiting for
you to get out of my way."

"Oh, is that what you're doing?" Chazz grinned,
stepped back one step, and cocked his head inquiringly.
Then he stepped back another smaller step and looked
at her again.

Teel began to descend slowly, walking in her most
sedate way. When she reached the bottom step, Chazz
flashed forward and locked his hands around her waist.

"I like this," he crooned. "Being face to face, nose
to nose with you, I mean." His grin widened as her cheeks
burned. "Did you know that you have tiny little gold
flecks that ray out from the center of your eyes?"

"Yes," Teel answered tersely.

"Did you know that the gold flecks match those in

my eyes?" he whispered, his tongue touching her lips in a quick caress.

"What?" Teel said.

"Don't you think our children will have beautiful eyes?" he murmured into her neck.

"Maybe."

"How many should we have?"

"The national average is two and a half, I think," Teel answered, dazed.

"Don't you think three would be better than two and a half?" Chazz chuckled into her throat.

Then she realized that her head was thrown back to expose all of her throat to his swift, hot kisses. She wondered vaguely who had pushed her head back. "Three is an odd number," she said vaguely.

"True. Would you like four, do you think?"

"That's a nice round number. Not too big, not too small."

"Right."

Teel's eyes refocused. She blinked at a grinning Chazz, her words repeating themselves in her mind. "Stop that," she told him, pushing his hand away from her thigh. "You're a menace," she hissed, shoving the sheets, pillow slips, and blanket at his chest. "Here. Make up your own bed."

"Yes, ma'am. I think that's only fair. Since we both work at demanding jobs, we should share the chores." He shifted the bundle of linens under one arm and took her elbow, leading her down the last step and across the small foyer into the living room. "What days do you want me to do the cooking?" he asked, setting down the bedding and glancing around the room. "You forgot the pillows," he said softly.

"Oh." She had been thinking about what he'd just said about cooking. "I'm sure you can't boil water." She whirled and rushed back up the stairs.

"Don't be too sure, love," he called up after her.

She ignored him, reaching up to the top of the linen closet to get her extra pillow. She looked at the striped ticking without seeing it. What if he liked two pillows? She ran into her own room, took one of the pillows off the bed, stripped the case from it, and carried both down the stairs.

Chazz was standing where she had left him, holding a pillow slip out in front of him. She noticed that the sheets were already on the bed. He watched her closely as she walked toward him. "This is beautiful work." He gestured toward the lace-edged linen. "It looks hand done."

"It is," Teel whispered, wondering how she had come to take Aunt Tessa's hand-embroidered pillow slips from the linen closet.

"The sheets match the pillow slips, but there's a tiny difference in the edging."

"Yes." Teel stared wide-eyed at the sheets that her aunt had made so lovingly, sheets that she intended to use only if she ever got married. She had been fairly sure that she would never use them. Now she had given them to Chazz. She really had to get her act together.

He grinned at her. "I'm flattered that you let me use such treasures, darling. Are they from your hope chest?"

"Yes—no!" she corrected as his grin widened and his golden eyes took on a speculative look. "They're just some old things I had around the house. I generally use them for drop cloths when I paint," she lied, gulping a silent prayer that Aunt Tessa would never know she'd spoken such blasphemy.

Chazz chuckled. "Liar," he told her softly. He reached for one of the pillows, catching it under his chin as he fitted the case to the bottom and let the pillow slide inside. "We'll have to take very good care of these. We'll want our girls to have them one day."

"Never," Teel snapped.

"Why darling, I never imagined that you would be selfish with our girls," Chazz reproved her, his eyes bright with mischief.

"You know damned well that wasn't what I meant at all," Teel hissed, her fingers curling into fists.

Chazz yawned. "Let's not fight now, love. I need my sleep." He looked at her sideways, watching her gnaw at her lip. "Are you going to get my hot milk?"

"Take a jump off a bridge!" Teel fumed, whirling and running up the stairs two at a time. She heard him laughing as she slammed her bedroom door shut behind her.

She stood against the closed door, her hand covering her mouth. That man! Now he was giving her stomach trouble. She, who had an iron digestive tract, was probably getting an ulcer, she decided as her stomach churned sickeningly.

She strode into the bathroom, stripping off her clothes and scattering them every which way behind her. She would take a long, hot shower. That would help her sleep.

The soothing warm water was sluicing over her and she'd just soaped herself thoroughly when the water turned ice cold, making her shriek.

Shivering, wrapped in two fluffy bath sheets, she rushed out of the bathroom, stalked across her large bedroom, and yanked open the door. "You hog!" she shouted down the stairs. "You took all the hot water! Who told you you could use my shower?" she demanded. "I'll bet you can't fit into the powder room, much less take a shower in it!" She was still shouting down the stairs, bent double, when Chazz appeared at the bottom, rubbing his wet hair with a towel.

"Did you want me to shower up there, darling?" he inquired pleasantly.

"What?" Teel snapped erect, fumbling with the slipping terry-cloth bath sheets. "Up here? No, of course I don't want you showering up here."

"Well, then." He shrugged, staring up at her as if X-raying her through the towel. "Shall I come up and kiss you good night?"

"Certainly not!"

"Okay, you come down here and kiss *me* good night."

"No!" Teel's voice was frigid. She whirled away, her chin in the air, and stumbled over the end of the towel. She stubbed her toe on the edge of the door and staggered into her room on one foot, then slammed her bedroom door closed and shouted through it, "And don't you dare take all the hot water again!"

She returned to the bathroom, rinsed herself quickly, cleaned up after herself and dropped the wet towels down the laundry chute. As she sprayed the bathroom tiles with cleaner and wiped around the sink, she muttered imprecations. "No doubt he left my powder room a mess," she grumbled into the cupboard under the vanity where she replaced her cleaners and sponges.

Once she was settled in bed, Teel tried to read. First she tackled some school work that needed her attention. When she couldn't concentrate on that, she reached for the novel she'd borrowed from Nancy, who'd told her it was well written, but steamy. Teel was able to picture the hero quite easily.

Before the first chapter ended the author had described him as Nordic with blue eyes. Teel saw him as dark with a slight hook to his nose and expressive gold eyes. She thought the blonde heroine was rather insipid and, as she read further, she was happy to see that the heroine's hair was darkening to chestnut.

By the third chapter she was yawning and blushing, picturing Chazz and herself in the panting corkscrew positions of the passionate duo in the book. "What am

I going to do," Teel whispered. "I can't get him out of my mind."

She yawned again, making her jaw crack. She lay down and couldn't get comfortable. But eventually sleep overtook her, soothing her. She dreamed she was held close in Chazz's arms. For once, her inner voice of caution was silent. She felt thoroughly relaxed.

When Teel opened her eyes and heard birds singing outside her window, she knew at once it was Saturday. Ahhhhh! She lay back and closed her eyes.

They snapped open again. Chazz was downstairs! Her body sprung into a sitting position. She listened. Nothing. Maybe he had left. No doubt he worked on Saturday. That would be a relief. He would be away all Saturday. She could rest.

She swung her feet out of bed and stretched, then went to the bathroom, where she brushed her teeth and hair. She padded back to her room, naked, not bothering with her robe.

Every morning, before she dressed, Teel ran in place for ten minutes, then slipped on her sweats, took the pressed clothes that she intended to wear that day with her, and drove to the local high school. There she would swim forty laps in the Olympic-sized pool. If the weight room was unoccupied, she worked out on the Universal Weight Machine before swimming. If the room was crowded, she skipped that portion of her physical fitness for the day. On weekdays she showered and changed there and drove directly from the high school to the Mary Dempsey School for Exceptional Children, skipping breakfast. On weekends she treated herself by having the special at the local Greek diner.

Now, out of breath from running in place, she made her bed before returning to the bathroom and splashing her body with cool water, then wiping herself dry and slipping on her sweats. She put a skirt, vest, blouse, pantyhose and sling backs into her canvas carryall.

Teel skipped downstairs, whistling—and stopped dead. Chazz stood there in a pair of slacks, his chest bare, holding his folded bedding. The bed was back in its original position as a couch. "What are you doing here?" Teel demanded.

"Did you forget that I slept here last night, darling? Where are you going?"

"No, I didn't forget. I just thought you might have left to go to your office."

"Never on Saturday, love, not unless it's an emergency."

"I'll pray for an emergency," Teel retorted frostily, grabbing her car keys from the hook near the door and opening the front door.

"Where are we going?" Chazz asked behind her.

"I don't know where you're going. *I'm* going swimming, then for breakfast." She held her nose high in the air.

"Suits me," Chazz replied, lifting a leather bag from the floor next to the couch. "Just let me get into my sweats." He pulled cocoa brown sweats from the bag, slipped off his slacks, and put on his sweats before she could protest.

Teel gulped and averted her eyes. "You don't have a swim suit."

"Yes, I do. Sibley always packs this bag with essentials. I'm ready. Let's go."

Teel discarded several scathing remarks that came to mind as they headed out the door. None seemed destructive enough to suit her mood. "I'm sure you won't like the diner," she said.

"Smug, darling? That's not like you." Chazz cocked his head at her Chevy Camaro. "Shall I drive?"

"Certainly not." Teel felt a ray of hope. "If you don't like being driven by a woman, then stay here. I like to drive my own car."

"That's fine with me." Chazz stepped into the carport that Teel had had built onto the carriage house and held open the door to the driver's side. When she had slipped behind the wheel, he closed the door and went around to the other side, then eased into the bucket seat next to her and smiled. "All ready."

Teel gunned the motor and shifted into reverse. The gears ground. Her annoyance soared. She had always prided herself on never grinding the gears. She loved to drive a shift car and knew she was both careful and confident. She ground her teeth as Chazz turned to look at her. "It may interest you to know," she began, "that I have never ground the gears on this car before this moment." She spun the wheel, making the car rock and spew stones.

"Of course," Chazz agreed, grinning wickedly at her when she threw him a glowering look.

Teel decided her best course was not to speak to him at all. That way she wouldn't be tempted to run her car up a tree.

Teel lived only a mile from the high school, which they reached in short order. She nodded and waved to the students who had Saturday duty at the door to the pool, then she and Chazz separated at the locker rooms. Since the weight room was filled with students, Teel decided to skip it.

There was only one person other than Chazz in the pool. Teel slipped into a lane next to his, admiring the slick, clean strokes that carried him rapidly through the water. Soon they were both creaming up and down the pool. Though Teel put everthing she had into her swimming in an effort to pull ahead of Chazz, she couldn't keep up with his powerful strokes.

After fifteen laps she was panting. Chazz stopped next to her, his own breathing scarcely affected by the vigorous exercise.

"Macho man," Teel breathed as she hoisted herself up on the edge of the pool. She felt rather than saw Chazz heave himself up next to her.

"I'll see you when you're dressed," he told her, laughing.

Teel crashed around the locker room, slamming the door, dropping her key, and nearly scalding herself in the shower. "Now he's going to burn me to death," she seethed, shampooing her hair with a vengeance. "Owwww!" Damn, she'd gotten soap in her eyes. It took a long rinse to relieve the sting.

Teel stalked away from the shower room muttering to herself, intent on dressing as fast as she could. Instead of soothing her, as her swim usually did, it had left her more frazzled than when she'd first arrived. And she hadn't even lifted weights. That man! He was even attacking her mind. Now, when she went out to the lobby, he'd be waiting for her—to do more damage. She straightened slowly from in front of her locker. Why should she hurry out there to him? Let him wait.

Suddenly Teel had an idea. The sauna! She rarely used the facility, but today she would—if only to keep him waiting.

Since the school had only one sauna, which was used by both men and women, the rule was to wear a bathing suit and shower afterward.

Grimacing at her soggy, cold suit, Teel pulled it on again and shivered. After grabbing a towel, she slammed her locker door shut and hurried through a short tunnel that led to where the sauna was situated, equidistant from the men's and women's locker rooms.

Teel stepped into the wooden cubicle and immediately felt suffocated, as she always did in it.

"Hello, love," Chazz said behind her.

Teel jumped in surprise, her heart pounding like a trip hammer.

"What are you doing here?" she demanded.

"It occurred to me that you might find some excuse to keep me waiting, so I thought of this. When I saw you run down the tunnel, I went back and got my own suit," he explained, stretching out beside her on the upper level.

When she sat erect and put her feet on the next level down, Chazz moved closer and put his head in her lap.

"Stop that." Teel tried to lift his head. Ignoring her, he turned his face into her abdomen and hooked one arm around her body. Teel felt his mouth on her navel. "I—I don't want to stay in here too long," she said. "Too hot."

"Right." He spoke into her body. "I'll be ready to leave when you are."

Chazz's hand burned into her spine. She shook her head to keep the perspiration from running into her eyes. Her blood pressure was rising, she was sure of it. "I want to leave now," she announced suddenly, standing up so quickly that Chazz almost tumbled off the wooden bench.

Good reflexes saved him from a hard fall, but he clutched at Teel to right himself. "Would you mind giving me a little warning when you decide to do things like that?" he suggested, both amused and perturbed.

"Sorry. Hot." Teel jumped down to ground level and pushed open the wooden door.

"See you in the lobby, angel," Chazz called.

Teel grumbled continuously as she sluiced herself with cold water, redried her hair, and brushed it into a gleaming chestnut fall. After dressing in her panty hose and a denim skirt and vest with a pale silk blouse, she studied herself in the mirror. She ignored the fact that the color of her blouse matched her eyes and was a perfect foil for her hair. She barely noticed her long, shapely legs and trim ankles and looked instead at her low-heeled sling backs, which were as comfortable as slippers. Most of all, she studied her face carefully for signs of defeat by the determined assault of a man called Chazz Herman.

"Don't you dare think he has defeated you," she admonished her mirror image as she pouted her mouth to apply lip gloss. "Tell him to go to hell." She nodded at the image, slapped the lip gloss into her shoulder bag, picked up her carryall, and left the locker room.

Chazz was waiting for her in the lobby, his hair still damp and curly from his shower. He wore beige slacks with a beige shirt in a deeper shade and a tan suede vest that he had left open. His shoes were beige loafers in finest suede. He looked like what he was, a modern Croesus, Teel decided grudgingly.

Chazz seemed to sense Teel's presence, and he looked around, his face lighting up when he saw her. "Ready, darling?"

Teel had no intention of smiling at him, but she couldn't help it. She just stood there and grinned and nodded. Maybe she really was coming down with something!

The change in Chazz was electric. He snapped erect, his own smile fading as he strode toward her.

Teel almost collapsed when he leaned down and kissed her mouth—not a light kiss, but a searching, passionate caress. "That's the first time you've smiled at me since we left the *Deirdre,*" he whispered, his mouth just above her own.

"Hello, Miss Barrett." Teel instantly recognized the cold, stiff voice. Miss Daisy Butler, teacher, spinster and member of the board at Mary Dempsey School, was staring at them in shock and amazement.

"Miss Butler." At Teel's stricken look, Chazz's eyes narrowed warily. He turned to Miss Butler, placing an arm around Teel's waist, and smiled at the tight-lipped woman. "Miss Butler, you are the first to congratulate me," he said. "Teel has just promised to marry me—next week."

"What?!" Miss Daisy's cry was louder than Teel's protest. The older woman's eyes darted to every corner, as if looking for someone to tell. Teel knew Miss Daisy loved news, yet was rarely the first to hear any.

"Yes." Chazz held a struggling Teel at his side. "I finally convinced her, and since neither of us can take another vacation now, we're going to get married right away and honeymoon later." His smile seemed to mesmerize Miss Daisy. "Of course the wedding will be small." Chazz had to tighten his hold on a now moaning Teel. But Miss Daisy took no notice of her. Her birdlike eyes snapped in anticipation of Chazz's next words. "But we'd like all of Teel's many well-wishers to join us for the reception.

"Never," Teel promised.

"Delightful," Miss Daisy exclaimed. "Where will you marry? Here in New York?"

"Never."

"We've haven't settled that yet," Chazz said over Teel's answer.

"Lovely. How romantic!" Miss Daisy clasped her hands and looked heavenward. Teel kicked Chazz in the shins, but Miss Daisy didn't seem to notice.

"And we hope," Chazz continued through gritted teeth, "that you'll tell everyone you meet. Teel and I are so happy—we want the world to know—owww."

"Oh, dear. What happened? Do you have a stitch in your side?" Miss Daisy focused her attention on Chazz's middle, giving Teel the chance to pinch his rear end. But Miss Daisy apparently forgot her question in the more delightful prospect of informing the town of Selby that Miss Barrett was to marry—"Oh dear, I don't know your name."

"Charles Herman, Miss Butler, but everybody calls me Chazz."

Miss Daisy looked over her glasses at him, frowning. "I shall call you Charles. I can't abide shortened names."

Chazz smiled and bowed gallantly from the waist, endearing himself to Miss Daisy for life, Teel was sure.

"I really must go. There are many people to see," Miss Daisy said vaguely, and she fluttered across the lobby and out the door.

"The old dear can really move when she wants to," Chazz commented wryly as he watched Miss Daisy skip across the parking lot to her Edsel.

Chazz was still watching her when Teel kicked him again. "Love, I wish you wouldn't do that." Without releasing her, he bent down to massage his ankle.

"Now you've done it," Teel accused him. "By nightfall she'll have everyone in the county talking about our marriage. How could you?"

"Don't be so surprised." Chazz looked down at her, his smile gone. "I'd do anything to get you, angel. I thought you knew that." He kissed her mouth again, paying no heed to curious onlookers. "Come on. I'll buy you breakfast."

- *8* -

TEEL PROTESTED CHAZZ'S high-handedness day and night. She was furious with him for going out of his way to inform anyone he thought might not know of their coming nuptials. She seethed when Nancy placed a copy of *The New York Times* on her desk, folded open to the proper page, and she saw the photographs of Chazz and herself.

"I'm giving you a shower," Nancy said, then ducked out the door when Teel took a firm grip on a paperweight.

The phone rang just then, distracting Teel from the newspapers. She reached for it absently and said, "Hello?"

"Hello, darling. How are you this morning? I'm sorry I had to leave before you—"

"How *dare* you put those pictures and that write-up in *The New York Times?*" she cried.

"Actually I'd have liked a full-face picture of you better, but there wasn't one, so we used the profile."

"You know what I mean." Teel took a deep breath and lowered her voice. She rubbed her forehead. "You're giving me another headache. I never had headaches until I met you," she complained. *Lord, I want to marry him. I'm a masochist,* she thought.

"You're too tense, that's the problem," Chazz told her. "Just stop fighting me, darling, and your ordeal will be over. Once we're married, you'll be in excellent health."

"Bull." *Fight him harder, you fool,* Teel's inner voice argued. *Drop dead,* Teel moaned to herself, *I want to marry him.*

"Oh, before I forget," Chazz continued, "I talked to Aunt Tilda this morning. She's relieved that her errant nephew is settling down—"

"Tell her to think again," Teel snapped, determined to go down fighting.

"—and ready to marry the woman of his dreams—"

"Twaddle." God forbid he should ever know how much she wanted to be his wife.

"—so of course I told her we'd be delighted to attend a party at her studio that she'll be hosting for some of our friends tonight."

"What?" Teel shouted. "What do you mean *our* friends? We don't have any friends together." Again she tried to rally her defenses.

"We will," Chazz soothed. "All my friends will be your friends, and all your friends will be mine," he instructed as though teaching kindergarten.

"Balderdash."

"Do you never run out of archaic epithets, my dove?" Chazz crooned, continuing on without waiting for her answer. "I'll stay in town to dress here and I'll send the plane for you. We can fly back home after the party. Bye, love."

Home! Did he really consider her house in Selby home?

She set the phone back on its cradle and stared into space.

Nancy entered the room with several application forms in her hand. For the rest of the day Teel was kept busy studying the forms and checking to see which pupils would be best suited for the facilities at Mary Dempsey School. But she had trouble concentrating on her work—thoughts of Chazz crept repeatedly into her mind—and the hours dragged. Finally, sometime after five o'clock, she cleared off her desk and headed home.

Her phone was ringing when she unlocked the door.

Because she had stayed later at work than she had intended, she was running behind schedule. She dropped her key, cursed, retrieved it, pushed open the door, and picked up the phone on the fifth ring. Somehow she knew it would be Chazz. She didn't wait to hear him identify himself.

"Do you have a cold?" Teel asked, a little out of breath, trying to wriggle out of her coat.

"I'm so glad you remember my voice so well, sweetheart." The laugh was too high—not Chazz's voice at all.

"Who is this?" Teel demanded, her body stilling into alertness.

"Darling, why are we playing games? It's Ben Windom. Didn't I just tell you that?" His voice lowered. "I've missed you, angel."

"Don't call me that!" Teel exhaled, her sudden, explosive anger surprising her. "What do you want? I'm in a hurry."

"I just wanted to wish you well. I'm sure we'll be seeing more of each other now that you're engaged to such a powerful man. Herman and I move in the same circles, you know."

"Crap. Chazz wouldn't travel in your circle because he doesn't frequent sewers. Good-bye, Ben."

"Wait—Teel—"

Teel slammed down the phone. She didn't feel elated by putting him down; she only felt relief that she would never have to see Ben Windom again. For a fleeting moment, she wondered how he had gotten her phone number. Perhaps he'd gotten her address from the newspapers and simply called information. She shrugged, then rushed up the stairs two at a time. Chazz's pilot would be sending the taxi for her soon and she wasn't anywhere near ready.

Teel showered and shampooed her hair in record time. While she blow-dried it, she pondered how she would wear it, finally deciding to leave it hanging free, the way Chazz liked it.

Her dress was a sea-green silk, almost the color of the ocean in the painting above Chazz's fireplace. Teel turned slowly in front of the mirror. She loved the feel of the silk material, which was caught under her breasts in an Empire fashion. The dress had puff sleeves and a hem that just touched her ankles. The square neck was low cut in the Regency style. The dress had a piquant, old-fashioned look that enhanced Teel's long neck and legs. The fabric fell straight, but when she moved, a side pleat parted to reveal a slit from ankle to mid thigh. One of Teel's friends from her college had gone into fashion design and made a respectable living in New York running a small boutique in Greenwich Village. She had designed the dress for Teel, who had then modeled it at the boutique's last fashion show. Teel's shoes were *peau de soie* sandals, the same color as the dress.

Teel frowned at her image in the mirror. Her hair was wrong for the dress and the jade earrings and pendant she was wearing. She recalled that Charine, the designer, had wanted her to wear her hair pulled into a topnot with a fall of curls on one shoulder.

Teel glanced at the clock and groaned but decided to

take a chance that she would have time to arrange a more intricate style.

Clutching the curling iron in one hand, she proceeded, grim-lipped, to curl several locks. Then she twisted her pile of straight hair into a coil on top of her head and pinned it tightly. Again she used the curling iron on the remaining locks of hair, twisting them into two curls that fell down one side of her face. "Good grief, I'm a giant," Teel whispered at her image, but as she turned in front of the mirror she had to admit that the style suited her, giving her a Junoesque grace.

The taxi honked twice as Teel fumbled for her clutch purse. She threw a short evening jacket in white velvet over her shoulders and ran down the steps, praying she wouldn't trip.

"The feller at the plane sez we wuz to be there in fifteen minutes...thirty minutes ago." Monica Binny, the taxi driver, glowered at Teel. "I hope I get a good tip for this."

"Monica, don't try to con me," Teel told her. "You've been tipped already."

Monica shrugged. "A girl's gotta make a living."

During the rest of the trip Monica regaled Teel with gossip about Selby inhabitants. As they pulled into the small landing field, Monica glared at her in the rear-view mirror. "It was Daisy Butler what told me about you gettin' married. You mighta told me yourself, Teel. That Daisy acts so uppity if she knows something first."

"Next time I'll arrange for you to know first," Teel promised.

Monica whirled in the seat, her face reddening from the strain of heaving her bulk around. "Ya mean it ain't gonna last? This one, I mean. You got another one on the line, Teel?"

Teel snapped alert, her eyes focused warily on Monica. "What? No—of course I haven't—oh, never mind. I have to go. The pilot's waiting outside the building."

Monica faced front again, looking slightly crestfallen. "Yeah, that's him. 'Bye, Teel."

Teel had never before flown in a Lear jet. She found the sensation exhilarating. Before taking off, the pilot doffed his cap and handed her flowers, a lovely nosegay of violets, the green of the leaves and purple of the flowers a perfect foil for her dress.

Teel was amazed. "How did Chazz guess what I was going to wear?" she asked, bemused, pressing her face into the flowers.

"I don't know," the pilot answered, smiling as he disappeared into the cockpit. Soon they were airborne.

The landing at La Guardia took longer than the flight itself, but Teel didn't mind circling the field. She was growing more nervous by the second about meeting Chazz's only relative.

When the plane taxied close to a small hangar, she saw Chazz, dressed in a silk evening suit, step from the building, the wind ruffling his hair. He spotted her in the window almost at once, and smiled and waved.

The plane came to a halt and an attendant opened the door for Teel. Chazz was waiting at the foot of the steps, grinning up at her, his eyes a leaping, liquid gold in his tanned face. "I've missed you," he said simply.

"Don't be silly," Teel said, feeling out of breath despite her protest.

When Chazz didn't move from the bottom of the step, she was forced to pause. They stood face to face Teel felt a silken net drop over her. "You just saw me this morning," she whispered, nonplussed by his nearness.

"So I did. I've grown accustomed to coming home to you when I leave work. I like that. Tonight I didn't go home to you. I didn't like that." Chazz rubbed his nose against hers.

"Oh!" She felt all her senses stir and come to life.

"I want my kiss." His nose moved alongside hers, his lips coming to rest on hers. When his teeth nipped her bottom lip, Teel groaned. "You look beautiful, my angel. I'm going to buy you a fur coat." Chazz nibbled her ear.

"No," Teel murmured, her hands clenching and unclenching on his shoulders. "Don't wear real fur. Save the seals."

"Right." He groaned and kissed her again.

"Ahem . . . sir . . . I should get the plane into the hangar." They looked up to see the pilot watching them from the door of the plane.

Chazz laughed and nodded. Teel reddened and thanked the man for flying her to Chazz.

Chazz was still chuckling as he led her to the Rolls-Royce. Behind the wheel sat Darby, dressed in an official uniform and cap. To Teel's delight, he bounded out of the car and came toward her, his arms outstretched.

"So, Sister Terese Ellen is no more, is it?" His elfin face was wreathed in smiles as Teel hugged him and kissed his cheek.

"Darby, please forgive me for deceiving you," Teel begged, glancing warily at Chazz. "It seemed like a good idea at the time." It surprised her when he looked grim instead of smiling.

"Well, all's well that ends well, isn't it?" Darby shot a searching look Chazz's way, then said, "I just got back from a trip to Ireland to see my folks. Had a lovely time."

"Oh, it sounds wonderful. How old are your parents, Darby?"

"My dad's ninety-seven and my ma's ninety-five, and both of them as chipper as the day they were married fifty years ago."

Teel's eyes opened wide. "Amazing."

Darby helped Teel into the back seat, then resumed his place behind the wheel. It startled Teel when Chazz closed the glass partition between them and the driver. "Ah, I like the violets," she told him. "How did you know what color to get?"

"I remembered this from when I went through your clothes the other evening and thought it might be the dress you would wear." Chazz stared at the back of Darby's head, his voice terse.

Teel was bewildered by his sudden anger. "What's the matter with you?" she asked. "Is something wrong?"

Chazz turned toward her, his eyes glittering fiercely. "I damn well don't enjoy being jealous of Darby."

Teel's jaw dropped. "You have an empty room in your upper works, buster," she breathed, watching his black eyebrows form a stiff bridge across his forehead.

"That I know," he growled. "You've never once come up to me and put your arms around me and kissed me, have you?" He looked furious. She was flabbergasted.

"No," she admitted.

"Damn you." To her surprise, Chazz hauled her into his arms. "One day you will." His mouth punished her. She felt his teeth against her lip; then all at once his lips softened, coaxing her, warming her. Teel forgot Darby, forgot that they were riding in the Rolls-Royce, forgot that she was nervous about meeting his aunt. She was annoyed when Chazz released her and she kept her arms around his neck. The frown melted off his face.

"Wait, darling, I have something for you." All at once he was serious again.

Teel looked down just as he pushed a square-cut emerald onto her third finger. "Chazz!" Her voice came hoarsly, and she tried to pull her hand free.

"This is yours," he told her, his voice solemn. "If you

try to give it back to me, I'll throw it down the nearest sewer."

"At least sell it and give the money to the poor," Teel offered in a dazed voice, not taking her eyes from the ring.

"Keep it. Wear it. If you do, I promise I'll give the equivalent of what it cost to the poor."

Teel's eyes flew to his face. "That's bribery," she cried.

"You're damn right it is." Chazz kissed the ring on her finger. "Do you like it?"

"Who wouldn't like such a beautiful ring? I can't believe it's real."

"It's real." Chazz chuckled. "It matches your eyes perfectly. That's why I had to buy it."

He pulled her into his arms, and she cuddled close to him for the rest of the trip into Manhattan. She didn't even try to move away. She was a prisoner of her own emotions. One moment she rebelled at his high-handedness. The next she melted at his tough, romantic streak. The ambivalence weakened her resolve to fight him.

When the car pulled up in front of a brownstone with a patch of grass and an old-fashioned iron street lamp in front, Teel's fears returned.

Seeming to sense her hesitancy, Chazz practically lifted her from the car and told Darby to return at midnight.

"Won't that be too late to fly back to Selby" Teel asked.

"Yes. We'll stay at my apartment tonight. You have clothes there. I'll have you flown back in the morning."

"I don't have clothes here," Teel mumbled, regarding the front door with its ornate knocker as though she were facing a rattlesnake.

"You do now, angel. I gave your measurements to Madame Delmar."

"My friend, Charine, designs my special clothes," Teel protested, trying to rally as Chazz opened the door.

"Fine. Next time you can get Charine." He paused. "I don't think I know the house."

"Snob," Teel sniffed as he led her into a small foyer decorated in gilt and a soft cerise color. It was both elegant and comfortable.

A woman who looked like an aging Barbie doll tottered toward them on the highest heels Teel had ever seen. Her makeup gave her a pale clown face. Two perfect circles of rouge drew attention to her high cheekbones. Her lips were bowed in cherry red, her eyebrows penciled thin, black, and arched. Her lashes looked as though they had been dipped in black mud. Her amber eyes twinkled with delight as Teel watched her approach. Her all-over curls were dyed a terra cotta red.

"You mustn't try to mask your shock at my appearance, my dear," the woman said. "If you don't look suitably laid low, I shall think I don't have enough makeup on." She stretched to press a kiss on Teel's cheek, her silk caftan, which was threaded with gold and silver, billowing around her.

"You have more than enough makeup on, Tilda," Chazz mocked as he leaned down to lift the woman into his arms and kiss her.

Tilda tapped him playfully on the cheek with a finger. "Don't be naughty. You know I must preserve my image."

"Why?" Chazz grinned, setting her back on her feet and putting an arm around Teel to bring her forward. "This is Teel Barrett."

Tilda Charles put one saberlike cherry-colored nail to her front teeth and tapped, her eyes narrowing on Teel. "So this is the woman who has taken the wind out of your sails, eh? She's a beauty. Would you mind if I painted you, my dear?"

Teel gasped. "But you don't do portraits!" She reddened when Tilda and Chazz laughed. Chazz squeezed her waist and whispered, "Nut."

Tilda took Teel's hand in both of hers, her eyes warm. "Yes, that's true—most of the time. But I have done a few people." She glanced quickly at Chazz. "This ne'er-do-well of mine insisted that I would want to paint you the moment I saw you, and he's right. So, for a wedding present to my nephew, I would like to paint you. Will you mind?"

Teel shook her head, bemused, knowing she should tell this woman that a marriage between Chazz and herself was impossible, that it couldn't possibly work.

"Thank you, darling," Chazz murmured, bending down to kiss her lightly on the mouth.

Teel reddened even more. Tilda Charles beamed and took hold of Teel's free arm. "Come with me," she said. "I want you to meet some friends and"—she shrugged, a tiny frown appearing on her penciled brow—"some hangers-on, I call them. I wonder how these people find out when one is going to entertain," she mused as if to herself. "You can't really throw them out." She shrugged to Teel. "But I resent their being here on such a ... a personal occasion."

"I have no qualms about removing anyone, Tilda," Chazz said. "Just point out the ones you want gone and I'll take care of it." He looked grim as he scanned the cluster of people, many of whom had turned in their direction.

Teel heard many calls of "Hi, Chazz," and "Chazz, how are you." She would have hung back, but a warm hand on her arm guided her forward.

Tilda Charles stopped, her hand on her cheek. "Chazz, my dear, we are both a couple of fools. Neither of us took Teel's lovely jacket from her. Here, dear, let me hold your violets while Chazz takes your jacket. Monroe will hang it up." Tilda gestured to a tall, thin woman dressed in black with a salt-and-pepper bun screwed tight to the back of her head.

Teel felt the jacket being lifted from her body; then she returned to retrieve her violets from Tilda, who was looking at her with wide eyes. "Dearest girl, that dress is gorgeous. You look like a sea nymph. I shall paint you in that dress."

Teel heard other comments as if through a thickening haze, for one look at Chazz's tight, angry face made her pulse race with fear. She looked down at the violets to hide her anxiety. What was wrong with him?

"Chazz, old man, you've snared the most beautiful woman in New York." Teel glanced up to see a sandy-haired man coming up to clap Chazz on the back.

"Yes, I have, haven't I?" Chazz's voice was like hot steel hitting cold water.

"Hello." The sandy-haired man sketched a slight bow toward Teel, who held out her hand. Instead of shaking it, he kissed the back. "I'm Trevor Mahon. Chazz and I attended Columbia grad school together. I'm a much better engineer than he is, and I'd would make a much better husband. Reconsider, o beautiful one."

Teel relaxed, letting her laughter bubble over, enjoying Trevor Mahon's nonsense.

Both men stared at her, unsmiling. "Trev, old man," Chazz mocked, "I'd hate to see your body mangled."

Tervor, who was inches shorter than Chazz but of equal breadth, said, "She'd be worth the risk." He smiled back at Chazz, then at Teel. "That dress is simply stunning on you."

"Yes, isn't it." Chazz folded her closer to his side and bent his head to her ear. "I love looking at your breasts, darling, but if I'd known this little number was cut so low, I'd have made you wear something else. Tell Charine I want higher necklines next time."

Teel looked angrily up at him and her lips barely moved, when she said, "I wear what *I* choose." She almost cried out as the pressure of Chazz's fingers on her waist increased tenfold. She bit her lip, then turned to Trevor Mahon. "You're not a native New Yorker," she guessed.

Trevor looked pained. "And I thought my New York accent was perfect." He smiled. "I was born in Sydney, Australia, but I've been in this country since my under-graduate days at Rensselaer."

"I visited Sydney with my parents," Teel commented. "It was a graduation present. I thought it beautiful, and the people were very friendly." She grinned. "Even though the topless bathing shocked my mother . . . and intrigued my father."

Trevor threw his head back and laughed, and even Chazz's frown disappeared in a reluctant grin.

Soon they were bantering easily back and forth, and Teel felt as if she'd known Trevor for ages. She began to relax and even enjoyed the attention when other guests crowded around to meet her and admire her ring. Some-time later, she realized that she'd been separated from both Trevor and Chazz for several minutes.

Suddenly a voice seemed to come to her out of the past. "Hello, darling. Do I say congratulations or best wishes?" She turned to find Ben Windom looking her up and down, his pale blue eyes boldy assessing her figure, lingering provocatively on the swell of her breasts.

Surprise and discomfort assailed Teel. One of her first thoughts was to wonder what she'd ever seen in the milksop standing before her in a black evening suit, his blond hair thinning but not gray. "Are you a friend of Chazz's?" she asked coldly.

Ben cocked his head. "I know him. Let's just say I'm better acquainted with Tilda Charles."

"Oh, then you must be one of the hangers-on she

mentioned earlier," Teel replied, her voice hard. She watched with very little feeling as Ben's neck flushed red. She wanted to be rid of him as quickly as possible.

"You'd better be careful, Teel," Ben warned her, his features set in an angry line. "How do you think that fiancé of yours would like it if I were to tell him I was the one who deflowered the virgin Teel Barrett at the tender age of eighteen?"

Teel was so angry that she decided immediately to call his bluff. "There he is," she said, "right over there. Why don't you wander over and tell him?"

Ben put his hand on her arm, his smile reappearing. "Now, now, angel, you know I wouldn't do that. I'm hoping we can all be good friends. I have some people who want to do business with your fiancé, and they'd like you—"

"Drop dead, creep."

Ben Windom's mouth fell open and his face twisted with anger as Teel turned away from him, thoroughly disgusted by his vile behavior. But she had only taken two steps when his voice rose behind her.

"Ladies and gentlemen, the newly engaged lady is too shy to tell you that she's a most accomplished musician, but I'm sure you would love to hear her sing and accompany herself on the piano."

Teel turned to see Ben's hard smile and fought to control the sudden fear that gripped her. Once, long ago, a very young Teel Barrett had confided to her hero, Ben Windom, that the reason she had never continued with a music career was that performing in front of people filled her with terror that rendered her immobile. "You bastard," Teel whispered through lips that had suddenly turned icy cold.

Ignoring her, Ben continued, his mouth twisting in amusement at her epithet, "I knew Teel the summer she modeled in New York. Sometimes I could persuade her to play and sing for me." He began to applaud, looking straight at Teel. Soon others followed suit.

Teel looked desperately around the room. The only face that registered on her was Chazz's, which seemed carved from white fury. Her eyes flew over the others blindly, then back to Chazz. His expression changed, and then he was pushing his way toward her, propelling people out of his path.

"Come on, Teel, play," Trevor said from somewhere.

Play. Play. Play. Teel heard the words repeated over and over as if in a dream and shuddered. She seemed to hear her first teacher telling her mother that the only cure for Teel's shyness was to make her play in front of an audience. She heard her mother's doubtful voice replying that she didn't want to force her daughter. Teel remembered her teacher's words later, when they were alone. "Think how disappointed and unhappy your parents will be if you don't play, Teel," she had said. Teel had played—and hated it. And as the years passed, she realized that Mrs. Curtin had forced her to play not from a love of music but because she hadn't wanted to lose a pupil—or the pupil's money. By the time Teel had reached college she was proficient in both voice and piano. It seemed natural to gravitate to the study of music at Nazareth College. But by her junior year she had switched to special education and was much happier. She still played for herself—and sometimes a few friends— but she had never played in front of so many people as were gathered here. Everyone was looking at her expectantly, yet she felt rooted to the spot, incapable of moving to the piano bench, much less making the ivory keys produce beautiful music. Panic engulfed her. She was trapped, humiliated.

"You're frightened, darling." Suddenly Chazz was there, putting his arm around her. "Tell me what's wrong," he murmured for her ears alone. "I don't want anything to frighten you ever." His deep, soothing voice penetrated her numb brain, warming her and unlocking the ice that seemed to encase her limbs. Chazz's touch generated new life in her, making her blood flow once again and firing her resolve.

"I'll play—if you stay with me," she whispered, biting her lip to still its trembling.

Chazz's eyes leaped with golden fire. "Oh, angel, why do you say such things in front of a roomful of people? Of course I'll stay with you." He kissed her lips gently, rubbing his mouth back and forth in a way that left her yearning for more of his touch and taste. "But you don't have to play if that's what's making you afraid. Is it?"

"Stay with me."

"Always." Chazz hooked her close to his side with one strong arm and turned to follow the assembled group, who were moving toward the grand piano by the floor-to-ceiling bow windows.

As Chazz pulled out the bench and seated her carefully on it, Teel felt as though she had crossed some invisible bridge. He released his hold on her and she swung around on the bench to look up at him. She needed him near her. "Will you put your hand on my shoulder while I play?" she asked quietly.

"Darling! Of course I will." Chazz's gaze remained fixed on her. The excitement she saw there, the golden fire, warmed her to her very core, releasing her from the fear.

His touch on her shoulder was her impetus. She bent over the keys with relaxed absorption and Rachmaninoff spilled from her fingers. She barely heard the 'Ohhs' and 'Ahhs,' as she switched to show tunes. Even after five songs she didn't sing, the whispered pleas from the onlookers failing to touch her.

Finally Chazz squeezed her shoulder and leaned close.

"Will you sing a song, love?" he asked. "Everyone's been asking you to sing, but you don't have to if you don't want to."

Teel nodded, her fingers picking out the notes before she knew what she would sing. The song, "I'll Always Choose You," had poignant lyrics and, as she sang them, some part of her seemed to stand outside herself and judge the quality of her singing. Her phrasing was good, she decided, her low register pleasing, even seductive, she realized with surprise. But why had she chosen this song? For Chazz. The answer came without volition. She paused, then finished, " . . . for the one to share my life with, I'll always choose you." And then she looked up into his face.

Absolute silence filled the room as Chazz looked down at her. The others seemed to fade away, and they were alone. Teel felt protected and cared for, as safe as she had felt on the *Deirdre*. For a moment she seemed to float free of the room, free of the planet.

Then Trevor said, "Well done, well done." He began clapping. The others joined him, and Teel's awareness of her surroundings returned. The old fear began to sneak over her once again.

Chazz helped her up from the bench. "You're so beautiful, and I'm so proud of you. I want you so much." His voice was hoarse with emotion, and he leaned down and closed his mouth over Teel's as if they were alone in the room.

Why hadn't he said he loved her? Teel sighed sadly to herself as her arms slipped up and around his neck. She held him fiercely, desperately. She could never hold him forever, but she would hold him for this one moment.

"Release her, will you, old man?" Trevor's sardonic voice broke the spell.

Teel pushed away from Chazz, and he lifted his head, his irritation at the interruption clear on his face. "Your aunt's guests," Teel reminded him.

"Damn them." Chazz kissed the tip of her nose and allowed Teel to push back from him, but he didn't release her entirely. One strong arm still fastened her to his side.

Teel accepted the congratulations of the guests, knowing that she could never have played for them if Chazz hadn't supported her.

Finally she met Ben Windom's malevolent gaze and flinched.

She sensed Chazz's eyes on her as her body tensed in rejection of her former lover. She felt Chazz's intent look follow the direction of hers. "What has Windom to do with you, Teel?" he demanded.

"I'll tell you later," she promised, looking up at him. "He's only a minor irritation."

"Is he? Is that why you looked so stricken when he announced that you would sing and play?" Once again Chazz's face appeared to be carved from marble, his flesh resembling the unfinished form from a sculptor's chisel.

Teel studied his expression, and was unable to read it. But she recognized his implacable desire to know the answer to his question. She nodded and sighed. "All right, I'll tell you, but first I must—" She glanced at the people around them.

"Yes, speak to them. You deserve their accolades. You are a most talented lady."

Trevor was there kissing her hand as Chazz melted into the crowd. Others took his place. Tilda appeared with tears in her eyes. "My dear, my dear. That was just beautiful. You love my boy, and you told him so, so sweetly." Despite her tears, Tilda Charles studied Teel with shrewd eyes. "You mustn't worry about it," she added confidentially. "He's too in love with you to read the signs."

Teel gasped. "He isn't in love with me. He—he just

wants me," she blurted out, then pressed her fist to her mouth, cursing her gaucherie.

Tilda Charles studied her critically, her sparrow eyes snapping, making the clotted lashes look even more unlikely. "Well, well." She nodded. "So the two of you are playing hide and seek with your feelings, eh? Perhaps that's best." She reached up and kissed Teel's cheeks. "I'm going to my studio to make some sketches of you. Come along in thirty minutes or so." She shrugged toward her guests. "They can take care of themselves. Monroe can handle everything for a while." She frowned. "I wonder why Chazz is being so chummy with that Windom fellow. I really don't like the man and can't imagine what he's doing here. He's such a fool. Thinks people don't realize that he looks down on them. Pluperfect jackass." She patted Teel's cheek, then tiptoed away on her ridiculously high heels.

For a moment Teel watched Chazz moving from guest to guest, then she wandered over to the small bar and poured herself a Perrier and lime with lots of ice.

Suddenly Chazz was looking down at her, his eyes conveying a fierce warning that he would stand for nothing but the truth. "Now tell me why you're afraid of that man," he demanded.

- *9* -

TEEL STARED UP at Chazz, assailed by an unexpected feeling of fate taking control of her life. Chazz might look at her with scorn and contempt, but there could be nothing but the truth between them. She would never allow a man like Windom to hold anything over her head. Let the sword of Damocles fall.

"I'm not afraid of him, Chazz," she answered quietly. "I despise him."

Chazz ran an anxious hand through his hair, tousling it in a way that made Teel's heart ache with yearning and led her to a bow window in the dining area, where there was some measure of privacy. "Were you in love with him?" he asked.

"I thought I was." She kept her eyes steady on him. "At eighteen my standards were high, my judgement low. I was just starting a summer modeling job when I met him. I thought he was the man of my dreams."

Chazz swallowed. "I see."

"I let him make love to me, thinking that we were going to get married. I was a virgin and fully intended to keep my virginity for the man who would be my husband." She felt her chin tremble and bit down on her lip. "I suppose most women feel that way."

"I suppose." Chazz's mouth hardly moved.

"Tonight he wanted me to intercede with you so that you would do business with colleagues of his. I told him to drop dead. That's why he introduced me as a musician—"

"You're a fine musician," Chazz broke in.

"—so that he could use my pathological fear of performing in front of people to humiliate me." Teel felt her face crumbling. "You gave me the strength to perform."

Chazz reached out to grip her forearm. "Windom tried to intimidate you?"

"Yes"

"I see."

"Do you believe me?"

"Of course." His voice was flat, almost vague.

Teel's stomach churned. "Tilda wants me to go to her studio," she told him, unable to stay with him a moment longer.

"What? Oh—all right." Chazz led her through an archway out to a hallway and pointed to a door at the end of the corridor. "There. If she's ready for you, she'll open the door. I'll be along in a few minutes. I have some calls to make."

Teel walked down the short hall like an automaton. Chazz hadn't looked at her with hatred, but after years of dealing in the business world he was adept at hiding his feelings. Her hand reached out to turn the knob, a numbness spreading through her body, mind and spirit.

Wasn't she getting her wish? Now that he knew all about her shameful relationship with Ben Windom, Chazz would leave her alone. Wasn't that what she had wanted all along?

She pushed open the door to see an engrossed Tilda Charles, a sketch pad on her knee, her small hand flashing rapidy across the page, then flipping to a clean sheet in rapid motion.

Teel stood there for long moments, staring at the woman without really seeing her. By the time she focused on where she was and realized that she should leave Tilda to her work, the woman looked up.

"Teel, dear, just the person I wanted to see. Would you step over to that platform? It will only take a few minutes."

Teel nodded, glad that no words were required of her. Her jaw seemed to be locked into place. She was almost sorry when, several minutes later, Tilda told her to come down from the platform.

"Ah—I wasn't sure about the eyes. I should have known they would be green, like that exquisite emerald Chazz has given you." Tilda smiled at her as she darted quick looks at Teel, then back at her sketch book. "You're bringing out the romantic in that tough boy of mine," she said, pausing for a moment, her pencil falling still. "You know you're the first woman to break through that barrier of his. For many years I thought I'd be the only one ever to really know him." Her face took on a dreamy look. "He's much like his father. What a wonderful man Itzak was. I think that's why I never married. I could never find a love like my sister had. How they loved each other! It was extraordinary to see. They seemed to mold each other with their love." She nodded once, her birdlike eyes snapping. "It was sad when they died, but I was glad that they died together. I don't think one could have lived without the other." She smiled at Teel. "I knew my boy would love like his father if he ever found the right woman."

"And he did find the right one," Chazz said from the doorway, making Teel jump and Tilda laugh.

"How many times have I told you not to creep up on people in that fashion?" she scolded her nephew, her eyes crinkling in amusement as he came over to Teel, bent down, and kissed her with an intensity that demanded a response.

Teel kissed him back with all the love she could never express directly until, through a warm haze, she heard Tilda chuckling. "Stop it," Teel gasped, pulling her mouth free and hiding her face in his shoulder. She felt Chazz's warm mouth on her neck. "Chazz, please behave," she told him, not really meaning it.

"Let's get married tonight," he murmured into her ear.

"What?" Teel exclaimed.

Tilda chortled. "I knew he wouldn't be able to wait once he'd made up his mind."

"We can't," Teel whispered, reeling.

"Why?"

"Shower." Teel blinked, feeling anesthetized under his probing gaze.

"What does she mean?" Tilda continued to sketch as she questioned Chazz.

He laughed "She means that a friend of hers has arranged a shower for her tomorrow evening in Selby, and she has to be there. Is that right, love?"

Teel gulped and nodded, wishing with all her heart that they could get married that very minute. Was she really going to marry him at all? It seemed impossible, yet Chazz had a talent for making things happen the way he said they were going to.

Chazz sighed. "All right. I'll wait until next Thursday when we can get married in that little church with your

Aunt Tessa in attendance"—he smiled gently—"even though you don't practice that religion any more."

"Chazz," Teel began, an idea flashing through her head that surprised her, "I'm going to ask the rabbi from Temple Beth David to take part in our wedding service."

Both Tilda and Chazz looked startled.

"Don't be so shocked." Teel felt laughter bubbling up inside her. "You've taken complete charge of this wedding—and—well, I want to do this for you. You don't mind, do you?"

"No, I don't mind, love. I'm glad you've reconciled yourself to the fact that you belong to me." Chazz frowned for a moment. "I wasn't raised in any religion. My parents wanted me to choose when I reached an age when religion would interest me." He shrugged, a half smile on his face. "I guess I was too busy to bother."

"I should have made him go to the Episcopal Sunday school at least." Tilda tapped the sketching pencil against her cheek. "You know, Chazz, I think having the rabbi there is what your father would have wanted."

Chazz looked at his aunt for long, pensive seconds, then nodded. "Since we're being married by a priest, which would have suited my mother's wishes, it does seem fitting." He smiled at Teel and pulled her close to him again. "Thank you, love. That was very thoughtful of you."

Teel smiled back, heaving a big sigh. She felt Chazz's lips feathering her temple and closed her eyes. She felt safe. Maybe she really *was* going to marry him.

"I'm taking my lady out to get her some of that food you have there. Then I think we'll leave. Teel has to get up early tomorrow and fly back to Selby."

Wrinkling her nose at him, Tilda put down her pencil and rose to her feet. "I suppose you're hinting that I'm ignoring my guests." She held up a hand palm outward as Chazz was about to speak. "Don't try to excuse yourself, nasty boy. I shall come out with you and sample my own food." She smiled up at Teel, who was molded tight to Chazz's side. "I'll enjoy painting you, my dear. You have the most expressive eyes."

"She's beautiful, isn't she?" Chazz said proudly. Teel's heart seemed to soar on wings of happiness.

When they re-entered the lounge area, she hesitated for a moment, reluctant to encounter Ben Windom.

"He's gone, darling. I kicked him out." Chazz spoke mildly, but Teel detected the gold fire in his eyes. "The word is out that I don't want Ben Windom around you— or near me. He won't bother you again." A muscle jumped in Chazz's cheek. "I had to hold back to keep from breaking his jaw. The thought of him touching you made me sick."

"Thank you," Teel whispered, slipping her hand into his.

Chazz looked down at their clasped hands, then back to her face. "For what, my angel?"

"For exorcizing my ghosts tonight. I don't just mean Ben. I mean for making it possible for me to do the impossible, play in front of so many people." She smiled up at him as they stood apart from the people at the long buffet table. "I don't suppose I'll ever really enjoy playing in public, but I don't think I'll ever be so afraid of it again. Thank you."

"You're welcome," Chazz said simply, and he leaned down to kiss her again.

"Chazz, old man, not only do you monopolize the girl all evening, but you don't stop kissing her," Trevor complained, coming up to them holding a plate laden with shrimp, paté, and flaky dinner rolls.

"Wait until it happens to you," Chazz murmured, his eyes never leaving Teel's face.

Trevor shook his head and offered some of his food to Teel, who assured him she was about to get her own.

"I will never be as bad as you, old man. No one could be." Trevor guffawed and sauntered away.

It surprised Teel to see red stain Chazz's face and neck. It gave her a funny surge of power deep within her.

He looked down to catch her interested stare and gave her a wry smile. "Trevor talks too much." He guided her to the stack of dishes at one end of the long refectory table and placed one of the hand-painted plates in Teel's hand.

"These are too lovely to use," said Teel handling the translucent china with care.

"When we come again, I'll show you Aunt Tilda's collection of Sévres plates. They were given to her by an admirer and are beautiful."

Chazz encouraged Teel to try everything and added more food to her plate when she would have passed it by. She laughed as the two plates became piled high with food.

They found a small table and chairs in a corner. "This is too much. I'll never be able to sleep tonight," Teel protested.

"Good. I wasn't planning on letting you anyway." Chazz grinned when she blushed. "Tell me about your modeling here in New York."

Teel tasted a shrimp and closed her eyes, savoring her favorite fish. She looked up to find Chazz watching her. "I could eat shrimp every day of the week. I love it." She reached over and speared one of his with her fork and popped it into her mouth, grinning at him with her mouth full.

"Devil." Chazz leaned over her, his tongue licking her lips. "You left a little hot sauce on the corner." When Teel fumbled for her napkin and glanced about to see who had noticed, he laughed, seeming to enjoy her confusion.

"Stop it." She looked away from a woman who was watching them. "People are staring at us." Teel tried to smile at the woman. "You've been kissing me all night," she hissed from the side of her mouth.

"And I intend to keep right on kissing you," Chazz hissed back. "And for stealing my shrimp, you get extra kisses." He leaned down again and kissed her full on the mouth.

"You're acting like a schoolboy instead of an executive of several successful firms," Teel told him, feeling giddy.

"I know," Chazz agreed. "You bring out the craziest feelings in me. I'm not the same man I was when we first met." He stared at her. "Colors are more vivid, grass is greener, flowers have a stronger scent, the air is fresher, birds seem to sing louder. It scared me at first, but now I accept that you have a powerful effect on me, lady."

"Check the exhaust on the Rolls. You're probably inhaling monoxide gas," Teel retorted, unable to suppress a happy laugh.

"Brat. Making fun of me when I'm waxing poetic."

"No doubt it's just indigestion." Teel retorted, a heady happiness ballooning through her. For a fanciful moment she thought she might have his words carved in wood so that she could keep them forever. But, no, there was no need for that. She would never forget anything Chazz Herman had ever said to her.

Chazz rose. "Time to go," he said, taking her plate and stacking it with his on the sideboard. Teel got up and opened her mouth to speak but Chazz covered her lips with two fingers. "Don't say anything, love," he whispered.

He pulled her behind him as they wandered from group to group, saying good bye. Chazz didn't hurry, but he didn't pause for long conversations either. "Come on, we have to pick up Darby in the kitchen. He'll be stuffing himself with the food Monroe will have made for him." Chazz retrieved Teel's velvet coat, studying it with narrowed eyes. "You won't let me buy you furs, but I intend to indulge myself by buying you other things."

Teel looked at him over her shoulder. "I—I don't want to be spoiled, Chazz."

"Impossible." He kissed her nose.

"You know what I mean. I don't want a—a meaningless collection of expensive trivia."

"I know exactly what you mean, love."

Darby glared at them when they entered the kitchen. "You're early." He lifted a forkful of paté into his mouth. "You wanta give me an ulcer, do ya?"

"That'll be the day," Chazz said drily. They watched the smaller man clean the mountain of food from his plate, delicately mask a burp, rise, and give an offended Monroe a pat on the backside. He pushed his chauffeur's cap to the back of his head. "I'm off, darlin'. Give my love to herself," he said to the stern-faced Monroe.

Teel bit her lip to keep from laughing at the way Darby gestured for Chazz to get moving, then chided him for being slow. Darby winked at her and continued to berate Chazz as they headed out the back and down the walk to the parked Rolls.

"Why don't I fire him?" Chazz asked once they were seated. He sighed and leaned back against the plush upholstery enfolding Teel in his arms.

"Because you trust him," she answered, gazing into the gold eyes so close to her own.

"How clearly you see things, my own," Chazz murmured. "God, I'm on fire for you."

All Teel's protests became meaningless as he began nuzzling her neck with his mouth.

"I almost went through the roof tonight when I removed your jacket and saw that dress," he said. "Lord, it was all I could do not to throw the coat back on you and my jacket as well." He loosened her coat, letting his mouth curve downward. "I have never felt like that in my life." He lifted his head, a rueful smile on his face. "I was ready to punch Trev in the nose. He knew it too. He told me I looked at every man in the room as though he were my enemy. I can't believe it." He looked down at Teel's mouth, his voice thickening. "But I don't deny it."

"I stopped necking in a car when I was a teenager," Teel told him, in what she hoped was a withering tone, but her voice came out as a whisper.

"I like it," Chazz murmured close to her ear. "After we're married, I'm going to take you out to the park once a week and we'll neck."

Teel tried to smother a laugh. "You fool."

"About you I am."

Chazz cursed under his breath when Darby stopped in the underground garage. "Of course he wouldn't dream of letting us off at the front entrance. He thinks this is more efficient." Chazz glared at a bland-faced Darby as he helped Teel out of the car.

"And so it is more efficient. Good night, Darby." Teel detected a thread of nervousness in her voice even though she smiled at the elfin man.

"Good night, Terese Ellen. I will see you at the wedding, if not before."

"Who says you're coming?" Chazz glowered at him.

"I'll be there, Chazz, my boy." Darby flipped his hand in a good night salute.

Silence fell between Teel and Chazz as the elevator sped them up to the apartment. One light burned in the private foyer as Chazz locked the door behind them.

"I have a key to the apartment for you, love," he told her as he ushered her inside and removed her coat. "Would you like a drink?"

"No—no, it's late." She watched him. "I have to get to sleep."

"Right." He took her arm and led her up the curving stairway to the second floor.

"Where are you sleeping?" Teel whispered.

"With you," Chazz whispered back.

"What about Mrs. Pritchett?" Teel protested, grasping at straws.

Chazz raised his eyebrows. "She would only crowd us, darling."

"You know what I mean," Teel hissed, trying to shake off his arm as he led her into a room she had never seen before, a huge circular bedroom with many doors opening off it. A huge bow window opened onto a terrace and revealed a spectacular view of Manhattan and the Hudson River. The bed was round and pulled Teel's eyes to it. "A seducer's camp cot if I ever saw one," she whispered, her lips numb.

"You're the only woman I've had in bed who has ever meant anything me," Chazz declared. "And you'll be the first to sleep in this bed. I had this room prepared especially for us."

"I'll feel like a lady of the evening."

Chazz stared at her, then pressed a button, making part of the wall slide back to reveal a closet. "To me you are virginal, my love, untouched, unspoiled, and sweeter than honey. When you marry me, it will be the happiest day of my life." He looked back at the closet. "Here are your clothes." He pointed to built-in drawers. "Here is lingerie of all kinds." He smiled at her. "I think it would be a waste of time to wear a nightie but suit yourself. I'm going to shower. I'll use the one that connects to my room. You can use this one." He pushed open a door to reveal a gold and cream tiled bath, then disappeared through another door.

Teel stared at the spot where Chazz had been for long minutes. Had he really said that to her? That she would make him happy when she married him? *Oh God, Chazz, please love me, for I will love you all my days, and I haven't the courage to tell you that I won't marry you. I want it too much.*

Coming out of her reverie, Teel hustled into the bathroom after grabbing a silk robe from the closet. "Eeeek!" she exclaimed at the enormity of the pool-sized bathtub. Its cream-colored tiles were repeated in the large shower cubicle. Everything but the wooden sauna was colored the muted cream, which shone with a quiet luster. Thick towels hung from several racks. Myriad soaps and shampoos filled the built-in shelves.

All at once jealousy streaked through Teel at the thought of all the women who had used this bathroom. But she shook her head, telling herself not to be silly. If Chazz said no other woman had used it, no other woman had. He would always tell her the truth. It was his way.

Teel showered and shampooed her hair, knowing she wouldn't have time in the morning. It would take awhile for her hair to dry, but at least it would be done. She dried herself in fluffy bathsheets and rubbed her hair with a smaller towel.

When she returned to the bedroom, she found Chazz in bed, reading some papers, half glasses propped on his nose. "I didn't know you wore glasses."

"Yes, for reading." He smiled at her and pushed the papers into a neat pile before shutting them into a briefcase. He swung around on the bed, putting his feet on the floor and the briefcase next to the night table. "Are you coming to me, or shall I come to you?" He removed his glasses and set them on the night table, not once taking his eyes from her.

Teel looked at him, mute, still holding the towel on her head.

"I'll dry that for you, love." Chazz walked over to her and took the towel from her hand. He rubbed gently for a few moments, then got a hairdryer from the bathroom. He blew her hair back and forth with the warm air, rubbing her head with his free hand.

The soporific effect stayed with her when he brushed her hair free of tangles, led her to the bed, and removed her robe. She blinked up at him, aware of his stillness.

"Your body is perfect," he whispered. "But I also know that if it were marked with scars it would still be perfect to me." He looked down into her eyes and smiled.

"You're blushing, love. Don't be shy with me. I'll always want to look at you."

"I'm not used to it."

"I'm glad of that," he chuckled into her neck, his hand running up her thigh to her waist.

"Will we live here?" Teel asked.

His laugh tickled her skin with warm breath. "Stalling, love? You know we intend to live in Selby so that you'll be near your work. I'll commute. We'll use the apartment when we want to stay in New York for one reason or another. All right?"

"Yes." Teel sighed, immediately forgetting what he had just said. Her body was warming to the feel of his body pressed against it. "I wear half glasses too." She slurred the words, her fingers picking at the short hair on his neck.

"Do you?" Chazz's body curved over hers, his mouth edging down her cheek. "Teel!" His breath grew ragged as his mouth took hold of one soft breast. "Darling!" He swung her up in his arms, his face still as he looked down at her. "You're the loveliest woman I've ever known."

"You're not so bad yourself." Teel's voice quavered as she felt the bed sink under his weight. "I love your hair with that little wave," she crooned, her fingers threading through the strands, feeling an electric tingle on her skin when a shudder passed through his body.

"God, Teel, you tear me apart." Chazz's eyes turned a darker gold, his passion building. "I need you," he murmured hoarsely.

She curved her body close to his, loving the velvet feel of skin against skin, warmth against warmth.

His hands convulsed on her body as his face moved down her, loving her.

Her stomach contracted as his mouth touched her. Her hands clenched on him as a volcano of feeling erupted within her. Her veins and arteries were lava, and she panted raggedly. Her heart was pounding erratically.

"I've never felt this way," she gasped into Chazz's shoulder. "I feel as though I were dying."

"Love me, angel, love me." Chazz's voice broke as he lifted himself over her, his body light yet pinning her, demanding yet giving.

A ringing sounded in Teel's ears. She seemed incapable of getting enough air into her lungs. Her body began to pulsate with a new rhythm as Chazz took her, claimed her, and joined with her. She felt as if she were breaking free and floating out of the atmosphere as the power built between them. "Chazz!" She didn't recognize the hoarse voice as her own.

They crested together, holding each other so tightly that Teel's bones felt fused to his.

The planets and stars before her eyes faded slowly. She was glad that Chazz continued to keep her in his strong grip. She had the feeling that her body would fall apart if he released her.

"Love?" Chazz leaned back from her. "I didn't hurt you, did I?" He wiped tears from her cheeks.

She shook her head, unable to speak. She saw him clearly in the glow of the lamp, a pale, urgent look on his face that she had never seen before. "You always think of making love in the darkness," Teel said dreamily, her finger traveling down his cheek. "It's nice with the light on, isn't it?"

"Yes." Chazz's face softened as he smiled down at her. "It is most enjoyable in the light. Looking at your body excites me more than anything." He grinned as her cheeks grew hot. "Still blushing? Will you be doing that when you're an old married lady?"

Teel yawned, covering her mouth with her hand, and nodded. "Probably. You say the most outrageous things." Her eyes fluttered shut, and she smiled to herself when Chazz folded her close. She fell asleep feeling utterly relaxed and at peace.

Twice more in the night Chazz woke her, and each time Teel was eager for his lovemaking, each time surprised that he could bring her up to heaven with his touch.

At last she curled her body into him quite naturally, murmuring, "I'll be a dishrag in the morning." His chuckle was the last thing she heard before a black velvet sleep claimed her.

When she opened her eyes, sun was streaming through the windows. She sensed it was late even before Chazz poked his head around the door of the bathroom.

"Sorry, love, it's my fault. I should have left a call with Darby or Mrs. Pritchett. We were both dead to the world." His chin was covered with shaving cream. "Come and take a shower." He smiled to see her gripping the sheet under her chin.

"I'll use the other bathroom," Teel said.

Chazz paused in his shaving, his smile slow, making the cream on his face part in an upward curve. "All right this time, but after we're married, we'll be showering together."

Teel's pulse rate soared, her hands trembling as they

clutched the sheet. "Maybe."

"Absolutely." Chazz's head disappeared from the doorway.

Grabbing the robe that Chazz had discarded the night before in such cavalier fashion, Teel sprinted for the bathroom that connected with Chazz's bedroom.

After her shower Teel wrapped herself in a bathsheet, cursing her lack of foresight in not bringing clothes with her to put on in the bathroom. When she opened the door to get some, she found Chazz standing there, her lingerie in his hand.

"Thought you might need these." He chuckled as he handed her the small bundle. "Of course, I'd prefer that you came out here to dress..."

"No." Teel shut the door in his face, smiling when she heard his laugh.

She hurried into the undies and stockings, twisted her hair in a loose knot on her neck, and did her makeup right there, impressed with the array of cosmetics. Back in the bedroom, wrapped in her robe, Teel quickly inspected the closetful of clothes, choosing a deep green suit in a silky wool material and a silk blouse with very thin green and pink stripes on an ecru background. She found low-heeled black pumps in soft kid and a matching bag.

For the first time she noticed the glow in her face, the elusive smile that played around her mouth, the sparkle deep in her eyes. She bit her lip and closed her eyes, but she couldn't mask the warmth that was spreading through her. She was happy.

"Hey, lady." Chazz's voice rose from downstairs. "Breakfast is ready."

Teel was emptying the contents of her clutch evening bag into the day bag just as Chazz re-entered the bedroom. He stopped and hitched his shoulder against the

doorjamb. "Is this what I'll have to do every morning?
Get your lovely rear in gear?"

"Don't be ridiculous. I'm always punctual," Teel retorted lifting her chin in the air as she tried to sail past
him.

One strong arm hooked around her waist and pulled
her against a long, hard body. "First, my kiss."

Teel opened her mouth to scold him, then changed
her mind and stretched up on tiptoe to fix her mouth to
his.

"There," she told him, a little out of breath, watching
his eyes turn dark with desire.

"Ummm, you taste good."

Chazz made as though to pull her more fully into his
arms, but Teel ducked away from him and sprinted down
the stairs, calling over her shoulder, "It's late. Hurry
up." She laughed when he cursed. She felt as if her feet
were touching ground at every other step as she waltzed
into the breakfast room and caroled, "Good morning,
Mrs. Pritchett."

"Good morning, miss." The older woman smiled at
her indulgently. "You look happy this morning."

Teel felt the blood rushing to her face, but she smiled
more widely. "I am, thank you." She looked past Mrs.
Pritchett to the sideboard, her mouth beginning to water
at the sight of eggs and ham, kippers and croissants, and
silver-dollar-sized hot cakes. Holding a plate in one hand,
she paused before the food and sniffed appreciatively of
the coffee Mrs. Pritchett was pouring from the silver pot.

A hand reached in front of her and scooped egg and
ham onto her plate. "Toast or hot cakes, love? The jam
is homemade."

"I can't decide." Teel assumed a stricken expression
as she gazed from Chazz to her plate. "I can't imagine
why I'm so hungry."

"I can." He leaned over and whispered, "Lovemaking is the next best exercise to swimming."

"Hogwash," Teel exclaimed, looking sideways to see if Mrs. Pritchett had heard him and feeling relieved when she saw that the older woman had returned to the kitchen. "You shouldn't talk like that in front of Mrs. Pritchett," she scolded as he set the plates on the table next to each other and held out her chair for her.

Chazz shrugged, watching Teel as he took his seat. "She didn't hear me." He lifted a forkful of egg from his plate and fed it to her, smiling when she, "ahhhhhed" her enjoyment. Even though they were rushed, they took time to enjoy their meal.

Suddenly Teel clamped a hand to her mouth. "I should have called Nancy."

"I told your office you would be a little late," Chazz informed Teel, wiping her chin with his napkin.

"Thank you." Teel felt shy. "I suppose she'll question me unmercifully." She sighed, lifting one shoulder in a fatalistic shrug, not really feeling uncomfortable.

"Ignore them all." Chazz went with her when she returned to the bedroom to brush her teeth and get her bag. "We'll be married soon," he added.

"There are a few more things to do first." Teel gulped. Her voice sounded thin and unsteady.

"Hurry it up then," Chazz told her. "I'm not waiting forever. I want to get married now."

"Yes," Teel capitulated, absolutely certain for the first time that she was going to marry Chazz Herman. The thought filled her with a quiet, steady happiness, a calm that entered every part of her body.

They went down the elevator in silence, hand in hand.

Outside, Darby wished them a good morning, his eyes twinkling.

Once in the car, Chazz pulled Teel close to him. "Love, I have a meeting, so Darby's dropping me off first. I'll see you tonight at home. All right? Alexander has to fly some of the corporate staff to a meeting in Pittsburgh, so I'll be flying the Cessna to Selby."

Teel nodded, suddenly sad at the thought of being away from Chazz for a whole day. When the Rolls pulled over to the curb in front of his office building, she clung to him for a brief moment and returned his kiss with fierce ardor. He seemed surprised but pleased, and with a last gentle caress on her cheek and a jaunty wave, he stepped out of the car and disappeared inside.

- *10* -

THE TRIP BACK to Selby was uneventful, but Teel's late arrival meant that she was buried in work until after six that evening. She was rubbing the back of her neck when Nancy and Clint Wills walked into the office. She looked up at them, surprised. "Hi. I thought you two had gone home. Are you here to pick me up early for the shower, Nancy?"

"No." Nancy's voice sounded strained, and she sniffed.

Teel stared at her, alarmed. Nancy had been crying. Teel glanced at Clint. His face had a pinched look to it. "What's wrong?" she asked, wariness assailing her, then panic. "Tell me. Is it Chazz? Tell me!" Her voice sounded shrill in the otherwise silent room.

"There was a plane crash," Nancy said hoarsely. "The announcement came over Clint's police radio. He called the sheriff."

173

"Les Tillman is my brother-in-law," Clint explained. "He said the man's wallet identified him as Charles Herman. Don't look like that, Teel. He's in the hospital. Les said he was unconscious, but that it didn't look bad." Clint swallowed hard and patted Teel's arm as she stood rigidly in front of him, both hands pressed to her mouth.

"The plane lost power and Chazz crash-landed in a field just short of the runway. He was all the way down and it looked all right, but he must have hit a tree stump or something because the plane flipped over." Clint took a deep breath. "I called Nancy because I thought you would want her along when I take you to the hospital."

Teel nodded numbly, unable to speak, and squeezed Clint's hand in silent thanks. The car ride seemed to take forever even though the hospital was located only ten minutes from the school.

Later, Teel had no memory of what Nancy or Clint said to her or what the nurses and doctor told her. She only knew that she had to see Chazz. She would make him get better no matter how bad it was.

When she stepped inside the door of the private room and saw him lying there, his face white, his eyes closed, she froze. Though her brain registered that there were no tubes coming from his body attached to life-sustaining apparatus, that he was not heavily bandaged, enervating shock coursed through her body.

To her surprise, his eyes opened and his mouth curved upward in a boyish grin. Was he all right? Suddenly he looked fine.

She stepped forward tentatively, still unsure. "Chazz," she breathed. "Are you badly hurt?"

"I'm fine, love. Fit as a fiddle," he replied blithely. "Just resting up a bit is all."

All at once Teel was angry. "You frightened me to death," she cried, trembling with relief and rage. "I thought you might be dying—or at least have broken bones." She shook a fist at him, tears streaming down her face as she shut the door forcefully behind her and stalked over to the bed.

Chazz sat up, wrapping his arms around her and pulling her down on the bed with him, soothing her as she cried out her fear and frustration. Several attendants entered the room, but Chazz said something to them, and then they were alone.

"It's all right, love," he murmured. "I made it down just fine, but I must have hit a rock or something as the plane was beginning to stop. No broken bones, nothing but a scratch on my arm and a bump on my head. Don't cry." Chazz held her close, rocking her. "They tell me that I landed not too far from the carriage house." He kissed her forehead. "I guess I was in too much of a hurry to see my woman." He chuckled softly.

"That's not funny." Teel sniffed and wound her arms around his neck. "I couldn't bear to lose you." She tightened her hold. "I just couldn't bear it."

The doctor came in just then to talk to Chazz about staying overnight for tests. Teel nodded in agreement, but Chazz shook his head. "Chazz, you must stay—just to make sure," Teel pleaded.

"I *am* sure." He kissed her nose, then turned to the doctor."You've run some tests already, haven't you?" At the doctor's slow nod, Chazz continued, "I'm getting married next week, and my fiancée and I have things to do that need our attention. Could you give me an educated guess about the state of my health? I know I feel fine except for the throbbing in my arm and head."

The doctor stared at Chazz for a few moments. "I'd prefer that you stay, but I feel that you're in pretty good shape and could be released tomorrow with a clean bill of health."

"Good." Chazz squeezed Teel.

"But if you feel dizzy or nauseated at all tonight or

tomorrow, come back." The doctor shook a finger at Chazz.

"He will," Teel promised, her voice firm, one arm around Chazz's waist.

The two men smiled at her.

As they left the hospital, they met Nancy and Clint in the waiting room. Teel suddenly remembered the shower, but Nancy reassured her. She had already telephoned everyone and rescheduled the event.

Chazz was fine. Chazz was fine. The words rang in Teel's head just over a week later as she dressed for her wedding. She looked down at the cream-colored lace that her Aunt Tessa had brought for her from Spain. Her friend Charine had fashioned it into a mantilla-like veil. The ecru silk gown that Charine had made for her swirled out behind her to form a train. Veil lace edged the sleeves and formed a bertha around the low neckline. Tiers of silk material were caught at the dropped waist to create a modified bustle, which made Teel's small waist look even smaller. Her neck rose from the almost off-the-shoulder style like a slender column. Her skin glowed like translucent porcelain.

Aunt Tessa was giving her away and, though she promised not to cry, she had pushed several lace-edged hankies up the sleeve of her sky-blue dress.

Nancy was her only attendant. "You're the most beautiful bride I've ever seen," she told Teel, sniffing discreetly.

Darby drove them to the church in the Rolls-Royce, patiently answering all Aunt Tessa's questions about the limousine.

At the church Teel looked down the aisle and saw Father Gargan and Rabbi Levine standing side by side. She was very grateful to both clergymen for rearranging their schedules so that they could assist at her and Chazz's wedding on such short notice.

When the organ played the processional, she walked down the aisle, never taking her eyes off Chazz. He stared back at her, heat leaping in his eyes.

Later, Teel couldn't remember saying her vows, but she did remember seeing both clergymen lift their hands in a blessing. Vaguely, she heard someone say, and "You may kiss the bride."

Chazz turned her toward him, and she looked up and smiled. "I love you," she murmured, her voice as clear as a bell in the sudden silence of the church.

Someone tittered. Someone whispered, "Did she say what I think she did?"

Teel didn't pay any attention. She only watched Chazz. She felt relaxed and serene as she stared up into his familiar face.

"Darling." His voice was hoarse.

"You may kiss the bride now," Rabbi Levine whispered once more.

As the organ music swelled, Chazz pulled Teel close. His mouth touched hers in a tender caress that held a promise of passion and enough love to last them all their lives.

The reception was held at the Selby Museum. Chazz had arranged the catering from a New York firm, but when the local ladies asked him if they might bring their own dishes as well, he had kindly encouraged them. Virtually the whole town was invited because Teel couldn't think of one family she could exclude. Few of Chazz's business associates attended, because Chazz had assured them that they would have another reception in New York in the near future. Nevertheless, he took great pride in introducing Teel to the small number of his associates who did attend. And he neither left Teel's side nor let go of her hand the entire time. "How does it feel to be married, Mrs. Herman?" he asked.

"Lovely." Teel felt unaccountably shy with him. The look in his eye was possessive, but even more than that, she had the feeling that she could step inside his eyes and revel in that golden world.

When it was time to change, Tilda and Nancy came with her. "I think it's nice that you're going to take a week on the yacht," Tilda said, and she smiled when Teel's mouth fell open. Tilda wrinkled her nose in dismay. "Oh, I wasn't supposed to tell you!" She shrugged, then grinned when Teel and Nancy laughed. "Teel, dear, one of the crew has taken your portrait to the *Deirdre,* so you'll have your own surprise for Chazz."

"How can I ever thank you?" Teel asked, hugging the small woman with sincere warmth.

"You can't," Tilda answered tersely, "so just go and enjoy yourselves."

In no time at all they were flying southward toward where the *Deirdre* was docked. "My lovely aunt told you, didn't she?" Chazz whispered as he held Teel against his shoulder.

"Yes." She laughed, hugging her secret about the painting to herself.

It was a relief to land and know that it was only a short drive to the ocean. With Chazz at her side, the time seemed to fly past.

"We'll just cruise in the Caribbean for a few days," Chazz said as he helped Teel out of the car and led her down into the forward cabin, looking surprised when she gasped at the size of the room and how it was outfitted. "That's right. You've never been in here before, have you? Do you like it?"

She nodded, staring around at the oak-trimmed stateroom, which was dominated by a king-sized bed.

"Tell me again," Chazz's voice demanded, bringing Teel's head around to him.

She didn't pretend not to know what he meant. She

swallowed once. "I love you," she whispered, her eyes steady on him.

"Thank God for that." His mouth quirked in amusement, but Teel knew that the fire leaping in his eyes expressed his deeper feelings. He reached out and pulled her into his arms. "When you said that at the end of the ceremony, I wasn't sure I heard you correctly. Lord, darling, you choose the most public places to tell me your most important—and most private—thoughts. I almost picked you up then and there and ran out of the church with you."

Teel smothered a sigh. She would never regret having told him she loved him, but how she yearned to hear the same words from his own lips.

"I've loved you since I leaned over the side of the *Deirdre* and saw you lying unconscious in the dinghy," Chazz told her.

"What?" Teel pushed back from him, her eyes searching his face. "You love me?"

Chazz frowned. "Of course I love you. I've told you often enough."

"You've *never* told me." Teel felt her sinuses open up and her head clear. Her body felt pliant, alive, and strong. Her thoughts seemed to regroup in an intelligible order. She suddenly felt capable of outstanding feats. Her spirit soared. "You love me," she repeated simply.

"Of course. Everyone knows that. How could you not know it?"

"Dumb, huh?"

"Very." Chazz enfolded her in his arms and slowly began to undress her. "Are you hungry? There's a lovely bridal dinner awaiting us."

"How nice," Teel answered, unbuttoning his shirt. "I hope it's a casserole. It will have to wait." She smiled up at him, confidence coursing through her.

"Quite awhile, I think." Chazz's breath grew ragged.

"How I've chased you, woman. You had me scared witless."

"Not true." Teel stood in front of him clad only in silk bikini panties, the flesh-colored fabric hiding nothing from her husband's ardent gaze.

"Very true, my love. I held you in my arms when you were unconscious, and all I wanted to do was make you well so that I could marry you. You were all the dreams of women that I'd ever had, all rolled into one bruised and scarred package. You have very few scars left now from your ordeal in Central America, but my love for you is the same." He took her hands, smiling down at her. "No, that's not true. I love you much more now and still more every minute." He lifted her hands to his mouth and kissed each palm. "You have a beautiful body."

"So do you," Teel said, feeling a little out of breath and giddy when Chazz chuckled. She watched his muscular upper torso rise and fall, the arrowed patch of curling black hair having an erotic effect on her senses. She couldn't control the urge to touch him and, wriggling one hand free of his grasp, she reached forward and gently pulled at his chest hair. She saw the leaping gold of his eyes and thought of the painting over the fireplace in the apartment. Painting! It was on board the *Deirdre*. Darby must have put it in the lounge area.

"Hey, beautiful wife, you've left me. Where are you?" Chazz demanded, nuzzling her neck.

"I want to go to the lounge."

"What?" He leaned back to look at her.

Teel took his hand and pulled him over to the cupboard, where she rifled through the clothes and pulled out two terry-cloth robes. She put on one and held out the other to Chazz.

He closed his eyes, then opened them and stared at

her. "Lady, I hope you have a good reason for breaking the romantic mood I was in."

"I do," Teel promised. She pinched his chin and smiled up at him, giddy with confidence. "Besides, I don't think it will take much to put us in the mood again."

Chazz grinned. "You're right." He led her from the stateroom, interrupting their progress with frequent kisses.

Teel ran ahead of him into the lounge and deliberately blocked his entrance until she saw the painting propped up on an easel facing the door. She gasped at how beautiful Tilda had made her look in the vibrant sea-green dress, her hair a chestnut fire, her eyes luminous with love. She seemed to be stepping through a sea mist. She and the dress seemed alight with an inner fire.

She stepped aside and let a puzzled Chazz enter. His eyes remained on her until she turned toward the painting.

At once his gaze was riveted to it. He swallowed and took a deep, shuddering breath. "Tilda has given me the best present of my life, except for the gift of the real you, which I received this morning." He looked down at her, and Teel saw the shimmer of tears in his eyes. "I love you, Mrs. Herman."

She reached up to cradle his head in her hands and kissed him gently. "I love you too."

He swung her up into his arms, looked at the painting for long moments, then left the lounge and made his way back to their cabin.

He set her down on her feet and removed the terry-cloth robe. His eyes roved hungrily over her body as she stood naked in front of him. "Woman, I hope you're going to take pity on me. I have a feeling I won't be able to deny you anything you ask me—ever." Again Chazz swept her up into his arms.

"Really?"

"Really," he murmured into her neck.

"Then...I would like a baby...right away."

Chazz leaned back from her, searching her face intently, his expression a mixture of hope and concern. "Are you sure that's what you want?"

Teel nodded, feeling warmth creep up her face. "Yes," she said lightly. "After all, since we're having four, I think we should get started."

Chazz kissed her cheek, sinking with her onto the king-sized bed. "Very efficient of you." A slow smile spread across his face. "Tilda will go out of her mind. She loves children."

"And you won't mind?"

"No, my lovely Teel, I won't mind. You can't know how much I want us to have children together." He nuzzled her chin, taking little bites of her skin. "Of course, I will demand some time alone with you."

"All the time you want, husband."

"Darling, you just promised me your every waking moment, not to mention all your sleeping time," he growled into her ear.

Teel traced his features with a light finger. "You're the first man I've ever met that I truly enjoy talking with, except my father."

"I want to do more than talk with you." Chazz stroked her body from shoulder to ankle, his mouth following his hand.

"Yes, I rather got that idea." Teel's breath came in short gasps, as though she had just run up two flights of stairs. "Will you always love me, Chazz?" Her voice had a hollow, detached sound.

"Till the earth falls off its axis and then some. You're both dream and reality to me. Without you, breathing is a waste of time," he murmured into the valley between her breasts.

"Oh Chazz, that's the way I feel, too. I love you so much."

The love flowing between them increased until they were caught in the vortex that spun through their own private world.

Teel's last coherent thought was how delightful it was going to be to have a baby who looked just like the man she loved with all her heart. Being enthralled with Chazz Herman was very sweet indeed.

Mystique

CHAPTER ONE

MISTY CARVER, KNOWN professionally as Mystique, enjoyed playing the piano in the Edwardian Room of Manhattan's Terrace Hotel, but she didn't like playing for private parties there, especially during the Christmas season. In the eight months since she'd begun working at the posh midtown hotel, she had discovered that private audiences tended to be more boisterous and undisciplined than regular guests. Tonight was the third party she had played for that week, and she was exhausted.

During her break, Willis, the maître d', told her, "The Manhattan Stuyvesant Bank always holds its employee Christmas party here. One of the directors of the bank is part owner of the hotel."

"Really?" Misty asked with mild interest, rising from the piano bench.

Willis placed a hand on her arm to stop her and spoke in a hushed voice. "Well, what do you know? The man himself is here."

Flexing her tired hands and arching her aching back, Misty followed Willis's gaze around the richly decorated room hung with maroon velvet draperies and bordered with oak wainscoting. "Who?"

"Lucas Stuyvesant Harrison, director of the Manhattan Stuyvesant Bank and part owner of this hotel . . . and half of the real estate on this island," Willis added under his breath.

"By island, do you mean Manhattan?" Misty asked. Willis nodded, and they followed Luc Harrison's tall, elegantly dressed figure as he threaded his way past tables clustered around the small dance floor. Pausing in the doorway, Misty watched the striking man stride into the opulent lobby.

As Willis turned to a newly arrived couple and asked to see their invitations, Misty took a deep breath and proceeded down the wide corridor past the powder room to the Elm Bar, where she often had a drink between sets. She had just reached the bar when a rich baritone voice coming from behind her sent a shiver up her spine. "Mystique?"

She fixed a smile on her face and turned. "I'm sorry, I'm in rather a hurry. I'm . . ." Her voice trailed off as her eyes traveled up Luc Harrison's tall, masculine form and encountered a pair of deep brown eyes.

"I know. You're taking a break. I've been waiting for a chance to speak with you. I'm Luc Harrison, and I wondered if you would join me at my table for a drink."

His hair was ash blond, almost silver. The short, tousled locks fell with a casual artistry that could have been achieved only by a master barber. His tuxedo was of dark brown silk. The pleats of his cream silk shirt had been sewn with matching brown thread. His eyes roved over her, lazy, calm, self-assured.

Anger rose unbidden in her at his slow perusal. Luc Harrison oozed arrogant male confidence. Obviously few women ever turned him down. But Misty had promised herself seven months ago never to let herself be a shadow in any man's life. No more giving herself away to greedy takers. She was her own woman now, and she liked it that way.

"Sorry. I'm on my way to the ladies' room." She flashed her most professional smile, whirled away, and strode back down the hall, nodding to staff members who greeted her and listening with half an ear to the hum of conversation coming from the nearby Terrace Restaurant.

Misty used the bathroom, washed her hands, and began to repair her makeup in front of the wide mirror. She paused after glossing her lips and stared at herself. "My, my, wasn't Mr. Harrison impressive?" she asked her mirror image, noting casually that her long red-gold hair was properly tousled and that the skintight green satin dress clung to every curve.

She never needed to wear heavy clothing when she was working. Energy and excitement bubbled through her, warming her, allowing her to lose herself in the music and forget for a time the emptiness of her life. There was no way she'd take on a man like him again, Misty told herself silently. She'd had enough of them. She was just beginning to climb out of the pit. She glanced up as another woman entered the powder room.

The woman flicked her a nervous smile. "You're Mystique, aren't you?" Misty nodded and smiled. "You play so well."

"Thank you." Misty smiled again, pleased by the compliment. It gave her a lift to know that her music, which meant so much to her, also gave enjoyment to other people. Music was her lifeline, the one thing that could chase away the shadows.

Misty left the powder room and headed back toward the Elm Bar. Suddenly she felt a hand cup her elbow. She stiffened and turned, her eyes widening at the sight of Luc Harrison. His eyes pinned her sharply. A muscle tightened in his jaw. "Mr. Harrison, if you'll excuse me," she said coolly. "I only have a few minutes."

"Of course." He released her, but his voice and eyes remained cold.

She entered the Elm Bar and went at once to a stool at the very end of the bar next to the pickup station for the cocktail waitresses. "Hi, Steve."

"Hello, Mystique. The usual?" When she nodded, Steve plunked down in front of her an icy cold glass of mineral water and lime juice.

"I'll have an Irish whisky on the rocks," said a deep voice behind her.

Without acknowledging Luc Harrison's presence, she sipped her drink and watched his silk-covered arm lift the glass of dark liquid and glistening ice. All at once, without reason, she felt a frisson of panic—as though someone had brandished a weapon under her nose. She shivered.

"Cold, darling?" The soft query shot through her, stiffening her spine.

She set the glass down on the bar, making sure it was dead center on the cocktail napkin, and swung off the stool to her feet.

"Stay. You haven't finished your drink," Luc Harrison said.

"I've had enough."

The muscle in his jaw jumped again. His mouth tightened into a thin, hard line. "As you wish."

A shudder ran through her as she wended her way past small tables crowded with people, many of whom recognized and spoke to her. Moments later, she was back at her piano in the Edwardian Room.

For the rest of the evening, as the staff of the Manhattan Stuyvesant Bank danced, drank, and laughed, Misty played the piano like an automaton, aware the whole time of Luc Harrison's cool dark eyes riveted on her.

The party began to break up at three in the morning. As Misty watched a man stagger out to the lobby, Willis leaned toward her and said, "The big boss has arranged for all his people to be sent home in taxis."

"That's a blessing." Misty tried to smile, but her face felt stiff with tension and fatigue. At least Luc Harrison hadn't made any attempt to approach her again.

Once the crowd had dispersed, she shot a quick glance around the room. Luc was gone. Relief . . . and disappointment . . . flooded through her.

Soon she was stepping out into the chill December night and inhaling the clear, frosty air. The doorman waved down a cab for her. "Thank you, Frank," she called, slipping inside.

"See you tomorrow night, Mystique."

Relaxing against the seat cushions as the cab shot forward, she sighed deeply, welcoming her weariness. Only when she was deeply tired did sleep come easily to her.

As she closed her eyes, Richard and Leonard appeared like ghosts in her thoughts. She knew she was remembering them because of her encounter with Luc Harrison that evening.

Richard Lentz had come into her life during her last year at the Eastman School of Music in Rochester. A shared love of music had drawn them together. Richard had been majoring in clarinet. She'd attended school on a piano scholarship.

At first they had talked for hours about their music, the subject uppermost in both their minds. Misty had been delighted to meet someone with the same consuming desire to excel. Music had deepened their interest in each other and formed the primary bond that tied their lives together.

During their last semester at school, when they had become inseparable companions, though not lovers, Richard had said, "I'm amazed that you don't live at home and commute to school, Misty. It would be so much cheaper."

"I just prefer to live near the school," she had said, hedging. "It's more convenient." She had hesitated to tell Richard that she was glad to be away from home, away from her parents. How could she explain that, after her happy childhood, her parents' attitude toward her had subtly but dramatically changed? She prayed she would never again feel about herself the way she had during the last few years she had lived with them.

Not until just before graduation had she told Richard that she lived with her aunt and uncle, not with her parents. "When I was sixteen I asked if I could live with Aunt Lizabeth and Uncle Charles, and they said yes."

"Didn't your parents mind?"

"No, not really. They have three other children to raise, and my aunt and uncle don't have any." Misty had smiled as she'd remembered the loving, strictly disciplined life she'd lived with her aunt and uncle before going to the Eastman School.

"Oh, I see. You did it to make them happy." Richard hadn't seemed to notice that she didn't actually agree with him. Nor had he questioned her further.

After graduation she and Richard had decided to move to New York, live together, and look for work in their chosen field. Their determination to succeed had been fired by mutual enthusiasm. They were sure that plum jobs would fall into their laps. Misty had been relieved when Richard had informed her he wasn't interested in getting married or starting a family. When she'd left her parents' home, she'd made a firm promise to herself never to have children. The fear that she might treat her own offspring as her parents had treated her gnawed constantly at her.

Misty's initiation into physical love with Richard had been a somewhat painful and disillusioning experience, but she'd hidden her feelings and told him she was content. Occasionally, she'd had the uncomfortable feeling that their relationship should be based on more than a shared interest in music, but she'd shrugged her doubts away.

Misty had found a job at a piano bar almost immediately, but Richard had held out for orchestral work and remained unemployed. Sometimes it had irked her to come home from work to find that he hadn't even made the bed or washed the breakfast dishes.

"You're just feeling superior because you have a job and I don't," he had stormed at her, his slight frame quivering with rage, his horn-rimmed glasses falling askew on his nose. "Well, let me tell you, Misty, I'll never waste my classical training by playing in a bar."

"It beats starving," Misty had shot back, furious.

Afterward, she'd spent an hour apologizing to him.

When Richard had finally landed a job, he'd helped out even less in their apartment. They'd quarreled about it.

"You never stop denigrating what I do," Misty had argued, "but you don't mind using my money to buy concert tickets for you and your friends."

"Concerts are an important part of a musician's education," Richard had retorted.

"I'm a musician. Why didn't you get a ticket for me?"

"You play piano in a bar," Richard had scoffed.

The next day Misty had found a tiny studio apartment just two blocks away and moved out. She and Richard had lived together for one year, yet she had felt only relief at their parting.

After that, Misty had dated other men, but she hadn't become seriously involved with anyone until three years later, at the age of twenty-five, when she'd met Leonard Glassman, a rising account executive with an advertising firm. After they had dated for three months, Leonard had insisted that she move in with him. He had been very caring, eager to shower her with gifts, and willing to help clean the apartment. She'd told herself she really didn't mind when he woke her up each morning to make love—even though she usually didn't get to bed until three or four in the morning. "For God's sake, Misty, I thought we cared about each other," he'd exclaimed. "Isn't that why we live together?"

"Yes, but caring goes both ways," she'd answered. "We have to be considerate of each other."

"You have a great place to live, I give you money for your clothes..."

"I don't spend your money. I have my own," she'd muttered as she'd let him make love to her exhausted body.

Leonard had also wanted her to meet his co-workers and entertain them at home occasionally. Although she'd done her best, she'd begun to chafe at his constant demands.

"Lord, why are you always so tired?" he'd complained.

Misty had felt confused and unhappy about what was happening to them. She'd gone to see a therapist and had begun to learn that, despite her anger and resentment at being taken for granted—first by her parents, then by Richard and Leonard—she was still worthy of being loved.

Misty and Leonard had stayed together for a year and a half, and Misty had to admit that she preferred a man like Leonard to one like Richard. But since neither man was a prize, she decided that men weren't for her. In her opinion, love didn't liberate; it enslaved. Frequently she pondered the thought that her parents' love for her had begun to fade when she'd become a teenager and demanded control of her own destiny.

Sometimes she could still hear her father shouting, "Slut! That's what you are—a slut! It's after midnight, young lady."

"Hey, lady, what's the matter? You sick or somethin'? This is your address."

Misty clapped her hand over her mouth to stifle a groan. "Ah, it's nothing," she told the cab driver. "Just thinking. Here you are." She handed over some money. "Keep the change."

Misty climbed out of the cab and trudged up the stoop

to the front door of the brownstone she owned with four other people. She'd been delighted when, after leaving Leonard, she'd learned that the small stock investment her uncle had made for her had grown into enough money to buy a good-sized co-op apartment. At a time in her life when her problems had loomed large, owning her own home had given her a sense of security. But tonight she was too weary to appreciate the joys of ownership.

As she often did, Misty climbed the four flights of stairs instead of using the tiny elevator, which made her feel claustrophobic. The exercise was good for her heart, she told herself. Besides, it made her tired, let her sleep.

Her apartment was on the top floor, a sunny studio with a wall of windows at the back. Best of all, a previous occupant had soundproofed the walls and floor so that she could practice her piano at any hour of the day or night without disturbing the other tenants. She'd bought the piano at a household auction in Connecticut and paid a king's ransom to have it hoisted up the rear of the building and through a window. She'd been broke for months afterward.

That night, instead of going straight to bed, she decided to play the piano before trying to sleep. After locking the door and slipping off her shoes, she crossed her frugally furnished apartment, sighing with pleasure as her feet sank into the soft Oriental rug covering the hardwood floor. Except for the rug and piano, the only other piece of furniture was the king-sized water bed she had purchased from the previous apartment owners. It had taken her weeks to adjust to the bed, but now she enjoyed it.

At the floor-to-ceiling windows Misty had hung a green curtain of plants. Across the floor she'd scattered colorful throw cushions. She could lower the rope blinds over the windows when she wanted privacy, but more often she pulled them up to let in as much of the scarce Manhattan sunlight as possible.

It was still dark, however, as Misty sat down at the piano and played every piece of classical music she knew from memory. She played to exorcise both Richard's and Leonard's ghosts from her life. In the last few months she had come to realize that in many ways both men were like her father. They had seen her not as she was or could be, but as a reflection of their own desires.

Misty's hands came down on a discordant arpeggio. She wanted no more men in her life! Lucas Stuyvesant Harrison was just like all the others, and she wanted no part of him.

Her fingers were once more poised over the keys when an image of the man rose before her. His brown eyes glittered with the hardness of granite. His ash blond hair flashed silver under the artificial light. His impeccably tailored tuxedo conformed to every muscle in his tall, lean form.

"Stop it. Stop it, Misty," she admonished herself. "Wipe him out of your mind. He's trouble. Your life is just beginning to be your own. You have a good job. You can pay your bills. You're playing the piano every day, and you get occasional orchestral jobs." Reciting the familiar litany of blessings in her life helped her to feel less anxious, less alone.

When the orange light of dawn filtered through the windows, Misty went to bed, falling instantly into a deep and dreamless sleep.

She awoke thinking the building was coming down around her. A terrible noise filled her ears. As her eyes popped open, it took her a moment to realize that someone was banging on her door.

"Misty! Misty, did you forget the twins' lesson today?" Aileen Collins called out. Aileen and her husband David lived on the parlor floor with their ten-year-old twins, Mark and Mary.

"Huh?" Misty sat up in bed, blinking and running a hand absently through her tangled hair. "Oh, wait, Aileen. I'm coming." She jumped out of bed, her flannel nightgown falling to her ankles as she staggered over to the door and unlocked it. "Sorry. I overslept."

She smiled groggily at her friend and the exuberant twins, who called out "Hi, Misty!" and bounded past her into the room. Heading straight for the water bed, they tumbled into the center amid squeals of laughter.

"Stop that, now!" Aileen called, rolling her eyes in exasperation. "I should have kept them downstairs. I'll bet you haven't even been to bed yet."

"Yes, I slept for several hours. Why don't you make me

some coffee, and I'll start Mary on her scales?"

"Done." Aileen grinned, but she couldn't quite mask her concern for her friend.

"Now, don't start mothering me again," Misty protested. "I'm fine. I don't need much sleep. I told you that." She laughed, moving toward the piano bench.

"But there's a great deal you've never told me about yourself, Misty," Aileen said softly. When her friend didn't answer, she shrugged and went into the small kitchen to fill the electric drip pot with coffee.

Misty showed Mary where to start in the *Dozen a Day* book of finger exercises for beginners and listened attentively as her pupil began to play. Misty was grateful for the income from these weekly lessons, which helped pay her bills each month. She also knew Aileen was delighted that her children didn't have to travel for the lessons she and David wanted them to have.

The hour passed quickly. Afterward, Misty and Aileen chatted over another cup of coffee while the children drank milk and munched cookies that Misty stocked especially for them.

"So, how was it last night?" Aileen asked, keeping a close eye on the twins, who were wrangling over a game on the oval carpet.

Misty shrugged. "The usual Christmas party scene. People getting drunk, laughing too loudly." She paused. "But at least they were all chauffeured home after this gathering. The boss arranged it."

"Oh? Who's the boss?"

"Lucas Stuyvesant Harrison. Isn't that some name?"

Aileen whistled. "I've seen his picture in the paper lots of times. That man has a veritable stable of women. I read in a gossip column that he has no intention of marrying anyone from outside his social circle. Keeping up the family name, don't you know?" Aileen curled her pinky finger and raised her cup in an exaggerated imitation of a pretentious person.

"Ah, yes, noblesse oblige." Misty grinned, but she could feel her stomach contract. Undoubtedly Luc Harrison had thought she would be eager to join his stable of women. She should be pleased to think he might want to set her up in an apartment, give her clothes, deign to see her on Wednesdays, perhaps even on Thursdays—but never on weekends. He must save those for the family, the little woman.

"Hey, what are you thinking, Misty? I can almost hear your red hair crackling with anger. Your eyes are sparkling like emeralds. What's going through your mind?" Aileen leaned eagerly forward, her chin in her hand.

"Nothing. That type of man irritates me, that's all."

Aileen shrugged. "He's got everything—money, women, a great position with the bank. He's sailed in the America's Cup race. He's a scratch golfer. He's even competed in the triathlon in Hawaii, and you have to be in superb shape to do that. You have to swim, run, and ride a bike twelve miles without stopping in between." Aileen refilled her coffee cup and added cream. "I suppose a man with that kind of record comes to expect good things to tumble into his lap." She smiled at Misty. "I know you've sworn off men for some reason." When Misty began to protest, Aileen held up her hand, palm outward. "And, no, I'm not prying again. I admit I'd like to know, but I'll wait until you're ready to tell me."

I'll never be ready, Misty thought. Even though you are the best friend I've ever had, I can't tell you.

"But it wouldn't hurt to flirt a little with a man like Luc Harrison," Aileen added.

"I doubt I'll see him again," Misty said. "He came with his staff for the party. He won't be back. Men like him go to private clubs."

Aileen shook her head. "Don't sell the Terrace Hotel short. Some of the most influential people in the world stay there. David says you can walk into the Elm Bar any night and see celebrities. From what you've said, quite a few frequent the Edwardian Room as well."

"Quite a few," Misty conceded.

She and Aileen talked of other things. Then Aileen rounded up the twins and said good-bye. Misty was tired by the time they left, but instead of going back to bed, she straightened the apartment, showered, and shampooed her hair. She was due for a fitting at Morey Weinstein's design studio downtown that afternoon, so she wouldn't have time for a nap. If Morey didn't have any clothes ready for her to try on, she'd shop for shoes and accessories instead. Morey designed most of the clothes she wore while performing. Although he wasn't a commercial success yet, Misty had no doubt he would be someday.

Misty left her apartment at three o'clock that afternoon, knowing she wouldn't be back until three the next morning. She shook her head, trying not to think of the fatigue that would soon weigh on her like an iron blanket. Luckily she had tomorrow night off.

It took Misty half an hour to get to Morey's garretlike studio on the top floor of a run-down building encrusted with grime. Morey had every intention of moving uptown one day, and Misty was sure that, considering his talent, he would eventually make it.

She rang the bell adjacent to a locked oak door and submitted to being scrutinized by an eye at the peephole. The eye disappeared, and the door was swung open by a whipcord-thin man of medium height who radiated energy and enthusiasm.

"Mystique! I've been thinking about you for two days. If you hadn't come this afternoon I was going to call you. I found some fabulous silk." Morey shoved his black-rimmed glasses up his nose with an index finger and grinned, his pale blue eyes sparkling with excitement.

"Silk, Morey? I can't afford silk. For that matter, neither can you." Misty laughed as her irrepressible friend tugged her across his littered workroom to the cutting board under the skylight.

"True," he conceded. "But this was water-damaged, so Fetler let me have it for almost nothing." He grinned and waved his hand when she frowned. "Now, don't worry. Fetler didn't bother to unravel the bolts. I did. The damage doesn't go through all the way. This is great stuff—the finest silk from Japan. Look at the colors—blue, green, burgundy, orange, cerise, lemon." He let out an ecstatic sigh as Misty bent over the material.

"It *is* beautiful," she agreed, "but I can't afford to pay you what it's worth."

"Listen, Misty, don't worry. The clients you've sent to me have a lot of friends. My business is really picking up.

I've hired two women to sew, and"—he paused, clasping his hands together—"there's a good chance I might get into that building I was telling you about, the one uptown. I could live in the apartment off the main room."

"Oh, Morey, that's great!" Misty gave her friend an enthusiastic hug.

"Now, don't get too excited. I haven't talked with the bank yet, and Manhattan Stuyvesant is tough on this sort of thing, especially since my only collateral is my talent."

"But that's very big collateral," Misty assured him.

Morey's expression became momentarily woebegone. "I hope the bank thinks so." Then he brightened. "Come on, get undressed. I want to see this stuff on you."

When Misty arrived at the Terrace Hotel for work that evening she was already bone tired. Morey had pinned, pulled, and draped material on her until she couldn't stand another moment. But by the middle of next week their efforts would pay off when she became the proud owner of two lovely silk gowns. The cost wouldn't even put too much of a hole in her savings. She shouldn't let Morey sell the dresses to her too cheaply, she thought as she took a black satin gown and matching pumps from her carrier. But she also realized she would never be able to afford them if he didn't give her a good deal. He was such a good friend.

That evening she played for a smaller Christmas party than the night before. "Thank God, this is the last of them," Willis commented wearily during her break.

"Amen to that. Only three days to Christmas, and I haven't put up my tree or finished my shopping."

Willis laughed and shook his head. "My wife takes care of that."

"Lucky you."

Misty left the hotel at two-thirty the next morning. Her head was throbbing painfully because she'd skipped dinner. Fatigue clung to her like wet cement, making every movement an ordeal.

At home, she barely took time to hang up her clothes and put away her dress carrier before she tumbled into bed and down, down into the well of sleep.

Hours later, the insistent peal of the telephone jarred her

awake. She blinked at the clock on her bedside table and was stunned to see that it was four in the afternoon. Her day off was almost gone. At least she had the evening to herself. "'Lo?" she said groggily.

"Misty, it's Morey. The bank turned me down!" Her friend's anguish came through to her with painful clarity.

"Oh, no! They couldn't have. How could they be so stupid?" Misty sat up in bed and pushed back her thick hair. "Did they give you a reason?"

"It seems I need more collateral than my talent." Morey tried to laugh, but Misty heard the heartache in his voice.

"Listen, Morey, don't give up yet. I'll put up my apartment as collateral. It's the least I can do after all your kindness to me. Let me help you out. Please."

"Misty, I can't. Your apartment is all you have."

"Please let me. I'll become your silent partner. Weinstein Couturiers must survive. Please. I want to do it."

"Misty . . ." Morey's voice cracked. "Except for Zena, you're the best friend I've ever had." As soon as his business was well established, Morey planned to marry Zena, who worked as an assistant wardrobe mistress in a downtown theater.

"It's too late to go to the bank today," Misty went on, "but we'll be there waiting when the doors open tomorrow."

When they walked into the awesome foyer of the Manhattan Stuyvesant Bank early the next morning, Misty stared admiringly at the three-story vaulted ceiling decorated with mosaic tiles in intricate patterns. Offices on the second and third floors opened onto a horseshoe-shaped balcony that afforded a clear view of activity on the main floor, with its long row of tellers' windows and intimate groupings of officers' desks and chairs. The open space and hum of subdued voices created a hushed, formal atmosphere.

"The silence is intimidating," Misty whispered with an uneasy smile.

"If you think you're intimidated now, wait until you meet Mr. Watson." Morey ushered her over to a chair. "We have to wait our turn," he explained.

Twenty minutes ticked by. Misty began to fidget. She kept getting the feeling that someone was watching her. But when she glanced around the bank and up to the second- and third-story balconies, she saw no one looking her way.

Finally, after they'd waited for thirty-five minutes, Mr. Watson ushered them to his desk on which a discreet sign said: Loan Information. They all sat down. "Now then, Mr. Weinstein," Mr. Watson began, "you said you wanted to see me again. I must tell you, however, that I don't think we can change our minds on this—" The phone rang, interrupting him. "Excuse me." Morey and Misty exchanged glances as Mr. Watson picked up the receiver. "Ah, good morning, sir." Mr. Watson sat straighter in his chair. "Yes, yes. A loan. Ah, no collateral." Mr. Watson shot a quick glance at Morey.

"But he has collateral—my apartment," Misty exclaimed, jumping out of her chair and leaning across Mr. Watson's desk.

Mr. Watson appeared to be taken aback by her forwardness. He quickly covered the mouthpiece of the phone and directed a quelling look at Misty, then spoke quickly. "Ah...I'm sorry, sir. No, there's no need for you— You want me to what? You're coming down here?" Mr. Watson finished weakly and stared at the receiver with a baffled expression. "He hung up," he muttered.

"Who?" Misty asked, still standing.

"Huh? Ah...never mind. What were you saying about your apartment? There could be extenuating circumstances." Mr. Watson took the papers Misty handed him and began perusing them, but his thoughts were obviously elsewhere. Several times he looked anxiously up toward the second-floor balcony. Then abruptly he jumped to his feet, his gaze going past Misty and a disconsolate Morey to a distinguished-looking man in a three-piece suit. "Mr. Damon, sir. Did Mr.—"

"Never mind, John, I'll take care of this," the man said. "Perhaps you could attend to the next person. Why don't you use another desk?"

"Of course." Mr. Watson sprung away from his chair and hurried toward an elderly couple sitting nervously some distance away in the cavernous lobby.

"Hello, I'm Lester Damon," the man greeted them. He shook Misty's hand, then Morey's. "Sit down, please, Miss

Carver. I'll just take a look at Mr. Weinstein's papers."
Silence fell as Lester Damon perused the sheets in front of
him. At length he paused and looked up. "Miss Carver, do
you plan to put up your apartment as collateral, so that you
will, in effect, become partners with Mr. Weinstein?" he
asked.

"Yes." Misty met Lester Damon's direct gaze without
flinching, but she had a terrible feeling that he was going
to turn them down. Why hadn't he let Mr. Watson consider
their loan application? Why was he stringing them along?
Her temper was beginning to rise.

But to her surprise, Lester Damon said, "Fine. Everything seems to be in order." He pushed the papers toward
Morey. "You have your loan, Mr. Weinstein."

"I do?" "He does?" Morey and Misty croaked in unison.

"It's all set," Mr. Damon assured them, shaking their
flaccid hands. "If you have any problems, Mr. Weinstein,
please call me. Don't bother going through Mr. Watson.
But I don't think you'll run into any difficulties. Pick up
your check from Miss Edwards at the cashier's desk. Good
day." Mr. Damon smiled at each of them, then strode swiftly
away.

Morey fell back into his chair. "I think I'm hyperven-
tilating," he wheezed, loosening his tie with trembling fingers.

"I'm having a little trouble myself," Misty whispered
back. "Come on," she said, urging her friend to his feet.
"Let's get out of here. Don't forget that stamped paper.
Let's pick up the check; then we'll call Zena and celebrate."

"Lord, Misty. Maybe Zena and I can get married this
year after all," Morey said in trembling tones as they approached a smiling woman behind a desk.

Minutes later, they left the bank arm in arm. Misty had
the feeling that at any moment Mr. Damon would come
rushing after them and declare that it was all a mistake.
"Hurry, Morey." She urged him along the street to the bus
stop, not pausing to take a breath until they were on the bus
and several blocks from the Manhattan Stuyvesant Bank.
They called Zena from Morey's apartment and agreed to
meet her for lunch at a nearby deli.

Morey insisted on buying the lox and cream cheese. Zena

sniffled all through the meal.

"Zena, honey, stop crying," Morey pleaded. "There's a policeman over there who keeps staring at me."

"I will, I will," she promised tearfully, kissing his cheek and turning grateful eyes to Misty. "You're the best friend we ever had, Misty. Thank you."

"Thank *you*. Not many people will have the privilege of saying 'I knew Morey and Zena Weinstein before they were famous.' But *I* will." She grinned happily at her two friends.

After lunch, Misty shopped for Christmas presents. She was delighted when she found a scarf for Aileen, a word game for Mark, and a stuffed animal for Mary. For Morey and Zena she bought a starter set of china in a pattern they had admired. She sent a poinsettia to her aunt and uncle at their new home in Florida. Since her mother and father had returned every gift she'd sent them, she planned to mail them a check. For her sister Celia she bought a chess set; for Marcy she bought tapes of the latest rock music; for Betsy, the youngest, she'd already bought a hand-crocheted vest at a church bazaar. Though she always tried to choose gifts her sisters would enjoy, she never really knew if they liked them. Her mother's terse thank-you note never provided details. Misty had buried her hurt so long ago that she rarely dwelt on it now. On her way home, she selected a small Douglas fir tree from a corner vendor.

Back at her apartment she just had time to set the tree in a container filled with water before she had to get ready for work.

The Edwardian Room was crowded that night, only two days before Christmas. A sense of anticipation filled the air, and Misty willingly immersed herself in her music. Then, abruptly, unaccountably, she stiffened and raised her eyes.

Lucas Harrison was sitting at a table directly in her line of vision. His eyes met hers for a brief, intense moment before she looked hastily away. From then on, whenever she looked up, she found his gaze riveted on her.

During her break she gestured to Willis with a shake of her head. "Isn't it a comedown for the director of the Manhattan Stuyvesant Bank to be here?" she asked.

Willis gave her a knowing look. "He's been here three

times since the Christmas party. Last night, when he heard you were off, he left right away. Usually he asks for a table in the back where you can't see him."

Misty was stunned. "He's been here every evening since the party?" she repeated incredulously.

"Yes. For at least an hour each night." Willis moved away to greet a couple who had been hovering at the entrance to the Edwardian Room.

Misty continued to play, but her head was filled with the fact that Luc Harrison had come to watch her play the piano several times.

During her break she strolled to the powder room, then to her usual place at the Elm Bar. She had just sat down when she felt the press of silken material against her bare back.

"Let me buy you a drink, Mystique."

She didn't bother to turn around. "All right. I'd like mineral water with lime, please."

Luc Harrison gave the bartender her order and his own for an Old Bushmills on the rocks. Once the drinks were in front of them he said casually, "You play very well."

"Thank you." Misty took a gulp of the cool drink and coughed when it went down the wrong way.

"Are you going to face me at all?" the voice asked, "or are we going to converse by looking at our images in the mirror?"

Misty's eyes flew to the reflection over the bar and caught the saturnine look on his face. "It's not necessarily a bad way to converse," she said.

"No, but I prefer the more personal way—face to face." He moved between her stool and the waitresses' pickup station. They were so close that their legs bumped. She only had to lift her eyes a few inches to meet his gaze.

Misty took a deep breath as his eyes scanned hers. A tingling sensation ran through her body. "I . . . I was in your bank today, the main one downtown. It's beautiful."

"Yes. It's an architectural marvel—or so the brochures describe it to sightseers."

"My friend procured a loan to move his business to a better location," Misty explained, glad to have found a safe topic of conversation.

"Is he your lover or just a platonic friend?" Luc queried smoothly.

The question surprised her. "What difference does that make?"

"None." The terse answer seemed to linger between them. The silence grew heavy.

"At first your bank turned down my friend's loan application," Misty said, feeling increasingly uncomfortable. She cleared her throat nervously.

"I know. I saw you at the bank today."

She stared at him, stunned. He was looking straight ahead into the mirror. "I had a feeling someone was watching me," she blurted out.

"I had come out of Lester Damon's office on the third floor and was waiting for the elevator when I happened to look down and see you."

"So, you sent Mr. Damon down to—"

"I called Watson from my office. Then I told Les to go down and handle it. John Watson is an honest man, but he would have required too many explanations, and he probably wouldn't have issued you the check."

"But I had collateral."

"Do you really think that one-fourth of a brownstone is equal in value to the third floor of the Beadle Building?"

She lifted her chin. "My apartment is worth a great deal more now than it was when I bought it. The neighborhood is good and—"

"And the entire building isn't worth a quarter of the Beadle property." Luc took a swallow of his Irish whisky and ran a finger slowly up her bare arm.

She stiffened at his touch. "I have to get back. My break is over," she managed to say. Her body felt both hot and cold. She felt both threatened and titillated. She had to escape!

Luc took hold of her upper arm and scrutinized her through narrowed eyes, a hard smile lifting his lips. "Yes, to your unspoken question, Mystique. I do want something from you in return for granting you that loan."

Cold dread pierced through to her very core. She raised stricken eyes to his, then fled as if all the demons of hell were at her heels.

CHAPTER TWO

WHEN MISTY WOKE up the next morning, Christmas Eve, the first thing that entered her mind was Luc's statement from the previous evening: *"I do want something from you . . ."*

Somehow she had managed to return to the Edwardian Room and continue to play the piano, but she had felt like a whirling dervish. Her thoughts had flown in all directions, and she hadn't been able to concentrate. At some point she had become aware that Luc Harrison was no longer at his table. She hadn't felt relieved or glad, just numb.

Now, the next morning, she wished for the hundredth time that she didn't have to work on Christmas Eve and Christmas night. At the time her schedule had been drawn up, she hadn't cared that she would be working those two nights. But now she was sorely tempted to quit her job and hide from Luc Harrison.

Stop it, Misty Carver, she told herself silently. Chances were Luc Harrison wouldn't show up either night. He had a huge family, and he would spend the holidays with them.

Feeling somewhat mollified, she cleaned her apartment

and began to prepare the buffet supper she would serve that evening for Dave and Aileen, Mark and Mary, Morey and Zena. Tomorrow she would join Dave and Aileen for dinner in their apartment.

Several times during the day the twins came charging up the stairs to look at the gifts under Misty's tree, their faces alight with excitement. "I like it when Morey and Zena come," Mark informed her, "'cause we go to their place for Hanniker, and we get gifts both times."

"Chanukah," Misty corrected absently as she arranged gumdrops into an edible wreath for the center of the table. She would put a fat bayberry candle in the middle. "You're lucky children to be able to join in both the Jewish and the Christian holidays. You can learn a lot from both traditions."

"Yes," Mary said solemnly. "You get the best foods on the holidays."

"Yes, dear," Misty agreed. "Mark, don't you dare shake one more package."

"Awww, Misty..."

"On your way now the two of you. Take your baths and get dressed. You'll be going to church with your parents after we have our supper."

"Why aren't you going to services with us, Misty?" Mary asked, tearing her gaze from the gumdrop wreath. "Are you Jewish like Zena and Morey?"

"No, she's working." Mark tapped his sister on the arm. "Race you downstairs."

"Nooo," Mary said with a moan as her brother raced out the door. She turned to Misty with a smile. "I always say no, but he never listens. Now I'll walk down real slow, and he'll think he's won the race." Mary's curls bobbed as she walked primly out of the room.

"How did you get to be so wise, Mary?" Misty asked softly. She was glad the twins had been around to distract her all day. They had kept her from thinking about Luc Harrison. She refused to consider what he might want from her. She was pretty sure she knew...and she was damn sure he wasn't going to get it.

Promptly at five, Misty's guests arrived. After coaxing and cajoling the twins into eating dinner *before* opening their presents, they all filled their plates with hot antipasto; cold prawns in hot sauce; and then pasta shells stuffed with ricotta, parsley, and sausage.

"I'd love to have some of these make-ahead recipes, Misty," Zena said, closing her eyes in delight as she tasted a stuffed shell.

"All my recipes are for dishes you can make ahead," Misty said, laughing. "That's the only kind I have time to prepare."

They all ate their fill, then settled down on cushions around the tree and opened their gifts over coffee, a fruit board, and Christmas cookies. Misty had such a good time that, long after her guests had departed, she felt as if she were floating on happiness. She hummed Christmas carols as she got ready for work and ran lightly downstairs and outside to hail a cab. Christmas Eve had been wonderful. She refused to allow the fact that she hadn't heard from either of her parents to dull her delight.

At the hotel, Misty passed out the gifts she had bought for her friends on the staff. She laughed when Willis put on his Australian wool sweater vest right over his shirt. "You can't wear your tuxedo jacket over a sweater," she protested, laughing.

"It's Christmas Eve. Of course I can," he insisted. "Thank you for the sweater, Misty. I love blue."

"And thank you for the lace hankies, Willis. Tell your wife they're just perfect to carry with the gowns I wear. My hands get damp when I play, but I'll look very ladylike using these hankies to discreetly wipe my palms."

That night Misty played some of her usual songs, but she concentrated on playing Christmas carols. She didn't think of Luc Harrison until she caught sight of his tuxedo-clad form entering the Edwardian Room. Her fingers faltered momentarily, and she hit a B-flat instead of an A-natural, but other than that she made no sign that she had noticed him.

During her break, she went directly to the powder room and stayed there until it was time to return to the piano.

As she sat down again to play, she saw a hand place a glass on the frame of the piano, where the mahogany surface was protected by a metal tray.

"Thank you, Willis," she said without looking up. "I was thirsty."

"I thought you might be," came Luc Harrison's velvet voice. Her eyes shot up to his granite-hard eyes.

"Merry Christmas," she managed to say through stiff lips. She watched dumbfounded as he placed a small package wrapped in silver paper on the piano, then turned and strode from the room before she could speak again.

Misty looked at the gift as though she expected it to explode at any moment.

"What's this? A gift from a fan?" Willis hefted the small package in his palm.

"You could say that." Misty smiled weakly and bent over the keyboard.

As usual, she was exhausted when she returned to her apartment very early Christmas morning. Yet, despite her fatigue, she was too keyed up and apprehensive to sleep. She felt as though she were carrying a time bomb in her purse instead of a very small package.

She stripped off her clothes, brushed down the green velvet dress she had worn that evening, and hung it in the bathroom where it would steam the next time she showered. She had learned to take good care of her clothing; she couldn't easily afford to replace it.

After putting away her clothes and shoes, she donned a flannel nightgown and crawled into the middle of the water bed, where she sat cross-legged and stared at her purse. Swallowing twice, she unzipped the bag and reached for the gift inside, holding it in her palm for a moment before inserting a fingernail carefully under the wrapping. That was another of her economies; she saved paper and bows.

After folding the paper along its crease lines, she rolled up the ribbon and stared at the box. The name Van Cleef & Arpels was printed across the top.

No doubt he had a charge account there, she thought. Calls up and orders a gross of aquamarines and sends them to his friends. Millimeter by millimeter she lifted the hinged cover. Her eyes grew wide. "Good God!" she exclaimed softly, blinking at the sight of emerald earrings arranged on apricot velvet. How dare he give her something so expensive? Did he think she was too stupid to know he was coming on to her with jewelry? She scooted back on the bed, putting as much distance as possible between herself and the exquisite jewels.

It took several minutes to get up the courage to lean forward and pull the box toward her. With great care she rewrapped the package and dropped it back into her purse.

Anger made her writhe and turn on her bed until dawn. Finally she fell into a fitful sleep. Her last thought was that no man was ever going to take charge of her life again.

Christmas Day brought laughter, good food, and several more small gifts for the twins, despite their parents' mild protests. As Misty played Christmas songs on the Collinses' spinet, they all sang, ate, and laughed.

Afterward, Aileen handed her a glass of eggnog. "I could swear I heard your phone ringing. You know how the sound sometimes vibrates in the old dumbwaiter. Even though we can't hear anything else, I sometimes hear the phone. Do you suppose you should go up and answer it?"

Misty hesitated. No, it wouldn't be her parents. They never called her. She would call them before she went to work that evening. "No, I won't bother," she said. "It's probably a wrong number."

She returned to her apartment in the early evening. Morey and Zena would be staying awhile longer with David and Aileen, and the twins were already in bed sound asleep.

That night the Edwardian Room was full to capacity with complete families as well as couples. Misty saw a few single people dining alone, and she tried to play just for them. She could empathize with their loneliness.

All evening she kept a sharp eye out for a tall masculine form. Even during her break she searched the corners of the room that she couldn't see while playing. She was determined to return Lucas Harrison's gift.

"Looking for someone, Mystique?" Willis asked with a smile.

"Just checking the numbers," she said, hedging.

Luc Harrison never came. Once again, Misty went home with the expensive emeralds in her purse.

She carried them twice more to the Terrace Hotel. Then, on the third day, she wrapped the package in brown paper, put it in a sturdy mailing envelope addressed to the Manhattan Stuyvesant Bank's main office, and carried it to the post office. Just before mailing it she wrote *Personal* on the front.

Since she had to work on New Year's Eve, she had wrangled special holiday reservations for Morey and Zena, Aileen and David. Neither of the couples planned to take advantage of the overnight accommodations or the breakfast, which had cut down on the cost for Misty. It delighted her to be able to do something extra for her friends, who had done so much for her, and she refused to take any money from David or Morey when they tried to press it on her.

How could they know what a relief it would be to have them with her on what was for her the worst night of the year? Misty mused when she arrived that evening for work. New Year's Eve was a night for couples. She was single. It hurt, but she was determined not to show it.

As she changed in her small dressing room, a niggling thought chased through her mind. Had Luc Harrison received the emeralds in the mail? She had insured them, but she was certain they were worth more than the maximum insurance the post office had allowed her. She felt as though she were waiting for the other shoe to drop. She didn't know what was worse—not seeing him and not knowing if he had received the jewels, or seeing him and knowing. She shook her head to clear it of such thoughts and studied her reflection in the narrow mirror on the back of the door. Morey was right. Her new silk dress was perfect.

The emerald green fabric was draped around her like a sari, delineating her lissome form in glittering silkiness as the faint gold thread caught the light. Her curly red hair was pulled to one side with an ivory comb, the tousled locks catching gold fire in the light. The four-inch heels of her pale green peau de soie pumps made her a svelte five feet eight inches tall.

As she studied herself, she felt an unusual surge of confidence, but immediately chided herself. She'd felt like that before and fallen flat on her face. She'd better be careful.

As she left the dressing room, she heard sounds of revelry coming from the Elm Bar. The rooms were already filling up for the partygoers' biggest night of the year.

Misty was stopped several times on her short walk to the Edwardian Room by men who had already had several drinks. Two men even tried to kiss her, but she easily eluded them, smiling good-naturedly.

"Happy New Year, Mystique," Willis greeted her. "We're almost filled already." It was only a few minutes before nine.

"Happy New Year, Willis." Misty smiled back at him and walked over to the piano. Before sitting down she scanned the room. She caught sight of Morey and Zena waving. David and Aileen hadn't arrived yet. No doubt they'd had to wait for the sitter. Then her casual gaze fell on a crowded table almost directly in front of her. Luc Harrison sat there facing her. He lifted his glass in a silent salute, and Misty shivered at the hard look in his eyes.

Immediately she began to play, hoping to lose herself in the music. Luc Harrison couldn't possibly harm her here at the Terrace Hotel. She was safe for now.

The room seemed to be seething with loud, laughing people. More than one man came up to the piano and asked her to play a special song. She always complied.

One minute time seemed to be crawling by; the next, she realized an hour had passed since she'd last checked her watch.

At eleven-thirty Misty took a break, knowing she would have to play "Auld Lang Syne" at midnight.

She left the piano and made her way past the tables to where her four friends were sitting. Passing Luc Harrison's table, she thought she heard a low comment aimed in her direction: "God, she's lovely. Why not come over here, pretty redhead?"

She wasn't sure, but she thought she heard Luc mutter a sharp reply.

"Hi," Aileen said, beaming. "This is too beautiful for words, Misty. And guess what? Our baby-sitter is going to spend the night so we can stay as late as we want. Isn't that great?"

"Wonderful," Misty agreed, squeezing into a chair and accepting the drink that one of the waiters brought to the table.

"You look gorgeous in that dress, Misty," Zena said with a sigh.

"And I'll have you know that several women have approached me tonight and asked where I buy my clothes. I told them, of course." The others laughed with her.

Morey poured her champagne, but she shook her head. "I really shouldn't. I'll get a headache, and I'm on until five in the morning." She held up her own glass. "Tomato juice. This will give me the energy I need. Say, why don't the four of you come up to the piano at midnight? Then I won't have to race down here to give you your New Year's kisses."

"Great!" David exclaimed.

Misty glanced at her watch. "Oops! Ten minutes. I have to go. In about five minutes, come on up." She rose and made her way back to the piano, staying well away from the table where Luc Harrison was sitting.

Minutes later, people began counting down the time.

From the corner of her eye Misty saw her friends rise from their table and move toward her. As she sent them a bright smile, she caught sight of Luc Harrison scrutinizing them for a fleeting moment before looking back at her. Then she was too busy to register anything but the guests counting down the seconds until midnight.

"Ten . . . nine . . . eight . . . seven," they shouted. "Five . . . four . . . three . . . two . . . one! Happy New Year!"

Misty laughed along with everyone else, nodding happily as her friends hugged her and her fingers moved over the keyboard. As soon as she finished playing "Auld Lang Syne," she jumped up and kissed Zena, Aileen, David, Morey . . .

"Happy New Year, darling." A masculine mouth covered hers as Luc spoke the words, his breath going into her mouth, his tongue touching her teeth, then her tongue.

Misty tried to suck in air, to release herself from his embrace, but all at once she felt herself free-falling through space, detached from her own body, wrapped in an aura of throbbing delight. She pressed closer to him and heard a groan come from deep inside her, then his answering growl of pleasure.

Misty fell back, ending the kiss, her eyes darting around her. Had anyone seen the soul-stirring kiss she and Luc

Harrison had just exchanged? People were laughing, hugging, joking. Her eyes shot back to him. His face darkened as he bent over her, his sensual mouth not an inch away, his brown eyes burning into her.

"I knew it would be like that, but it was even better than I imagined. You're wonderful." His hand brushed downward over her breast. "You shouldn't have sent your gift back. The earrings belong to you. They're so like your eyes," he whispered.

"No," Misty croaked out. "I don't want anything from you. Get away from my piano. I have to play."

She ran her hands up and down the keyboard and then broke into "Auld Lang Syne" once again.

Gradually people stopped talking and kissing, and faced the piano. Their party hats askew, they began to sing the words of the Robert Burns poem, the poignant lines touching Misty deeply.

She played the song at least four times, until everyone had had a chance to sing at the piano. Then the dancing began. As usual on special occasions, she had the support of two backup musicians, Roddy on drums and Lem on bass.

She was glad to be distracted by her music. She didn't look at Luc Harrison at all, though at intervals she looked up and smiled into the audience. When the set ended, she went straight to her friends' table, where she sat and talked with them.

At three-thirty in the morning her friends rose to leave. They came up to the piano to say good night.

"I won't bother to call you for breakfast . . . or brunch . . . or dinner," Aileen said, yawning and leaning on David. "But I have to tell you that this has been one memorable New Year's Eve. Thank you, Misty."

"Yes, thank you, Misty. And you look beautiful in my dress." Morey kissed her on the lips, as did David. Then the four of them were gone.

"Happy New Year," Misty whispered after them, more grateful than she could say for their presence there tonight.

She watched the crowd dwindle, though several groups remained until after four-thirty. She felt both relief and emptiness when she saw Luc Harrison's party depart. No doubt he and his date would stay in one of the best suites and have breakfast in bed, then a nice long sleep . . . in the same bed. She was glad she hadn't been able to figure which of the women at the Harrison table had been Luc's date.

At ten minutes to five on New Year's morning, the Edwardian Room was empty except for a few busboys and waiters. Misty said good night to her backup men and leaned against the piano for a moment, rubbing her throbbing temples. It had been a long night.

"Tired, darling?" Luc Harrison crooned, his hand slipping around her waist. "Come on. I have some food ready for you."

Misty blinked up at him. "I'm not hungry." She hadn't sampled food from the buffet because she played better on an empty stomach.

"You didn't eat anything tonight," he told her firmly, leading her from the room.

"I don't want to go anywhere. I'm exhausted."

"We'll eat right here," he reassured her.

"You're crazy. The dining rooms are closed for the night."

"We'll eat in my suite upstairs."

"I'm not joining your floozies!" Misty sputtered as he led her into an elevator. He inserted a key into a slot and pressed the top button on the panel. "You have the penthouse suite. That's disgusting." Misty lifted a hand to cover her yawn. "I'm not staying. I have to get some sleep." She struggled against him for a moment, then subsided. She just didn't have the strength to fight him. Exhaustion weakened her resolve to get to her dressing room, change, hail a cab, and go home.

"Fine. First you'll get a little nourishment," Luc said. "You can't live on tomato juice." He still had an arm around her when the elevator doors opened onto a small foyer.

Misty walked into the living room of the penthouse. She scanned the curving stairway that led to the second floor. She squinted at the table set for two in front of sliding glass doors that led onto a terrace. She noted the Christmas tree and sundry decorations outside. "Pretty . . . but I can't stay." She yawned again, feeling a bit weary.

Luc put her carrier down on a couch along with the fleece-lined velvet cape that Morey had designed for her. "This is quite nice," he said.

Misty glanced at him, trying to stifle another yawn. "My friend Morey designed it for me. He's fabulous." Fascinated, she watched Luc's eyes turn hard, and a muscle tightened in his jaw. "You change expressions like a chameleon," she said.

"Chameleons change color," he corrected tersely.

"Whatever." She shrugged and ambled over to the couch, where she sank down into the velvet depths, her eyes sliding shut.

"Is he the man you arranged the loan for? This Morey?" Luc demanded.

"Huh?" Misty's eyes blinked open. "Ah, yes. He's my special friend." She tried to focus her thoughts but couldn't. "I really have to go."

"I see..." Luc's voice sounded from far away. "Wake up. The food will be here in a moment."

Misty yawned widely and struggled to her feet as Luc took hold of her elbow. "Didn't you see Morey tonight?" She wet her dry lips with her tongue. "He and Zena and Aileen and David were there."

Luc guided her into a chair at the table and went to answer a knock on the door. A waiter entered the room, pushing a covered cart ahead of him. He laid out the dishes and was gone, like a wraith.

Misty looked fuzzily after him. "That was fast." She stared at the array of food, feeling all at once hungry. "I think I would like some of that soup." She watched Luc ladle some into a small bowl, her mouth watering. "Zena makes marvelous soup. She says the trick is to let the schmaltz rise to the top and skim it off." Misty sighed. "I'm sure she and Morey will be eating a great deal of soup until his business takes off. But at least they'll be able to get married now." She yawned again and rubbed her face. "Aren't you going to have some soup?" she asked as Luc continued to watch her, the silver ladle poised above the tureen.

"Ah, yes." He served himself, then cut each of them thick slices of warm bread. "So Morey is going to marry Zena?" he asked.

Misty nodded, spooning the hot chicken broth into her mouth, feeling warmth spread through her.

She ate four bowls of the broth, which surprised her. She'd never been especially fond of soup. But, barely able to keep her eyes open, she refused the casserole and the side dishes. "I really have to go," she mumbled, glancing around for her cape.

Luc stood up and helped her out of the chair. "Not yet. You're dead on your feet. Lie down for a bit. Then I'll take you home."

With an effort, she looked up at him. "I really shouldn't . . ." But her head flopped forward onto his chest.

"Just a short nap," he urged, reaching down to lift her into his arms. "You're such a tiny thing."

Misty felt the comforting motion of being jostled against his shoulder as he carried her into another room. Then, before she knew it, she was asleep.

When she woke, she ran her eyes around the gold and cream-colored room, then closed them again. She was still in a dream. Good. She was too tired to get up anyway. She snuggled back down under the covers, not questioning the great comfort of the bed, but wondering why her water bed wasn't undulating as it always did. She didn't even question the solid warmth at her back. After all, her water bed was heated. Grateful for the extra sleep, she burrowed deeper into the warmth, certain that she couldn't have heard someone groan.

Nevertheless, she opened her sleepy eyes and blinked once again at the cream and gold room. She lay perfectly still, trying to orient herself. "If I didn't know better, I would think I fell asleep in the Queen Victoria Dining Room," she muttered, the sheet up to her chin, her eyes registering each opulent article in the large bedroom. "I must be drunk."

"On tomato juice," a deep voice murmured in her ear.

She snapped her eyes shut in a futile effort to hide from the sudden horrible realization that she had gone to bed with Lucas Stuyvesant Harrison! Stunned, she kept her eyes tightly closed, wishing she could disappear. What a way to start the New Year! After all the promises she had made to herself about how she would live her life. This was awful! She'd had no intention of doing such a thing! Was she losing her mind?

She turned her head slowly and looked into glittering brown eyes so close to her own that she could see the tiny gold and green flecks in the irises.

"Happy New Year, darling." He leaned forward and kissed her, his mouth a gentle caress, his tongue a hot, questing spear that set fire to her bloodstream. His arm slid over her bare middle and pulled her to him. "I wanted you to wake up, love. I've been waiting."

"You mean we haven't . . . ah, made love—euphemistically speaking, that is?"

His eyes narrowed on her, the sparkle in them turning to a hard glitter. "No, we haven't made love—euphemistically speaking."

Misty let out her breath in a long sigh and rolled away from Luc's loose hold, out of bed, and to her feet, snatching up a blanket to cover herself. She fumbled awkwardly, and the blanket slipped, revealing a generous amount of skin.

She stood rigidly straight, almost naked, facing him, her chin up and her hands clenching and unclenching on the blanket. Her face flushed and her skin burned under Luc's hot gaze as his eyes traveled over her. She took deep breaths, trying to steady herself as he lay on his side watching her, the sheet barely covering his lower body. She couldn't seem to force her voice from her throat.

"Do I take it you're telling me no, my darling, even though we've spent the night in each other's arms?"

"That's right—and I'm not your darling." Misty forced the hoarse words from her throat, shivering not so much from cold as from nervous tension.

Luc saw her shudder and reached behind him for his robe. He tossed it to her. "Put it on, Mystique. It will keep you warmer than the blanket."

She slid her arms into the voluminous sleeves, which hung past her hands. Only when the belt was tied did she drop the blanket. "My clothes," she said, keeping her eyes on him as he pointed behind her. Without turning, she stepped backward.

His expression darkened. "From your cautious behavior

I gather you expect me to jump out of bed and rape you.
For some reason you don't trust me, Mystique."

"And all men like you," she snapped, shooting a quick
glance at her silk dress lying on a chair. "Where's my
carrier?"

"Downstairs in the living room. Shall I get it?"

"No!" With effort she controlled her anger. She didn't
want to see him out of bed, naked and...beautiful. She
closed her mind to the thought.

"Dammit, stop that," he railed. "I said I wasn't going
to rape you, and I'm not. I don't know what the hell kind
of men you've been dealing with, but I'm not what you
think." His anger raised goose bumps on her skin, and she
backed away. "Dammit, stop it, I said. You think I was
wrong to climb into bed with you. Well, I don't, and I sure
as hell don't feel guilty because I'm attracted to you. I
haven't done anything to hurt you."

She didn't stay to hear more. In a flash she raced out of
the room and down the stairs to the living room, grabbed
up her carrier, and looked around wildly for a place to
change.

"Try the bathroom over there." Her eyes shot upward.
Luc was standing on the balcony overlooking the living
room, a cheroot in his hand, a lighter held to the cigar. He
was naked.

"Thank you," Misty mumbled, sliding her eyes quickly
away from his form. God, he was beautiful...

She got dressed in the bathroom, his brown eyes and ash
blond hair filling her thoughts. No way! she told herself.
No way would she get caught in that trap again.

After dressing hurriedly and combing her hair, she
emerged from the bathroom.

Luc stood in the middle of the living room, dressed in
brown cord jeans with a champagne silk shirt and brown
vest. "I'll take you home," he said.

"No need," she retorted, clutching her carrier to her.

"I said I'll take you home, and I will."

"I'd rather go home alone. I'll call a cab."

He ran a hand angrily through his tousled hair. "Dammit,
Mystique, what the hell is the matter with you? I'm sorry
if I offended you. I thought I made it clear that I had no

intention of hurting you. But I also have no intention of hiding my attraction."

"That's why you sent the earrings. Since I sent them back, you should have gotten the message."

A smile fluttered across his mouth. "Yes, you did send them back, damn you." He took several restless steps and turned to face her. "What does it take to convince you that I want a relationship with you?"

In her anger, the words popped out before she considered them. "Two things: a certificate from the Board of Health saying that you're free of disease, and a proposal of marriage."

For once she had caught Luc Harrison by surprise.

CHAPTER THREE

ALL THE WAY home in the cab and for the rest of the morning Misty couldn't get out of her mind the expressions that had crossed Luc Harrison's face when she'd answered his question. Shock and incredulity had been followed rapidly by contempt, anger, and finally icy disdain.

"I'm afraid marriage isn't what I had in mind," he'd told her coldly. Then he'd helped her with her cape, called down to the doorman to hold a taxi, and watched her walk into the elevator. Neither of them had said good-bye.

In the shower, as she shampooed her hair, she wondered if Luc Harrison really thought she expected him to marry her. She turned the water on full force, trying to wash away the unclean feeling from her body and soul. He was no different from Leonard and Richard . . . and her father. He thought of her as a toy. She didn't know when her tears began mixing with the shower water. All at once harsh sobs were issuing from her mouth into the loofah sponge.

She emerged from the bathroom like a somnambulist, wrapped in an old terry-cloth robe. She would not go through that again, she vowed. How many sessions with the therapist had it taken before she realized that her parents felt threatened by her maturity, by her budding womanhood, so they had punished her as though she were evil. Then Richard and Leonard had used her, taken advantage of her. She raised a fist to her mouth and shook her head. "No, no, no!" Moving like an automaton, she began neatening her apartment.

As soon as she finished straightening up the room, she fell into bed and slept deeply, dreamlessly, not wakening until early afternoon.

Immediately she jumped out of bed and got dressed. She had promised to take the twins to Rockefeller Center to skate. Thank goodness she felt rested after her nap. Eager to do anything that would keep her from thinking of Luc Harrison and the pain she had buried deep inside her, she hurried downstairs to Aileen and David's apartment.

"Are you sure you want to take the twins by yourself?" Aileen asked, covering a yawn.

"I'm sure. You and David go back to bed. I know you were up early with them. Honestly, I feel good, and I'm looking forward to the fresh air and exercise."

"I could call the U.S. Marines and have them give you a hand." Aileen warily eyed her progeny, who were at that moment arguing over the multicolored laces in their skates.

"Don't worry," Misty told her and shepherded her charges out the door.

The twins enjoyed themselves so thoroughly during the bus ride that Misty began to relax and have fun, too.

"Look at that building, Misty," Mary pronounced in awed tones, her nose pressed against the window. "It's all wrapped in ribbon with a big bow." She pointed at the Cartier building on Fifth Avenue.

"I saw that before Christmas when I went with Dad to pick out the tree," Mark announced importantly.

"You're just bragging," Mary accused through pursed lips.

"All right you two, this is our stop," Misty announced, urging them off the bus.

The twins were so excited about skating that they forgot to argue as they walked through Rockefeller Center. It didn't take long for Misty to rent skates for herself. Although she usually found the rentals too tight or too loose, this time they fit comfortably. The twins, who had already put on their own skates, urged her to hurry.

"I am hurrying," she protested. "Mark, I want you to retie yours. You've skipped a few eyelets with the laces."

"Aw, Misty, do I have to?" Mark moaned.

"Yes, you do. It will make skating much more comfortable."

"I didn't miss any of the eyelets with my laces," Mary announced primly, making her brother glower with indignation.

"Let's go, let's go." Misty forestalled an explosion by clasping an arm of each and hurrying them out to the ice.

There were fewer people than she had anticipated. They were probably sleeping late after partying most of the night.

Misty kept an eye on the twins, who were making a rapid if somewhat erratic circle around the rink, and she began to skate herself. She had always been a good skater. As a young girl she had even daydreamed of winning a gold medal in the Olympics. But her father had refused to pay for the expensive coaching that would have been necessary. When she'd begged to earn the money herself by baby-sitting, her parents had told her she was being selfish. Her mother had explained that there were other children in the family who needed more important things, that they couldn't buy luxuries for one child without buying them for all the kids. Misty blessed her aunt and uncle, who had given her not only an old upright piano but also a pair of secondhand skates that she had loved and used for years.

She smiled as she recalled the telephone conversation she had had with her aunt and uncle on Christmas Day. They had urged her to visit them in Florida, and she had made up her mind to do so as soon as she saved enough money for the trip.

Coming out of her reverie, she looked for the twins again and found them in the middle of the rink trying to imitate a young girl about their age who was doing skillful turns and figures. A man and woman skated up to the girl. Then the man lifted his head and looked right at Misty. The smile froze on her face. Luc Harrison! What was he doing here? She looked away from him and continued skating. How was she going to get the twins away? Of course! She would take them to Rumpelmayer's and buy them some ice cream.

But before she could act, she felt her arm being taken in a light but firm grip. She stiffened, and one of her skates caught on an uneven patch of ice.

"Sorry. Did I startle you?" Luc's mouth curved up in a smile, but there was no amusement in his face. His eyes were like icicles that stabbed through her. Tightening his grip on her arm, he kept her moving forward around the ice. The woman he was with remained on his other side toward the center of the rink. "Linda Caseman, this is Mystique Carver. She plays the piano at the Terrace Hotel."

"I've always wanted to be able to play as well as you, but I'm afraid I'm a rank amateur." Linda gave Misty a friendly smile.

Misty smiled back, not sure if the woman was being sarcastic or sincere. Good grief, Luc Harrison had made her paranoid! "It's nice to meet you, but I really have to go," Misty said, trying to pull her arm free.

Luc's grip tightened. "Whose children are they?" he asked, his mouth still smiling but his face tight with tension.

"Aileen and David's . . . my neighbors." Again she tried to jerk her arm free, but she succeeded only in bumping into an older man who was skating by. "Oh! Pardon me."

"No respect—that's the problem today," the senior citizen grumbled, glaring at Misty.

"I think I'll go get a hot chocolate," Linda announced brightly, beginning to skate away from them. "Nice meeting you, Mystique," she called over her shoulder.

"Nice meeting you," Misty mumbled, then dug her fingers into the gloved hand holding her arm. "Will you let me go?" she demanded.

"Stop doing that. You'll knock down someone else." Still Luc didn't release her.

"I didn't knock anyone down," Misty sputtered. "You were the one who— Oh, excuse me." She smiled weakly at the frowning teenager she had just rammed into. "See? You made me do that. Let me go."

"No." Luc put his arm around her waist and began skating faster.

"Stop. I can't skate fast. It makes me dizzy," Misty

argued as the twins' startled faces flashed past her. Finally
Luc slowed to a stop. Misty leaned against him, panting.
"What . . . in blazes . . . did you think you were . . . doing?"
she demanded. "Trying to set a speed-skating record?"

"Tired?" He shot the word at her like a whip.

"No!" She gulped, then whirled away and skated out to
the middle of the ice, where Mark and Mary were still trying
to master the complicated turns being performed by the
young girl Misty had first seen with Luc.

"Hi, Misty," Mary called. "I saw you skating with that
man. Janie says he's her uncle. Isn't that funny?"

"Hilarious," Misty said flatly.

"This is Misty." Mark paused in doing figure eights and
introduced Janie, who smiled and held out her hand.

Misty admired the young girl's poise. "Hello, Janie."

"Hi. Are you a friend of Uncle Lucas? He said he called
a friend today and found out she'd gone skating. Was it
you?"

"No," Misty denied. "Ah, what I mean is, I hardly know
your uncle. It was very nice meeting you, Janie, but if Mary
and Mark want to go to—"

"Rumpelmayer's!" Mary interrupted gleefully. "I want
a hot chocolate and a milk shake. Nice meeting you, Janie.
Maybe we'll see you again when Misty brings us."

"Yeah," Mark put in, a trace of reserve in his voice as
he turned from the girl, and followed Misty and Mary off
the ice.

"Mar-rk likes Janie. Mar-rk likes Janie," Mary chanted
as they removed their skates.

Misty glimpsed a sheen of angry tears in Mark's eyes.
She moved between the twins as she returned her rented
skates. "All right, that's enough, Mary," Misty admonished.
"If you want to go to Rumpelmayer's, don't say another
word."

Mary made a face but fell silent.

Not wanting to catch sight of Luc, Misty kept her eyes
on the two youngsters until they were out on the street. She
hailed a cab to take them to the ice cream parlor. The sun
was shining, but the wind had a cold bite to it. Had Luc
called her? Misty wondered. If Aileen had heard the phone
and answered it, would she have told Luc that she had gone

skating? Misty struggled to keep from thinking of him.

As usual, Rumpelmayer's was a great success with the twins, but somehow the luster of the afternoon was gone for Misty. She had to fight to concentrate on the children who were chattering about their new friend Janie.

That night she shared a supper with David and Aileen after the twins were in bed. "Mary said you know Janie Patterson's uncle," Aileen said, sipping her coffee and watching Misty over the rim of her cup.

"Yes. The girl's uncle is Luc Harrison."

David whistled, then coughed when Aileen glared at him. "He called asking for you," Aileen told Misty.

She shrugged. "The twins loved Rumpelmayer's."

"They always do," Aileen agreed, not protesting Misty's abrupt change of subject. But several times that evening Misty felt her friend's anxious gaze fixed on her, and soon afterward she rose to say good night.

"Just be careful, Misty. Don't get hurt again," Aileen said at the door, hugging her.

"I have no intention of getting hurt," Misty assured her. But her smile wavered.

Because New Year's Day had fallen on a Sunday, the following Monday was a holiday for most people. Not for Misty, however. She was expected at the Edwardian Room at nine that evening.

She was waxing her piano in the morning when she heard the clatter of the twins' feet on the stairs. In the next moment the door flew open and banged against the wall. Mary stood there grinning, Janie smiling shyly at her side. "Look, Misty, isn't it great? Janie came over to take us skating again, and she wants you to come with us."

Misty's gaze flew to the stairs behind the girls, where she expected Luc Harrison to appear at any moment. "I, ah...I don't think so. I have to work tonight, and...I should practice."

Mary's face fell. "But you *have* to come. Janie wants to go on the bus. She's never gone on the bus before, and you're the only one who knows the way. We can't go without you," Mary wailed.

Janie must have come without her uncle, Misty decided.

She smiled. "All right, I'll come. But remember, I have to be home early so I can take a nap before I go to work." The two girls broke into loud whoops and raced down the stairs.

Misty hurried through the rest of her chores, took a shower, and put on thermal underwear, cord jeans, a blue wool sweater, and a down vest.

When she arrived downstairs, the door to the Collinses' apartment stood open, and she walked in. "All right, slow-pokes, let's move it—" She stopped short, her mouth falling open at the sight of Luc Harrison sitting at Aileen's kitchen table drinking coffee. The three children were already tugging on their coats and boots.

"Isn't this great?" Aileen exclaimed, rushing into nervous speech. "Janie wants to go for a bus ride, and Luc says he'll go, too." She laughed gaily, watching Misty the way a bird watches a snake.

"I see," Misty said calmly, though she wanted to shake her friend. She glared at Luc, who saluted her with his coffee cup, his eyes steady on her, his mouth lifting in a polite smile.

He rose from the table and drained the last of his coffee before putting the cup in the sink. "Very good coffee, Aileen. Thank you. Well, shall we go?" he asked the three youngsters, ignoring Misty's mutinous expression.

The children swept out the door, chattering nonstop. Luc and Misty followed side by side in silence.

Half a block from the bus stop, Misty said, "You had no right to come to the house."

"Janie wanted to skate with Mark and Mary again."

"Then you should have sent her alone. I would have been glad to take her with the twins."

"Thank you so much, but *I* can take care of my niece." Luc's voice was frigid.

"Then do so. But don't include me."

"I won't ever again."

"Good." Misty ran to catch the bus and stepped inside with change in her hand. But another hand pushed past hers and dropped money for all of them into the box. Ignoring that, she made her way to the middle of the bus where Mark, Mary, and Janie were crowded into two seats. Misty tried to sit down next to a plump woman with a big shopping bag on the seat, but the woman glared at her.

"There's an empty seat farther back," the woman muttered, making no effort to move her shopping bag.

"Come along, darling. We'll sit behind the children," Luc said smoothly.

"Yeah, sit behind your kids. Disgusting the way these modern mothers ignore your brats. I never done that," the woman observed to an old man in another seat.

"You're just trying to make trouble," Misty accused Luc.

"*I'm* not the one ignoring our children," he teased mildly.

"They are *not* our children!"

"Mystique, that woman is looking back here again," he whispered. "She probably heard you say that and plans on turning us over to the Society for the Prevention of Cruelty to Children."

"Oh, you . . . you . . ." Misty sputtered.

"What's the matter, Misty?" Mark turned awkwardly around in his seat.

"Nothing, Mark," she said.

"Temper, temper," Luc whispered, a thread of laughter in his voice.

Misty shot a glance at him, surprised by his amusement. Earlier, he had been so furious with her.

Janie turned around, too, and smiled at her. "I like to skate. Do you, Mystique?"

"Her name's Misty," Mary informed her friend. "And she teaches us piano, too."

"Oh? Uncle Luc calls you Mystique, doesn't he?" Janie asked.

"That's the name I use professionally," Misty explained, acutely aware that Luc had draped an arm along the back of the seat.

"I think it's pretty," Janie assured her.

"So do I," Luc murmured.

"We call her Misty," Mark insisted, shooting a suspicious glance at Luc.

When they got off the bus, the three children ran ahead, shouting over their shoulders that they would be careful.

"They have fun together," Luc observed.

"Yes, they do," Misty said, not looking at him.

"Will you have dinner with me this evening?"

"No, thank you. I'm working." Misty was relieved to have an excuse.

"Join me for a meal first," Luc insisted, directing the children across the street.

"I generally don't eat before work. I have a light lunch a few hours before I leave, and that's enough." She clamped her mouth shut, annoyed with herself for having explained it to him.

"You're too thin," Luc observed.

Stung, Misty pulled away from his hold and hurried after the children.

"Stop being so defensive with me," Luc called, catching up with her. "I just meant that I think you should eat more nourishing meals."

"I thought we said everything there was to say to each other yesterday," Misty snapped.

"Yes, we did say quite a bit. I've been wanting to talk to you about that."

"Misty, hurry," Mary wailed. "We want to skate."

"Coming." Misty trotted after them, glad of the diversion as she ushered the children past the kiosk, not bothering to try to pay for them when Luc's hard eyes glinted at her.

She rented a pair of skates and stood on the sideline watching the children as they skated to an open area in the center of the rink and began practicing turns and twists.

"Shall we skate?" Luc took her arm in a firm grip and tugged her out onto the ice. "Don't worry, I have no intention of racing. I just thought you might like to waltz to the Strauss music." His brown eyes held a spark of recklessness that sent a frisson of alarm down Misty's spine.

"I like Strauss's music," she conceded grudgingly.

"Good." Luc spun her around the ice in a gentle waltz. As always, she was caught up in the music. She felt her body and spirit melt into the graceful rhythms of old Vienna.

"You're good," Luc whispered to her, bringing her out of her reverie. "So very, very good. I love the way you move."

"Oh!" Misty tried to look away from his mesmerizing gaze, but she found it too difficult to do so.

They danced close together across the ice for six waltzes.

When they finally slowed to a stop, Misty felt out of breath, partly from the exercise, partly from Luc's lips hovering so close to hers.

"The children," she gasped, pushing away from him. The man was hypnotizing her!

"They're fine," he whispered in her hair.

"See? There they are. Just about where we left them."

"I have to watch them," Misty said, breaking free of his hold and skating to the center of the rink. The children looked up at her and smiled.

"Hi, Misty. Look what I can do," Mary crowed, twirling around with her hands clasped over her head.

From then on, Misty stayed close to the children. Sometimes she skated with one or the other. Once when Luc came close, she went off by herself. Wherever she was on the ice, she was constantly aware of his piercing gaze.

When it was time to go, both Mark and Mary held back. "Aw, Misty, just a little while longer," Mary begged.

"Come on, Misty," Mark wheedled.

"It's nice today. Not as crowded as other days," Janie offered.

Misty hesitated, wanting to please the children but knowing that if she didn't leave now she wouldn't have time for a nap before she had to go to work. Luc took the decision out of her hands.

"Everybody off with the skates," he commanded, sending the twins and Janie scurrying to the sidelines.

Misty stared after them, amazed to see that they appeared neither angry nor sullen. She glanced up at Luc. "Thank you. I should get home."

"But you would have given in to them," Luc said softly, a flicker of warmth in his brown eyes.

Misty shrugged. "I suppose so."

"You need someone to take care of you."

She stiffened; her temper flared. "No, thank you," she said coolly. "I take care of myself." She skated away, her back ramrod straight.

As they rode home on the bus, Luc and Misty sat close together but didn't speak. Misty was content to listen to the children's chatter. Gradually her ire settled into a renewed resolve not to get caught in any man's trap ever again.

Luc walked with them to the house, saw them inside, and left with his niece, his quiet nod toward Misty in marked contrast to the children's noisy good-byes.

Misty didn't stay long either, although she could tell Aileen was dying to ask her about the afternoon she had spent with Luc Harrison. "I really do have to get some sleep, so I'll pass on the offer of coffee," she told her disappointed friend.

Misty went up to her own apartment, deliberately erasing Luc Harrison from her thoughts. After packing the carrier with makeup and accessories, she climbed into the water bed, curled into a ball, and willed herself to go to sleep.

In the end she overslept and had to race through the apartment, making her bed, showering, and pulling on a pair of pale green velvet jeans and a matching chamois vest. Her emerald green blouse was almost the same color as her eyes. She wore tiny earrings that she would later exchange for dangling gold ones to complement her persimmon-colored silk dress.

She took the elevator downstairs, her purse and carrier bumping against her legs.

"Good night, Misty. Take care," Dave called out from the doorway of his apartment. "Why don't you hail a taxi instead of taking all that stuff on the bus?"

"I'm fine," she assured him, closing the heavy oak door behind her and hurrying down the stoop. Since she could afford a taxi only once a day, she saved it for coming home.

She had reached the sidewalk and was hitching the carrier higher on her shoulder when a familiar voice said, "I'll take that for you." She turned, aghast. Luc was standing beside her, removing the carrier from her shoulder and stuffing it into the trunk of a bronze-colored Ferrari parked at the curb.

Her mouth agape, Misty made no move to protest when he opened the passenger door and ushered her inside. "Where did you come from?" she demanded. "I didn't see you when I came out the door." She sank back against the soft leather upholstery; she knew she should get out of the car but for some reason she was unable to do so.

"You were too busy wrestling with that carrier. Do you take the bus to work every night?"

"I don't work every night." Feeling his gaze on her,

Misty kept her eyes focused straight ahead.

"You're a proud little thing."

"I don't know why you keep coming around. We said everything there was to say yesterday morning."

"Not quite," he disagreed, firing the powerful engine and pulling smoothly into heavy traffic.

"But why do you keep coming?" she repeated, confused. "I won't change my mind."

"I know. I've changed mine."

"About what?"

He didn't answer. Instead he concentrated on maneuvering the sleek car through the congested traffic. Misty gazed distractedly out the window at the people hurrying along the sidewalks. Where were they going? Home? Out to dinner? To a show?

Finally Luc drew the car up outside the Terrace Hotel. As Misty began fumbling with the door handle he said mildly, "Don't bother, darling. It's locked on the wheel." He parked and turned to her. "I've thought over what you told me yesterday, and I realize your request has merit." He pressed a button on the steering wheel, and the door on her side of the car unlocked. Then he got out, removed her things from the trunk, and ushered her up the steps to the entrance.

"What do you mean?" Misty asked as a thin thread of panic uncurled inside her.

"Shall I park your car, sir?" the parking attendant asked Luc.

"No, thank you," Luc replied. He walked with Misty into the lobby, handed her the carrier, kissed her on the cheek, and left without explaining how he'd changed his mind.

Misty stood staring after him, thoroughly perplexed. But in another moment she realized it was time to change and she hurried to her dressing room. Once dressed, she studied herself in the mirror. Morey had been right again. For some reason the persimmon-colored gown seemed to enhance her hair rather than clash with it. She applied pale gold eye shadow—tonight she would have cat's eyes—and leaned closer to the mirror. Was the gown cut a shade too low in front?

The crisp silk was molded tightly to her bosom and clung as though magnetized to her form. The wide neckline skimmed her shoulders, and the long sleeves ended tightly above her wrists. There was no extra material to get in her way as she played the piano. The dress was light and very comfortable, and it gave the skin on her neck and above her breasts a peachy pearlescence. Misty laughed with delight at her image as she put on dangling gold earrings, her only jewelry except for a thin gold watch. She found costume jewelry a distraction when she played and rarely wore it.

Misty strolled out of the dressing room twenty minutes early and went over to Willis, who was gesturing to her. "Hi. How's the crowd in the Edwardian Room?" she asked.

"We're full up, as we've been since you began playing here," Willis told her. "Here. You have time to eat some soup and bread and drink a glass of milk. I've put it all out for you on the little table behind the palm tree."

Misty blinked at him in surprise. "Willis, you know I never eat before I play."

"But this won't be a lot of food. Come on and sit down." He ushered her to a chair at the small corner table and gestured to one of the waiters.

"I don't think I should do this," she protested faintly, tantalized in spite of herself by the fragrant soup.

"Eat," Willis commanded.

She did. The clear beef broth with vegetables tasted great with the French crackers, while the glass of milk was a welcome addition. "Thank you, Willis. That was delicious. I do feel better." Misty put her hand on the maître d's sleeve.

"It's about time I fed you. I don't know why I didn't think of it before," he grumbled, then turned away to speak to a portly man in a cashmere suit.

Misty wanted to ask Willis what he meant, but he was busy and, besides, it was time to begin playing.

Her sense of well-being affected her playing in a positive manner. She found herself straying from her usual repertoire of popular songs and show tunes to play a rousing piece by Nicolai Rimsky-Korsakov. She smiled at the audience's burst of applause, then moved immediately into Rachmaninoff, chuckling when she heard a collective sigh rise from some of the diners. She returned to her standard repertoire feeling refreshed.

The evening passed quickly. At midnight she realized she felt less fatigued than usual. She looked up to smile at her audience . . . and gazed right into Luc Harrison's brown eyes. He raised his glass to her and tipped some of the brown liquid into his mouth. She caught her breath as a tingling warmth started in her toes and worked its way upward.

After that, she couldn't seem to control her eyes. They strayed at will toward Luc. Each time, she found him watching her. Adrenaline rushed through her veins. Her fingers seemed to take on a life of their own as they skimmed skillfully over the piano keys. A few stragglers lingered in the dining room and applauded loudly after each song as she continued to play, putting all her heart and soul into the music.

Finally there was no one left but Luc. In accordance with house rules, she could have quit for the night, but she didn't. Instead, she continued to play ever more difficult pieces.

At two-thirty a hand came down over hers on the keyboard. "That's enough, darling. You're tired."

Misty nodded, staring mesmerized at Luc as his determined gaze kindled a warmth in her such as she had never felt before. "I think I could play all night," she whispered to him.

"I know," he told her, lifting her from the piano bench and slipping an arm around her. "Go and change. I'll drive you home tonight."

"Isn't this awfully late for you? Don't you have to work at the bank in the morning?"

"Yes to both questions. But I think I may have a solution to the problem."

"Oh?"

"Never mind that now. I'll tell you later." He led her to the wide corridor and patted her backside. "Go and change."

"I . . . I . . ." Misty stood, irresolute.

"Stop thinking up excuses, Mystique. I'll just have to refute them."

She turned away, frowning as she said good night to Willis and went into her dressing room. After scrubbing the makeup off her face, she changed into the velvet jeans and emerald green blouse she'd worn on her way over to the hotel. I don't understand him, she thought. He confuses me. Tonight I'm going to tell him again that I want nothing to do with him. She stifled the ache that the words brought deep inside. If she was to survive, she had to keep men like Luc Harrison out of her life. It was the only way. She left the dressing room, wearing no makeup except a little lip gloss.

Luc was waiting for her. He took the carrier out of her hands. "You look twelve years old," he said, staring at her.

"I'm not."

"I'm glad," he said, imitating her stern tone. But his eyes glinted with amusement.

"Mr. Harrison..." she began as they walked out the front door to the Ferrari. Louis, the parking attendant, was holding open the passenger door. "Thank you, Louis." She tried to smile.

Luc got in, started the car, and pulled away from the curb. "Put your head back and rest," he told her. "You can say anything you want when we get home."

Misty turned in the seat to face him. "I want to tell you now, Mr. Harrison.

"Luc."

"All right, Luc. I want to tell you—"

"Put your head back and relax, love. Then you can talk to me."

Misty settled back, her eyes skimming the facades of the buildings they passed and the darkened interior of the car. "You keep interrupting me," she complained.

He laughed lightly. "I promise not to do it anymore," he said, pressing his hand on her knee for just a second, seeming not to notice when she quivered at his touch.

"Good," she said, suddenly hoarse. "Luc, I want you to stop coming to the Terrace Hotel."

"Darling, how can I? I'm one of the owners."

"You're doing it again," Misty said, rolling her head to stare at him.

"Sorry, sweet."

"We talked this through on New Year's Day, in your apartment."

"My suite in the hotel," he corrected her.

"Stop interrupting!"

"All right," he whispered.

"Luc!"

"I'm listening."

"We talked, and we decided we wouldn't see each other again."

"Now I *have* to interrupt," he said, trying to soothe her with a squeeze on her knee that made her jump. "I did not agree that we shouldn't see each other again. I admit that I was a little thrown by your demands, but I did not say that I wouldn't see you again."

"Well, now you can," Misty declared.

He shook his head. "I can't do that. Primarily because it would be a lie." He turned the car onto the entrance ramp leading to a small underground garage where only two other cars were parked.

With a start of surprise Misty sat up abruptly, looking around her. "Where are we?" she demanded.

"Now, don't panic. We're in the underground garage I share with three other brownstone owners in the neighborhood. Although the cost is outrageous—"

"I don't want to hear how expensive it is to park your Ferrari." Her voice rose to a shriek. "Take me home."

Luc parked the car, removed the keys, and got out. He went around to her side, opened the door, and leaned in to take her arm. She shrank back, cringing. Luc's mouth tightened ominously. "Darling, don't ever flinch from me." He went down on his haunches so that they were eye to eye and lifted her hand to his mouth, his eyes never leaving her face. "Please come in for a moment, Mystique. I want to show you something." He pulled an envelope from his pocket.

"I want to go home. It's late." She swallowed, her throat dry.

"Just let me show you these papers." He glanced around the garage. "This place is well lit, but not for reading. Besides, I want to show you something else."

Reluctantly she swung her legs around and let Luc help her to her feet. "I won't stay long."

"It won't take you more than fifteen minutes to read these papers," Luc assured her, leading her to a doorway with a steel nameplate that read: Lucas S. Harrison. "This stairway leads to the basement of my brownstone," he explained. "Above us are the owners' four backyards. Each one is separated by trees and fencing to ensure a measure of privacy for all the tenants." He led her up cement steps, his hand enveloping hers. At the top he unlocked another steel door and switched on a light. "This is the wine cellar. It feels cool, doesn't it? Through here, Mystique." He ushered her down a wide pathway with wine bottles on either side to a thick oak door, which he also opened. It led onto a more spacious area of the basement. "I keep gym equipment down here." He gestured toward a weight machine, a punching bag, and a padded exercise board.

"Nice," Misty murmured, glancing at the unfinished brick walls.

"If you'd like an exercycle, we can get that, too," he said.

Misty stared at him. "I don't care what you put in here. I swim at an athletic club three times a week."

Luc considered the room. "I don't think we could fit a pool in here, darling."

"I'm not your darling," she snapped, preceding him up a wide staircase that led into what Misty surmised to be the front foyer of the house.

"That's the front door leading to the street," Luc confirmed, pointing to an oak door inset with a stained-glass window. "We'll go into the living room. On the second floor is my library, on the third floor is the master suite, and on the fourth floor are three more bedrooms. There are four bathrooms. Down here, besides the living and dining rooms, is the kitchen and a larger room that I use for entertaining. I have day help, but no live-in—"

Just then Misty heard a rhythmic clicking coming across the oak floor. A large brown Doberman stuck his head around an open door. Misty stepped back, paralyzed with fright. A thousand remembered nightmares filled her thoughts, foremost among them the image of the dog that had bitten her when she was thirteen. The growling, snapping, and snarling seemed to be all around her, as fresh in her mind as the moment the animal had attacked her, leaping out at her as she walked past his house. Later, when the

owner had suggested to her father that she had provoked
the dog, her father had agreed without hesitation that she
probably had.

"Darling, for God's sake!" Luc exclaimed. "Are you
afraid of dogs?" He took her into his arms, cradling her,
protecting her, trying to lift her chin, which she burrowed
against his chest. "Bruno, down," he ordered. "Good boy."

Misty took several deep breaths. "A dog like that bit
me," she said shakily. "It wasn't my fault."

"No, of course it wasn't. You're trembling." Luc tipped
up her chin. "Don't be afraid."

Gradually, feeling warm in Luc's embrace, she grew
calm. She turned her head to study the dog, who was lying
on the floor, his head between his paws, whining softly.
Misty gave a weak laugh. "He thinks I'm crazy, doesn't
he?"

"I think he's worried about you. I found him on a country
road when he was just a pup. He's been with me ever since.
He's gentle and very intelligent."

"Yes," Misty agreed, though she still wasn't sure of the
animal.

"I'll send him into the kitchen."

"Should I introduce myself?" She gasped at her own
boldness, afraid yet wanting to rid herself of the fear.

"It might help," Luc agreed. "I'll hold you. Don't worry.
Bruno, come." The Doberman rose in one fluid motion and
stepped toward them, stopping inches away from Misty.
She closed her eyes. Fear turned her legs to jelly. "Open
your eyes, darling, and say hello," Luc whispered.

She opened one eye. "Hello, Bruno."

The dog wagged his stub of a tail.

"That's enough for the first lesson, I think." Luc ordered
the dog to the kitchen and led her into a huge room with a
fireplace and walls paneled in hand-carved oak. "Sit here."
Luc gestured toward a couch that matched the green in the
Persian carpet. He sank down near her feet and put a lit
match to the kindling in the fireplace, then turned and handed
her the papers he'd shown her in the garage. "Here's what
I want you to read."

Misty tried to smile. "Why don't you just tell me what
they say."

He rose from the floor to sit close beside her. "All right."
He put the papers in his lap, lifting the first one. "This is
my bank statement certified by my board of directors and
accountants. With it is a list of my tangible assets and
liabilities. I'm a rich man, Mystique."

"That has nothing to do with me," she said in a faint
voice, staring from the papers to his face and back again.

"Shhh. You mustn't interrupt me. There, you can peruse
my financial statements at your leisure, and of course you
are free to ask further questions and get any additional proof
you might want."

"Proof?" she repeated.

He lifted the second paper. "This is a statement from my
personal physician with a copy of all tests that I've had in
the last three years. I'm very healthy and, as you specified,
free of disease."

"Lord . . ." Misty groaned.

"Shhh. You can look at all the X-rays and tests I've had,
and of course you can question my doctor."

She shook her head, unable to say anything. A terrible
dread had settled over her. She could almost guess what
was coming next.

"This last paper is our marriage license, which is valid
as of today. Since I see no reason to wait, I've arranged for
us to be married tomorrow afternoon, upstate in the town
of Hudson. I managed to get your blood test waived, so
we're all set."

Misty sagged against the back of the couch, staring in
shocked speechlessness at the man beside her.

CHAPTER FOUR

MISTY SURGED TO her feet. "I have to go home." If need be, she'd run to Alaska to get away from Luc Harrison.

"You're tired, darling. Why don't you sleep here tonight? Then we'll have a leisurely drive up to Hudson tomorrow." He stood up, clasping her lightly to his side.

"I can't marry you," Misty said with a gasp.

From Luc's expression she could tell he felt affronted. "I won't accept that," he said firmly. "I fulfilled all your specifications. There is no insanity in the family—well, no *overt* insanity. I have a few strange relatives, but what family doesn't?"

"You don't know me," Misty protested.

"I *do* know you. The day I first saw you playing the piano in the Edwardian Room I hired a private investigator to learn all about you."

"You what!" She was shocked. "Checking to see if I was a social pariah, I suppose," she said with deadly sarcasm.

"No. Checking to see if you had a husband I would have to take care of."

"What would you have done? Bought him off? Killed him?"

"Yes," Luc said promptly.

Misty stared at him. Her mouth had gone dry. "I won't marry anybody who's investigated me like the FBI."

"Why not? You're free to investigate me. I've never been married, though I've had a mistress or two."

"Or forty," Misty shot back with scathing anger, feeling less and less numb as she began to recover from the initial shock.

"All right, I shouldn't have had you investigated. But I had to know all about you. I couldn't wait to court you and ask you questions about your marital status. I was in a hurry. You *are* going to marry me."

"You don't know anything about me. I . . . I've had my share of problems. I'm not the kind of woman who will fit in with your family." She had no intention of telling him that her father had once accused her of being a whore.

"Then we won't see my family," Luc assured her. "I'm fond of them, but I don't see them all the time. Of course I'll want you to meet my father and mother." Luc smiled down at her. "Father thinks you're beautiful. He told me my mother's hair was just a shade lighter than yours when they were first married, but my mother says her hair was more blond."

"Your parents know who I am?"

"Yes, but they'll really get to know you after we're married. I took them to hear you play at the hotel, and they were very impressed, as I knew they would be. You play so well."

"Luc, you didn't . . . I didn't see them with you," Misty babbled.

"We were sitting at a corner table out of your line of vision." He opened the double doors of the living room and led her out to the foyer. "Shall we say good night to Bruno?"

"If you have to walk him, I'll wait here," Misty said, her mind awhirl.

"You're thinking that you'll run out the door and go home while I'm walking the dog. But I'm not about to let you roam the streets of Manhattan at this time of night. Besides, I would come after you and take you up to Hudson to get married anyway."

"We aren't in love."

He shrugged. "Define *love* for me. I know I want to marry you. I know you told me you wanted no other type of relationship with a man. So, I'm all set." He looked down at her, determination showing in his rigid stance and hard jaw.

Misty was at a loss for words. She felt as if she'd been swept up in a strong current and washed helplessly downstream.

"Didn't you tell me that you wanted marriage?" Luc queried.

"I said I wouldn't have any other type of relationship, but . . . but I didn't—"

"I'm holding you to that, Mystique."

"Misty. Everyone calls me Misty," she declared, losing her patience.

"Except your husband-to-be."

"We can't get married. People like us don't get married. They live together until they're sure, and then . . . then . . ."

"You don't want that, and I've found that I don't want it either. You can sleep alone tonight if you wish, but no matter what you decide, I want two things from you now."

"What?" Her voice had a hollow ring.

"I don't want you to try to leave this house alone, and I want you to promise that you won't go back on our agreement."

"What agreement? I didn't make any—"

"We're just going around and around in circles, love. You're tired. We'll talk in the morning. Come on, I'll show you our room. You can sleep there tonight. I'll sleep upstairs."

"This is crazy, this is crazy," Misty kept whispering to herself all the way up the stairs.

She was too distraught to appreciate the beautiful beige and cream-colored bedroom with the huge bed in the center. "I have a water bed," she said inanely.

"We'll toss this one out and get a water bed," Luc offered.

"I have to have my piano. It costs a great deal to move a concert grand," she informed him as he unzipped her jeans.

"I know. I had three Steinways moved in here two weeks ago. They're all in perfect tune, so you should have no trouble."

"Three Steinways? That's disgusting," she told him, her voice going hoarse. Without thinking, she stepped out of her jeans.

"Would you like to sleep in the buff, sweets, or do you want the top of my pajamas?"

"I sleep in a flannel nightgown, and sometimes in flannel pajamas," she babbled.

"With feet in them, I'll bet."

"I used to until we were able to buy a better heating system for the house," Misty told him blankly. "This is a dream." Her voice was muffled as he slipped his silk pajama top over her head. "What will you wear now that I have your pajamas?" She looked down at herself, noting that the hem of the top fell below her knees.

"My mother buys them for me so that if the place burns down I won't have to run naked into the street. She has high hopes that I'll at least keep them at my bedside."

"You sleep in the nude," Misty pronounced solemnly.

"Yes. You'll get used to it."

"I am signing myself into an asylum tomorrow," she told him, wiping at the tears on her cheeks.

"I'll make you happy," he promised.

"You'll hate me in three months," she vowed.

"Never." Luc led her to the bed and stared down at her with an expression that sent warmth to all her extremities and set off a throbbing pulse in her very core. After a few moments he urged her under the sheets. "Would you like some company to keep you warm?" he asked, his voice sounding thick to Misty, who was half asleep.

"No." She yawned. "I always sleep alone. You go walk the dog."

"After tomorrow you won't sleep alone," he muttered, his voice growing fainter as Misty sank deeper into sleep.

The sound of an insistent buzzing almost awakened her. Then the noise stopped, and she snuggled into the warm down quilt that covered her, rolling over onto her stomach.

"Wake up, darling." Luc shook her gently, chuckling

when she groaned as he pulled the quilt off the bed. "I fully intended to let you sleep longer, but we have a problem that—Lord, where did you get those scars on your backside?" He cursed softly as he lifted the pajama top higher and examined her. "If you hadn't twisted the top up, I might not have noticed these. I sure as hell didn't notice them when I undressed you." He muttered another low curse as his hand gently traced the raised welts.

Misty shivered and, pushing the pillow off her head, turned on her side to face him, trying in vain to pull the pajama top down. "Give me back the covers," she mumbled, regarding him through bleary eyes.

Luc didn't bother to remove the towel from around his waist before he slipped into bed beside her and gathered her close to him. "Tell me. Was that where the dog bit you, darling?"

Misty nodded, burrowing her face into his neck and reveling in his warmth. "I hadn't teased the dog. I was just walking past on the sidewalk."

"And your father accused you of teasing the animal," Luc said in low tones.

"Yes." She gulped. "He and Mr. Marris, the owner of the dog, said that I must have provoked it because Sandy was usually friendly." The words bubbled from her like air escaping from a balloon.

"Why didn't the doctor recommend cosmetic surgery?"

"My father didn't take me to the doctor until the bites were infected."

"Damn him! You might have contracted tetanus from being left untreated." Luc cuddled her closer.

"My mother poured iodine on the bites." Misty shivered as she remembered how much it had hurt. She'd screamed so loudly.

"Good God," Luc whispered, his hand trembling as he stroked her hair.

They lay there in silence, Luc's slow hand soothing her. Then, abruptly, he stiffened. "I forgot. I got a call from Aileen. It seems we have visitors. Your three sisters have come to stay with you."

"My sisters?" Misty shot up to a sitting position in bed and whirled to face him as he rolled onto his back, his hands clasped behind his head. "Are you sure? My sisters?"

He nodded.

Misty bit her lip. "I haven't seen them in years. Gosh, they must be—"

"Eighteen, nineteen, and twenty-one," Luc supplied. He reached up and twisted a finger in her thick hair. "Don't worry. I called my sister Alice, and she's going right over to your apartment. She has three grown children, two boys and a girl, all of whom are living on their own in various parts of the country. She and her husband John love their family and miss them. When I told her she might get the chance to have young boarders, she was ecstatic."

"They came to *me*," Misty said in wonder. "They need *me*. I have to go to them." She jumped out of bed, jerking the pajama top down over her backside when she heard Luc suck in his breath.

"Okay, darling. If you want them to live with us, that's fine with me. We have plenty of room. But this morning we'll explain that it's our wedding day and arrange to have them stay with Alice and John."

"Surely you don't mean to go through with this charade," Misty protested.

His face grew taut. "We *are* getting married."

"Today?" Misty asked weakly.

Luc rose from the bed. The towel had slipped, and she averted her gaze. "As much as I would like to dally with you in this bed, I think we'd better get dressed. You'll find clean underwear in the left cupboard in the dressing room. I indulged myself one day in Saks. I enjoy shopping for you. See if you like my choices. I'll use the other bathroom on this floor." He padded out of the bedroom, leaving Misty still sputtering.

Without thinking, she went automatically into the dressing room and pulled open the door he had indicated. "Buy me underthings," she fumed, fingering the silky, peach-colored briefs and bra, as she slipped into them. She pulled on her velvet jeans and now wrinkled blouse and ran a comb through her long curly red hair, then ran out of the bedroom and down the curving staircase to the foyer, looking for Luc.

"Out here, darling," he called to her from under the stairs. "Come and sit down."

"We have to hurry," she whispered, smiling politely at a heavy-set woman whose plump face was wreathed in smiles. She glanced warily at the Doberman, who cocked his head at her.

At once, Luc was at her side, leading her past the dog to a chair in the dining room, where he seated her. "I know, love. I just want you to have some freshly squeezed orange juice and—here you are. A vitamin pill and one toasted English muffin. Mrs. Wheaton makes them herself."

"How do you do, Mrs. Wheaton?" Misty could feel her smile trembling as the dog rose and ambled over to her side.

"How do you do, miss?" Mrs. Wheaton greeted her. "May I offer you my best wishes?"

"Ah, thank you." Misty turned to glare at Luc as he picked up her vitamin pill and gestured for her to open her mouth. Snatching it out of his hand, she popped it into her mouth and swallowed. His kiss of approval emboldened her to risk patting Bruno's sleek brown head.

After they had finished eating breakfast, Misty urged Luc down the stairs to the garage. In the car he glanced at her pinched face and, loosening her clenched fingers, clasped his right hand around her left one. "Stop worrying," he scolded. "Everything will be fine. You're not to worry ever again."

"But I want my sisters to be all right."

"I will personally see to it that everything is just the way you want it, darling," he promised. "But nothing is going to interfere with our marriage at four o'clock today."

Misty didn't respond. Images of impending doom sprung up in her mind. By the time Luc parked the car in front of her brownstone, she was trembling, and her teeth were chattering.

Luc helped her out of the car, his arm tight around her, her carrier slung over his other shoulder. "Take it easy, love," he soothed.

As they walked up the stoop, the front door was flung open, and Mary stood bright-eyed on the threshold. "They're in our house, and I'm going to take Betsy skating, and Marcy wants to see the New York Public Library, and Celia is pretty," she exclaimed all in one breath, beaming at Luc and Misty. "Oh, and another lady is here, and she's nice, too." Mary chattered nonstop all the way down the hall to the door of her apartment.

As Misty walked in, her eyes alighted immediately on her sisters. She opened her arms, and the three young women ran into them.

Celia, Betsy, and Marcy cried. Misty felt raw pain, but her eyes remained dry.

"We made up our minds to come a long time ago, Misty," said chestnut-haired Celia, wiping her tears away. "But we couldn't leave Betsy behind, so we waited until she was eighteen. It wasn't as bad for us, but Father was getting worse, especially with Marcy when she said she wanted to go to college."

"I'm so glad you came to me," Misty said, her voice husky. "I've missed you." All at once she felt guilty. Why had she always assumed that her sisters would be spared the parental coldness and censure she had suffered once she began to mature? She had always been so certain that some flaw in herself had caused the gap between her and her parents. Despite the progress she'd made in therapy, she had never quite shaken that feeling.

"I was afraid you might not want us," Betsy said, her voice trembling.

"Of course we want you," Luc said, stepping forward and introducing himself. "You will always have a home with Mystique and me."

Misty heard Aileen gasp, but her attention was diverted as an unfamiliar woman came forward, her hand outstretched. "Hello, Mystique, I'm Luc's sister Alice Hemings. Luc has told me all about you. I'm so pleased to hear you're getting married today." Aileen, Mark, and Mary all gasped at this piece of information. "I would so love to have your sisters come and stay with me until you and Luc return from your honeymoon."

After that, pandemonium broke loose. The babble of voices filled the room as everybody but Misty spoke at once, firing questions, shouting congratulations, expressing surprise. Misty felt cut loose, disoriented, unable to respond.

Finally Luc succeeded in getting across the message that he and Misty wouldn't be going on a honeymoon right away and that they would be back in a few days.

"Well, not too soon, I hope," said Alice. "I want the girls to have some fun—go riding, shopping, sight-seeing." She ticked off the activities on her fingers.

Mark stared open-mouthed as Alice explained to him that her family owned horses and that he was welcome to come out to Heath Farms at any time to ride. Both he and Mary gazed at Alice with saucer-eyed delight.

After a while Misty and her sisters excused themselves and went upstairs to Misty's apartment for some private conversation. "We couldn't stay any longer," Celia said. "We thought about it a long time. He was so smothering, so critical."

"He wasn't always like that," Misty interjected softly, knowing that it was true, also fully aware that she couldn't have made such a statement a few months ago. "When I was small, they were both good to me."

"But they changed as we grew older," Marcy mused. "One by one we all felt the change."

Her sisters nodded.

"Why did they even have children?" Betsy asked, her voice anguished.

"I don't know, Bets, but I do know you'll be happy here," Misty promised, her heart aching for her sisters. Why had she never suspected that the girls were going through the same painful experience she had endured?

"Don't look like that, Misty," Marcy pleaded. "We didn't have it as bad as you did. Honest." Marcy's glasses glinted in the light coming through the wall of windows. "He was never after us like he was after you. But he was getting worse, and Mom never seemed to care about anything as long as she could do as she liked."

"They hated watching us become independent," Betsy said with sudden insight.

Awhile later Luc knocked and entered the room. "Darling, I hate to rush you, but it's time for you to get dressed. Alice wants to take your sisters to Saks to do a little shopping before driving to Long Island." He chuckled as Misty's sisters whooped with joy.

"Imagine us shopping in Saks," Betsy said dreamily after Luc had left. "By the way, Misty, I think Luc is terrific. I hope I find a husband just like him."

"Me, too." Marcy pushed her glasses back up her nose and grinned at Misty. "It's so good to be here."

"I should stay with you," Misty said, feeling as though she were caught in a whirlwind. Both pain and joy assailed her at the thought of becoming Luc's wife. She realized she wanted to marry him! The mere thought was like sliding off the top of a mountain into wonderland!

"No, don't stay with us," the girls chorused.

"Marry Luc. It will make us happy to see you happy," Marcy added. "I think you should have a nice quiet ceremony with just the two of you—even though I *would* like to be there."

"We can have a party when you come back," Celia suggested.

"You don't mind staying with Luc's sister?" Misty asked, aware that she had accepted the idea of marrying Luc that day. Still, she couldn't seem to get off the emotional roller coaster she'd been riding since she'd met him at Christmastime.

"Alice is nice," Marcy went on. "As soon as she arrived, she told us she would be delighted to have us come and stay with her." Marcy smiled. "Besides, you'll be back soon."

Celia and Betsy added their agreement.

Later, her sisters returned downstairs while Misty went through her closet, trying to decide what to wear. She wanted to talk herself out of marrying Luc, but she couldn't summon the will to do so. Gradually she was fully accepting that she would be his wife. "Damn the consequences," she muttered. "I'll handle them as they come." She was staring into her closet when someone knocked on the door. "Come in," she called. She turned in surprise as Morey and Zena walked in.

"Get away from those mundane clothes and look at what you're going to wear," Morey told her.

"Whoever would have thought you'd get married before me," Zena said. "And he's so nice."

"How do you know?" Misty had one eye on her friend

and one eye on the cream-colored silk suit Morey was pulling from a garment bag.

"He called and offered to let us use your apartment,"
Zena explained, biting her lip. "I realize now we should
have asked you first."

"Oh, no," Misty said, hugging first Zena, then Morey.
"You'd make me so happy by moving in here. Can you
imagine how good it would be for Aileen, David, and the
children? Oh, please, please, live here."

"We will. Now never mind that business," Morey said,
separating the two women and urging Misty out of her
clothes so she could try on the suit. "Let's hope Superman
doesn't come through the door when you're standing in your
undies. He's liable to blacken my eyes."

"Don't be silly," Misty scoffed.

"That's all right, Morey. I'm here to protect you," Zena
assured him.

"I may blacken his eyes anyway," Luc said from the
doorway. Misty whirled around. Luc's eyes pinned her to
the spot, heating her flesh with their burning intensity.

Zena jumped up and hurried over to Luc, reaching up
to cover his eyes. "You can't see her in her wedding outfit.
It would be bad luck." She ushered him out the door.

It didn't take Morey long to complete the small adjust-
ments needed. Misty pulled out of her closet a pair of cream
satin pumps that went perfectly with the suit.

When she finally descended the stairs on Morey's arm,
she wore an ivory comb in her hair and carried a tussie-
mussie, an old-fashioned bouquet of cream-colored tea roses
that Luc had bought her.

He was waiting at the foot of the stairs. As she reached
the final step, he came forward to take her hand and stood
silent while her friends and sisters all talked at once.

"I don't think even Saks could upstage this moment,"
Alice said as she kissed Misty's cheek. "How beautiful you
are. Thanks for letting me take care of your sisters. My
house is just crying for them." She lowered her voice. "Be
happy. I think you're just what the doctor ordered. Luc's
cynicism had begun to run too deep. Love will change that."

Misty looked blankly at Alice. "I don't understand."

"Never mind. You'll find out." Luc gave his sister an

irritated glance, but Alice just grinned.

"Come on, darling," he told Misty. "We have to hurry. Good-bye everyone." He placed a fox fur jacket around her shoulders, and she felt his strong arm propel her out of the house.

"But I don't wear furs," she protested. "I don't believe in killing animals." Despite her words, she couldn't help noticing how warm the coat was as she stepped into the cold wind whistling down the street.

"I should have known." Luc chuckled and kissed her cheek as he held open the car door before walking around to climb under the wheel. He tooted the horn and they both waved to the people huddled on the stoop as he pulled the car into traffic. "I won't make that mistake again, love," he promised. "But indulge me this time, won't you? I don't want you to catch cold."

"Thank you," Misty said. "It really is lovely. I don't want to sound ungrateful."

"You don't. You sound like a woman who doesn't like to see animals killed for their skins. You're sweet."

Misty drew in a deep breath. "I can't believe we're really going to get married. It's crazy."

"Maybe, but we're going to do it."

"Luc, will you admit that we don't have much in common, that all things that should be in a good marriage— knowing one another well, love—"

"Forget it, Misty. We're getting married at four o'clock today, and our marriage will be a good one." Misty let her head fall back against the cushioned seat. Neither one of them spoke for several long moments. Finally Luc said, "Don't worry about your sisters. Alice is the kindest person I know, and her husband is an old softie. I intend to make sure your sisters have happy lives from now on."

"Luc, thank you."

"We'll be happy, Mystique." He reached over and clasped her hand warmly. She looked with amazement at their entwined fingers.

"Will we be coming back today?" she asked.

"No. I've made reservations in an old country inn where I used to stay when I went skiing upstate."

"Oh."

"I think you'll like it."

"I don't ski," she mumbled, feeling like Alice falling into a deep, deep rabbit hole into Wonderland.

"I'll teach you, darling. Not that I plan on doing much skiing during the short time we'll be there." He chuckled, then shot her an annoyed glance. "Don't scrunch up to the window like that, Mystique. Nothing bad is going to happen to you."

"You don't know me."

"I've already told you I know everything I need to know about—"

"But you don't know what I'm like deep inside. And I still resent your having investigated me."

"I know. I'm going to try to change. It won't happen right away or all at once, but I want to be the kind of husband you can be proud of." Luc paused before adding, "I overheard what Alice said to you about my cynicism." He sighed and reached out to squeeze her thigh. "I am . . . I *was* a cynic about almost everything, but especially about women. But in the short time we've known each other, my feelings have changed. I'm not the same man I used to be. I want to be a man you can be proud of," he repeated.

"Please, Luc, don't say that. I don't want you to change for me . . . or do anything for me." Misty fought to keep the stridency from her voice.

"Calm down, love. Everything will be fine."

Misty was about to argue with him, but it was so much easier to lie back and watch the countryside roll past the window. Luc snapped a tape into the player, and soft piano music filled the car. Misty recognized the skill of the musician who was playing and listened carefully, taking note of his careful phrasing and meticulous technique. As she absorbed the music, her gaze ran desultorily over the landscape through which they were traveling. The thrumming of the music, the rich purr of the engine, and the pulsing rhythm of the piano were like narcotics to Misty. Gradually she fell asleep.

She began to dream. Her father appeared, making her shift restlessly, though she didn't waken. Lord, she didn't want to remember. But she couldn't help it. Suddenly she was sixteen again.

"No, Father, I didn't do anything wrong. I didn't," Misty pleaded, her stomach churning with anguish.

"Slut! You're pregnant with Howie Breston's kid. Even his parents know about it!" Misty's father shook his fist in her face. "I never laid a hand on you, but I'm sorry now. Whore!" He turned to his wife, who was standing next to him, wringing her hands. "See! See what your daughter is, Marilyn? A whore."

"Alvan, don't use that coarse word in front of me."

"But, my dear, you can see what she is." He turned back to Misty. "Look at her. Her lips are blue, and she's shaking. She hates to hear the truth about herself. She's a stupid slut."

"I'm not, I'm not," Misty whispered, nausea rising inside her. "Howie wouldn't say that about me. It's not true. I never let him . . . Stop saying those things and listen to me. No one ever touched me."

"Don't you raise your voice to your father," Marilyn Carver said coldly.

"Let me tell you what happened," Misty pleaded, her voice rising in desperation.

"I don't want you talking in front of your mother about what you did with that boy!" her father roared.

"Listen to me. I didn't do anything." Misty's voice quavered.

"Slut, slut," her father bellowed.

"I'm not, I'm not . . ."

In her dream, her father's face grew and grew and became distorted into a grotesque mask. Then she saw herself standing between Aunt Lizabeth and Uncle Charles, her parents facing them, her gaze going from one couple to the other.

"I don't care if you are my brother," said Aunt Lizabeth, "I won't let you do this to her anymore."

"I tell you she had an abortion," her father yelled.

"How do you know that? Has she ever been examined by a doctor?" her aunt shot back.

"No," Misty answered softly. "Never."

"Misty, be quiet," her mother said through pursed lips. "Don't interrupt. Nice girls do not speak until they are spoken to."

"You never talk to me," Misty told her mother, earning a glare from her father.

Aunt Lizabeth and her father argued for hours. In the end it was decided that Misty would stay in school but live with her aunt and uncle.

In the car on the way to Misty's new home, her aunt had looked over the seat at Misty huddled in the back. "No wonder you called me, child. Now, don't you worry. We have a piano, so you can practice at home instead of going to the music room at school after classes. Why did that fool brother of mine sell the piano?".

"Mama told him it disturbed her, and he said he didn't like the noise, either."

"Damn fools, both of them," her uncle muttered.

"Charlie, there's no need to swear," Aunt Lizabeth said mildly as Misty was jostled in the back seat by the car's movements.

Gradually she emerged from the depth of sleep and realized someone was gently shaking her shoulder. "Come on, darling, wake up. We're here." Luc frowned down at her and gently pushed curling tendrils of red-gold hair away from her forehead.

What was wrong? Misty tried to clear her sleep-befuddled mind. Why was Luc scowling at her like that? She became instinctively defensive. "We can always turn around and drive back," she told him sharply. "I'll pick up the girls at your sister's house—"

"What are you babbling about, love?" he interrupted, helping her out of the car and taking her arm to lead her through the gate in a picket fence.

But now Misty was wide awake. She paused to admire the series of humpbacked mountains that circled the town of Hudson. "They're beautiful," she murmured.

Luc pointed toward the distance. "Do you see that bare snakelike area on that mountainside? That's Sweetgum, the ski resort where we'll be staying tonight."

Suddenly Misty knew she couldn't go through with the marriage. Panic churned inside her. She inhaled deeply of the crisp winter air and turned resolutely to face him. "Listen to me, Luc. This marriage is a mistake. We can't do it."

The words seemed to echo in the cold air. "I . . . I've been through two failed relationships." Her eyes slid away from his.

"I know all about that." He led her up several steps to a wraparound porch with a grass doormat in front of the oak door. A sign pasted to the glass window said Enter.

Misty stopped in her tracks. "Come on, darling," Luc said in low tones.

"I've never done anything like this before," she muttered, dragging her heels.

"Neither have I," he said, opening the door and waiting for her to precede him inside.

"That's true." For some reason his words sent an unaccountable feeling of relief through her. "We can help each other during the hard parts," she said.

"That's my thought exactly."

A plump woman well past middle age came forward from a back room to greet them. She was wearing a gray dress with a white lace collar and cuffs. "Hello, I'm Judge Latimer. You must be Lucas Harrison and Mystique Carver."

"Yes," Luc answered for both of them, removing the jacket from Misty's shoulders.

She was about to explain that Mystique wasn't her real name, then decided that if that's what Luc liked to call her, she might as well let him.

Judge Latimer led them into a spacious parlor with a bay window in which a marmalade cat sat washing its paws. It looked up briefly at the company, then resumed it's methodical licking. "I've arranged for my housekeeper and my lawyer to serve as witnesses to the ceremony. Is that all right with you?" asked the judge.

"Of course," Luc said, his hot gaze roving over Misty. "You look lovely, darling." He slid an arm around her waist and hugged her to him as the judge excused herself. "Here. I have something for you." He took a jeweler's box from his pocket and handed it to her.

Misty stared at it in confusion. "I can't put the wedding band on until the judge—"

"This is your engagement ring," he told her, leaning forward to let his mouth graze hers.

"We're not engaged. I mean, I don't need one."

"Indulge me by wearing it," Luc whispered into her hair as he lifted her right hand and slipped a square-cut emerald on her finger. "Do you like it?"

Misty slowly lifted her hand, letting the stone catch a ray of late afternoon sunlight. "It looks too large to be real."

Luc laughed. "It's real, all right."

"Don't do too much for me," Misty requested, overwhelmed by everything that had happened that day. How could she explain to Luc that she feared becoming too dependent on him? Not because of the material things he could give her, but because the sweetness and passion he had shown her were already binding her to him irrevocably. If, later on, he took away the caring, withdrew the tenderness, she would be utterly bereft.

"I am giving you my life this afternoon. What you do with it is up to you," he said solemnly, his eyes holding hers, his hand clasped warmly in her own.

"It will be spoiled," Misty said with a moan, shutting her eyes in momentary pain, her left hand coming over to protectively cover her right one.

She felt Luc's hand grasp her shoulders to draw her close just as Judge Latimer returned with a balding man and a thin woman, both middle-aged.

"Mr. Harrison, Miss Carver, this is George Lemond, my lawyer, and this is Esther Gregson, my housekeeper. Shall we begin?" Judge Latimer pressed a button on a stereo system, and Mendelssohn's Wedding March played softly in the background.

Following the judge's instructions, Misty and Luc took their places side by side in front of the fireplace between the two witnesses. Judge Latimer faced them.

"Dearly beloved," the judge began, "we are gathered here . . ."

Misty supposed the judge must be speaking because her mouth was moving, but Misty couldn't hear over the roaring in her ears. Her eyes didn't seem to be focusing properly. Blinking to keep the judge's face from becoming blurry, she was grateful for the strong grip of Luc's hand in hers.

When he looked down with one eyebrow arched, Misty knew he wanted her to respond to the judge's query. "I do," Misty said. He smiled with what looked like relief and squeezed her hand. Misty watched his mouth move in response, reading his lips as he repeated his vows. The roaring in her ears faded away.

"Now, by the power vested in me by the sovereign state of New York, I pronounce you husband and wife." Judge Latimer beamed at them as Luc bent to kiss her.

"I will make you happy, darling," he promised against her lips.

"Thank you," Misty said, and then she felt silly at her inappropriate remark. Her smile slipped on and off her face.

Congratulations were spoken all around, and Mrs. Gregson produced a bottle of New York State blanc de blanc with which to toast the bride and groom.

Soon they were saying good-bye and Luc was leading Misty out onto the porch. He insisted that she button her jacket up to the neck.

"I don't care if the fur tickles you; you have to keep warm," he insisted. "It's colder up here, but you don't notice it because the air is so dry." He frowned down at her feet. "I should have insisted that you wear boots instead of those pumps."

"Don't be silly. The car is warm," she answered as Luc hurried her into the front seat and started the engine. All at once she remembered something. "I put a ring on your finger. I didn't know you were going to wear a wedding ring."

Luc held out his hand to show her the heavy gold band, which exactly matched her own. "I decided I'd like to wear one. Do you mind?"

"Oh, no. I'm glad. I mean, it's a very nice ring."

"Yes, it is. So is yours. Are you going to put your engagement ring on your left hand now?"

"Ah..." Misty held out both hands. "No, I think I'll wear them this way. Then my wedding ring won't be overshadowed by the emerald."

Luc threw back his head and laughed as the car shot forward. "You also have emerald earrings coming to you, my pet." He glanced at her. "I called you on Christmas Day to see if you liked them, but you weren't home."

"I was at Aileen and Dave's."

"Then you sent the earrings back to me." He shook his

head. "That angered and confused me." Suddenly he smiled. "But now you're getting them back."

Misty glanced at him. "Why don't you keep them?" she suggested, laughing out loud for no particular reason. She was still chuckling when she noticed that Luc was giving her peculiar glances. "What is it?" she asked. "Did I say something?"

"No, my lovely wife, it's your laugh. I haven't heard it enough. I find that I want to hear it as often as possible."

Misty sighed. "I really like to laugh."

"But that wistful note in your voice tells me you don't do it often enough."

Misty didn't answer him. Her attention was taken by the narrow, winding road that was leading them into the mountains. "Look at all the snow!" she exclaimed. Snow had often fallen in the area where she was raised, but it had never looked so white and sparkling.

As they rounded a curve at the top of a driveway, the Sweetgum Inn appeared like a jewel in the snow.

"Luc, it's perfect," Misty whispered, staring at the rough-hewn exterior that had weathered to a deep brown. The rambling building had an open front porch, and smoke was coming from a stone chimney.

"We'll eat here, but we'll stay in one of the guest cottages," Luc told her, grinning at her wide-eyed expression. He parked the car in front of the entrance.

Luc came around to her side of the car and reached in to help her to her feet. "Like it?" he asked.

She nodded, then pointed. "Oh, look! Skiers." She shaded her eyes against the rays of the dying sun and watched black dots sliding down the slopes. "I think I would like to try," she said.

"Then we will."

"But I haven't got any ski clothes," she pointed out as he led her up the steps to the front door, gesturing to a bellman to carry their luggage. She gasped at the amount of baggage being pulled out of the car. "We have a great deal for just one night."

"Yes." He grinned unrepentantly at her.

"You bought me clothes," she accused as he shepherded her through the lobby. "Oooh, it's nice." Immediately forgetting her quarrel with him, she gazed around her, her attention caught by the knotty-pine interior of the lodge. Tables and chairs were grouped casually throughout the spacious lobby.

"Mr. Harrison, welcome back to the Sweetgum Inn," said the smiling desk clerk, nodding to Luc and running curious eyes over Misty.

"My wife and I will be staying a day or two," Luc said, signing the register.

"Your wife?" The clerk looked momentarily discomfited. "May we at the Sweetgum Inn wish you well, sir?"

"Thank you. We were married today." Luc's mouth lifted at the corners as he glanced at a blushing Misty. "I'd like some ski attire sent to our cabin for my wife. Size six in clothing, size seven in boots."

"Of course, sir." The man bowed slightly and signaled to a bellman.

Misty stopped often on her way to the guest cottage to gaze, fascinated, at the skiers coming down the mountain and at the powdery snow that covered the trees and crunched under their feet.

Luc put his arm around her and hurried her along. "Come on. Your feet will get cold."

The bellman opened the door of their cottage, which was actually a small bungalow. It had a bedroom, living room, kitchen, and dining area, plus a picture window that looked out over the mountains.

"Oh, a fire in the fireplace." Misty sighed as Luc removed her fur coat, then sat her down to remove her shoes and rub her feet. He tipped the bellman and came back to her as she sat on the low couch in front of the roaring blaze.

"It's beautiful, Luc."

"I've never stayed in this cottage before, because I thought it was too big for just me."

"You and your stable of women," Misty heard herself say tartly in a voice she didn't recognize as her own.

Luc turned toward her, his eyes searing into her. "There's no need to be jealous about my past, darling. I'm not jealous of yours."

"Neither am I," she shot back, coming to a ramrod straight position on the overstuffed couch. "I . . . I have never discussed Leonard or Richard with you."

"Now is not the time," Luc said, throwing his suit jacket toward a chair, not noticing when it fell to the floor. He loosened his tie and jerked it off. "We'll have plenty of time to talk, darling. The rest of our lives, in fact. But right now I want to love you, to show you how I feel. I want you to know how much I need you."

Misty's heart began pounding as he unbuttoned his shirt and pulled it off his powerful shoulders.

CHAPTER FIVE

IN THE NEXT instant Luc lifted her into his arms and carried her to the spacious bedroom decorated in peach and brown tones. Sudden shyness overcame her as he placed her on the peach-colored bedspread covering the king-sized bed. She felt her face redden. Something about making love with Luc embarrassed her. Sex with Richard and Leonard had been a mechanical act that didn't involve her mind and spirit. But she knew instinctively that Luc would demand all of her, heart and soul. The idea of such total intimacy with him made her flush with both reluctance and anticipation as he followed her down onto the bed, pressing her into the firm mattress.

He quizzically regarded the heightened color in her face. "Mrs. Harrison, do you mind that I'm going to undress you?"

"No," she whispered. *But I do mind*, an inner voice shouted. With Richard and Leonard she'd always undressed in the bathroom, and she'd worn a robe until she climbed into bed. With them, sex had been an obligation, and not a completely comfortable one . . .

"Good, because I'm going to enjoy this, my sweet," Luc

murmured. "And so are you." His voice was thick as he peeled the pantyhose down her legs. "You know, my love, I think I'm going to buy you some underthings with garters. I saw some in Saks that would be perfect for you." He lifted her hips and slid the skirt down her body. "Ummm, pretty panties." He kissed the silken briefs, pressing his open mouth to her pelvic area in a caress that awakened a slow throbbing.

Misty gasped, and her body moved involuntarily in surprise at his tender loving. No one had ever kissed her like that! She was stunned. A tingling sensation began in her hands and feet as Luc raised her to a sitting position and removed her cream-colored jacket and the frilly blouse with the lace jabot.

"Pretty bra, darling." He ran a gentle finger around the embroidered edge. "Did I buy you this one?"

"Yes," she said breathlessly as he reached down and unfastened the tiny clip between her breasts. His mouth followed his hand, his arm supporting her arching back. Her hands came up to grasp his hair, her fingers threading through the thick locks.

"You're so sweet, wife of mine." Luc lifted her up against his body with ease, suspending her with one arm, taking her breast more fully into his mouth and with infinite tenderness sucking slowly, sweetly.

"Luc!" Misty cried out, her hands clenching in his hair, her eyes closing as hot, pulsing sensations seared through her. "What . . . what . . ." She tried to speak, but her mouth couldn't form the words.

"Shhh, my angel. Let me love you." Luc's hoarse words sent a thousand tiny electrical charges over her skin, like lightning bouncing off mountaintops. He pressed her down, down onto the peach coverlet. "Let me cover you . . ."

"I'm warm," Misty said with a gasp. "I don't need any covers." Her hands slid free of him, her fingers clutching air as he stepped away to remove his trousers and briefs. Her body tingled with delight as she stared up at him—at the thicket of chestnut hair that arrowed down his body, the color a surprising contrast to the ash blond locks on his head. Her sisters would describe him as a hunk, Misty thought giddily. His legs were long and muscular, his shoulders broad and powerful. At this moment he looked every inch the athlete Aileen had said he was. Misty reached for him again.

"Easy, darling, I'm not leaving you," he crooned, stretching out at her side.

"I love your hair," she whispered, reaching again for his head, her fingers spreading and closing in delight at touching him.

"Good. I love everything about you," he murmured back, sliding his mouth down her body, touching every inch, caressing every curve, exploring every intimate crevice. His mouth traveled lower and lower, and then he was touching the very core of her desire, setting off a kaleidoscope of overwhelming feelings. Her blood seemed to turn to molten lava in her veins. She trembled and writhed in uncontrollable passion.

"Shhh, darling. I'm loving you."

"Ohhh . . ." She pulled his hair, impatient with him, but he merely chuckled against her skin. She pulled harder, and he inched upward until they were touching lips to lips. "I didn't realize," she whispered, awed.

"I know, my treasure." He pressed her thighs farther apart and positioned himself over her. "I'm glad, because I want to be your first real lover." He pushed himself gently into her.

His heart was pounding against hers. Her breath was coming in staccato gasps as the tempo between them increased. Never had Misty been an eager participant, but now she clasped her lover and held him tight. Together they soared, higher and higher, until the world exploded, flinging them up to the stars, around the sun, and gently back down to earth.

For long moments afterward they held each other tightly. Gradually their breathing slowed, their glistening bodies relaxed.

"Does anyone know about this but us?" Misty whispered up at Luc, her eyelids drooping.

"About what, Mystique?" He nibbled at her neck.

"About . . . about lovemaking?"

Luc chuckled and raised himself on one elbow to look

down at her. "I doubt it," he teased. "Shall we make it our secret?"

"Yes!" But her laughter vanished as his grin faded. "What is it? Why are you looking at me like that?"

"I told you before, I love to hear you laugh."

"I feel like laughing. In fact, I wish we had a piano so I could play and we could sing." Feeling sleepy, she burrowed her nose into his neck.

"Going to sleep on me?"

"Yes," she admitted with a tiny smile.

"I forgot to tell you that that was only the beginning. I intend to make love to you all night." He took her earlobe between his teeth.

"Wonderful. Don't start without me," she muttered, yawning.

"Don't worry, I won't." He chuckled again. "I've never laughed quite so much either, my little wife," he whispered, pulling her closer to him and closing his eyes.

In the night Misty dreamed again. She saw her father coming toward her, ever closer. But when she called out, Luc was there, and her father vanished in an instant. She sank deeper into sleep.

Later, Misty smiled, her eyes closed, as she felt soft kisses on her neck and face. "Luc," she murmured.

"Yes, my darling wife, it's Luc," he murmured gently.

She felt his mouth move lower, caressing her breasts and arms. Her body wriggled in response, but still she didn't open her eyes. She had the irrational feeling that, if she looked, Luc wouldn't really be there, and that she would find that she had only imagined the ecstasy of their wedding night. Beautiful, wondrous emotions had cascaded over her. It would be terrible to wake up and find he had been just a figment of her imagination. But once again he proved his existence with the reality of his lovemaking.

His hands coursed down one side of her body and began working their way up the other. He gently bit each toe. His mouth massaged each kneecap. He nuzzled her thighs with his mouth in a tender quest. He kissed her arms, her fingertips, and the crook of each elbow with special loving attention. He was nibbling her chin when she opened one eye.

"Don't be a ghost, Luc," she whispered.

"I'm not," he assured her. "Open both your eyes, Mystique."

"All right." She opened them and sighed. He wasn't a ghost; he was real. With a deep, shuddering breath she touched his cheek with her fingertips.

"Do you mind if I continue to enjoy my breakfast?" he teased with a wicked gleam in his eyes.

"Am I sunny-side up?" She smiled at him. Then she felt herself being lifted and turned over, face down in the pillow.

"Now you're sunny-side up, angel. Ummm, how luscious." Luc nipped at her backside, his open mouth gentle on her scars. He explored her back from her neck to her ankles, setting her on fire.

When he turned her over once again to enter her body, Misty was ready for him, eager to be swallowed by the hot, piercing rhythm they created together.

They strove mightily to give the other the utmost satisfaction, and once again the world exploded. They lay close together, open mouth on open mouth, their eyelids fluttering, their breath mingling.

"My goodness." Misty gazed lovingly at her husband. "That was more powerful than anything on earth."

"Yes." His brown eyes were somber for a moment; then he smiled and rolled from the bed to pull her to her feet. "Let's take a shower."

"Together?" Misty asked, recalling how Leonard had always insisted on having the bathroom first, leaving her to clean up after him.

"Forget them," Luc growled, reading her thoughts and pulling her to him in a fierce embrace. "You're thinking of those two fools. Don't. I don't want to be compared to them."

"That would be impossible. You'd get a nosebleed if you dropped down to their level," Misty said, the words popping out before she could stop them. She felt her face flush.

Luc chuckled and kissed her cheek. "Mystique, that was a sweet thing to say. I think I'll run out in the snow and thump my chest."

"Not without clothes on, you won't." She took a deep breath. "I won't let you."

"Lord, I've married a bossy wife!" Luc lifted her in his arms and carried her into the bathroom.

"Yes," she said firmly, marveling at her own daring as she clung to his neck, not letting go even when he let her slide down his body. He turned the spigots in the shower stall. "Will we fit?" she asked, laughing again. She had never laughed or giggled so much! Luc would begin to think she was silly.

"Of course we'll fit." He watched with lazy amusement and flinched from the cold spray. After readjusting the knobs, he tested the water. "There." He lifted her into the stall and stepped in himself. "Isn't this nice?"

"Yes," she said softly, loving the feel of his hard-muscled body against hers. "Luc . . ." She lifted her head to look at him as he began running a loofah sponge down her arm.

"Uh-huh?" He seemed to be completely absorbed in the task.

"Don't stay with me when we go skiing today. I'll get an instructor to teach me."

He handed her the loofah, and stood still while she scrubbed him. "I've already arranged for an instructor, Debbie Allen, to give you a preliminary lesson. Then I'll take over." His eyes went to her breasts as she raised her arms to rinse the soap from her body. "Darling, are you finished? Good, because I think you'd better get out of here if you want to go skiing today." His eyes glinted with laughter as her eyes darted away from the most blatant sign of his obvious arousal. "I'm beginning to think I may have to move my office to our house."

"Would you like to postpone skiing?" she asked, stepping out of the shower stall and taking a towel from the warming rack. Skillfully she wrapped it around her body like a sarong.

"Yes, I would." He closed the shower door with a snap, then abruptly opened it again. "Don't think I don't know you're teasing me, wife." He grinned at her and banged the door shut once more.

Misty skipped into the bedroom, hugging herself. This can't be happening to me, she thought. Luc can't be real.

She was standing in her bra and panties in the bedroom

when he came out of the bathroom, naked and rubbing his hair with a towel. She smiled, then laughed out loud when he closed his eyes and groaned. In a few swift strides he closed the space between them, a determined expression on his face.

"Skiing," Misty muttered, laughing.

"Skiing, hell," Luc snarled, scooping her up into his arms. "How can you stand there in those peach-colored underthings and expect me to go skiing? It's insanity." He carried her to the bed.

"Luc, you haven't had breakfast yet," she protested laughing.

"Tell me about it," he muttered into her skin, removing the bits of lace from her body.

The fire storm took them again, yet to Misty it seemed brand-new—fresh and exhilarating. Afterward, she was sure she must have misunderstood the words Luc murmured against her flushed skin. He couldn't have said he loved her, could he?

They were holding each other, their hands sliding over each other's bodies, waiting for the love tremors to subside, when a knock sounded at the door. "Mrs. Harrison, I have your ski clothing," said a voice muffled by the door.

With a sharp yelp, Misty jumped out of bed and streaked into the bathroom. When Luc handed her a pair of slacks and a shirt through a crack in the door, she poked her tongue out at him.

"Don't do that, love," he warned, "or we'll be back in bed again before you know it." She gasped, and he chuckled.

"Answer that door," she told him.

It didn't take long to try on the skiing togs, but Misty was surprised at how picky Luc was about everything for her. At last, after the bellman left, they finished getting dressed, Luc's eyes going over her in lazy assessment of everything that came into his view. "You are one beautiful woman, Mystique Harrison. Even in those skiing togs you send me into a spin."

Misty looked down at her pale green ski outfit, which felt incredibly warm but as light as a feather. She moved her feet in the heavy green ski boots.

Luc, dressed all in black with black goggles dangling

from one hand, ran his other hand over her short battle jacket. "The man at the desk assured me that this was the lightest, warmest outfit. How do your long johns feel?"

"Comfy." Misty wriggled inside her suit.

"You look damn sexy, too, my little siren," Luc said in low tones. "Here, these are your goggles, and I want you to wear them. The lenses are tinted to prevent glare, but they also react to growing darkness and allow clearer night vision."

"The wonders of science," Misty murmured, hooking her gloves onto her sleeves in the way Luc had shown her and placing her hand in his as they left the cottage and walked the short distance to the lodge.

Misty inhaled deeply of the numbing air, feeling warm and comfortable in her thermal clothes. "My goodness." She pointed to the chair lift rising up the mountainside. "That looks as though it's going up at an awfully steep angle."

"It is," Luc agreed, watching her. "The ride up can be cold, but coming down makes it all worthwhile. Here, let me take you over to the instructor's office and get you settled."

"No," Misty said, "it's right there." She pointed to a small shed attached to the back of the lodge. "You go ahead and get some skiing in while the sun is still shining. I'll be fine."

"You're sure?" Luc kissed her and glanced around him as if searching for hidden dangers. He scowled at several skiers who were lounging near an outdoor stove, then looked back at Misty.

"I'll be fine," she repeated, giving him a slight shove. After kissing her again, he reluctantly left her.

She went to the open window of the instructors' office. Seeing no one, she called, "Hello, I'm Misty Car—Harrison. I'm supposed to have a lesson with Debbie Allen."

A tall blond man came up to the window. "I'm Roger Larsen, Mrs. Harrison. Debbie isn't finished teaching her youth group yet, so I'll be your instructor this morning." He smiled broadly, deepening the dimples at the side of his mouth and making his widely spaced blue eyes twinkle.

Misty decided she preferred tall, athletic men with ash blond hair and brown eyes.

"Ah, fine," she said. "Shall we go out now?"

"Just let me get my gear."

Roger demonstrated several basic maneuvers—the snowplow, a simple stem christie, and paralleling—on a slight incline nearby. As Misty gained confidence, they progressed to a more advanced beginners' slope. Roger skied closer to her as she tried to put her lessons into practice.

Misty grew exhilarated as she continued to ski without falling and was able to perform most of the turns with ease. Soon she was eager to try the rope tow that would take them up an even longer and slightly more precipitous incline.

She fell on the rope tow, receiving a faceful of snow, but she held on steadfastly until they reached the crest of the hill. "I really don't like that rope tow," she told Roger. "I suppose I will *hate* the chair lift."

Roger laughed. "Don't worry. You'll like the chairs better. But we'll try this hill a few times first."

Misty was amazed and pleased at how rapidly she progressed under Roger's instruction. As she skied down the gentle slope, she was delighted with the sensation of flying through space.

"Now we'll try the chairs." But Roger fell abruptly silent as he gazed past her shoulder, a wrinkle of puzzlement in his forehead. Misty turned to see Luc striding toward them, looking like the very devil in his black attire. His mouth was a tight slash in his face, and his hair shone silver in the sunlight.

"Mystique," he said angrily, tearing the goggles from his face and glaring at Roger. "Where is your ski instructor?"

"Debbie was still with her youth group, so I volunteered to instruct your daughter, sir," Roger explained.

Luc seemed to swell with anger.

"Luc, you look like Darth Vader," Misty exclaimed, then clamped a mittened hand over her mouth when Luc's head swung abruptly toward her. "Ah, thank you for the lessons, Roger," she called. "We have to go." She pushed her poles into the snow and glided forward—straight into Luc! He caught her with his hands, struggling to maintain their balance. "Thank you." Misty leaned up and kissed Luc's chin, confirming with a quick sideways glance that Roger was skiing away from them.

"Where the hell does he get off—" Luc fumed, glaring after Roger, his arms around Misty.

"He was only teaching me to snowplow and stem christie, and tomorrow he wanted to show me—"

"I'll be teaching you tomorrow," Luc said firmly, his hands tightening on her. He brought icy lips down on hers. "Damn him," he said against her mouth before lifting his lips a fraction of an inch. "Thinking I was your father. I'll kill him." He ran his ungloved hand down her cheek. "You do look young. No more than seventeen."

Misty leaned against him, reveling in his warmth as his body sheltered her from the wind. "Roger's harmless," she assured her husband.

"Ha!" Luc laughed harshly and leaned over Misty, his body shielding her. "Are you warm enough? Would you like to go inside the lodge and get some soup?"

She did feel a little damp, but she was eager to show Luc what she'd learned so far. "I'd like to go up on the chair lift and ski down that slope first."

Luc studied her for a moment and finally nodded. He checked to see that her poles were in the proper position and skied with her to the end of the short line of skiers waiting for the lift. A stiff breeze momentarily chilled her. "Did you just shiver?" he demanded.

"Uh-uh," Misty lied, sensing that Luc would whisk her back to the lodge in a moment if she gave him the slightest indication that she was cold.

But she hadn't anticipated the blasts of frigid air that assailed her on the chair lift. Although she and Luc went to only one of the intermediate hills, the frosty wind left her stiff and chilled when she alighted with Luc's help.

"You *are* cold," he accused her. "Your lips are turning blue. Damn you, Mystique."

"I'll be better once we get moving," she said, trying to control the shivers that wracked her body. Turning away from Luc, she skied toward the lip of the hill. Looking down, she felt sure that the descent would be relatively easy, even for a beginner like herself. But the cold had begun to stiffen her hands, and her feet were chilled. She pushed off, wanting to get down to the bottom and into the warm lodge as soon as possible.

"Mystique!" Luc called from behind her, alarm in his voice.

Abruptly Misty forgot how cold she was in the stunning realization that she was going to need all her concentration to get down the slope without falling. She was moving faster than she cared to. "Plow, darling, plow," Luc called. "That's it . . . good. Now traverse. That's fine."

Suddenly he was at her side, guiding her past a group of skiers. Sudden confidence infused Misty. Luc was there! He wouldn't let anything happen to her.

Cautiously she tried to parallel. But her left ski slipped, and she felt herself falling. The heel and toe bindings on her left ski came undone, and she tumbled several yards down the hill, the collar of her jacket filling with snow, her face pushing through the soft powder. She was laughing as she raised herself from a snow bank.

Before she could stand up, Luc was taking her in his arms and lifting her high. "Darling, are you all right? I shouldn't have let you do it." Cradling her close with one arm, he wiped her face with his other hand.

"Ptui." Misty giggled. "Will Sweetgum Inn charge you extra because I'm eating up all their powder?"

The beginning of a smile softened Luc's rocklike visage. "You're a good sport." He kissed her nose, then placed her on her feet. "Come on. Let's get down this hill."

Misty helped Luc brush the snow from her clothes. "I want to ski down, Luc. Please. It isn't far."

"All right. But traverse." She nodded, brushing some snow off him.

Luc stuck to her like glue the rest of the way down the hill, talking to her, encouraging her, instructing her in soft, sure tones.

When Misty reached the bottom, she wobbled, then regained her balance and came to a full stop facing Luc. "I did it!" she exclaimed, grinning and shivering at the same time.

Luc scowled at her, gestured to an attendant, kicked off his skis, and loosened hers. In seconds he was hurrying her into the lodge. "But Luc, you can't walk away and leave our stuff out there," Misty protested. She looked over her shoulder to see if the young attendant was giving proper attention to Luc's equipment.

"Never mind that. I have to get you inside."

Another attendant rushed forward as Luc half lifted her, hustling her through the doorway into the basement ski room. A group of skiers was clustered around a blazing fire in a rough-hewn stone fireplace. "Was there an accident?" a young man asked anxiously.

"No, of course not," Misty denied, whispering furiously at Luc to let her go.

"My wife is cold," he said. "I want some soup and hot chocolate *now.*" He turned to glare at the people sitting on a couch next to the fire.

"Stop that," Misty exclaimed. "You can't act like Attila the Hun in here." A flush of embarrassment warmed her cheeks as three people scrambled up from the sofa.

"Put her here," one offered.

"She can have my spot," said another.

"Did she fall?" asked the third. "Has she seen a doctor?"

"Luc," Misty said with a moan as he settled her on the couch and unfastened her boots. She looked up at a semi-circle of concerned expressions and tried to smile. "I'm fine," she said weakly.

"She's very cold," Luc said, as if accusing the world. He rubbed her bare foot, then blew on it.

"Stop," Misty said with a gasp, feeling tendrils of warmth begin to uncurl deep inside her. "You're tickling me."

"Am I, darling?" He caressed her with his eyes.

Misty tried to sink deeper into the cushions. "Have you no shame?" she whispered with a forced, lopsided smile.

A young red-haired man hurried up to them, carrying a bucket of warm water. "Here. This will help," he said, lifting one of Misty's hands and plunging it into the water. "We have to gradually heat the extremities, you know." He stared at Misty wide-eyed. "I put baby oil in the water so your hands won't be chapped."

Misty smiled weakly. "That was very kind of you."

Someone bustled up carrying a small tureen of soup.

Another hurried over with hot chocolate in a white china mug.

"Luc," Misty begged. "Stop this."

He looked up at her with surprise, then glanced around the room. "Stop what, love?"

Lord, she had married a sweet despot! Luc was so used to having people jump up and run errands for him, that he saw nothing out of the ordinary in being waited on. When he took the soup spoon and tried to feed her, she glared furiously at him. "That's enough," she snapped, snatching the spoon from his hand.

"Poor thing is still jumpy," someone said sympathetically.

"Yes, it must be nerves," another concurred.

"I'm fine," Misty insisted, her exasperation turning to resignation. She looked into the depths of the vegetable soup and raised a spoonful to her lips. It was good. She tasted several more spoonfuls, then took a tentative sip from the mug of hot chocolate, assuring everyone between sips that she really didn't want anything else.

Almost half an hour went by before people began to disperse. "Luc," Misty said, feeling exhausted from all the attention, "I'd like to go back to our cottage now."

"Are you sure you're strong enough?" He ran a worried glance over her.

"If I were any stronger, I'd be pulling a trolley car in San Francisco," she retorted.

Luc's eyes narrowed on her momentarily. Then a smile lifted the corners of his mouth. "Irked with me, love?"

"Yes," she declared, swinging her legs off the couch and getting to her feet, resisting with effort the urge to jerk her arm free of his hold.

"Sorry, but you'll have to get used to it. I'm not letting anything happen to you."

"Must I remind you that I'm not helpless? I've been on my own for some time now and—"

"You're my darling." Luc fastened her jacket and kissed the tip of her nose. Then he dropped down to the floor and lifted each foot to put on her boots.

Misty balanced herself by placing one hand on his head.

She was torn between the longing to savor the tactile delight of Luc's crisp, clean hair and the irritated urge to give his head a good yank.

They said good-bye to all the people who had been so concerned about Misty. Luc seemed to feel none of the embarrassment she experienced. He promised that he and his wife would meet them for a drink if they decided to stay an extra night.

On the short walk back to their cottage, Luc kept his arm tightly around her, now and then pressing his lips to her hair. Misty felt as though she were traveling in a pink bubble that they alone inhabited. "Luc, you mustn't worry about me," she said, forgetting her irritation in the relaxing aura of his presence.

"I can't seem to help it, my dear." He gave her a bittersweet smile. "Marriage is proving to be tougher and more complicated that I ever imagined."

Misty stared up at him as he held the door open for her. A shiver of panic zigzagged down her spine. Was he already regretting their marriage? Never! She wouldn't let him! He was hers now. She stood in the center of the living room, staring at the empty fireplace, crossing her arms in front of her, hugging the pain to her. Blinking, she watched Luc bend to light a fire. Soon a roaring blaze was radiating heat into the room. But still Misty didn't move.

"Hey, what's so interesting in those flames that you can't tear your eyes away?" Luc asked, lifting her chin and staring down into her eyes. "I'll be back in a moment. I'm going to run a bath for you."

Still Misty didn't move. I really can't survive without him now, she thought. Damn him. I hate him for making me love him. Why did he have to make himself such an important part of my life? There won't be anything left of me if he ever goes away. Damn him!

Luc came back into the room. He paused momentarily on the threshold, studying her. "I should never have let you get so chilled," he said grimly. "Come on, darling." Misty went with him, loving the feel of his warm body as he led her into the bathroom, keeping her close to his side. "Have I told you yet that I enjoy undressing you?" he asked, removing her clothes in the steamy warmth of the good-sized room.

"I like sunken bathtubs," she mused, feeling a sense of defeat because she couldn't muster the strength to tell Luc to get lost . . . before he took over her life completely. She'd been able to do it with Leonard and Richard. Even with her father she'd summoned up the courage to ask to live with her aunt and uncle. Now she had a feeling of falling through space, of spiraling down toward the crash that would inevitably come when Luc left her. Until then, she was helpless to erect barriers between them to protect her emotions against him.

She looked down at him as he rolled her long johns down her legs. Damn you to hell, Lucas Stuyvesant Harrison. You've hooked me like a fish and thrown me into the boat. I'm yours until you toss me back into the water. How did you manage to soften my backbone? I used to be so full of fight.

"Darling? Darling, are you daydreaming? Not that I don't want you to, but I'd rather you concentrated on me." Luc leaned forward from his kneeling position and kissed her navel. "Because I sure as hell can't think of anyone but you."

"That will pass," Misty mumbled as she slid into the tub.

"What did you say?" Abruptly he stood to remove his clothes and stepped into the tub with her. "Whew, isn't this too hot for you?"

"No, it's nice." She closed her eyes and leaned against his chest, opened one eye and noticed an array of powders and oils on the shelf next to the tub. "What's this?" She raised a languid arm and grasped a tall plastic bottle. "My goodness. Opium is a perfume. I didn't know they made a bath oil, too. You'll like this, Luc."

"Mystique, for God's sake don't—" Luc half laughed, half groaned as she poured the fragrant liquid into the tub.

"Aren't we sweet?" she simpered.

"You little devil. I should paddle your bottom."

"Lovely." She looked up at him, wide-eyed. "Why not?"

Luc stared down at her for long moments, his skin flushed.

"And when did you turn into Circe?" he quizzed hoarsely.

"The minute you married me, I think," Misty muttered, watching his face come closer.

"I agree." His mouth teased her lips apart. "I want to have you all the time." She caught a note of disbelief in his voice, as though such a realization had shaken him.

"I want you all the time, too, Luc," she admitted.

"Darling . . ." He pulled her on top of him and massaged her backside with gentle, possessive strokes, his teeth nibbling at her neck. "You're so sweet. Each day I learn something new about you."

"Me, too."

"You find something new about you every day?" Luc chuckled and buried his face in her hair.

"Not about me, about you." Her fingers kneaded the muscled flesh of his shoulders. Erotic sensations flooded through her as she explored his chest and lower body.

"Yes," Luc said, his face still in her hair. "Touch me, love. I want you to."

Misty had never especially wanted to touch either Richard or Leonard. With them, she had tried to convince herself that sex wasn't particularly important. Having similar goals, tastes, and ideas about life were of paramount importance.

But now! Every pore of Luc's body hypnotized her. "You're gorgeous," she whispered. "I don't think men are supposed to be so gorgeous."

"I never want you to stop thinking that . . . Ohhh, Mystique, don't stop. That feels so good."

Luc's own hands became busy on her body. Misty felt a familiar heat begin to spread deep inside her. Her flesh became a liquid flame. Her pulse sped out of control. Her breath grew harsh and heavy. "Luc, you're teasing me." She clasped him fiercely, exulting when she heard him groan.

He rose abruptly to his feet, wrapped them both in huge towels, and hurried her to the bedroom. Their love play became fire play as both of them went up in flames of passion.

"Darling . . . not so fast. I can't . . ." Luc's face was a mask of sensual feeling, his cheeks crimson with blood, his eyes glazed with passion.

"Luc!" Misty heard the hoarseness in her voice when she

called out to him. She was awed by the power of feeling between them.

Once again they scaled the heights to a peak of emotion and fell back exhausted, still clutching each other fiercely.

"I never wanted anything so much in my life as to satisfy you in our lovemaking," Luc murmured against her breasts. "I've wanted that since the first moment I saw you."

"You have satisfied me," Misty whispered, her eyes heavy with contented weariness.

"Your eyes are like dewy green violets," Luc said. His grin was lopsided, as though he were trying to hide the tumult only now subsiding inside him.

"I thought you were a banker, not a poet." Misty ran her fingernail lightly down his nose.

"I'm finding that, since meeting you, wife, I've become a multifaceted person." He took a deep breath. "I find that I want to tell you things I've never considered telling anyone else. You've changed me. I'd heard of sensual love, but I didn't believe it really existed. I never believed that anyone could take over my life, yet at the same time fulfill it with beauty and warmth." His body shuddered as he drew in an unsteady breath. "There were always women. They were as matter-of-fact about sex as I was. I was certain that was all there was to it . . . until the night I first saw you playing the piano. You turned my life upside down."

Misty giggled and snuggled closer to him.

He took all her weight on top of him and pulled the satin quilt over her back. "Shall we stay one more day?"

"I can't. I have to work tomorrow night."

"Have you forgotten that you're now part owner of the Terrace Hotel?" Luc smoothed his hand over her backside. "The very best part, too," he murmured, kissing her hair and trailing a finger over her face.

"Don't be silly. I'm not the owner. I'm married to the owner." Misty sighed. "Could we really stay one more day?"

"Yes. I'll make a few calls." He lifted her chin. "You *are* part owner of the hotel, darling. I arranged for quite a few properties to be put in your name."

"Take them out of my name, Luc." Misty leaned back, her hands braced against his chest. "I really would rather not own anything. I can always work and—"

"Mystique," Luc interrupted her firmly. His face was grim though his voice was soothing as he added, "I don't give a damn what you do with your money and property, but it's yours and it will stay yours until you sell it or give it away."

Misty laid her head on the sinewy comfort of his chest. "I'm not the rich type," she muttered, kissing a flattened nipple.

"We're never going to get out of this bed and go to dinner if you do that," Luc warned. He shifted her to one side so that they were lying face to face. "But I do like it."

"I like to do it." Misty kissed him again.

In moments they were flesh to flesh, locked in another journey through the dynamic world of love.

A long while later they finally left the bed and began to dress. Misty paused in putting on silky, flesh-colored briefs and turned to catch Luc's gaze on her. She grinned. "I thought I felt someone looking at me."

"Your husband was looking at you, Mrs. Harrison." He let out a long breath. "And if I don't get dressed in the bathroom, we'll never get out of here." When she chuckled, he grimaced at her.

At last they left the cottage and strolled hand in hand to the main lodge.

Dinner was a gourmet's delight, much to Misty's surprise. "Sweetbreads en brioche in the mountains!" she exclaimed. "And prawns Pernod!" She took another bite of the succulent shellfish broiled in lemon and rosemary with a touch of dill. "Isn't that just like you to find a place in the middle of nowhere that serves gourmet food."

"Now that you're a Harrison you'll have all the benefits the family enjoys."

"I'm a Harrison," Misty mused, testing the words.

"Yes, you are, wife. For the next eighty years." Luc lifted a forkful of his boiled lobster for her to taste. "Good?"

Misty nodded. "Yummy."

"Yummy?" Luc laughed. "I like the word. You're a yummy wife."

After they finished glasses of cognac and sampled assorted cheeses, they danced. "Why do I get the feeling that my wife doesn't like cognac?" Luc murmured as they turned and swayed to the slow rhythm of the music.

"It's terribly strong stuff, isn't it?" Misty said, her mind on Luc, not the cognac. "I imagine you could get roaring drunk on it."

"Ummm," he agreed. "But not on the amount you drank, love. I've put down a good bit of it a time or two, and the next day I felt as if the dentist was drilling my teeth through the back of my skull."

Misty lifted her head from his shoulder to look at him and smile. "Dopey."

"Yes." He kissed her nose.

They danced for a while longer, then went back to their room to make love again. The next day they skied all day. Luc never left Misty's side. After dinner that evening they packed and began the drive back to New York.

Misty had the sinking feeling that the paradise they had shared at the Sweetgum Inn was coming to an end.

CHAPTER SIX

LUC HEADED STRAIGHT for his house. "I think Alice may have brought the girls back today," he told Misty.

"Shouldn't we stop at my place and pick up some of my clothes?"

"I think what you'll find in our room will be adequate until we get your clothes tomorrow." Luc grinned at her.

"Luc, tomorrow I won't have a car to carry them in. And you'll be at work."

"Do you have a driver's license?"

"Yes, I learned to drive Uncle Charlie's truck when I was sixteen. But I won't have a car." She was still trying to persuade him to turn back to her apartment when he drove into the garage under his brownstone.

"There." He pointed through the windshield. "That's yours—all gassed and checked and ready to go. There are two sets of keys in our bedroom upstairs, and"—he fumbled on his key chain—"another set right here. I also made another key to the Rolls in case you want to drive it."

"Never," Misty said faintly, her eyes glued to the pale

green Lotus he'd pointed to. "Can we look at it?" she whispered.

"Yes," Luc whispered back, teasing her and kissing her ear.

"You're spoiling me," Misty said with a gulp. "Please don't buy me anything else. I mustn't forget how it is to work for things. If I have to take care of myself again—"

"I'll be taking care of you for the rest of your life," Luc declared. He got out of the car and came around to open her door. His face was taut, and his eyes slid uneasily away from her.

"Luc, please. I didn't mean to hurt your feelings. The car is so beautiful."

He glanced down at her and sighed. "I know. I guess I'm a little too sensitive but I don't like you talking about being away from me, being on your own."

"I won't do it again."

They walked hand and hand over to the sleek car. Misty wouldn't let Luc unlock it until she'd walked all around it and studied each piece of chrome and pale green steel. "It's not quite the color of your eyes, but almost." Luc grinned at her over the top of the roof.

"It's beautiful. I hope I'll know how to drive it."

"Let's find out." He opened the passenger door and climbed inside, reaching over to unlock the driver's door. "Get in, Mystique."

"But, Luc, the luggage. We just got home." She bent down to look at him through the window and bit her lower lip when her eyes encountered his steady gaze. She nodded and sank down into the leather driver's seat. "Nice," she whispered, accepting the keys Luc handed her. She took a deep breath and inserted the key into the ignition. The engine fired with a low growl. Misty took another deep breath and shifted into reverse.

"I thought you might prefer a standard shift to automatic," Luc said, lounging back in his seat, watching her.

"Yes, I do. I just hope I won't strip the gears." She checked the rearview mirror and backed out with scarcely a jerk. She swallowed with nervousness as she turned the car toward the ramp that led to the street. "Here goes," she called with forced brightness.

"Don't worry, darling. Even if you dent it, it can be fixed."

"Luc! Don't say that." Misty turned left at the corner and cruised down Fifth Avenue along the east side of Central Park.

"For someone who hasn't driven in a few years, you're doing fine," Luc said. "I'm proud of you. The only thing I ask is that you never park in a dangerous neighborhood. Use a chauffeur when you go anyplace that might be risky. Promise."

"But, Luc . . . Oh, all right, I promise."

They returned to the underground garage. Misty felt exhilarated at having driven the sophisticated machine.

"That was fun," she told Luc once she'd parked the Lotus and they'd begun to unload the Ferrari. "My sisters will be wild about it."

Luc laughed as he retrieved two large pieces of luggage and gestured to her to take the two smaller ones. "The key with the gold cross on it is the house key."

Misty unlocked the door and preceded him to the basement. While they were still in the dark, she said, "Luc, thank you for the lovely honeymoon. It was wonderful."

He pressed the switch with his elbow, lighting their way, his eyes finding her at once. "It was great for me, too, darling. But we'll have a longer honeymoon in a few months. How would you like to go to Jamaica? A friend of mine has a place there."

"It sounds wonderful, but can you get so much time off?"

"A man is entitled to a honeymoon," Luc insisted.

"How many, do you think?" Misty laughed as she stepped into the hall, glad to set down the two small bags.

"As many as we want." Luc set down his cases with a sigh and kissed her nose. "What do you say we raid the freezer and see if there's a casserole? While it defrosts in the oven, we'll unpack, shower, and change."

"Good thinking." Misty felt her heart turn over when he took her hand to lead her into the kitchen, but she stopped short when Bruno padded down the hall to greet them. "Hello, Bruno," she whispered tremulously, though she felt nervous delight when the dog wagged his short tail and rubbed his muzzle against her hip.

"You've made another conquest." Luc chuckled and kissed her hair.

A note on the counter from Mrs. Wheaton informed them that a casserole was in the refrigerator, needing only to be warmed, and that there were homemade rolls and a pie in separate containers.

"We'll have a feast," Misty said, pulling out the covered dishes. "Ummm, nice salad."

An hour later they finished their meal as strains of Rachmaninoff came from the stereo. Arms around each other, they went upstairs to bed in a sensual, languid eagerness to make love again, which they did all night long.

When the phone rang very early the next morning, Misty grumbled and didn't open her eyes as Luc got out of bed to answer it. "Hello? Alice? Yes, how are the girls? Yes, we had a wonderful time at Sweetgum. We're going back to ski later this winter." He glanced warmly at Misty and smiled. Then the smile left his face, and his brows came together over his eyes. "What? When did this happen? Yes, all right, keep the girls with you until then. Yes, we'll see you tomorrow. John is coming with you? There's no need for that. All right."

Misty stared at Luc as he hung up the phone. He hit his fist lightly against the wall several times and stared at the small print of the French wallpaper. Finally he turned back to Misty. "It seems your father called. He's in town."

"My father?" Immediately she felt as if all the blood had left her body. She wet suddenly dry lips. "Why?"

"He didn't say. He spoke to Aileen. She called Alice." He sat down on the edge of the bed and turned to face her. "Apparently your sisters became very quiet and withdrawn when Alice told them your father was here. So she decided to keep them with her and have Aileen tell your father to call tomorrow. I'll call Aileen and tell her to send your father here."

"I . . . I don't know what I'll do if he tries to take them," Misty said, more to herself than to Luc.

"Darling, it's as much my problem now as yours. Together we'll handle your father and your sisters." Luc held her cold hands in his and stared into her eyes. "No one is going to hurt you again, or bother your sisters. I intend to see to that. You are not to worry about anything."

"But you don't know him," Misty almost whispered. "And you don't know me. I've never told you."

"Darling, were you a victim of incest?"

Misty jumped and started to shake. "No," she said honestly, embarrassed. "My father never touched me . . . not in any way."

Luc stood up, pulling her to her feet and slipping her arms into a robe, then pulling on one himself. "It hurts you so much." He clenched his teeth. "Do you want to talk about it now?"

"No," Misty said. "I want you to hold me."

"That I will gladly do, my love."

Misty held on to him as if for dear life. *I will be strong, I will be strong,* she repeated silently over and over again. *I will not let father do that to me again. I won't.*

"Mystique." Luc's voice sounded harsh. "Stop thinking about it. You have nothing to fear from anyone."

Misty pushed away from him and looked up into his face, which was twisted with concern. "I'm not afraid," she said, letting her head fall back against his chest. But deep inside she knew that wasn't true. She did fear something— that Luc would want to leave her when she told him the terrible story of her life. And she didn't think she could live without him now.

"Your eyes are talking to me, darling," he whispered. "Tell me what you're thinking."

"If you have time before you go to work, I would like to tell you something."

"I'm not going to the bank today."

"You'll be fired for malingering," she said in a feeble effort to lighten the mood.

"I'll find work," he assured her, threading his hand through hers and leading her to the dining room. He smiled at his housekeeper, who was putting a pot of coffee on the table. "We'll serve ourselves, Mrs. Wheaton," Luc said. "We don't wish to be disturbed unless my sister or a Mrs. Aileen Collins phones."

Luc seated Misty at the round table and opened the drapes

to let in the morning sun. At the sideboard he filled two plates, then brought a pitcher of iced orange juice to the table. "Here we are."

"I'm not hungry," Misty said, wringing her hands nervously under the table. "I want to tell you this before I lose my courage."

"All right." Luc sat down beside her, inching his chair close to hers. His eyes held hers. "But first, remember that nothing you say is going to shake our marriage." He lifted her hand to his mouth, kissing each finger and sucking gently on her thumb.

"Luc, you don't know." Misty tried to free her hand, but his grip tightened.

"Tell me."

She let out a long, shuddering sigh and looked out the window to the snowy terrace. "My parents are close to each other. As you know, I'm the oldest. I remember being happy as a small child, but the older I got the more they seemed to turn away from me. By the time I was a teenager my father was finding fault with everything I did. I couldn't please my mother either. From the time I was thirteen, I knew they didn't want me. Each day my mother would recite a list of my deficiencies to my father, and he would rant and rail at me, telling me how I'd failed them, how I wasn't what they wanted, how troublesome I was." Misty swallowed. "Neither one of them ever hit me, but they never hugged me either." She shot a quick look at Luc, then turned back to the window, unable to meet his eyes. "I remember thinking that it was strange they'd had children when they disliked them so much. But as my other sisters grew up, it didn't seem so bad for them. I began to think that it was only me my parents hated, not the others. I was absolutely sure I had failed them, but I didn't know how. I saw a therapist when I came to New York. He taught me not to hate myself."

"You're beautiful," Luc said huskily.

Misty felt a smile tremble on her lips, then disappear. "I used to work so hard to get A's in school. But when I brought my report card home, my father would accuse me of having cheated." She paused but didn't look at Luc. "I had started taking piano lessons when I was seven, but my parents stopped paying for them when I got older. They even sold our piano. After that, I took free lessons at school. I got a job cleaning classrooms after school for a few dollars and the right to practice on the piano in the music room. I liked sports and was on the swim team. But neither of my parents ever came to see me compete, even though I was written up in the newspapers for setting three county records."

Misty's voice faltered, her eyes stinging and her throat going dry. "Then, when I was sixteen, I was asked to the senior prom." Her voice dropped. "My aunt made my dress. I had fun. We went out for breakfast. We came home at six in the morning. My father met me on the front porch. He . . . he called me a whore right in front of my date, Howie Breston. Howie was shocked, but he tried to explain that we'd been with other people the whole time. My father . . . my father said that if I was pregnant, Howie's father would have to pay for the abortion. It wasn't true, Luc. I was a virgin." Misty forced herself to say the words. "After that, I went to live with my aunt and uncle because my father said he wouldn't have a whore in his house. But I'd never . . . never . . . " Misty raised a hand to her trembling mouth. "When I didn't have a baby, my father said that I had gotten rid of it."

"I'll kill him." Luc's harsh voice penetrated her pain-filled thoughts.

"No." She took in a deep breath. "I honestly didn't think it would be so bad for my sisters. Otherwise I would have tried to do something. I really thought it was just me."

"Your parents needed other targets after you left," Luc told her.

"My mother never said very much." Misty shrugged and gave a crooked smile. "But she wasn't much help either."

"No?" Luc kissed each of her palms. "So you went to school while you were living with your aunt and uncle."

"Yes. I got a scholarship to attend the Eastman School of Music. I considered myself lucky to be studying piano." She looked up at Luc. "That's where I met Richard Lentz. We came to New York together."

"I already know all I want to about Richard and Leonard," he said mildly, running a finger down her nose. "As long as I'm the man in your life now, they aren't important."

"I realize now that they never were." Misty wanted to tell Luc what his coming into her life had meant to her, but she couldn't seem to find the words.

Luc remained by her side for the rest of the day. Misty knew it would have been a nightmare without him. That evening she talked to her sisters on the phone. They seemed fine.

The next day Luc rose with her, showered, and dressed. He insisted that she sit down and have a good breakfast. They were finishing their coffee when the phone rang. Mrs. Wheaton brought the phone to the table.

"Yes, Aileen," said Luc. "No, that's fine. In about twenty minutes? Thanks. I'll call my sister." He hung up and dialed. "Alice? Yes. In about twenty minutes. Fine."

Luc gazed at Misty. "I'm sure you know what's going on. We'll entertain your parents in the living room. I'll have Mrs. Wheaton make more coffee. Don't worry, love. I'll be right beside you."

Luc's smile warmed her. "Yes, I know you will," she murmured. "I'm not afraid, not now." And she wasn't. She felt as if a great weight was being lifted from her shoulders. She felt lighter, freer. "You did it," she murmured to her husband as he took her hand and walked with her down the hall to the living room.

"What did I do?" he asked, slipping his arm around her waist.

"Saved my life." She leaned her head on his shoulder. "No matter what happens now, I know I can face it. I'll be strong."

"You *have* been strong, every step of the way. The only thing you've lacked is an appreciation of your own courage."

"And you gave me that." Misty wanted both to laugh out loud and to cry. "You've given me a great deal."

Luc left her for a moment a while later to put a match to the tinder under the fresh logs in the fireplace. He was coming back to her, a now familiar glint in his eye, when the doorbell chimed.

Misty was aware that Luc saw her start, but he just squeezed her hand, saying nothing. She heard him tell the housekeeper that he would answer the door himself.

The murmur of voices came closer. Misty stood facing the door, her hands clasped in front of her as her mother and father entered. Her mother's hair was pulled back in a stiff knot, and she wore a plain dress. Her father was of about the same medium height with freckled skin and thinning sandy hair. His eyes were green; her mother's were pale blue. Both of them were tight-lipped and tense.

Misty was surprised that they looked so small. How alike they were—pinched, stiff, narrow-eyed. "Mother, Father, how are you?" she said.

"Much you ever cared—" her father began.

"Unless you would like to be thrown through that window into the street, you will speak politely to my wife," Luc informed them casually as he closed the door.

"Hey!" Alvan Carver said, his eyes shooting from Misty to his wife to Luc.

"I mean what I say," Luc added, each syllable ringing with conviction in the high-ceilinged room.

"It would seem that Misty has married a bad-mannered person. She isn't like us," her mother pronounced in low tones.

"Neither Misty nor I wish to be discourteous," Luc said formally. "Perhaps you would like to be seated." He gestured toward some chairs near the fireplace.

"Alvan, ask him where the girls are. We can't stay long." Marilyn Carver swallowed, and her eyes became mere slits in her face.

"Yes, we've come to fetch our daughters and take them home," Misty's father declared. But his eyes slid away from her face.

"I don't think they'll be going," Misty said coolly. "But in any case I think they should be allowed to make that decision for themselves."

"You be careful what—" Alvan Carver glanced at Luc and coughed nervously. "We have a right to take our girls home."

"They're of age. They can decide for themselves," Luc said bluntly.

Just then Bruno padded into the room, the irritated voices bringing his ears forward. He went straight to Misty's side and put his muzzle into her hand.

"You hate dogs," her mother grated, her eyes fixed on the animal. "He'll bite you."

Misty stared at her mother with sudden insight. She was a bitter woman, filled with fear and anger. But Misty's own pain was gone. With deep gratitude for her therapist and, most of all, for Luc, she realized that she no longer hated her parents.

She looked at Luc, trying to convey all the love she felt for him. Her world seemed complete.

In the silence that followed, the doorbell chimed again, and Alice and John entered, followed by Misty's sisters. Alice launched immediately into angry speech. "I don't know what the trouble is, but my lawyer, Willard Harter of Harter, Harter and Young, will join us here this morning if we need him. And he tells me that Mr. and Mrs. Carver don't have a leg to stand on." Alice placed her arm in front of the three Carver girls like a protective barrier. Misty's sisters looked wary but unafraid.

Misty watched Betsy bite her lip, then lift her chin, and she felt her own face break into a tentative smile. She glanced at Celia, who nodded and gave Misty a shaky smile. Marcy shrugged, and kept a sharp eye on her parents.

"Girls," their mother greeted them, pursing her lips.

Misty's sisters nodded warily in greeting.

Alvan Carver nodded, too, puzzlement flashing momentarily in his eyes.

"Darling, this is Alice's husband, John." Luc indicated a tall, rather stoop-shouldered man to Misty's right.

"I'm also backup for Alice," John explained *sotto voce*. "She's fully committed to your sisters." His eyes glinted with amusement. "I'm going to try to prevent her from running your parents out of the country."

Misty felt a knot of tears in her throat as John patted her shoulder and went to stand next to her sisters. Why had she been worried? Hadn't Luc told her he would take care of everything? She stayed in the comfort of her husband's arm as she faced her parents. "The girls will be staying with us, Father. Marcy and Celia want to go to school, and Betsy may decide she wants to go, too. They'll make their own choices."

Misty's mother was struggling visibly with her anger.

"You know what you are," she said threateningly. "I'm too much a lady to use the word, but you know what you are." Her mother's sharp eyes darted to each sister in turn. "All you wanted to do was chase the boys. You didn't want to stay home with me and learn to cook and sew as I did when I was a girl. None of you is like me."

"How dare you speak to your own daughters like that!" Alice shot at her. "You will not be allowed to intimidate them." She looked down her nose at Misty's mother.

"Intimidate them!" Alvan echoed. "We're their parents. We've come to take them home."

"We won't go, Daddy," Celia said. "We want to live here and go to school."

Misty's mother turned red. "How dare you! Alvan, listen to what they're saying. Do something." She whirled on Misty. "You were never pretty! Never! You were an ugly child, and so were they. They never—" Abruptly she stopped herself. She looked around at the people staring at her. "We . . . we have come to take our girls home with us. The neighbors—"

"They aren't going, Mother," Misty said in a quiet voice, feeling a rush of pity for her mother and her bewildered father. "Perhaps someday they'll want to see you, but not for a while." She gestured for her sisters to come toward her. "They're staying here."

"At our house," John said mildly, taking a pipe out of his pocket and putting it in his mouth. "Alice has already registered them at a small college near our home. If after a time they choose to do something else . . ." He shrugged, smiling owlishly at Misty's parents.

As Misty's father looked at each of his daughters in turn, he seemed to age ten years right before their eyes.

"I think that settles it, then." Luc turned as Mrs. Wheaton pushed a coffee cart into the room. "Ah, I'd love a cup. I'll fix you one, darling. Betsy, will you pour for our guests?"

Misty felt deeply sorry for her parents. But she felt no rancor, no bitterness. Luc had freed her of those destructive emotions. The heavy weight she'd carried for years was gone. She was finally at peace with herself.

"Coffee, Mother? Father?" Betsy quizzed, smiling as she took charge of the refreshments.

"I think we'll leave," Alvan Carver said flatly. Again he looked at each of his four daughters. Then he took his wife's arm, and they walked to the door.

"I'll see you out." Misty followed them, Luc at her side. She took a deep breath at the touch of his warm hand at her waist. "Mother, Father, you're free to visit any of us at any time. Just call first." Her voice was low and sure.

"My wife and I will welcome you to our home," Luc said formally. "And of course you may see your other daughters, in either my presence or in my wife's."

"I see." Her father's face had taken on a gray cast. "I think maybe we might see you someday, girl." He glanced at his thin-lipped wife. "Come along, Marilyn. I'll take you home."

Her mother scarcely looked at Misty before she clutched her husband's arm. "Let's go."

"Father . . ." Misty took his arm, the first physical contact she'd had with him in many years. "I want you to know that I truly believe it's never too late to start over in life."

Without meeting her eyes he nodded, then walked through the door with his wife. Misty watched them as they got into their car and drove away.

"Are you all right, love?" Luc asked her.

"Yes, I'm fine. I feel so sorry for them—for my father— for all of us really. It all seems very sad." She looked up at him. "But you've given me hope." She pressed his arm. "I saw them with new eyes today."

Luc shrugged. "Your mother needs counseling. So does your father. Maybe they'll begin to realize that."

"Luc, I want to keep in touch with my father and see that my mother gets the help she needs." She turned to face him. "But I never would have seen any of this without you. I would have kept all that insecurity to myself forever." She smiled at him.

Luc kissed her nose. "You hid too much of your pain, my love. Especially from your parents. But you've come a long way since you lived with them. Even before I met you, you were well on the way to coming to terms with yourself. When you left Richard and Leonard, you were already beginning to question your reasons for doing things."

"I swore off all men."

"Lord, what a close call I had," Luc teased, kissing her lightly.

They walked back to the living room, where Alice announced, "Lucas, the girls have decided to come with me. They'll be starting school soon, and there will be riding and music lessons and of course we must begin to prepare them for their debut."

"Debut?" the three girls and Misty said in unison.

Luc looked accusingly at his brother-in-law. "Don't glare at me, Luc," John said mildly, returning his pipe to his pocket when his wife gave him a long-suffering look.

"A debut isn't necessary," Misty began.

"Don't be silly, Mystique, dear," Alice said. "And you mustn't worry about the money. Lucas has scads of money, and I intend to bill him for everything." Alice smiled, unrepentant.

"Of course," Luc agreed dryly. "But the fuss is what I hate. I'll be damned if I'll wear white tie and tails to a debutante cotillion. It isn't necessary," he told his sister.

"How like you to act the village idiot, Lucas," Alice commented. "Well, if you don't wear tails, you shall be the only one who does not." She rolled her eyes at Misty, who smiled back weakly. "How can you think of shaming your new wife that way?"

Betsy giggled. "Misty's not ashamed of Luc. Are you, Misty?"

"No, of course not."

"Well of course she's not ashamed now, but think how she'll feel when you arrive at the club without any clothes on."

"I could put a jewel in my navel," Luc offered.

"Fig leaf would be better," John said, then coughed behind his hand.

"Come, girls, this is getting us nowhere. We have to get you some clothes. We'll go to Saks. We'll get your shoes at Lord and Taylor. I like their shoes." Alice's voice floated behind her as she urged the girls to kiss Misty good-bye and herded them into the foyer.

"John," Luc said in a warning tone.

John held up his hand, palm out. "Don't start with me, Luc. She's your sister. Besides, I wouldn't interfere if I could. Alice is having a marvelous time. She's sunny in the morning, and she greets me at the door in the evening with a smile."

"What? No rose in her teeth and martini in her hand?" Luc teased, reaching out to pull Misty to his side.

"Ummm? Not a bad idea. I'll suggest it while I'm following the group through Saks. I relish the thought that all the bills will be going directly to you."

"Pirate," Luc accused mildly as he and Misty followed John to the front door. "Don't forget that they'll need recreational clothes, not just ball gowns."

"I'm sure Alice has a list." John laughed and closed the door after himself.

Misty turned at once to confront Luc. "Wait until we're back in the living room, darling," he said. "You can ring for more coffee before you berate me." He chuckled and chucked her under the chin.

"Luc, it isn't funny! You can't let Alice run up big bills for my sisters. They have enough clothes." Misty bit her lip.

"Would you mind buying wardrobes for them if you had the money to do it?" He sat down on the couch and pulled her into his lap, cuddling her close.

"Stop. Mrs. Wheaton will come in any minute." She pushed against him, laughing. "And, no, of course I wouldn't mind buying clothes for my sisters." She paused as he chuckled. "You tricked me," she accused, pulling gently on his hair.

"Maybe a little. The point is, darling, we're well able to pay for any number of wardrobes Alice thinks necessary. If you like, I'll arrange for your accountant to pay the bills instead of mine."

"I have an accountant?" Misty asked, her voice faint.

"Of course. A very good man from the same firm the family has always used. You won't mind that, will you?"

"Huh? No, I guess not. Oh, here comes Mrs. Wheaton." Misty's voice failed as the older woman entered carrying a silver coffeepot, which she put on the serving cart. She smiled at Misty and Luc.

Misty wriggled on Luc's lap, feeling embarrassed, but

he held her still with a minimum of effort. "Darling," he whispered in her ear as the housekeeper replenished the cream and sugar, "you're arousing me."

"Eeek!" Misty squeaked. "Stop that!" she hissed, giving Mrs. Wheaton a weak smile when the older woman looked up in query. "Ah, nice weather we're having," Misty said.

Mrs. Wheaton looked momentarily puzzled. "There's a travelers' warning out, and the snow has turned to sleet, but I guess you like cold weather, don't you, Mrs. Harrison?" Mrs. Wheaton lifted the empty silver pot and left the room.

"Yes, you do like cold weather, don't you, Mrs. Harrison?" Luc teased, burying his nose in her neck. "In fact, the next time we go to Sweetgum, I'm going to make love to you in the snow."

"You'll be arrested," Misty said, trying not to laugh. "You're much too sure of yourself."

"I'm sure of the way I feel about you." He settled her more comfortably on his lap. "Now, I talked to Mother this morning, and she's inviting us over on Saturday to introduce the new Mrs. Harrison to some friends. I told her I thought we could make it, but that I had to check with you first."

Misty stiffened. "How many friends?"

"Just a few. She doesn't like to seat more than thirty in her dining room, even though she has room for sixty."

"Thirty? Sixty? Oh, my goodness," Misty groaned.

"If being the guest of honor bothers you, I'll tell Mother we can't come."

"We can't do that to your mother." Misty raised her head from his chest. "Doesn't your family ever do anything on a small scale?"

"I guess not," Luc said thoughtfully.

She tightened her arms around his neck. "Luc, it rather frightened me that my sisters made no move to kiss my parents, or express a wish to go with them. It makes me think I've been blind all these years not to have seen that they were going through the same thing I did."

"I don't think they suffered as much as you did. Truly, honey, I mean that. The three of them are close in age, so they could support one another, while you, being consid-

erably older, had to face it on your own. I watched your
sisters while your parents were here. I saw the same pity
in their faces that I saw on yours, but not the same anxiety."

"Oh, Luc." Misty sobbed into his neck.

He held her for long minutes, comforting her. Then he
stood and pulled her up to face him. "Now we're going to
change and go to see a designer I know."

"One that you used with your mistresses, you mean,"
Misty teased. She punched his arm, feeling buoyant with
happiness because she was with Luc.

"Mrs. Harrison! I'm shocked," he exclaimed with mock
indignation. "Insinuating such a thing about your husband."
He cupped his hands on her bent elbows, and hoisted her
up his body until they were mouth to mouth. "Shame on
you," he whispered against her lips. "My feelings are hurt.
Kiss me and make it better."

"You fool." Misty's laughter faded as his mouth claimed
hers. They kissed deeply, their mouths moving on each other
as though they were seeking the secret of life.

Luc pulled away first, breathing hard. "Lord, wife, we'd
better go now, or we'll be up the stairs and in bed before
you know it." He let her slide down his body.

"So? Who's arguing?" Misty stretched up and licked the
corner of his mouth.

His face flushed, his eyes narrowing on her. He placed
his palms on either side of her face. "Siren," he whispered.

"Yes."

"When we come home, we're going to have a nice,
leisurely soak in a hot tub, then—"

"Let's do it now," Misty urged.

"No. You're just trying to turn me away from my ob-
jective."

"But, Luc, Morey designs all my clothes. I like his work."

Luc regarded her for long minutes. "All right. But let's
just see if Charine has anything that would suit you. Then
we'll drive to Morey's place and take a look."

Misty nodded. "But please don't buy me too much. I'd
like to give some of what I have to the poor." She paused,
watching him. "I . . . I can use the money I earn at the Terrace—ah, I know you give to many charities . . ."

"Darling, I'll write out a check to any organization you

name." He shook his head. "Just when I think I have you figured out, you show another unexpected facet of yourself."

They freshened up, changed their clothes, and went down to the garage after Mrs. Wheaton informed them that Melton had arrived.

"I asked the chauffeur for the Rolls to come over today," Luc explained. "I thought it would be easier if we didn't have to fight traffic." He held open the door for her, nodding a greeting to Melton. "Comfortable?" Luc asked Misty.

"Luc . . ." Misty had pressed a switch that opened up a small bar with a desk and a telephone. "A person could practically live in here!"

"Great place for a seduction." He grinned when she glared at him. "No, I have never seduced a woman in the back seat of the Rolls. Would you like to be the first?"

"Yes." She laughed when his mouth dropped open. It delighted her to catch him off guard for once. He was always taking her by surprise.

"Next time I'll drive the Rolls, we'll park it someplace, and we'll see what we can do," Luc promised.

"Not in the middle of Manhattan!"

"And why not?" he teased.

They were still bantering when the sleek vehicle pulled up in front of a posh shop on Madison Avenue.

"It looks very expensive," Misty said as they got out. She watched over her shoulder as the Rolls merged into traffic.

"Just take a look at a few things," Luc urged. "We won't buy much. We can get most of your things at Morey's. In fact, how about suggesting to Alice that he make your sisters' debutante dresses? Alice would be bound to tell her friends about Morey." Luc shrugged as they approached a glass door bearing the name Charine in gold scrollwork. "Come on, darling."

The salon was lavishly decorated in cream and turquoise colors. Misty was a little nervous. She didn't feel comfortable in places like this, where the salespeople were often patronizing. Although she had learned to handle that sort of behavior at the Terrace Hotel, she preferred to avoid such places.

A tall woman with black hair in a French twist and

wearing a beige silk dress came toward them, smiling. "Mr. Harrison, how nice to see you. I'm afraid Charine isn't here today, but may I help with something?"

"Hello, Lois." Luc smiled. He spoke quietly to the woman, and she nodded agreeably and walked toward the back of the shop.

Misty felt as if she'd just received a hard blow. Unreasoning anger and jealousy swept over her because her husband had just smiled at the woman. She sucked her breath in sharply, trying to control her irrational emotions.

"Darling? What is it?" Luc bent over her.

"I'm going to sock her if she smiles at you again. How did you know her name? How many women have you brought here?" The questions tumbled from Misty's mouth. She pressed her lips together in an effort to stop them. Luc grinned, and her temper flared. "And don't you dare laugh, Lucas Harrison," she fumed, which made him laugh out loud. Just then Lois and another woman arrived carrying several dresses over their arms.

Still chuckling, Luc turned to face them. "Would it be possible for someone to model them for my wife?"

Lois looked momentarily overcome by surprise. "Your wife? Well, congratulations, Mr. Harrison. I didn't see an announcement in the paper."

"No doubt it will appear this week sometime."

Lois nodded. "Won't you both follow me?" She led them into an inner room with several Louis Quinze chairs arranged in a semicircle in front of a tiny stage one step up from the floor. In minutes the curtains parted, and a model glided forward wearing a low-cut flame-colored dress.

Luc frowned. "That's not your color."

Misty was about to agree when the model turned, and the color took on more cherry tones. "It might suit me," she mused.

"I don't want anything to detract from the color of your hair," Luc said, reaching up to wrap a strand around his finger.

Dresses, suits, and coats followed in quick succession, but Misty's thoughts kept returning to the first dress she'd seen. When the women finished showing her the garments, she asked to try on the red dress.

It fit perfectly. Misty stared at herself in the three-way mirror in the dressing room. "You were right, Mrs. Harrison," said Lois. "That dress suits you wonderfully. It emphasizes your glorious hair."

Misty looked down at the dress. "I'd like to show it to my husband, please."

The medium-heeled black pumps she was wearing didn't look quite right with the knee-length silk chiffon that wafted about her like scarlet flames. The many-tiered skirt was cut on the bias with a ruffle that went from breast to hem, delineating her every curve.

Luc was lounging in a chair talking to a salesclerk next to him. When he saw Misty he rose at once. "Darling, you were right. That dress is sensational on you. We'll take it, Lois. And I want all the accessories." He leaned down to kiss Misty, his smile wide, his eyes hot. "Are you sure there's nothing else you'd like to try on while you're here?"

"No, thank you, Luc. This dress is all I could possibly want."

He nodded and kissed her. Misty watched as he signed the bill, chatting with Lois, who stood at his shoulder laughing. Misty's temper rose.

When they stepped out into the crisp January day, she took hold of her husband's arm. "I don't know what you ever were to that woman, but I do know she has designs on you."

Luc looked down at her in amazement. "She didn't have a chance before I met you. She has a lot less chance now."

Misty let out a sigh of relief. She was beaming up at him as Melton pulled up to the curb in the Rolls. But Luc didn't seem to notice that their driver had arrived. He was taking her into his arms, his eyes alight with passion.

"Luc!" Misty stared up at him, perplexed by his determined expression. "Melton is here."

"What? Oh, yes. Let's go." He ushered her into the car and climbed in after her, keeping her close to his side as he reached into his breast pocket and brought out a jeweler's case with the name Cartier's inside the lid.

"A diamond pendant!" Misty exclaimed. "Oh, Luc, it's too much."

"I think this necklace will go very nicely with that new

dress. I bought it when I had your engagement stone reset."
His lazy grin widened as she gasped in astonishment.

"A necklace and earrings and two rings," she whispered,
studying the diamond pendant.

"The emerald in your engagement ring isn't new. It belonged to my Grandmother Stuyvesant. I purchased the other
items right after Christmas when I decided that you were
going to be very special to me. Do you think the pendant
will go nicely with your new dress?"

"I think it would look exquisite with a washcloth," she
muttered.

"Mystique, what a great idea! Tonight after dinner I want
you to wear your diamond and a washcloth."

Misty laughed and snuggled closer to him. When he
gasped she looked up at him. "What's wrong?"

"Nothing. I've just discovered what my favorite thing
is." Luc kissed her hard, forestalling further any questions.
"It's your wonderful laugh, my sweet."

CHAPTER SEVEN

MARRIED LIFE WAS EXCITING! At least Misty found it so. She was contemplating the thought as she bent over the keyboard in the Edwardian Room of the Terrace Hotel. She smiled to herself as she thought of Luc and how he would be coming soon to pick her up. He'd take her home . . . and make love to her. Imagining it sent a tremor of excitement through her, and she hit two keys at once with her middle . finger. Don't think of Luc while you're playing, she chided herself, forcing herself to concentrate on the music.

But in moments her thoughts had slipped back to Luc. He held her continually in thrall. He had merged her life completely with his. They had been married for only six weeks, yet Misty could scarcely remember what life had been like without him. She performed only two nights a week now, Tuesdays and Thursdays, and instead of playing until two or three in the morning, she finished at twelve, when Luc arrived to drive her home. Her breath rasped in her throat at the thought of going home with him.

"Hey, Mystique," Willis whispered, "you just played 'My Man' three times in a row."

Misty looked up at Willis, biting her lip. "I have to concentrate better."

"Not that it wasn't nice." Willis winked at her.

She shook her head and gave a half-laugh, half-groan. "No more daydreaming, I promise."

She switched to the Ravel Bolero, welcoming the intricate fingering since it forced her to concentrate on every nuance.

When she looked up sometime later in response to a burst of applause, the first person she saw was her husband. Her face broke into a brilliant smile. She had given up any pretense of acting aloof with him. Although she hadn't said the words "I love you" out loud, she was more committed to Lucas Stuyvesant Harrison than she had ever been to anyone.

She moved her hands on the keyboard in a complicated introduction to one of her favorite love songs, "Something Was Missing," from the musical *Annie*. On impulse she did something that she rarely did; she tilted up the piano mike and sáng the lovely words of the melody. Not once as she sang did she take her eyes off Luc.

When she finished several people came up to the piano and made requests. She played the songs they asked to hear, but she didn't sing.

At midnight Luc left his seat and walked up to her. He took her arm and lifted her from the piano bench, keeping his arm around her waist as they walked along the hall to the small dressing room. "Uh-uh, not tonight, angel," he said when she paused. "I had your clothes put in the penthouse suite. You can change there."

"Luc, I thought we went all through that. I don't mind that the—"

"Dressing room is so small. Yes, I know. But I thought we'd stay here tonight and go home in the morning, so I had your clothes moved to our suite."

"Why? I mean, it's just as easy..." Her voice trailed off as she saw the harsh look on his face. "Luc?"

"We've been married for six weeks today. I thought you might want to celebrate," he said stiffly as they stepped into the elevator.

"Oh, I do." Misty slipped her arms around his waist under his jacket. "I didn't think you would remember." She glanced up at him. "I thought men always ignored those things."

"I'm not likely to forget my own marriage." She noted a slight edge to his voice.

The elevator doors opened. Misty kept her arm around him as they walked into their suite. "I didn't mean to hurt your feelings," she said.

Luc loosened her arm from around him and headed toward the bathroom, his back rigid. Misty stood looking at the closed door, then walked over to the windows and stared out at the Manhattan skyline. The bathroom door opened a few minutes later, but she stayed where she was. She sensed Luc's presence close behind her.

"I'm sorry. I was hurt," he murmured. "I didn't think I could ever feel that way—like a child."

She turned slowly and looked up at him. "I know. We still don't know each other well enough not to be sensitive about what we say."

"Smile at me, darling," Luc said huskily.

"You always say that to me." Warmth suffused her face.

Inch by inch he pulled her toward him until they were lightly touching all along their two lengths. "I thought by now you knew that your smile was one of my favorite things."

He nibbled on her throat, trailing a line of tiny bites from one pulse point to the other.

"This happens to be one of *my* favorite things," Misty murmured as Luc's mouth traveled over her bare shoulders. "You nibbling on my skin."

"Another one of mine as well." His answer was muffled as he lifted her up his body with one strong arm. "I want you all the time." He sounded almost fierce as he swung her up into his arms and carried her to their bed. "I like your sisters very much, but I'm glad they've decided to stay with Alice and John most of the time." His voice held both anger and puzzlement as he sat her down on the edge of the bed and removed her shoes, then asked her to stand so that he could pull the long silken dress from her body. "I love my work, but sometimes I can't stand to leave you. You have such power over me." Ironic amusement filled his face.

"I hit a sour note tonight, and I played the same song three times, because I was thinking of you," Misty admitted.

"I know. I was there." He grinned. "You didn't see me. Don't be embarrassed, my love."

Misty loosened the studs on his evening shirt. "Maybe we should tell each other more, not hide so much from each other."

He laid her back on the bed—she was still wearing her silky briefs—and divested himself of his remaining clothes. He was holding the sleeve of his shirt when he looked down at her, his eyes appraising her hotly. "Do you know what you look like at this moment, my child-woman? Your red-gold hair looks like sunlight. Your eyes are like the most precious jade. Your skin is creamy pink. Your breasts are beautiful." His rakish grin almost masked the passion in his eyes. "And you have the cutest bottom in three counties."

"Not four?" Misty teased, thanking the fates that Luc thought her lovely.

"Mrs. Harrison..." Luc sat facing her on the bed. "I'd like to talk further with you, but I find that my mind can't hold any thought except how beautiful you are."

"Luc." Misty's body surged forward with a passionate need to love him. She raised her hands to explore his chest, tugging gently on his nipples, her energy building as she saw that he was already aroused.

"I feel I should warn you that I don't have a high tolerance for your loving," he said, his eyes following her hands as she probed, caressed, teased, and touched him.

"Just be patient," she cooed. As his body jerked and bent in response to her every touch, she felt consumed with a thrilling sense of power. "Luc, you're so beautiful." She squeezed the taut muscles of his stomach, then boldly let her hands slide lower and lower until she grasped his man-hood, massaging gently.

Luc groaned and reached out to grab her waist. "Much as I love your sensual massage, darling"—he lowered her fully onto the bed and leaned over her— "my restraint just blew apart." In a feverish frenzy his hands and mouth ministered to her.

When he gently parted her thighs to enter her, she was whimpering with desire for him. At once they went up in flames, holding each other, calling out each other's name.

Afterward they kissed good night, their mouths remaining only inches apart as they slept.

Misty woke once in the night with a strange longing. But she was too sleepy to analyze it. Tightening her arms around Luc's waist, she fell back into a deep slumber.

When she woke again, she was alone. She blinked in confusion at the sight of the unfamiliar room, then remembered that they had stayed at the Terrace Hotel suite. "Luc," she called, masking a yawn behind her hand.

"Yes, darling, I'm here. Come and take a shower with me."

Delighted, Misty leaped out of bed and ran unclothed to the bathroom. She paused just inside the door to watch Luc wipe the last traces of shaving cream from his face. "Oh, you're already finished," she said, disappointed. "I like to watch you shave." Her body tingled from the way he was looking at her.

"You do?" He sounded distracted. "From now on I'll call you before I shave." He took a deep breath and pulled her into his arms. "You're too much of a distraction, Mrs. Harrison. Seeing you like this makes me want to cancel my meeting this morning."

"You can't." She gave a breathy laugh. "It's with the board of directors, and you told me last week that it's very important."

"So it is." He sighed, dropping the towel from around his waist and leading her to the shower stall. "I've enjoyed my work since the first day I joined the bank after graduate school, but when I see you naked in front of me, I could chuck the whole thing."

"Don't you dare, Mr. Harrison. You have to support me."

"And the little Harrisons who will be coming along." Luc pulled her forward and began to scrub her back with the loofah sponge.

Misty clutched at him, stunned by what he had said. Children! She couldn't have children! She'd vowed long ago never to have them. What if she turned out to be a terrible mother like her own had been? She shuddered. Why had it never occurred to her that Luc might want children?

"Darling, you're cold. Let me make the water warmer."

"No, no. It's fine." She tried to smile up at him, but when she saw his eyes narrow in concentration on her, she pulled his head down and kissed him deeply. She kept her mouth on his until she felt his lips begin moving against hers, his mouth opening, his tongue thrusting against hers.

As they toweled each other dry and put on their clothes, Misty kept up a ceaseless round of questions concerning the board of directors' meeting.

"You've always been a good listener," Luc drawled, "but you seem obsessed with business this morning." He regarded her speculatively. She shrugged and didn't respond.

Even as they descended in the elevator to the hotel foyer, Misty felt him studying her. Melton was waiting for them outside the front entrance when she and Luc emerged.

Luc pulled her close to him. "We promised to be open with each other," he reminded her in low tones, his eyes piercing hers.

"We are open," she said weakly.

"Then tell me what's on your mind. What's making you frown?"

"Ah . . . I was trying to figure out what music to play on Thursday." As soon as she said the words, he stiffened beside her. He knew she was lying, but he didn't contradict her.

They were silent in the limousine on the way to the bank. Misty's head was filled with worries. How long had it been since she'd been to a gynecologist? When had she had her last menstrual period?

"Luc . . ." She licked suddenly dry lips as the car came to a stop in front of the bank.

"I'll be a little late tonight," he told her.

"Luc, we promised your mother and father we'd go out to the house Friday night and stay the weekend. They're giving another dinner party and—"

"Mystique, I really am in a hurry." Luc kissed her lightly

on the cheek and hurried out of the car. Melton pulled away
from the curb, not seeming to notice that his passenger was
pressing her fist against her mouth. She was bewildered and
upset. She had withdrawn from Luc, and he had sensed the
change at once.

Back home, Misty was greeted by Bruno and Mrs. Wheaton. She listened to what the older woman said about preparing dinner, promptly forgot it, and raced up to her
bedroom, Bruno at her heels. Nowadays he rarely left her
side when she was in the house, and she had come to love
the dog.

She dialed her gynecologist's number and made an appointment, feeling frustrated when she had to make it for
two weeks away. "Would you put me on a cancellation list,
please?" she asked the nurse.

She paced the bedroom rug, back and forth, back and
forth. She couldn't have a child. She couldn't take the chance
that she would be like her mother. To hurt a child that way!
She buried her face in her hands as tears filled her eyes.
Bruno whined at her side, and she patted his head. Why
had she stopped taking the pill? The headaches they caused
weren't so bad! Why had she assumed she wouldn't get
pregnant when she went off the pill? She started in surprise
when Mrs. Wheaton entered.

"Mrs. Harrison, I knocked, but— Why, what's wrong?"
the older woman queried, coming farther into the room.

"It's nothing, Mrs. Wheaton. Just a slight headache,
that's all." The housekeeper frowned, but she left when
Misty assured her she was fine.

That evening Luc was silent and aloof as they drank
coffee after dinner, a silver tray between them. The thought
of making love with him worried Misty, but the thought of
alienating him was an even greater fear. Nothing must come
between them! Hesitantly, she stood up and went over to
sit on his lap, cuddling close to him.

At first he did not respond. Then, gradually, his hold on
her tightened. "Witch," he whispered into her hair. He began
to caress her with slow, seductive strokes. Moments later
he surged out of the chair, holding her in his arms, and
strode up the stairs, his cheeks flushed with passion.

That night their lovemaking was frenzied. Misty felt as

though they were joined not just in body, but in blood and in spirit as well.

Unlike other nights, when they had cuddled and joked softly for a long time before falling asleep, now they held each other in fierce silence until welcome sleep took them both away.

The days remaining before she and Luc were scheduled to drive to his parents' house on Long Island were fraught with tension. Not all of Misty's efforts succeeded in melting the frost between them.

"It's unfortunate that I love you, husband," she whispered to the framed picture on her dressing room table that Friday afternoon as she packed her clothes for the weekend. "I was a fool not to go back on the pill as soon as we were married, but I got headaches...Maybe Dr. Wagner can suggest an alternative."

Just then Luc came into their bedroom, stripping the tie from his neck. "Since I'm here, why not talk to me instead of to my picture?"

"Ah...I was just asking your image if you would like two pairs of jeans packed or one." Misty watched his relaxed features tighten. *He knows I'm lying,* she moaned to herself.

"I'll pack the rest of my things," Luc told her, striding to the second bathroom attached to their suite.

"Luc," she whispered aloud. She couldn't explain to him how she felt, even though he'd met her mother. He would tell her she was wrong, she supposed, but she couldn't take a chance with their child. What if she was as twisted as her mother? No...no...

Talk between them was sporadic as they finished packing, checked with Mrs. Wheaton, and left the brownstone. "In the time since I've lived in New York, I'd never gone to Long Island until I visited your parents' and Alice's homes," Misty said as they left the city. She cleared her throat. "I enjoyed dining with them last month."

"So you told me." Luc's words were clipped.

"So I did." Misty began to burn from discomfort. "I was only trying to make conversation."

"Yes, you make conversation, but you're not honest with me. Is that how it should be?"

"What are you trying to say?"

"Look, Mystique, I'm not the one who's being evasive."

"I am not an evasive person," she shot back, her temper beginning to let go.

"What you mean is, you're not evasive or dissembling with most people. With your husband you are." His words seemed to echo in the confines of the car.

"Where the hell do you get off telling me what I am or am not, Mr. Perfect!"

"When did I ever do that to you?"

"When didn't you?" she retorted.

"There's no sense in continuing this discussion."

"Don't patronize me," she cried. As Luc pulled off the expressway and headed toward the North Shore, she faced out the window, ignoring the tree-lined avenues, open fields, and glimpses of Long Island Sound.

Silence reigned for what seemed like hours to Misty. Then the car was turning into a curving driveway bordered with rhododendrons, their brown leaves like claws snapping in the cold wind. The denuded trees looked to Misty like phantom guardians of the large sandstone and brick house they were approaching. Situated in the middle of a tremendous expanse of lawn, the building seemed to brood over the barren landscape.

Before Luc had pulled the car to a complete stop under the porte cochere, the double oak doors were flung open, and two boys of five and seven raced down the steps. "Good Lord," Luc muttered with evident amusement. "Attila the Hun and Genghis Khan are here." He turned to Misty, grim humor on his face. "My sister Deirdre's brood has arrived. My two nephews, Greg and James, who are now assaulting my car. Wait a minute, you two, until I get the door open. Their baby sister Jennifer, who has mastered the dubious art of smiling and spitting up at the same time, is also undoubtedly here." Misty gave a tentative laugh as the boys clambered onto the hood of the Ferrari. Wincing, Luc bounded out of the car and tackled them. "All we need now is for Velma to show up with her gaggle from Chicago. Janie, whom you met, is their only civilized child."

"Luc, you cad. Are you trying to kill my angels?" A tall, slender woman with gray eyes and ash blond hair similar to Luc's stood at the top of the steps, dressed in a simple pink cashmere dress. She hurried down as Misty stood uncertainly next to the car. "And you must be Mystique, the beauty who finally corralled the famous Elusive One. Good for you. What did you use? Bear traps?"

"A lasso," Misty answered, watching Luc pluck the two boys from the car and imprison one under each arm. "As a last resort I was planning to use poison—nothing lethal, you understand, just something to slow him down."

Deirdre threw back her head and laughed. "Oh, I love it. He has, indeed, met his match." Not seeming to mind the cold, she held out her hand. "I'm Deirdre. And I still think you *should* consider poison."

"Thank you for the advice." Misty chuckled at the boys, who were making faces at their uncle and smiling at her.

"Very funny," Luc said, panting and red-faced as they all climbed the steps to the open doors. "Stop wriggling, you monsters," he admonished. "Ah, Hawes. Get the bags, will you? Thanks."

"They drive him crazy, but he loves them," Deirdre explained. "How many will you have, do you think? Oh, Lord, Luc, watch them, will you? That's mother's Tang vase."

Misty felt vastly relieved that Deirdre had been momentarily diverted from the question of children.

"Lord, Dee, couldn't you peel one of them off?" asked a tall blond man coming into the massive foyer. He watched as Luc wrestled with the boys on the marble floor, again coming dangerously close to a Louis Quatorze table on which stood a rare vase of roses and baby's breath. He came forward to introduce himself. "I'm Ted Manning, father of the twosome that's assaulting your husband on the floor."

"Hello," Misty said, grinning back. All of Luc's family made her feel so at ease.

"Is that you, Mystique, dear?" Althea, Luc's mother, came out of the mammoth living room carrying a baby girl dressed in a pink pinafore, the one blond curl on top of her head tied with a pink ribbon. "Those are the boys, dear," she explained, casually handing her the baby. "And this is Jennifer. She's very good, but you should have this towel just in case." She adjusted the flannel square on Misty's shoulder.

Deirdre chuckled. "Let me take the baby until you can get your coat off." She hefted the baby onto her hip, and Ted took Misty's coat. "I've just met your sisters, and they're delightful. I like the idea of holding a Mardi Gras party to introduce the girls to society rather than waiting until the fall, don't you?" Deirdre handed Jennifer back to Misty.

"Ah . . ." Misty couldn't remember having heard about a Mardi Gras party.

"What the hell are you talking about?" Luc asked from the floor. Ted told the boys to behave, and Luc managed to shake them off for a moment. "We don't know about any Mardi Gras party. What in the world has Alice been up to?"

"You should see the girls." Deirdre giggled. "They look so preppy in their skirts and sweaters, and they love their schools. They seem very excited about Mardi Gras. Ted and I have decided to fly back for the occasion, and I know Vel and Ken will want to come, too. I understand just everyone will be there—at least three hundred guests."

Misty gasped. Luc stared at his sister in astonishment. "She's lost her mind," he declared.

"McLaren will do the flowers," Deirdre continued, "and Bijou is handling the food, and a couturier by the name of Morey is making all the clothes, including mother's dress." Deirdre finished breezily, apparently unaware that her brother's face had turned brick red.

"Oh, that's lovely. Morey's a friend," Misty offered, then bit her lip as Luc glared at her.

"Do you realize that she's creating a . . . a . . ."

"A bang-up do?" Deirdre suggested sweetly.

"A stampede," Luc corrected angrily. "And you can stop laughing, Ted. You'll be ordered to wear white tie, too."

Luc's brother-in-law chuckled and held up a hand. "Not me. This is your party, right, honey?" He glanced at his wife, who scowled back at him. "Now, Dee, surely you don't intend for me to—"

"Are you going to be the only one who lets those lovely girls down?" Deirdre demanded, seeming to swell with indignation.

"Yes, will you be a cad?" Luc quizzed.

"Quiet, Lucas." Ted shot his now chuckling brother-in-law a dirty look. "Dee, listen to me. Boys, quiet down. Dee . . ." His voice trailed off as he followed his wife back into the living room.

"Come inside and have some tea, dear," Luc's mother offered serenely. "We're just having a quiet evening at home. Hildebrand and George have joined us, but no one else will come until tomorrow night." She smiled at Misty and took her arm.

"You invited those bores?" Luc demanded.

"That is an unkind way to speak of your cousins," his mother admonished as she led Misty into the living room, which seemed to be filled with people, all of them talking loudly and gesturing wildly.

Ted was still pleading with Deirdre, who was talking to John and flapping her hand at Ted. John was nodding to Deirdre and shrugging at Ted. The twins were sticking their fingers in the clam dip and trying to get their grandfather to catch the crackers they were throwing at him. Luc's father was instructing the butler to make drinks at a small bar to one side of the Adam fireplace and telling the boys over his shoulder that he would be with them in a minute.

Misty cradled the baby and stared open-mouthed at a balding man sitting at the grand piano near the terrace doors. His singing was loud and flat, and his playing wasn't much better. At the same time, another plumpish man was reading him stock quotations from *The Wall Street Journal*.

"I lied when I said they were only slightly insane," Luc said into Misty's ear. He chuckled and cooed at the baby. "They're all mad."

"That's not true, Lucas Stuyvesant," his mother reproved him. "Hildebrand has a bit too much money and George tries to show him how to invest it, that's all."

"George lost a half a million dollars in oil wells last year," Luc told Misty.

"Yes, but I know for a fact that he gave an equal amount to charity," his mother supplied. She blinked rapidly at Misty. "My dear, you mustn't think my cousins gamble blindly." Her smile was indulgent as her gaze went from Misty to her son.

"They might as well just throw their money away and get it over with," Luc said dryly.

"Ah, but they have you, dear, to keep them steady." Mrs. Harrison glided away to speak to her other guests.

Misty coughed, choked, then laughed out loud. "It's so wonderful to be with your family." She gasped as the baby cooed at her. "Isn't she beautiful, Luc?"

"She's a heartbreaker," he agreed, sliding an arm around Misty's waist and leading her farther into the room.

Betsy spied them from the piano, where Hildebrand was trying to show her how to place her fingers on the keys. "Misty! Hi, Luc." She sped across the room and hugged them, then began talking nonsense to the baby. "I'm not supposed to talk baby talk to her, but she's so smart already that I don't think it will make a difference. We took care of her yesterday when Deirdre had an appointment. Marcy read her a few pages from *War and Peace*. Jenny loved it, didn't you, lovey?" The baby gurgled and waved her fists in the air. Misty and Luc laughed. His hand tightened at Misty's waist, and he kissed her on the ear.

"Oh, yuk." Betsy grimaced at them and assumed a long-suffering look as Misty's two other sisters joined them. "Are you going to drool all over each other this weekend?" Betsy asked. "I thought you were through with that stuff. You've been married for ages."

"Six weeks is not ages." Luc tapped Betsy on the nose and hugged the other girls. "You three look like bona fide collegians. Tell me what's new on the campus these days."

The three girls tugged him toward a group of chairs on one side of the room, leaving Misty alone with the baby. She chuckled as she watched her husband's family. Everyone was talking at once, all of them earnestly trying to persuade each other on whatever subject they were expounding. "It's just you and me, kid," she told the gurgling baby, who seemed to be growing restless and uncomfortable. She checked the diaper. "Ah, just as I thought. You need a change," she told Deirdre, who was still arguing with John and Ted.

"Oh, there's a diaper bag on the bed in our room. The green wing," Deirdre explained, returning immediately to her argument.

Misty shrugged. "I should be able to handle this," she said to herself. "What do you think, Jenny?"

Jenny squeezed her eyes shut and let out a howl.

No one in the room seemed to notice. Misty hurried out into the foyer and up the floating staircase to the second floor. From a past tour of the house she knew that the green wing was the biggest guest wing in the house.

After making two false turns she finally opened the correct door into Deirdre and Ted's bedroom. The diaper bag was in the center of the bed.

After placing the now squalling baby in the middle of the bed and putting pillows on either side of her, Misty stripped off the soiled diaper, disposed of it in the bathroom, and found a warm wet cloth with which to clean the baby. "Jennifer!" Misty wailed when she returned. A wet spot was spreading on the satin coverlet. "You weren't supposed to do that." The baby kicked her legs as Misty sponged her off and moved her to a dry portion of the bed, then pinned on the clean diaper. "I don't think your mother is going to appreciate my help," she told the child as she picked her up and gazed down at the dark spot in the center of the bedspread.

As Misty carried the baby down the stairs, she encountered Luc near the bottom on his way up. "I was looking for you," he said. "Where did you go?"

"Jennifer needed changing," Misty explained.

"Of course, Deirdre couldn't do that." He shot an exasperated look over his shoulder.

"I didn't mind. She's such a good baby."

Luc studied her through narrowed eyes for a minute, then came up two more steps so that their faces were even. "You look beautiful holding her," he began, then frowned. "You're pale. What is it?"

"Nothing." Misty looked away.

"You're lying to me, Mystique, and I damned well intend to find out why and what about."

"Jennifer needs her mother," she said, passing him, trying to escape his scrutinizing gaze. She hurried down the last steps and charged into the suddenly silent living room, almost tripping over the carpet in her haste.

All heads turned toward her. Hildebrand rose from the

piano. "Ah, here is the musician that Luc has married. A bit clumsy, I think." He turned to his cousin George for confirmation. "What do you say?"

"Perhaps she's a bit uncoordinated. Probably the result of poor blood lines."

"Ahhh," Hildebrand concurred, his index finger tapping the side of his nose. "That must be it."

"Shall I hold the baby while you murder them, or shall I do the deed for you?" Luc asked at her back.

"What did he say, George?" Hildebrand demanded, blinking at Luc in owlish dislike. "Lucas, must you always be so damned physical? So untidy." Hildebrand sniffed.

"If you make one more crass remark to my wife, I'll send you to the hospital, cousin. Not even my mother will protect you from that," Luc announced coolly.

Hildebrand looked for help, first from George, then from Luc's mother. "Althea, must I be subjected to this?" he demanded.

"Oh, do be quiet, Hildebrand," Luc's father said testily. He crossed the room to Misty, a broad smile on his face. "Pay no attention to him. He's a twit."

"Yes, I noticed that," Misty said clearly, the words reaching every corner of the room.

Luc's bark of laughter overrode the sighs, groans, chuckles, and exclamations of "Well, I never" that rose from the assorted company. His hand settled at Misty's waist, kneading the firm flesh.

"Perceptive little thing, isn't she?" Mr. Harrison commented to his son.

"Very," Luc agreed. "Here, darling, let me take Jennifer. She must be getting heavy."

"No," Misty said, her hands tightening on the baby. She gave her husband an apologetic glance. "I mean, I don't mind holding her for a bit longer." Unable to meet Luc's probing glance, she turned to his father. "She has your eyes," she observed, jiggling the baby in her arms and laughing out loud when she blew a bubble.

"Yes." James Harrison's shrewd gaze went from her to his son. "The Harrisons tend to have brown eyes. Perhaps you and Luc will have a brown-eyed baby."

"No, I don't think so," Misty said abruptly. "Excuse me.

I must take Jennifer to her mother." As she hurried across the room, she heard Luc and his father exchange surprised whispers, but she didn't stop.

Deirdre was still holding forth with John, while Ted was listening and grinning. Misty coughed to gain their attention.

"Ah, Mystique." Ted's grin broadened as he reached for his daughter. "How is Daddy's best girl?" Misty felt a tug on her skirt. She looked down at young James, laughing softly at his gap-toothed smile.

"Would you like to play Indians, Aunt Ma-steek? Greg and me, we gotta fort."

"Greg and I have a fort," Misty corrected absently, biting her lip as she recalled how many times her parents had corrected and criticized her. It had been so demoralizing never to hear an encouraging word from them.

"You and Greg have a fort?" James looked at her, goggle-eyed. "I didn't know that."

Misty chuckled and touched his cheek. She glanced around the room. Luc was still deeply absorbed in conversation with his father. Luc's mother and Alice were arguing about decorating. Misty's three sisters were comparing outfits. "Yes, I think I would like to see your fort," she told James. "Of course, I don't know if I can play Indians." Misty felt herself jerked forward by a strong five-year-old hand. She followed along behind, aware that Luc had lifted his head to watch her leave before refocusing his attention on his father. He was irritated with her, too, she could tell. He hated the fact that there was something she wasn't telling him. How could she explain that she wanted his child but was afraid to have it? She couldn't bury her fear that somehow she was tainted with her mother's twisted tendencies.

She shook off her dread as she followed James down a long hall and through the kitchen.

"Hi, Mabel," he called to the cook.

Misty said hello to the plump woman who was up to her elbows in flour. Her two young assistants smiled as James and Misty paraded past.

"James, why don't you call me Misty instead of Mystique?" she suggested. "It might be easier for you to say." They stepped from the kitchen to a damp outdoor corridor. "Isn't it too cold to play outside?"

"Yep. We're playing in the pool room. The pool is covered so it's okay to play there," James explained, leading her down a covered path to a huge bubble. "See, we could swim, but since no one is down here, the pool is covered. That way we won't fall in the water." He opened the door, letting out a blast of steamy air.

Misty welcomed the heat. Standing just inside the door, she looked around her. The olympic-sized pool was covered with a taut tarpaulin. She noted that it would be impossible for the boys to unhook the tarp from its grommets.

On the far side of the pool Greg sat on the tile floor arranging twigs as if for a fire. "He isn't going to light that, is he?" Misty's eyes widened at the thought of what a fire could do in the enormous air bubble.

"Naw. We aren't allowed to play with matches," James said matter-of-factly. "And we can't jump on the tarpaulin either, or Grandpa will skin our backsides."

"Good." Misty sighed with relief and followed the boy around the tile deck to where Greg was sitting. He ordered them to be quiet as he placed the last twig in the pile.

"There, it's done." He sighed and grinned up at Misty. "I didn't think you'd want to come, but James said you would, Aunt Ma-steek."

"We're supposed to call her Aunt Misty now," James announced importantly.

"Oh." Greg reached behind him and pulled a pheasant feather from a bag. He handed it to her. "Here. We found these on our farm. You wear it with this." He searched in the bag again and pulled out a garter, which he also handed to her.

Misty lifted an eyebrow at the blue satin garter with pink rosebuds and ruffles. "This is a bride's garter." She paused at the sight of their guarded expressions.

Greg shrugged. "It's ugly, I know, but it was all I could find in Mom's drawer. Grandma gave us these round ones. Aren't they neat?" He held up two more garters. "She said her mother used to roll her stockings in them." He looked puzzled for a moment, then shrugged. "I can't figure it out, but in the old days they did weird things."

"Right." Misty was glad now that she and Luc hadn't changed out of their travel clothes. She had no trouble sitting with the boys around their "fire." She slipped the garter over her head, inserted the feather, and passed the peace pipe, an intricately carved meerschaum. She was afraid it belonged to their father or grandfather.

"Ugh," Misty answered when Greg gestured that they stand and dance around the fire. "Whooo, whooo, whooo..." Misty chanted as she danced with half-closed eyes.

"Good God, she's a primitive." Hildebrand's voice carried clearly across the room. Misty gasped and whirled around. The sight that met her eyes made her want to sink through the floor. Luc's whole family was clustered just inside the door, watching her with astonished expressions.

CHAPTER EIGHT

MISTY PAUSED WITH one foot in midair, her palm inches from her open mouth, her eyes going as if in slow motion from one member of the family to the next. She froze when she saw Luc, his arms folded across his chest, standing next to his mother. "How, paleface," she said, turning her palm outward in a greeting.

"How," Luc murmured, raising one hand in imitation of hers.

"Me Red Eagle," Greg said, thumping his chest.

"Me Running Deer," James said with a fierce scowl.

"Me Purple Chicken," Misty finished lamely.

"Me Great Hunter coming to get Purple Chicken," Luc announced in deep tones, setting off peals of laughter among the family.

George and Hildebrand tutted and muttered. "No one need know she's related to us," said Hildebrand. "We could say she's a bit soft in her upper works," said George.

"Damnation, is that my meerschaum pipe?" Ted exclaimed.

"Is that my wedding garter around your head, Mystique?" Deirdre asked shrilly.

"What do you mean, yours?" Alice swelled with anger. "I let you borrow it. It's mine."

Misty turned questioning eyes to the boys. They shrugged sheepishly. "Fine braves you are," she mumbled as she pulled the offending garter and feather from her head. "Now it's every man for himself, I suppose."

"Just don't say too much," Greg whispered from the side of his mouth as the grownups came toward them from both sides of the pool. "Uncle Luc and Dad will take care of it."

"Yeah. Act like it never happened, Purple Chicken," James advised.

"Thanks, you two," Misty muttered as Luc ambled toward her, a gleam in his eye, his mother at his side.

"Not that I don't think you look absolutely smashing with the feather, dear," said Althea. "I do. You have marvelous clothes sense, but I'm not sure how our other guests will react. Of course, when all is said and done, who really cares what others think?" She smiled reassuringly at Misty. "I think you're perfect for Lucas." She kissed Misty's cheek and glanced over at the boys. "You've made good use of those garters. What smart lads you are!" Her grandsons beamed.

"They're brilliant," Luc's father insisted, skillfully inserting himself between the boys and their irate mother and aunt. "Come along with me, now. Mabel has a nice drink for you." He put his hands on their shoulders. As they walked away, Misty thought she heard him add conspiratorially, "Now, let's get out of here." But she wasn't sure.

"After dinner I'll have Hawes remove the cover and take you swimming," called their grandmother.

"This isn't the end of it," Deirdre warned her sons, glaring when her husband chuckled.

"I do believe they're almost as bad as our sons were," Alice said thoughtfully.

"Never," John denied, ushering his wife back to the main house. As the others departed, one by one, Misty and Luc were left alone.

"Great Hunter think Purple Chicken very sexy." Luc

leaned toward her and ran a hand over her suede-covered thigh.

"It will cost you much wampum to flirt with Purple Chicken," she informed him.

"Oh? How much?" Luc bit her earlobe and blew in her ear, sending tingles down to her toes.

"The scalps of those two braves who left me holding the bag." With effort Misty suppressed a smile.

"Old Indian maxim say: Never trust any of the Harrison tribe."

"Heap good advice." Misty closed her eyes as Luc's mouth touched hers. The kiss deepened, and her body sagged against him. His arms took her full weight as they swayed in sensual enjoyment.

"Shall I take off the tarpaulin so we can swim?" he suggested.

"Could we?"

"Uh-huh. I'll lock the door when we leave and tell Hawes what we've done. He won't let the boys in here alone."

"But we need suits."

"Hell, no." Luc held her back from him for a moment, his eyes serious. "You don't trust me fully yet, Mrs. Harrison, but you will."

"Luc," Misty began, but he turned away from her and strode along the deck to a cabana, returning a moment later with what appeared to be a large wrench. He knelt down at the far end of the pool and twisted off several grommets with the tool. After releasing that end of the tarpaulin, he folded it over, then went from side to side, loosening the rest of the grommets. Misty tried to help him fold the tarpaulin, but she found the sagging canvas too heavy. Instead, he used a hand crank to lift it off the pool.

"There. We'll leave it at one end like that," said Luc. "Hawes and a couple of the other men can put it away." He rose to his feet and stared across at her. "Come along, Mrs. Harrison. We'll undress in the cabana."

"Luc, what if someone comes?"

"Don't worry. I'll lock the door and put a sign on the outside." He held up an oblong cardboard that said in big letters: DO NOT DISTURB—SWIMMING NUDE.

Misty gasped. "Where did you get that?"

"John had it made for Mother and Dad as a joke, but they've actually used it a few times." He chuckled.

"And you?" Misty asked sharply.

Luc's eyes glinted. "I've swum nude with women a few times."

"More than a few, I'll bet," Misty said tartly.

"Darling, how you talk." He came around to lead her to the cabana.

She struggled to control her anger and jealousy at the thought of Luc swimming nude with other women. But the emotions burned in her, like raging flames. When she tried to close the cabana door against Luc, he pushed it open. "No way. We undress together."

Misty turned her back to him as she undressed, too upset to speak. The man had the power to make her temper go wild for no sensible reason! It angered and befuddled her to think that she was so easily riled by him.

"Ummm, so nice. You have the most gorgeous skin of any woman I've ever known." Luc's hand feathered over her backside.

"Spare me the detailed catalog of the women you've known," she snapped.

"Am I getting to you, darling? I hope so." He hung her vest and blouse next to his trousers.

She whirled around to retort, clad just in her briefs, but the sight of his naked body brought her up short. As she scanned his strong, muscular form, his skin taut and glistening, throbbing desire came alive in her. He took hold of her upper arms. "I hope I'm getting to you because you get to me. I'm frustrated. My wife is keeping something from me. Don't try to deny it."

"I'm not," she mumbled.

"And it makes me furious. So I dig away at you, trying to make you irritated enough to tell me what's buried under that red-gold hair of yours." Luc stared grimly down at her.

"Luc, I . . . I have something to sort out."

"Damn you, Mystique, why won't you tell me?"

"Are we going to swim?" she asked, desperate to change the subject.

He ground his teeth in frustration, then reached out and

slipped the silky briefs from her body. "Now we are."

Relief flooded through her as he took her hand. She needed him so much . . . But she couldn't tell him about how she felt about giving birth.

Luc lifted her in his arms. "Don't." Misty laughed, anticipating what he meant to do.

"It's you and me, love, all the way." Without further preamble he jumped into the deep end of the pool, taking her down with him into the chlorinated depths.

Misty didn't panic at the sudden loss of oxygen. She relaxed completely as Luc turned her to face him. His mouth came over hers, and he breathed his own life-sustaining air into her as they reversed direction and rose slowly to the surface.

Misty lifted her head above water with oxygen to spare, but she saw at once that Luc was gasping for breath. Humility coursed through her. Luc had given her the very air from his lungs, as well as shown the caring and sharing she had found as a married woman. He had done all that for her, although she had never expected it from him.

She paddled closer. He treaded water, watching her warily. He expected her to dunk him, she realized as he took a deep breath. "Darling," she murmured, tracing her fingers over his open mouth, his slowly moving feet keeping her easily afloat. Her mouth followed her fingers, and her hands crept upward into his hair. It struck her like a blow that there was no need for her to *tell* Luc she loved him. She need only love him at every opportunity. The realization left her feeling as light as air. For a moment she forgot to kick her legs and began to sink.

Luc's hands were immediately at her waist, hoisting her up again before she knew it. "What are you thinking, love?" he asked hoarsely. "Damn you. All you have to do is touch me, and I start to crumble like a cracker."

"My mind's blank," she told him serenely, her eyes half closed as she moved her body against his, her breasts tingling at the touch of his slick body. The softened hair on his chest rubbing against her skin created a sensual massage.

Luc clenched his hands on her hips. She was driving him wild. "Who would ever think that making love standing up in fifteen feet of water could be so delightful?" he said with a growl, manacling her to his hard thighs.

"I thought cold water was supposed to make that impossible." Misty rubbed her thigh in a gentle rhythm against his aroused body.

"With you, cold water is only another inducement, darling," Luc crooned, caressing her with skillful fingers, making her cry out with need for him.

She slid her arms around his neck and twined her legs around his waist. "I surrender," she whispered in his ear.

"Damn you, Mystique. Darling..." Luc sank with his burden under the water, then shot to the surface. He lifted her to the tile deck and vaulted up beside her. But instead of letting her rise, he pressed her down on the tiles and reached for a stack of fluffy towels.

"Your mother will think you're very extravagant using all those towels," she murmured as he spread them out, then lifted her onto their softness.

"I don't want your delicate flesh to get bruised, darling." Their wet bodies slid together with mounting need, awakening a thousand nerve endings. Misty was overwhelmed with throbbing, pulsating sensations.

"I'm here, Mystique." Luc kissed her ankle and nibbled on her Achilles tendon, setting off a series of exquisite shocks.

"My goodness," she said, gasping. "Whoever would have guessed that a leg could be so sensitive?" Her head rolled back and forth on the soft towels.

"I've had crazy sensations since the first time I saw your legs, darling," Luc muttered, his tongue searching for and finding her most intimate source of feeling.

"I...I..." Misty forgot what she was going to say as her body lifted and arched in an ecstatic consummation. Luc joined with her, and together they shot through the roof of the world, wrapped together in the ultimate joy of giving to each other.

His chest was still heaving when he pulled her on top of him and pressed tiny kisses on her face. "You're my angel."

"I want to be," she told him, aware that she had just given over a bit more of her life to him, that each time they made love he possessed more of her. It frightened her to give so much of herself, but she couldn't help it. She knew that she was far and away deeper into Luc's life than she had ever approached with Richard and Leonard.

"Misty, don't withdraw from me into that private corner of your mind where I can't go. I hate it when you do that," Luc grumbled. "I want to dynamite my way into your most intimate thoughts."

"Violent man," Misty chided.

A banging on the outside door startled both of them. "Hey, you two," called Ted. "The ponies are in the corral, and it's time to eat, and Hawes would like to get in there, and—"

"All right, Ted, we hear you," Luc interrupted, rising and pulling Misty to her feet, cuddling her to his body. "Tell Hawes not to worry. I took off the tarp. He can put it away. We'll be there in a minute."

"Right. I brought down the clothes that were laid out on your bed. I'll put them on the bench out here. Hurry it up. You wouldn't want your clothes to freeze." Ted chuckled, his voice fading as he returned to the house.

Misty looked anxiously up at Luc. "They'll know what we've been doing."

He nodded, unperturbed. "I should hope so. We've only been married a short time. My sisters and parents can't be so dense that they don't remember what it's like." He kissed her nose. "Darling, stop looking so worried." He strode over to the outer door and cursed the blast of cold air that swept in as he retrieved their clothes. "Hurry up," he called. "I want to take a warm shower." Grinning, he rushed her into the dressing room, holding up her outfit. "See? Your silk dress will be nice and fresh from the steam."

"How can you be so unconcerned!" Misty demanded, her hands clenching into fists. "We'll have to walk into that living room."

Luc shot out his wrist to look at his watch and shook his head. "I shouldn't think so. They'll be sitting down to dinner about now. We'll walk into the dining room."

"That's worse," Misty cried, sagging against him as he led her into the shower and helped her wash the chlorine from her hair and body.

"There's a hair dryer, darling, and an infrared lamp." He showed her where everything was. "Don't worry."

In her embarrassment she fumbled more than once, slowing her progress. Finally Luc fastened her dress for her. "Ummm, I love you in silk. So sexy . . ."

"Luc, we're late." Misty slapped his hand away from her thigh and glared at him when he laughed. In spite of herself she could feel her own mouth lifting in amusement. "You're awful."

"So sue me. I'm a bridegroom," he drawled, kissing the corner of her mouth, which she had just put lipstick on.

"Luc, stop," she wailed as he scooped her into his arms again and gave her a deep kiss. "Ohhh . . ." she moaned, "I should hit you."

"Umm, lovely. Hit me." He nibbled on her neck.

She pushed against his chest with both hands. "We have to go—right this minute." Scrambling past him, she raced out of the dressing room to the outer door.

"I think there's a law against abusing husbands," he crooned in her ear as he followed her at a trot along the path to the back door of the house.

Misty inhaled the warm, yeasty smell of the kitchen just as Mabel came through the swinging door leading to the dining room.

"Aha!" she declared, facing them, arms akimbo. "Love may be a fine thing, but the soup's getting cold." Misty blushed, and Luc chuckled.

"Sorry, Mabel, my darling." Luc placed a smacking kiss on her plump cheek just before swinging wide the double doors to the dining room and propelling Misty through them into the crowded room. Murmured conversation and the clinking of china and silver greeted them.

"There they are," young James caroled. "We get to stay for the soup, Aunt Misty, and then we're going to the pool. Did you have a nice swim?"

All eyes turned to Misty as everyone awaited her answer. "Ummm, great," Luc drawled. He let out a burst of laughter, bringing every eye to him. The adults shot quick glances at the boys as they, too, joined in the laughter.

"If I'd known you like swimming that much, Aunt Misty, I would have had gone with you," Greg interjected.

The adults' laughter grew louder as Luc led Misty to her seat. She was burning with embarrassment, blushing to the roots of her hair. "Thank you, dears," she mumbled to the boys, earning beaming smiles in return.

Misty lifted a soup spoon to her mouth, noticed that everyone was quiet, and looked up to find every eye on her. She swallowed the soup, hoping it wouldn't go down the wrong way and returned the spoon to the plate.

"You don't slurp," Greg observed from across the table. "That's good. Now you won't have to leave the table."

"And isn't that a blessing?" Luc whispered in her ear.

"Why does Uncle Luc keep biting your ear, Aunt Misty?" James asked.

Laughter rose again, then was masked behind coughs and throat clearings.

"Because, James," Luc answered for her, "Uncle Luc loves Purple Chicken."

Misty's heart seemed to soar away on a cloud of happiness. Everyone around her was laughing. Even she was laughing. But deep inside she knew it was a matter of deepest importance to have heard Luc say those words.

"Love agrees with you, Mystique, my dear." Her father-in-law leaned forward in his chair as Hawes led the twins away from the table to go for their swim. "You're positively glowing."

"She's beautiful," Luc said simply, rubbing his lips against her temple in a sensual massage.

She stared at him. "Stop it," she whispered, flushing.

"Don't try to control Luc, Mystique," Alice advised her. "He was always unruly as a boy."

"He was a knothead," Deirdre announced irreverently.

"Now, girls," Mrs. Harrison said placatingly.

Misty was stunned by the feeling of outrage that took hold of her at Luc's sisters' teasing. They were joking, she knew. Families often talked like that among themselves. But an irrational part of her resented the remarks, because she remembered how her parents had criticized her.

"Misty doesn't like you saying that," said Celia.

Betsy giggled. "I'll say. I remember her looking that way sometimes when we were small."

"Yes, I remember when Roddy Gordon pulled the cat's tail," said Marcy. "Misty socked him in the eye and brought the cat home, but Mother wouldn't let us keep it. Aunt

Lizabeth and Uncle Charlie took it. They had it for twelve years." Marcy's voice faded as the sisters regarded one another.

"That's my girl," Luc said, kissing Misty's cheek. "Defender of the weak and homeless."

Chuckles rose from around the table. As Misty gazed at each of the family members, her anger faded, she lost her self-consciousness, and the warmth of acceptance enveloped her.

After dinner everyone went into the living room for coffee, each one settling into a favorite chair. Mrs. Harrison sat down in front of a massive coffee service on a marble-top table.

"I suppose Mystique will play for us," Hildebrand said with a long-suffering expression.

"Only if you pay her," Luc snapped. "My wife is a professional musician, not a bumbling amateur like you."

"Really, Althea! Can't you control your son?" Hildebrand sniffed with disdain.

Mrs. Harrison seemed to consider his comment for a moment. "No, I don't think I can. Luc has always been strong-minded." She smiled at Misty. "Dearest Mystique, you don't have to play, but I must say I enjoyed listening to you that evening in the Edwardian Room when Luc took us to hear you. You have such a light touch."

Misty rose, smiling at her mother-in-law. "Of course I'll play for you, if you like."

"Please." Mrs. Harrison beamed, ignoring Luc's irritated gaze.

Misty went to the piano, flexing her fingers and rubbing her wrists. She raised her hands over the keys, and Rachmaninoff flowed forth before she had consciously made the decision to play his music. The driving rhythms and haunting melody seemed a perfect expression of her inner turmoil. As she swung one of his rhapsodies, she lost herself completely in the music.

When she paused, suddenly worried that Luc's family might have preferred to hear something lighter, there came a burst of applause. She looked up, surprised. A sigh of relief escaped her as Luc approached the piano.

He leaned toward her and whispered in her ear, "I feel

so proud of you. You never fail to surprise me, darling. You play magnificently." He kissed her hand. "Would you play 'Something Was Missing' just as you played it for me the other night?"

Misty nodded happily. So, he *had* known she'd been playing the song just for him that evening in the Edwardian Room. "Will you stand there"—she pointed in front of the piano—"where I can see you?" Luc nodded and positioned himself in the curve of the grand piano, his relaxed stance belied by the kinetic energy flashing in his eyes.

Misty sang the lovely lyrics straight from the heart to him.

As the last notes died away, applause once more filled the room. "Bravo, darling, bravo," Luc murmured to her alone.

"Oh, Luc," she began, tears stinging her eyes.

"Gee, Misty, you're good," Betsy said. "I'd forgotten how well you played."

"My dear . . ." Tears shone in Althea's eyes, too, as she came forward with her hands outstretched. "How beautiful you are."

Misty basked in the sunshine of their attentiveness. Her glance slid to her sisters, who were assuring Alice that there was no need to buy a grand piano; they had never studied music.

"But I always wanted to," Betsy finished wistfully.

"Ha!" Alice declared, a zealot's light in her eyes. "We shall find you a top-notch teacher on Monday."

"Lord," Luc muttered, holding Misty to his side, his eyes on John. "How many Steinways will you have to buy, do you think?"

"I'm not sure," John mumbled, a fascinated eye on his wife as she told Misty's sisters how well rounded they would be once they had studied both music and watercolors.

"It's very good for the spirit to paint," she finished.

"But I can't draw a straight line," Betsy said faintly.

"Don't worry." Alice patted her arm. "I'm sure John can find a teacher who would rather work with circles and curves than lines."

"Can you do that, John?" Luc queried his brother-in-law, tongue in cheek.

"You're a rat," he said mildly.

"Luc, rescue him," Misty pleaded. "Don't let Alice get all those teachers for my sisters."

Luc's eyes were like brown lasers searing her with sudden desire. "Let's go up to our room...Then I'll talk to Alice." His husky words filled her with longing, but she was acutely conscious of the people around them.

"Luc, please. Your father is looking at us."

Luc shrugged. "I don't care who's looking. Tomorrow when all those people arrive we won't have any time alone."

She couldn't help but chuckle at his woeful expression, which became thunderous when she laughed. "It's not funny," he declared.

She ran a fingernail down his nose. *"You're* funny."

"Take me to bed," he drawled, bending over her, his hands sliding to her waist.

"Not now," she said, chuckling. "We were in bed just a while ago."

"We weren't in bed. We made love on the pool deck. Now I want to make love in our bed. Let's go home."

"We can't!" The blood grew hot in her veins as Luc continued to look down at her with undisguised desire.

"Why?" He rubbed his mouth on hers. "Your heart is beating as fast as mine." He pressed the palm of his hand to her chest, his fingers splayed on the soft flesh.

"Luc," she whispered hoarsely as her pulse skyrocketed. "Maybe we could..."

They were turning to leave the room when Hildebrand come up to them. "Well, Mystique, you really surprised me," he said loftily. "Your technique isn't half bad." He paused momentarily as he noticed Luc's furious expression. "Ah, you're all red, cousin. You look—" he laughed "—as if you want to kill someone." Hildebrand's mouth slackened as Luc lifted his hand from Misty's waist and flexed it into a fist. "Pardon me. I have to see someone." With a shudder Hildebrand walked stiffly away.

"Luc..." Misty rested her head on his chest. "You shouldn't intimidate him like that. He thinks you're serious about hitting him."

"I am," Luc said, hugging her when she laughed. "Umm, I love the feel of your breasts pressed tight to me."

"Stop!" She was laughing out loud now, attracting the attention of several people nearby.

"Let's take a walk," he suggested.

"We'll have to get our coats."

"No. We'll walk through the house. This place is huge. I'll show you some of the galleries that are closed off most of the time."

Misty's skin tingled in delight as Luc took her hand and they walked up the wide staircase. They passed through the corridor to their room and went down another narrower hallway that lay beyond the master suite occupied by Luc's parents. At the end, double oak doors led to a small foyer. "This is called the turquoise wing," Luc explained, "but I suspect the only turquoise thing here is the mold." He grinned at her and reached up to take from the lintel a key which he inserted in the lock. "Just as I thought—a little musty."

"It's not too bad, Luc." Misty's whispered words echoed in the unused room. Her eyes settled on a painting of a woman working at a loom. "That reminds me." She nodded at the painting. "Did I ever tell you how grateful I am that you granted Morey a loan?"

"Yes, you did. Now be quiet so I can kiss you." Luc pulled her into his arms, and his mouth came down on hers.

"But—" Misty gasped and pulled slightly away from him. "I don't think you realize what you did for him. It was so kind."

"I was kind because he was your friend. Don't make it out to be more than it was. I would have done anything to get in your good graces."

Misty's heart flipped over. How she loved to hear him say things like that! "It was still very kind of you," she insisted, "and he won't fail you, Luc. He's an excellent designer."

"I agree. I've seen some of his designs—the clothes you wear for work." He frowned. "Not that I like to see you so bare . . ."

"Luc!" She was chuckling as she took his head between her hands. "You're very sweet."

Powerful silence filled the room as they stared intently into each other's eyes, facing each other like living, breathing statues frozen forever in a moment of perfect love.

Gently Luc placed his hands over hers on his face. "Mystique." The whispered word echoed in the empty room. "I want us to have a baby."

CHAPTER NINE

ALL DURING THE rest of their stay Misty was aware of Luc's hurt and frustration with her. She'd stiffened in his arms at his mention of children, and, despite his frequent efforts to get her to reveal what was troubling her, she was still unable to share her fears about becoming a mother.

When they returned home Sunday evening, she told him, "Luc, I'm not hungry. I'm going straight to bed."

"I want to talk to you."

"Please, not now. In the morning." Misty felt his anger radiating like heat waves on her back as she turned and left the kitchen. Wearily she climbed the stairs to their bedroom.

Much to her surprise, she fell asleep immediately after a quick shower. When she awoke the next morning Luc was already gone, and though his blankets were mussed she had no recollection of him even having come to bed. She had a splitting headache, one so severe that she became sick to her stomach. She was holding a cold cloth to her forehead when the phone rang.

"Mrs. Harrison, this is Dr. Wagner's office. You said to call you if there was a cancellation."

"Yes?"

"We have an opening at two o'clock today, if you'd like to take it."

"Yes, I'll be there." Misty hung up the phone and sat back in bed. Did she have the flu? She sighed, determined to keep the appointment with her gynecologist no matter how ill she felt.

By noon she was feeling somewhat better, much to her relief. She took a vitamin pill, but she didn't eat anything. Her stomach hadn't completely settled down.

At one o'clock she left the house, on impulse taking the bus to Henri Bendel, something Luc had been urging her to do since the beginning of their marriage.

As she walked into the quietly elegant establishment, she felt relaxed. She found some gloves in the softest white kid that she could use for evening wear and purchased several handkerchiefs with which to wipe her hands between musical arrangements at work.

By the time she left the store she was running late and had to take a taxi to the doctor's office, instead of waiting for the bus as she had planned.

She didn't have to wait long to see Dr. Wagner, and the examination was thorough but not uncomfortable. Afterward she got dressed, ran a comb through her hair, and met the doctor back in her office.

"I hope you'll be able to suggest another method of birth control," Misty began. "As you know, I was on the pill, but—" She stopped short in response to the quizzical look the doctor was giving her. "What's wrong, Dr. Wagner?"

The doctor closed Misty's folder and placed her elbows on top, her chin in her hands. "Misty," she said gently, "you're several weeks pregnant. Didn't you know?"

Misty's stomach seemed to sink to her feet. She stared at the doctor in stunned disbelief as a horrible sense of unreality swept over her. "I was tired," she said through stiff lips, "but I thought I might have the flu. I've never had regular periods." She let out a strangled sob. "I can't have this baby."

Dr. Wagner sat back in her chair and regarded Misty with concern. "You're very healthy, Misty, and I foresee no problem with the pregnancy, but if you insist on an abortion, I can suggest a colleague."

"Abortion? No, I don't want that. I'll give the baby up for adoption."

"You're married, Misty. Why would you want to do that?" Dr. Wagner asked with evident confusion.

"I'm married, that's true," Misty said dully.

"Doesn't your husband want children?"

"He loves them," Misty choked out, then bit her lip and fell silent. She stared sightlessly down at her hands.

"Misty," Dr. Wagner said, "something is deeply troubling you. Please tell me what it is so that I can try to help."

Misty studied the other woman's kind, concerned face, and suddenly knew she wanted to tell her everything. Words began to pour out of her in an unstoppable flood. She began at the very beginning, by describing how her essentially happy childhood had led to a traumatic adolescence. She explained how her parents had constantly corrected and criticized her and finally condemned her as an unworthy daughter. She went on to describe how her life had improved under her aunt and uncle's loving care, but how the vestiges of her low self-esteem had allowed her to get involved with Richard and Leonard, two men who used rather than loved her. Finally she told how Luc had entered her life and made her recovery complete. Except that she knew she must never have a child and risk becoming a destructive and hate-filled mother like her own.

When Misty finished, Dr. Wagner shook her head. "Misty, I grant you that there is sound evidence to support your belief that many emotionally abused children become abusive parents. But you've already faced and dealt with your problem. That makes all the difference in the world."

"But what if I ... I ..." To Misty's horror, tears filled her eyes and spilled onto her cheeks.

Dr. Wagner came around the desk, pressed a tissue into Misty's fingers, and laid a comforting hand on her shoulder. "Talk to your husband, my dear. Then come back to me, and we'll all three talk together. I sense that you do want this baby."

"Yes," she admitted with wrenching pain. She drew in several deep, steadying breaths, struggling to regain emotional control.

"Don't deny motherhood because you fear yourself," Dr. Wagner added. "Go back to your therapist. I'm sure he will tell you the same thing."

"Yes, yes, I'll make an appointment to see him." Misty wiped her eyes, a whisper of hope uncurling deep inside her.

Once outside, Misty began walking home, too deep in thought to even think of taking a bus or a cab. By the time she walked in the front door, she was tired and cold.

The sounds of someone in the kitchen surprised her. Mrs. Wheaton should have gone home hours ago. "Mrs. Wheaton, I'm home," she called. "I sure would love a cup of tea." She pushed open the door and stopped in her tracks. "Luc! What are you doing home so early?"

"Where the hell have you been?" he demanded. "More to the point, why didn't you take your car? Did you go on the subway? Damn it, Mystique, don't you know how dangerous that can be?"

Misty remained stunned into speechlessness as Luc rattled off question after question. When he received no answers from her, he strode forward and pulled her into his arms. She sighed with delight and weariness as his muscular heat enclosed her. "Ummm, you're so toasty warm," she murmured.

"Damn you, Mystique. I don't want you riding around Manhattan on a bus or subway." He leaned back to look at her. "Now, where were you?" He spotted the bag crushed between them. "Bendel's! So that's where you were. But why didn't you drive?"

"Sometimes I forget that I can take a cab or drive a car whenever I choose," she answered truthfully.

"Well, try to remember from now on, okay? I don't like coming home and not finding you here. I called Mrs. Wheaton to tell her to defrost some fish for us." He frowned. "That's why I came home early, so we could fix lemon sole together."

"Wonderful. Just let me take a shower and change first."

"I'll shower with you."

"No. We'll never get around to eating."

"Yes, we will. At midnight."

Misty shook her head and backed out into the hall. "No way. I'm hungry." She was laughing as she ran up the stairs, finally able to push her problem to the back of her mind.

She'd finished her shower and was humming to herself as, clad only in a silky bra and briefs, she searched through her closet for something to wear.

"I knew I'd find you like this." Luc's silky voice sent shivers up her spine and wave after wave of sensual shocks through her.

"It seems to me," Misty said sternly, straightening slowly but not turning around, "that you're always finding me in my underthings."

"Right," Luc said huskily, walking up behind her. "I was trying to think up an excuse for barging in on you like this, but"—he leaned down and kissed the nape of her neck—"I knew you'd see right through every one of them."

"Right," she agreed dryly, closing her eyes and letting herself relax against him.

"Ahh, good," he whispered, satisfaction in his voice as his hands began an intimate exploration of her rib cage. "You're gaining weight," he murmured. "That's good."

Misty reeled back in shock. Was it possible that he'd already noticed a slight difference in her shape? She closed her eyes, trying to resummon her quickly vanishing emotional equilibrium.

"Luc . . ." She lifted her hands from where they lay on top of his around her waist. "Let me go, please." The words were barely audible.

Immediately his hands fell from her, and he stepped back. "Are you going to tell me what's wrong?" He sounded angry.

Misty met his steady gaze. "Let me get my dressing gown first."

"I'll get it," he snapped, striding over to the bed where she had thrown the robe after emerging from the bathroom. He faced her with the dressing gown in his hands. "Turn around. I have a feeling I'm not going to like this."

She put her arms into the gown and belted it at the waist, then walked to the elegant chaise longue and stood behind it, facing him. "Luc, I went to the doctor today . . . to get a prescription for birth control pills."

"Mystique, if you don't want children right away, we can discuss it."

"Luc, listen. Dr. Wagner examined me. It was a very thorough examination." She took a deep breath. "The fact is, I'm pregnant."

His mouth dropped open. A smile lifted the corners and glinted in his eyes. "Darling . . ."

"Luc," Misty said on a sob, biting her lip, "I . . . I'm not going to keep the baby."

"You want an abortion?" he barked furiously, his hands clenching at his sides.

"No . . . no, I couldn't do that to our child. I intend to carry it full term, then release it for adoption." She watched miserably for his reaction, pleading silently for him to understand.

"And what if I don't want my child to be raised by strangers?"

She forced herself to say the words. "If you insist on keeping the child, I'll leave you."

"I see," he said with a calmness belied by his tense stance. "I thought you loved children. Were you only pretending to enjoy playing with Greg and James? Did you actually feel loathing when you cooed at Jennifer?"

"No, of course not," she shot back, stung that he should think such things. "I love them."

"What about Mark and Mary?" he demanded as though she hadn't spoken. "Did you only pretend to be fond of them? And what did you feel for Janie Patterson, my sister Vel's girl, whom you met at Christmas? Was it all a charade when you took them all skating?"

"No, no, no!" Misty denied, shaking her head and holding out a hand to make him stop. "Can't you see?" she screamed. "I can't take a chance that I might become like my mother!"

Luc's face twisted with anger. "Do you have so little faith in yourself that you'd rather give our child away than trust your own strength?" he demanded incredulously.

Misty felt as though he'd slapped her face. "But don't you see?" she wailed. "I can't take the risk."

"Damn you for being a coward, Mystique," he said

harshly, conflicting emotions of anger and love warring in his face.

"Yes, yes, I am a coward!" she cried.

He didn't reply. They stood facing each other like hostile opponents, their breathing harsh in the stillness.

"Get dressed. We have to fix dinner," Luc said with calm authority.

"I'm not hungry."

"You're eating for the baby," he reminded her. "And stop looking at me as though you think I'm going to strike you."

"I don't think that," Misty whispered, shivering. No, she knew he wouldn't ever hit her, but his anger was almost as frightening as physical violence.

He regarded her through narrowed eyes. "Dammit, do you think I'm going to attack you the way your father did? Berate you? Unfairly accuse you? Cut you down with words?" He inhaled a furious breath and exhaled it shakily. He studied her for long minutes. "I freely admit I'm angry with you, but that does not mean I don't understand how you feel. I don't agree with you, that's all. And I intend to spend the next eight months or so proving that you can trust me and yourself." His voice softened. "You *can* trust me, Mystique. Do you hear me?"

"I think they hear you on Long Island," she said dryly.

"As long as *you* hear me," he replied with faint amusement. "Now, are you going to get dressed or shall I do it for you?" His eyes went to her middle. "You *are* getting bigger," he said with quiet satisfaction. "Are you well? There aren't any complications, are there?"

"No problems. I have to take vitamins and eat whole cereals." She shrugged. "You know, the usual stuff for a pregnant woman."

Luc patted his shirt pocket as though looking for something. "No, I don't know, but I'll learn. Do you have paper and pencil? I want to get this down." He went to her desk, found some paper, and began writing rapidly. "Didn't you get any more details? Never mind, I'll call the doctor in the morning."

"Luc..." Misty reached into her closet for a pair of velvet jeans in a soft rose color and a matching silk blouse.

"I made an appointment with Dr. Mellon, the therapist I used to go to."

"When you first began taking charge of your life. Now you want to see him, but you don't trust your instincts."

"I do for myself, Luc," she tried to explain, "but I can't take any chances with our child. I just can't."

"Fine. Neither can I. I'll go with you to see Dr. Mellon. I have a few latent eccentricities he can begin to deal with. No, I am not laughing at you," he assured her. "I'm as serious as you are. I fully intend to be a very good parent... and a better husband." He held out his hand to her. "If talking to a therapist will help me in any way, then I'll work with him." Luc dropped his hand when she made no move to take it.

"I believe you, Luc," she said.

He let out a deep breath. "Well, that's a start." She pulled on soft rose-colored ankle boots, then straightened. "You look very beautiful in that color," he said. "Renoir would have loved to paint you. Your hair is red-gold. Your eyes are far more luminous than your emerald ring." He gave her a half smile. "I think I should be your PR man as well as your husband."

"Yes," Misty agreed softly, grateful that his anger had faded. She wanted back the teasing, loving Luc who was hers alone.

He reached out to pull her toward him. "I tossed a coin to see who'll make the salad. You lost." Together they headed downstairs.

"Was it a two-headed coin?"

"Why, wife, how you talk!" he drawled, running the flat of his hand down over her backside. "Ummm, you do have everything in the proper place, don't you?"

Misty laughed, leaning against him and daring to hope that, just maybe, they would find a solution to her problem, that just maybe Luc was right and she wouldn't have to give up her baby. She erased her thoughts of the pain and concentrated on the man walking down the staircase beside her, their bodies bumping gently at every step.

In the kitchen Luc rinsed the fish in cold water, soaked it in fresh lemon juice, and let it drain. Misty paused in tearing fresh spinach leaves for a salad and watched him, delighted by his off-key whistling.

"Stop goofing off," he chided her with a grin, wiping his hands on a towel he had thrown over one shoulder. "I'm doing all the work."

"Poor baby," Misty cooed.

He breathed in sharply. "When you pout like that, my blood pressure goes up thirty points. Love, your face is getting red. How far does your blush go?" Chuckling, he reached for the belt at her waist and brought her close, her hands still full of spinach leaves. "All the way down there," he whispered, lifting the neck of her silk blouse so that he could look down.

"You should be arrested," Misty declared, laughing. "You're a devil."

"Uh-uh, just a husband."

"Do you think all husbands are so interested in their wives?"

"They would be if they were married to you. But no one except me is ever going to have that privilege. You're mine for the next ninety years. After that you're on your own." Luc kissed her open mouth.

"By the same token, you're mine for the next ninety years."

"By George, I think she's got it. Now finish that salad. I have to make a few phone calls." He kissed her temple and left the room.

"Bossy." Misty sighed, feeling free from worry for the first time all day. "Don't get too comfortable," she muttered to herself. But her admonition didn't dispel the happiness that filled her. She was here with Luc. They were together!

"Daydreaming?" Luc asked from the doorway. She looked up to see him lounging against the frame.

"Never." Forcing herself not to smile, she pretended to glare at him.

"Looked like it to me." He ambled over toward her and leaned down to kiss her. "I'll put the coffee on."

"You usually do that after we've eaten."

"Tonight we might be having guests before we're finished."

"Oh? You didn't mention that anyone would be stopping by." Misty popped a spinach leaf into her mouth.

"That was before I informed my mother that she's to have another grandchild in September." Luc licked the corner of her mouth. "Piece of spinach there," he explained.

"Ah, Luc, do you think you should—"

"Yes, I do think I should inform the family. In fact, I'm thinking of putting an announcement in *The New York Times*."

"Luc!" Misty laughed as he left her to check the saffron rice and the sole, which was turning golden brown under the broiler.

They took their food into the dining room and sat at right angles to each other. Misty tasted the fish. "Ummm, good." She smacked her lips. "I've been so hungry, lately."

Luc grinned at her. "Expectant mamas have big appetites, but I intend to see that you go on a very special diet. You and our child will have the best health care."

Misty stared in awe at the gleam of determination in his eyes. "Dr. Wagner didn't say I needed a special diet," she began, falling silent as Luc glowered at her.

"What does she know?"

"She's the doctor," Misty pointed out softly.

"I'll talk to her in the morning."

Misty argued with him, but nothing she said shook him from his stand. They were still discussing the subject as they cleared the table and did the dishes. As they finished, the doorbell rang.

"That must be my mother and father," Luc said, smiling.

Misty turned to him in astonishment. "You let them drive all the way in here from Long Island tonight?" she accused.

He shrugged. "I only said they were going to be grandparents. I didn't tell them to come."

"But you didn't dissuade them either." Misty gave an irritated shake of her head, but he just grinned, unrepentant, and followed her to the door.

"Darling!" Althea Harrison burst into the foyer. "A baby! It's so exciting." She hugged Misty and then her son.

"Congratulations, my dear," Luc's father said more quietly but no less happily, if the light in his eyes was any indication.

Althea sailed into the living room, the others following in her wake. "I called everyone, and, of course, they're all delighted. Alice insists that we make a formal announcement at a special little party."

"There's no need," Luc said, his laughing glance going to Misty, who was staring in amazement in response to Althea's suggestion.

"But we must do something," Luc's mother wailed.

"We could put it in the morning's listings on the stock exchange. They go worldwide," James Harrison suggested.

"Could we do that?" His wife's eyes glittered.

"No, of course not. Dad's teasing you." Luc laughed at his mother's crestfallen expression.

"Well, I'll think of something," she declared.

"No doubt," her husband murmured, winking at Misty.

"Now, dear, tell me how you're feeling. Who's your doctor? Will you go to a hospital or have the baby at home? Are you going to continue to work?"

The last question brought Luc's head up. He stared at his wife, waiting for her answer.

"I think I'll work for a little while longer," she said hesitantly.

"All right, darling," he agreed, "but I reserve the right to take you off the job if I think you're getting too tired."

"Luc, I'll be fine." She smiled at him, feeling even more relaxed in response to his concern. She turned to her in-laws. "You will stay the night, won't you? It would worry me to have you travel back to the Island so late at night."

Althea glanced at her husband, who nodded, "Of course, we will, dear. It's so kind of you to offer."

"That will be great, Dad," Luc interjected. "You can come to the office tomorrow. You said you wanted to take a look at the Gennser plan."

"Good idea." James grinned at Misty.

Althea rolled her eyes. "I should have known he would insist on going to that foolish bank."

"I could go to that foolish bank every day if I wanted to, my dear. Have you forgotten that there are branches all over New York State, including several near us?"

"Yes, but it's always been the main branch that drew you. 'That's where all the action is,' you used to say."

"Ummm. Did I say that?" he mused, grinning.

Misty was delighted to watch Luc's parents interact.

When his mother described Luc as a boy, she had to laugh. "My dear, he was the original *enfant terrible*. He took a frog to dancing class, and seven mothers called me to complain. Oh yes, you laugh now, but you'll have to be on your guard with your own child. Those same awful genes may be passed on," she pronounced in mock funereal tones.

For Misty, Althea's teasing revived very serious fears. What if she *did* pass on bad genes to her child? She caught Luc watching her and gave him a shaky smile.

He relaxed visibly. "I like to see you smile."

James Harrison set his brandy glass down on an inlaid rosewood table next to his chair. His shrewd gaze remained on Luc for long moments before going to Misty.

Luc grinned at his father. "She's beautiful, isn't she?"

"Yes," James Harrison agreed, nodding solemnly.

"Stop it, both of you," Althea said tartly. "You're making Mystique blush."

Luc rose from his seat and pulled Misty to her feet, wrapping an arm around her. He sank back into his wide chair and pulled her onto his lap. "Is my darling blushing?" he asked softly.

"Luc, for heaven's sake." Misty pushed against his chest with one hand, trying to keep her blouse from riding up with the other.

James laughed. "Relax, my dear. A man always likes to hold the woman he loves. Occasionally I still chase Althea around the house."

"It's true," Luc's mother admitted readily. "But we never cavort in front of the hired help," she added sternly. She beamed at Misty. "Don't worry, my dear. You only have day help."

"See?" Luc said in dulcet tones, his eyes alight with amusement as he looked down at her spread across his lap.

Helpless laughter assailed Misty as she clung to him, taking in the indulgent glances of her in-laws. "You shouldn't encourage him," she told Althea.

"Too true. The Harrison men need very little encouragement to be arrogant." Althea lifted a stubborn chin and nodded insistently when the men protested.

"And no crowing from you, mama-to-be." Luc kissed Misty's hair and held her closer.

The evening was one of the happiest and most carefree Misty could remember.

That night after she and Luc had gone to their room, she undressed while Luc did some paperwork in his study. Wrapped in a silk robe, she peeked in to see how he was doing and decided not to disturb him, since he seemed to be completely absorbed.

Feeling restless, she went down to the kitchen to get a bottle of mineral water from the refrigerator. But when she opened the kitchen door, she saw that the light was on.

"Come in and shut the door," Luc's father greeted her. He was wearing Luc's maroon robe, and his hair was still damp from a shower. "Althea's asleep, or I wouldn't be down here. She's trying to break me of my nocturnal eating habits." He chuckled and, sticking his head inside the refrigerator, brought out two plastic-wrapped packages. "Turkey, chicken, or ham?" he offered.

Misty chuckled. "Actually, I'd rather have some mineral water and unsalted crackers."

James nodded. "Ah, yes. Easier on the digestion."

"But I've always enjoyed raiding the refrigerator." She refrained from telling him that scrounging for food at night when her parents were sound asleep had been the only way to avoid the constant carping that had become habitual during mealtimes in the Carver home.

"Good." James Harrison paused, then grimaced. "My dear, forgive me. I've been rude. This is your home, and I've encroached. My children are used to my eccentricities, but you—"

"I want you to feel completely at home," she assured him, taking the meat packages from his hands, then retrieving pickles and other condiments from the refrigerator.

James kissed her cheek and gently pushed her into a chair. "I'll be the waiter."

When they settled down at last, they had a table full of food from which to choose, plus milk and mineral water to drink.

"Mystique," James began, swallowing a bite of a chicken sandwich, "I have never seen my son so relaxed and carefree. I noticed in the last few years that he'd become colder and more cynical. I didn't think he would ever find the happiness he's found with you." He patted her hand.

Misty flushed with pleasure. "I didn't think we would be so happy, either." She shrugged. "We seemed poles apart at first."

She and her father-in-law chatted easily on a variety of subjects. Misty was pleased to have this chance to get to know James better. In some ways he was so like Luc; in other ways he was very different. Comparing the two men fascinated her.

They had just finished eating when a voice said from the doorway, "So here you are." Luc was standing there, glaring at his father. Now what was wrong? Misty wondered.

James chuckled. "Feathers ruffled?"

"A little," Luc admitted, going behind Misty's chair and leaning over her. "I didn't know you were hungry, darling."

"Want a cracker?" she asked.

He took the cracker she offered him, then pulled a chair up close to hers.

"I thought your wife might enjoy a little intelligent conversation," James told his son. "I don't imagine she gets much, living with you."

Misty laughed and Luc glowered as his father rose from the table and leaned over to kiss her on top of the head. "My dear, we will do this again. I enjoyed it."

"Don't count on it," Luc retorted.

"Thank you," Misty said simultaneously.

"Good night." James was chuckling softly as he left the kitchen.

Sudden silence filled the room. Misty couldn't control the giggle that escaped her. Luc stared at her, then lifted her hand to nibble on her pinky finger. "All right, so I was jealous."

Stunned, Misty stared at him. "You were not!"

He moved his mouth to her next finger and nodded without looking up. "Yes, I was. Why do you think Dad was enjoying himself so much? He knew."

"Luc." Misty was confused.

"It's stupid, I know, but I didn't want him feeding you down here. I wanted to do it."

As Misty stared at his scowling face, a surge of love swept over her. "Your father was already here when I arrived," she explained. "I came for some mineral water and crackers." She leaned forward and kissed him on the nose.

Before she could pull back, he slid his mouth over hers. "Do you want more crackers?" he whispered.

"No," she whispered back.

"Good." He stood up and pulled her from her chair. "Shall I bring the mineral water upstairs?"

"Not unless you want some," Misty murmured, leaning against him.

"No, I'm fine. But the next time you want something, tell me and I'll get it for you," he insisted, a mulish look returning to his face.

"That's fine with me." Misty felt kitten-comfortable cuddled to his chest, yet she was tingling with excitement because she knew Luc was going to make love to her when they returned to their room.

CHAPTER TEN

IT WAS THE evening before the event that Luc, his father, and his brothers-in-law had begun calling "the Stampede," the coming-out party for Misty's sisters. Misty had been deliriously happy all day. She and Luc had met with Dr. Mellon for two hours, and she'd begun to hope that her fears regarding motherhood might someday be put to rest. She intended to continue to meet with the doctor at least once a month during her pregnancy.

She'd been flattered and surprised by the reactions of Luc's family to her pregnancy. Alice had insisted on planning a baby shower to be held at the family's Long Island country club.

"With three hundred guests, you can be sure," Ted had whispered to her.

Her sisters had been thrilled to learn about the baby. They had come to New York to visit and dragged her to F.A.O. Schwarz, where they'd tried to talk her into buying a six-foot-tall stuffed bear. She'd laughed and shaken her head.

"I suppose Misty is right," Celia had finally conceded. "It might scare the baby."

For some time now Mrs. Wheaton had been preparing meals according to the diet Luc and Dr. Wagner had worked out together, despite Misty's protests.

Dr. Wagner had taken Misty aside. "Indulge him on this, Misty. He's so worried about you."

"But I'm as normal as can be."

"I know, but he's so used to being in control, and having this baby is one thing he *can't* control. He needs to feel he's taking part somehow."

"Not Luc!" Misty was incredulous.

"Oh, yes, Luc," Dr. Wagner had insisted, laughing.

Now, as Misty packed their clothes for a weekend on Long Island with his family, she smiled to herself.

"You'd better be thinking about me," Luc murmured directly behind her, making her jump. He slipped his arms around her waist and pulled her back against him. "That dreamy expression had better be for me."

"It is. But I didn't expect you home for another two hours."

"I know. But I started to miss you and decided to come home and help you pack."

Misty turned in his arms and lifted a hand to his cheek. "We're only going for the weekend. There isn't much to pack."

His arms closed around her. "You aren't supposed to do any lifting. Yesterday Mrs. Wheaton said she found you cleaning the bathroom."

"Luc, I was only wiping around the tub after my shower."

"That's what we hire people to do. A cleaning woman comes in three days a week."

Misty stared up at his truculent expression and laughed. "I love your little-boy look."

He leaned closer, his nose rubbing hers. "I like hearing you say things like that." He stared at her for a moment, his eyes going over her face and hair before returning to her mouth. "I don't suppose you love the little boy behind the little-boy look."

"I don't love the little boy," Misty agreed, seeing a flicker of emotion in his eyes, "but I do love the man." She finished in a barely audible voice, feeling as if the few remaining barriers between them had abruptly fallen away.

Luc's arms fell to his sides, and a muscle in his mouth twitched.

"Luc," Misty whispered, feeling the blood drain from her face. He must be angry with her for saying those words, for threatening to destroy the casual rapport they shared by declaring her love.

But to her relief he touched her chin with one finger and said, "And will you stay with me always?"

"You told me only ninety years," she said.

"Now I want ninety-five."

"Is this a bargain?"

"Yes. I love you, Mystique Harrison, and I never thought it would mean so much to hear you say you love me. You did say that, didn't you?"

"I did."

"Angel . . ." His voice broke. "Would you like to renew our vows in a church?"

Misty blinked. "Oh! I never thought . . . Well, yes, I would."

"Good. I want to be married five times — in three churches, one chapel, and a garden," Luc said lazily, not taking his eyes from her face.

Misty felt the power of his passion like a physical force that threatened to overwhelm her. "Luc, sometimes I'm frightened by the intensity of our feeling for one another."

"But you trust me, don't you, darling?"

"In every possible way."

The brilliance of his smile dazzled her. "We're getting there, aren't we, love?" he said. "Step by step, word by word?"

She nodded, too filled with emotion to speak. Feeling suddenly shy, she sought to direct the conversation to a lighter subject. "Do you think my sisters will have a good time tonight?"

He let his hands fall to her waist but didn't pull her closer. "Yes, I think the girls will have a good time. My sisters will have invited every eligible young man of a suitable age in the whole county for them."

"Ummm. No one ever did that for me," she quipped,

glancing flirtatiously up at him. It surprised her to see irritation cross his face. "Can't you take a joke?" she chided.

"Not about you, I can't."

"Silly." She stretched up to kiss his chin.

Being sure of his love gave her such confidence. She felt completely at ease with him. And all of a sudden she wanted to tell him everything about her past. They would have no secrets from each other ever again—nothing but complete honesty from this day forward.

"Luc," she began, "you once told me you didn't want to know anything about Richard and Leonard, but I want to tell you about them now. I don't want to hurt you, but I do want to settle once and for all any doubts you might have about me because of them."

Luc's expression was unreadable. "I don't have any doubts about you."

"Please, Luc. It would make me feel better."

He regarded her uncertainly. "All right," he said at last. "Tell me."

She gathered her thoughts. "I want you to understand that I didn't get involved with them out of love. I didn't know what love was. I thought it was an illusion, a fancy name for need, desire, lust. When I got involved with first Richard and later Leonard, I just wanted to be happy. I knew I didn't love them, and I didn't think they loved me. I neither wanted nor expected such an emotion." She lifted a palm to either side of Luc's face and didn't flinch at his intense gaze. "Sex with them meant nothing to me. It wasn't even very pleasurable."

Luc's taut muscles seemed to relax. "It wasn't?"

Misty shook her head and smiled. "If you want to know the truth, I felt more sensually aware while taking a hot mineral bath than I did when I was in bed with either man."

Luc chuckled. They grinned at each other in a silent sharing of intimate secrets.

"I didn't know anyone like you existed," Misty resumed. "Until you started making such a pest of yourself at the Terrace Hotel. Thank goodness you're a persistent man, Luc Harrison." She grew more serious. "At first I thought that what I felt for you must be an illusion. But it grew stronger and stronger every day, blowing apart all my pre-

conceived notions about commitments and relationships."
She laughed. "I have to admit that, in the beginning, I
expected you at any moment to turn from Dr. Jekyll into
Mr. Hyde."

"I noticed," he murmured.

"I didn't want to love you."

"I know."

"But you wouldn't leave me alone."

"I was fighting for my life," he said, massaging her waist
with strong fingers.

"Am I your life?"

"Yes."

"But how can you love me?" As soon as the words fell
from her mouth, she bit her lips. "I didn't mean to sound
self-deprecating, but all the newspapers in New York said
you would marry someone from your own social set. That
made sense to me." She clutched his shoulders. "Even though,
now that I have you, I won't let you go."

"Feel free to chain me to you, love," Luc murmured
against her cheek. "And as for my set, as you call it, you
are my set. You fit in perfectly with my family, and they
all love you."

"They do?" Misty felt herself swell with pleasure. "Oh,
Luc, I'm getting so conceited being married to you."

"Not true. You've just gained a sense of your own worth.
You're beginning to realize how much you mean to me,
how important you are. That realization has given you confidence."

She rubbed her cheek against his shirt. "I do feel better
about myself."

"Good. And are you beginning to believe that you and
I will make good parents?"

She nodded slowly. "I suppose I'll always have some
doubts."

"No, you won't, darling. After a time you'll begin to
know what I know already—that you'll be a fine mother."

Together they finished packing, teasing and laughing,
pausing frequently to share quick kisses and brief caresses.
Finally they left for Long Island, wrapped in their own
special aura of love.

The next day was a hectic one for the Harrison family. Luc's sister Velma and her husband Ken arrived, and Misty was able to renew her acquaintance with their daughter Janie, who chatted excitedly at Misty's side.

"My mother said Mark and Mary are coming with their parents and some of your other friends will be coming."

"Yes. Morey and Zena will be here, too, and—"

"I can't wait," Janie cried, clapping her hands. Then she covered her mouth. "I didn't mean to interrupt, Aunt Mystique."

"You didn't." Misty put her arm around the girl, delighted at being called Aunt Mystique. "Shall we go get Jennifer and take her for a walk?"

"Yes!" Then Janie looked around her and whispered, "But we'll have to take James and Gregory, too."

Misty nodded.

"Well, Aunt Mystique, we better watch out. The last time I took the boys for a walk, they jumped into the fish pond, and I ruined my best jeans getting them out."

Misty laughed. "Well, we'll have to keep a sharp eye on them, then. It's way too early to go swimming in Long Island."

Misty and Janie were both kept busy entertaining the boys as they pushed Jennifer in the English buggy provided by the housekeeper.

"I wish Uncle Luc didn't have to go with Grandpa and Daddy to help at the club," Janie said wistfully. "Then they could have walked with us. James and Greg would have behaved better." She ran off to retrieve the two boys from a thicket of bushes at the end of the curving driveway.

As they retraced their steps, Misty heard a car behind them and quickly ushered the boys, Janie, and the buggy to the side of the road. "Janie!" Mary shouted from the car window as she sped past with the rest of her family and Morey and Zena.

Misty and her troupe hurried back to the house, where they were greeted by a flurry of activity. Everyone was talking and laughing, making the old structure seem to echo with happy sounds and good feelings.

Since the very young children would not be accompanying the adults to the dinner dance that evening, they were indulged with an early dinner party of their own. Misty played the piano and sang "The Rainbow Connection," which the Muppets had made famous. The children crowded around her and sang boisterously.

"I think my wife is enjoying herself," Luc said, coming up behind her.

Misty laughed, a little out of breath. "I'm having a great time. Come and sing along with us."

Without further urging, Luc joined in, his lusty baritone standing out among the children's high voices and Misty's clear mezzo-soprano.

When it was time to go, Misty regretted having to leave the youngsters with the housekeeper. "Any fool can see that you love children, darling," Luc said as they left the room and climbed the stairs to their suite. "Soon you'll be able to see that for yourself."

"I think so," Misty said, squeezing his hand. "I think so."

Half an hour later they were on their way to the country club, where Luc's family had been members for generations. As soon as she stepped into the foyer, Misty could tell that the evening would be an unqualified success. The rooms were already crowded with beautifully dressed guests, and she was immediately caught up in the glamour and excitement. Alice was beaming, and Althea's cheeks glowed pink with the warmth of good feeling.

After chatting over cocktails, everyone sat down to a sumptuous dinner. Misty could only taste a bit of each of the many dishes. Afterward, she was standing with Morey, Zena, David, and Aileen when her mother-in-law sailed up to the group, her eyes sparkling. "Morey, I must take you with me." She turned to Misty. "Wanda Gump is green with envy over the girls' dresses. She insisted on meeting Morey, but I told her he's so exclusive that he'd have to interview her before taking her on as a customer." Althea grinned impishly, Misty laughed, and Morey went limp with nervousness. "Don't worry, dear, Alice and I will carry the ball," Althea assured him. She left with Morey in tow.

Zena and Aileen laughed out loud. "Morey will be as limp as a rag when we see him next," Zena predicted.

"A rich rag if Mrs. Harrison has her say," David mused,

smiling at Misty. "She's quite a woman."

"She's absolutely wonderful," Misty agreed.

"And I've never seen you looking better, Misty," David added.

"You do look wonderful, Mist," Aileen concurred.

"Thank you. If I do, it's because I'm happy," she answered, knowing that she could never begin to describe what she and Luc shared. How could she convey the delirious feeling of freedom that love had given her? What words could she use to draw a picture of the sweet ecstasy that was theirs alone?

Luc had led off the dancing by escorting Celia onto the floor while John danced with Marcy and Ted danced with Betsy. Now, as the three young women continued to dance with fresh-faced college men, Luc came up to Misty and asked, "May I borrow my wife for this dance?"

Misty slipped eagerly into his arms, and they whirled onto the crowded floor. "I thought I was never going to be able to dance with you," Luc complained, holding her close.

"You looked very good out there with my sisters," Misty said.

"And you look gorgeous in that sea-green silk dress. But I can see your legs through that slit every time you move, Mrs. Harrison." He shook his head in mock reproof, making her laugh. "It's not funny," he chided.

She lifted both hands and locked them behind his neck. "I love it when you act possessive, Mr. Harrison."

"Watch it, lady. See what I mean?" He pressed intimately against her.

"Darling, you're aroused! Shall we excuse ourselves?" Misty teased.

"Damn. If we only could," Luc muttered, glancing around.

"I was only teasing, Luc," Misty protested, laughing. "We can't leave, so take that mulish look off your face."

When the dance ended, they found themselves standing next to Betsy, who turned to introduce them to her escort.

"Luc, Misty, this is Kevin Short. Kevin, this is my sister, Misty Harrison, and my brother-in-law, Luc Harrison." Betsy's eyes shone with delight. "Kevin is in my Irish literature class."

Kevin smiled. "Hello."

"Misty is going to have a baby," Betsy announced proudly. Although Misty's cheeks flamed with embarrassment at the announcement, and Luc gave a muffled chuckle, Kevin remained coolly poised.

"I know, your Aunt Alice already told me, as did your grandmother. Your family seems to be pretty excited about the news."

"Yes," Misty said shyly. She glared at Luc, who laughed out loud.

"Sorry, darling. I guess I'm excited about the baby, too," he explained.

Kevin's puzzled look cleared. "Yeah." Then he glanced at Betsy and the couples gyrating on the floor to a fast rock beat. "Want to try it again?" he asked.

Betsy grinned. "Excuse us, please."

Misty took Luc's hand and pulled him into the surging crowd, too. "Are you sure it's okay for you to do this?" He frowned down at her as they moved to the wild rhythms.

"Absolutely. And stop treating me as if I were going to give birth to the first two-headed donkey."

Luc laughed. "I know I'm being difficult, but you'll just have to bear with me, darling."

Misty was about to answer when Ted and Deirdre swept up to them. "Misty, if it's a boy, you could name him after me—Edward. That's a great name."

"Don't be silly," Deirdre admonished. "She won't know the sex of the child for months yet. But you know, Edward isn't a bad name. If it's a girl, you can call her Edwina."

"Good Lord!" Luc exclaimed.

"I had an Aunt Edwina," Ted said defensively. A reluctant grin spread across his face. "Of course she weighed one hundred and eighty pounds and was five feet three inches."

"True." Deirdre sighed. "Do you think you'll choose one of the family names, Mystique?"

"We haven't even had a chance to think about it yet," she said.

"Family names," Luc mused, his arm still around Misty. "Didn't Mother have a cousin Eufemia?"

Deirdre closed her eyes. "Don't start."

"And she had a brother Eustace," Ted added with relish.

Misty began shaking her head, looking from one to the other.

"And wasn't there one named Tadpole?" Ted asked.

Misty gasped.

"That was Claypool," Deirdre corrected tartly as her husband burst into laughter. "That's the southern branch of mother's family—the Carters," she explained to Misty.

"Oh."

"I forgot to mention Cousin Lipscomb," Luc continued. "We called him Lippy."

"That can't be true!" Misty exclaimed.

"Of course it's true," Ted said, looking hurt. "Cousin Lipscomb was one of the most renowned icthyologists in all of Nevada."

"An icthyologist? In Nevada?" Misty said faintly.

Deirdre shrugged, sidestepping an energetic dancer who had come too close. "Strange, isn't it? He *was* eccentric."

"And subject to seasickness," Luc finished.

Misty looked blank as Ted chuckled and Deirdre smiled.

"Hadn't we better dance or something?" Misty suggested.

"I'd rather eat," Ted said, distastefully eyeing the jouncing couples on the floor.

"Would you like something to eat, darling?" Luc glanced down at her, his eyes alight.

"I'm not hungry, but I *would* like something to drink." As Misty took his arm, she noted that several women were assessing her husband from the dance floor. They passed into a smaller room with a round table set with assortments of canapés. "I can't believe anyone could want more food after the dinner we just ate."

"I heard that," Ted said, spearing a shrimp. "I'll have you know, sister-in-law, that I need continual sustenance when dealing with the Harrison clan."

"Amen to that," Luc murmured.

"Do you really have a cousin named Lipscomb?" Misty asked Luc when Ted and Deirdre had turned away to speak to someone else. "Or were you just trying to make me laugh?"

Luc paused, a glass of Irish whisky and water poised at

his lips, his eyes sparkling with amusement. "You know me too well, dear wife."

"And I like what I know." Her eyes widened, and she watched fascinated as Luc's face flushed with embarrassment.

He leaned closer and whispered, "Tell me that tonight, will you, when I'm holding you in my arms and your bare skin is rubbing against mine."

"Luc!" Misty gasped and looked around to see if anyone had heard. "Stop that."

"Too late. The image of you naked on our bed is implanted in my brain." He tipped the rest of his drink into his mouth and set down the glass. "Enough of that."

"But, Luc, you haven't had much of anything to drink. Just a few champagne toasts and this glass of whisky."

He grinned at her. "Checking up on me? But you're right, I haven't had much to drink. I find I don't want much when I'm with you. I want nothing that will cloud my thinking or blunt my awareness. You're all the stimulation I need. In fact, sometimes you're too much stimulation."

"Oh, dear, I do hate to interrupt you, but I was wondering, Mystique dear, would you play for us?"

Startled out of their tête-à-tête, Misty and Luc turned to see Althea. "Mother," Luc warned, obviously not approving of her suggestion.

"I know, I know. You don't want any of us to bother Mystique in any way. You made that very clear. But, Luc, surely it isn't a bother to ask her to play for us."

"Of course I'll play for you, Mother," Misty agreed.

Luc's mother beamed. "Did you hear that, Luc? She called me Mother." She stretched up and kissed Misty on the cheek. "We all love you, dear, and you needn't play if you don't want to. You're such a beautiful woman. I just know your babies will be beautiful, too."

"See?" Luc led Misty across the massive solarium and into a front room, where a piano stood on a small platform. "I'm not the only one who knows what a wonderful mother you'll make."

"Oh, Luc," Misty said, her eyes filling with tears.

"Don't cry," he whispered, "or I'll have to carry you out

of here and up the stairs to make love to you."

She gave him a watery smile. "Oh, Luc, Luc, I love you so . . ."

Misty's mother-in-law had just finished quieting the guests, and Misty began to play, her eyes rarely leaving Luc's face. Afterward, her enraptured audience burst into enthusiastic applause.

As Misty rose from the piano bench and accepted Luc's kiss, she felt that her world was complete. She had Luc, a loving family, and, coming soon, a baby she would love with all her heart. She'd come so far in such a short time— and all because of Luc's fierce and unwavering love. "I adore you," she whispered, the words coming easily to her now.

With a brilliant smile, amid the compliments and congratulations of the guests, Luc led Misty out of the room and home to their bedroom, where they made love far into the night.

Two years later, Misty and Luc went on a skiing trip to Sweetgum Lodge. As they removed their heavy clothing after spending a morning on the slopes, Misty turned to find her husband's eyes on her. "What is it, darling?"

"I can't believe we've had two children only ten months apart. Ten months!" Luc shook his head. "You leave me reeling. My mother and father are still bragging to all their friends, and your husband is at your feet."

"Never," Misty exclaimed in mock disbelief, happiness welling up inside her. "You don't regret having Mary Deirdre so soon after Stuy, do you?" she asked.

"I regret nothing, my lovely wife, except that I wish we had more time alone." He grimaced when she chuckled. "Even though I work at home two days a week, I still don't have as much time with you as I'd like."

"You'll get tired of me," Misty predicted, teasing him. She had perfect confidence in Luc's loyalty to her. He had made her whole. She knew that she was a good mother and, although Lucas Stuyvesant Harrison II was a little devil who kept his mother and his nurse chasing after him every waking moment, Misty was confident in her dealings with both children.

"How is it that your waist is still so tiny after having had two babies? Your legs are so slender, so long." Luc tossed his ski vest toward a corner of the room. The thermal shirt he was wearing emphasized his muscled chest. "You're still the sexiest woman in the world."

"I always want to look attractive to you. That's a thrill for me," she said softly.

Luc stopped cold and stared at her. "I'm five feet away from you, yet I feel as if we're making love. I'm most alive when I'm in your arms, my sweet. Your very special loving aura surrounds me," he whispered. "I'm constantly captivated by the mystique of your personality. That's the main reason I continued to call you Mystique even after you told me your name was Misty." His voice dropped lower. "From the first moment I saw you that night in the Edwardian Room of the Terrace Hotel, I was drawn to you, and I've never wanted to leave you since then. At first, I thought it would be great to have you as a lover. Then I imagined the moment when I would have to leave you, and I realized I could *never* leave you." He took a step closer. "That realization had the impact of a bomb dropped on my life." He smiled. "You're my Mystique, and I belong to you. No matter how many wonderful children we have, no matter what challenges we face, that will never change."

"I know, Luc. And I love you."

Misty smiled serenely as she glided into his arms.

No Gentle Possession

Chapter 1

"ARE YOU TIRED, Aunt Zeno?" Seven-year-old David clasped Zen Driscoll's arm as she leaned back in the cushioned seat and closed her eyes. The thought flashed through her mind that it was typical of the Aristides family to demand first-class air travel even for someone they didn't really want to see—herself.

"No, love, I'm not tired," she told David. "Just glad to be through the hassle of customs and on our way." Silently she added, I'm also nervous about leaving my job, which I love, to return for three months to a situation that I ran from three years ago.

She stared at David beside her. Large-boned, dark-haired, and dark-eyed, he had become her world. Seamus Dare, her friend and occasional escort, often told her she was too wrapped up in the boy, but even Seamus was not immune to David's charm.

"Will we ever come back to Dublin?" David asked, a faint quaver in his soft Irish brogue. Zen regarded him tenderly. Ireland had been his home for three years, ever since she had taken him there at the age of four. As soon as she had been officially declared his guardian, she had leaped at the chance to take a job in Dublin with Deirdre Cable, the world-renowned designer of woolen fashions for women . . . and to leave the United States and Damon Aristides behind.

"Will Daniel remember me, Aunt Zeno?" David tugged on her arm and scooted to a kneeling position on the seat next to her.

"Yes, of course he will." Zen tried to sound more confident than she felt.

"Will Nonna Sophie remember me, too? And Uncle Damon?" David questioned with stubborn persistence.

"Of course they will. I've sent pictures of you to them, just as they sent pictures of Daniel to us."

"Oh." David nodded, but his brow was still creased. "Robbie says that if I have a twin, he's s'posed to live with me."

Zen felt a wrench in her chest. Robbie was right, she thought, pushing back a strand of David's black hair. "That's why we're going to America, so you can be with your twin brother Daniel." Zen tried to swallow the lump in her throat as David screwed up his face in thoughtful concentration. Finally his brow smoothed, and he nodded.

"Then we can bring Daniel back to Ireland with us, and he can play with Robbie, too," he concluded brightly.

David's words conjured up in Zen a vision of Damon Aristides as he'd looked that day three years ago, standing outside the courtroom just after she had won the right to take David to Ireland with her. Thrown into shadow, Damon's dark good looks had taken on a satanic cast.

"This isn't the end of it," he'd warned her angrily. "And don't think you'll ever have Daniel."

"Don't you dare threaten me! You're the one who forced this court fight, not I," Zen shot back. "As David's guardian, I was within my rights to petition to take him with me to Ireland."

Sophie, Damon's mother, came up to them and pleaded

for them to be calmer, more understanding. But Zen shook her head and walked away, knowing her emotions would spill over if she said one more word to anyone.

She and Damon had parted bitterly, leaving so many thoughts and feelings unsaid, refusing to acknowledge all that they had meant to each other.

Now, three years later, a much-changed Zen was flying back to Long Island and the Aristides estate in response to Damon's request that she come home. Sophie, he claimed, wanted to see David.

Zen wondered if Sophie would find her much changed. Through her association with the world of fashion Zen had acquired an aura of sophistication, a confidence and grace that made her feel like an entirely different woman from the Zen Driscoll Sophie had known. Zen knew she was good at what she did, and that she was getting better all the time, just as her name was becoming better known. Designing fabrics fulfilled an artistic need in her, just as caring for David fulfilled a need to love. She was content with her life in Dublin.

"We can bring Daniel to Ireland, can't we, Aunt Zeno?" David persisted, pulling on her sleeve and rousing her from her reverie.

"Ah, no, love, I doubt we can bring Daniel back to Ireland," she said.

"Just for a visit?" David thrust out his jaw and scowled at his aunt. "He'll want to see Dublin and Robbie and play football...I mean soccer."

Zen smiled at the boy. "We'll ask," she said, but her heart contracted painfully at the thought of making such a request of Damon. She pushed him out of her mind and concentrated on the boy at her side. She was proud of his healthy good looks and vibrant personality. David was already involved in a soccer club for boys. His close friend, Robbie Parnell, often visited their apartment in Dublin, which Zen rented from the design company she worked for.

"Did my daddy and mommy like you and Uncle Damon?" David asked, his eyes fixed on hers.

"Your mother, Eleni, was my older sister," Zen explained, "and your daddy, Davos, was Uncle Damon's younger brother."

"And that's why you take care of me and Uncle Damon and Nonna take care of Daniel," David recited proudly. "That's what I told Robbie, but he said twins should be together."

Zen saw that David's eyes were questioning her now, but would they accuse her someday? She tried to smother the guilt that assailed her. She was responsible for having separated the boys . . .

"Do you like Uncle Damon, Aunt Zeno?" David quizzed, playing with the buckle of his seat belt, then looking out the window.

Like him? Zen's brain reeled. *Like* could never describe the tumultuous, overwhelming relationship she had had with Damon Aristides. She tried to dispel the memory of a twenty-year-old Zen meeting him for the first time when they'd both been honor attendants at Eleni and Davos's wedding. In that one instant her life had changed forever.

"I admire Uncle Damon's business acumen," Zen stated truthfully.

"What's an ak-a-min?" David asked.

"It means your uncle is an intelligent man and a well-known shipping industrialist. He also owns an airline. His company is called Olympus Limited," Zen explained, half wishing David would stop asking questions.

"Is this his airplane, Aunt Zeno?" David was looking out the window, watching the swirl of fluffy clouds that formed a blanket beneath the plane.

"Not this plane, but others like it." Zen masked a sigh. She was tired of speaking of the great Damon Aristides, an American born of Greek parents, a man who, in her opinion, still held an archaic view of women.

She tried not to think of him, but her mind betrayed her and carried her back to that day at Eleni and Davos's wedding when Damon had taken her arm as they followed the bride and groom back up the aisle. The way she remembered it, he had not released her hand for the rest of the day.

The next day she had returned to college in upstate New York, sure she would never see him again. But she hadn't been able to get him out of her mind.

At her sister's insistence Zen had stayed with Eleni and Davos on her holiday break. Since the young women had no other relatives, they were very close.

Each time Zen stayed at Eleni's, Damon arrived and took her to a show or dancing. But, although Zen wanted desperately for him to be more than courteous, more than friendly, he never kissed her, hardly ever touched her. Then, one day soon after she turned twenty-one, and just before she graduated, she went sailing with Damon. They dropped anchor and swam off the side of the boat, then went down to the cabin to change.

Their relationship had always been stormy, full of emotional highs and lows, but this time something seemed to snap in Damon. Like a dam bursting, he lost control and swept her into his arms, both cursing and muttering endearments to her. The moments had run together in a pleasure-filled blur as he initiated her into the tender joys of physical love. His touch had left her breathless and totally committed to him. He became the center of her existence.

Zen moved restlessly in her seat as she remembered. Oh, the arguments they had had! How often she had run away from him . . . then back to mend the rift. How wild and passionate their reunions had been.

How he had comforted her that day when the twins were three-and-a-half years old—the day Davos and Eleni had died in a sailing accident. She and Damon had stood close together when the will was read, and they'd learned that they were to share custody of the boys. She was named David's guardian; Damon was named Daniel's guardian. If they married, they would become the boys' legal parents.

They had supported each other in their grief until the day Damon's Aunt Dalia had informed Zen that Damon had another woman in New York, a woman he kept in an apartment. Zen would have laughed in her face if Damon's mother, who had been standing nearby and overheard, had not flushed a deep red.

"Is it true, Mrs. Aristides?" Zen had begged. "You were my mother's friend. As her daughter, I ask you to tell me the truth."

Sophie had remained silent.

"Why should she tell you anything?" Dalia had interjected. "As for your mother, young lady, she married beneath her...an artist from Greenwich Village, a man who was not even Greek."

A shaken Zen had lashed out at her. "My father was a successful painter. My parents were happy. They made our lives wonderful..." Zen swallowed painfully. "When the plane crashed they were on their way to Paris for a showing of my father's works. The money from the sales paid for Eleni's and my education."

She could see in her mind's eye a younger Zen storming out of the room, confronting Damon that very night with the charges his aunt had made. "And do you keep a woman?" she shouted.

"You're often angry with me, Xenobia," he said. "Should I be without a woman's company at those times?" Damon regarded her haughtily. "When we are not together, it's none of your business what I do." His body was taut with anger.

"Damn you, Damon Aristides!" Zen whirled away from him. She didn't answer his phone calls, and she refused to see him when he came to her apartment. When Deirdre Cable offered her a job, she sought a court order to retain custody of David and left for Ireland.

"What is Seamus doing now, Aunt Zeno?" David asked, interrupting her painful thoughts. He yawned and blinked, the long trip beginning to take its toll.

Zen glanced at her watch. "I suppose he'll be sitting down to his dinner soon."

"I like Uncle Seamus. He knows how to play football...I mean soccer...and he said he would like a boy like me," David pronounced proudly.

"So he did, and I don't blame him." Zen hugged her nephew, who hugged her back. Zen welcomed the obvious affection he had for her.

"Would Seamus like Daniel?" David waited expectantly for her answer.

"I'm sure he would," she assured him.

"Then if you marry Seamus, Daniel can come live with us, can't he?" The idea had taken firm root in his mind.

"Honey, Seamus and I have not been talking about getting married." Zen noted the stubborn thrust of David's chin, which was so like his father's . . . and his uncle's.

"But if you did, he could, couldn't he?" David persisted, worrying the question like a dog with a bone.

"Yes, of course he could."

"Good. I'd like having my own playmate living with me."

"I know you would." Zen kissed David's cheek, loving him, pleased with the grin he gave her.

The trip was long and tiring and, despite the many distractions offered by the flight attendants, David grew restless and cranky. By the time they had landed and gone through customs, he was complaining frequently and loudly.

"I don't like it here." He pushed out his lower lip and scowled at his aunt as they reached the baggage claim area.

"We'll be there soon. You'll feel better after a nap," Zen said absently, searching for their luggage on the moving conveyor belt.

David stopped in his tracks and twisted out of her grip.

"I don't want to take a nap. I want to go home and play with Robbie."

"Listen here, young man . . ." Zen bent to grab his arm, but he moved swiftly out of her reach just as she spotted her suitcase. "David, come back here or—"

"Can't you control him better than that?" a deep,

masculine voice interrupted, sending a frisson of panic up Zen's spine just as she swung her overnight case off the conveyor belt. She caught Damon Aristides in the midsection with a resounding thwack. He doubled up, all the breath knocked out of him.

Zen stared in dismay, then all her long-repressed anger at Damon Aristides boiled to the surface. "Well, it serves you right for startling me that way," she said stiffly, thrusting out her jaw. "Anyway, it was an accident."

Damon straightened, grimacing with pain and irritation. "It always is . . . an accident, I mean. You are the most dangerous person to be around."

Zen inhaled sharply at the full sight of him and swooped to retrieve David's suitcase as it moved past her. "I only have accidents with you," she retorted somewhat breathlessly. "David, please mind your suitcase while I get the others."

"For God's sake, let me take those," Damon interrupted. "Yanos, get the other cases," he told the liveried chauffeur at his shoulder.

"Is he Uncle Damon?" David asked in an awed stage whisper. "Is he the one you don't like?"

Zen flushed with embarrassment. She had never discussed her personal feelings for the members of the Aristides family. It occurred to her that children were far more perceptive than adults gave them credit for being. She stared in wonder up at Damon as his face grew taut with anger and his eyes glinted darkly.

He seemed bigger, more threatening than she remembered, all black like the Brian Boru of Irish folklore— hair, eyes, brows, even the curling hair that could be seen at the cuffs of his shirt. He was tall and broad-chested with high cheekbones and steely muscles. His body was conditioned to fighting form, Zen thought, her heart plummeting. She struggled to keep her courage high. She damn well wouldn't let him intimidate her.

Her heart squeezed into a knot when she saw the gray hair at his temples, but the rest of it was still black and thick and straight as it had always been. His huge body dwarfed her tiny frame, and his dark coloring contrasted sharply with her curly blond-red hair, brown eyes, and white skin.

God, he looked angry! She'd better try to explain. "David meant—"

"I'm sure I know what he meant." Damon's harsh words stunned her into silence. "Shall we go? Yanos will bring the luggage to the car."

"He might not find my soccer ball." David stood with his legs apart, looking belligerently up at the man who had yet to speak to him.

Damon studied him for a long moment, then squatted down in front of him, showing a careless unconcern for his pearl gray cashmere suit, which molded itself to his body as though it had been sewn on him. "You're a soccer player, are you?" he said softly. "I used to play soccer."

"You did?" David's expression lightened.

"Yes. Perhaps between the two of us we can convince your brother to play, too." He paused, touching the boy's cheek with one finger. "You look like Daniel, but I think you may be just a little bigger. You're older, you know. By three minutes."

"I know. Aunt Zeno told me." David pushed out his chest. "I'm as big as Robbie...almost...and he's the biggest boy on our team."

"That's great." Damon rose to his feet, holding David's hand in his. "Don't worry about your ball. Yanos is very thorough."

They headed for the exit, but David stopped and looked anxiously back at Zen. "You come too, Aunt Zeno." There was a quaver in his voice.

"I'm right behind you, love." Zen deliberately avoided Damon's intense gaze.

"That's good." The boy looked up at Damon. He did not free his hand, but a stubborn expression came over his face again. "I live with my Aunt Zeno. She takes care of me."

"I see," Damon said, looking from the boy to Zen,

who stood several feet away. "Come along . . . Aunt Zeno."

David looked relieved. Avoiding Damon's eyes, Zen stepped to the other side of David and took his other hand.

In the limousine, David chattered with excitement, asking endless questions and supplying random bits of information about himself. He exclaimed repeatedly over the vehicle's special features and kept Yanos busy explaining how they worked. Zen was soon lost in her own thoughts. Just seeing Damon had stirred memories she'd thought long dead . . .

"How are you?" Damon's terse question startled her. She stared blankly at him. "There's no need to be frightened," he snarled, his voice low.

"I'm not frightened of you or your family," Zen snapped, alert now. "I was just thinking of someone . . . something." Her voice trailed off. She wasn't sure what she had been thinking.

"Ah, yes, the boyfriend . . ." His soft voice was underlaid with steel.

"Why don't we agree not to talk about personal matters?" she suggested frostily, struggling to keep her anger from her voice.

"How can we not discuss personal matters when you have custody of *my* nephew," he retorted.

"And you have custody of *my* nephew," Zen riposted.

"True. And since I will be marrying in the near future, my mother feels I could provide a better home for—"

"Not on your life!" Fury curled through Zen like smoke from a forest fire. "If that's what it takes, then I'll marry Seamus." She said his name without thinking. "Then I'll be able to provide a home for Daniel as well as for David."

"Seamus? He's the man you're involved with?" Damon's words dropped like bombs.

"Seamus and I are not *involved,* as you put it, but David likes him, and so do I."

"Don't you dare subject David to your series of lovers." Damon said the words as if he were throwing spears.

"Then I'll marry Seamus," Zen said with measured sweetness, wishing Damon would leave her alone.

David turned to face her, a pleased smile on his face. "You *are* going to marry Seamus? Goodo! Then I can live in Dublin again, and Daniel can come live with us...maybe. I like Seamus," he added wistfully before leaning forward again to ask Yanos how fast the car could go.

Zen didn't look at Damon, but the goose bumps on her skin warned her of his anger. "You shouldn't listen to David."

"Don't tell me what I should or shouldn't do," Damon said stiffly.

Zen glared at him, then shifted away and stared sightlessly out the window.

David didn't seem bothered by their strained silence. He continued to hit Yanos with a barrage of questions. The old man answered him patiently. "This car doesn't have the best mileage, but—"

"Why does it need twelve cylinders?" David asked.

By the time they reached the Aristides estate, a huge gray stone building on Long Island's north shore, Zen was ready to jump out of her skin with impatience.

With effort she stilled a fluttering panic when she saw Sophie Aristides standing on the fan-shaped cement steps leading to the front entranceway, a slightly smaller version of David standing next to her. Sophie's hand lay possessively on Daniel's shoulder.

As the car drew up, Zen pulled David down next to her on the seat. "There's your grandmother and your brother Daniel," she whispered, her hands tightening on his shoulders.

"Oh," David whsipered back, all at once quiet as they got out of the car and stood uncertainly in the driveway.

For a moment Zen felt a fiery resentment because Sophie stood three steps above them, like a queen looking down on her subjects. Zen bit her lip, deliberately pushing aside those feelings. Suddenly, looking up at Daniel, she felt a great rush of love for the boy.

"Hello, I'm your Aunt Xenobia. But you can call me Aunt Zeno, as David does." Zen paused, studying the boy. He looked very much like David, but there was a subtle difference. David had the stockier build of the Aristides, while Daniel was smaller with somewhat lighter skin and a more delicate facial structure, like his mother Eleni. Yes, Zen thought, there was more Driscoll in Daniel than in his twin.

"Hello." Daniel's smile was like sun coming through clouds on a rainy day.

David responded instantly. "Hi." He bounded up three steps. "Do you like football?" he asked, referring to the soccer of Ireland, the Irish lilt in his voice sounding more pronounced.

"Oh, I do," Daniel replied quietly. "I've been to see the New York Jets."

"Huh? Do they play for the World Cup, Aunt Zeno?" David asked, clearly puzzled.

"No, darling. Remember I told you that in this country football is called soccer."

"I forgot," he said solemnly, but with a twinkle in his eye as he came back down the steps and took her hand.

Zen turned him around. "Now go back and say hello to your grandmother."

"Oh . . . that's right." David ran and grabbed Sophie's right hand. "How do you do, Grandmother, I hope you're well," he recited, just as Zen had taught him. He laughed up at the stern-faced, older woman, totally at ease with her. "Are you going to kiss me now?"

Sophie's rigid expression softened; then she seemed to collect herself. She leaned down and kissed David's cheek. "You are full of vinegar, I can see that. Do you speak Greek? Your brother Daniel does."

"Mother," Damon said softly but firmly, "it's not necessary for the boy to know Greek since both of them will be speaking English."

"That's all right. I don't mind teaching David to speak Greek," Daniel offered with a maturity beyond his years.

"Okay," David said with a shrug, "but not now." Zen

followed his gaze across the wide expanse of manicured lawn that sloped gently down to Long Island Sound. "We can play foot—I mean soccer—here. There's lots of room."

"After you change your clothes... After you visit with your grandmother... After your rest," Zen told him.

"Aunt Zeno," David wailed. "All those things to do first... I'll never get to play." He pushed out his chin, and glared at Zen, but she remained firm. "All right," he relented, "but I won't like it." He hung his head and paced the stone step, scowling, then grimaced at his twin. "Aunt Zeno is nice, but when she makes up her mind, ya havta go along." David's brogue thickened emotionally as he and Daniel stepped into the cavernous house, following a butler.

Zen studied Sophie's steel-colored hair and black shoe-button eyes and thought she looked much the same as she had three years ago. She had a few more lines in her majestic face, but she stood as straight and as strong as ever.

"Hello, Mrs. Aristides," Zen said. "It's been a long time." Zen was surprised at how stiff her words sounded. She was finding it hard to face this woman.

"Hello, Xenobia. You look well... and prosperous. You didn't used to style your long hair like that... or wear such high heels. You've grown up."

"I'm twenty-eight years old," Zen replied defensively.

Sophie regarded her in thoughtful silence. "The April wind has a chill," she finally said. "Why don't we go inside?" She turned regally and walked slowly into the house.

Following, Zen was temporarily blinded by the suddenly dim light after the bright sunshine. She stumbled slightly and instantly felt a hand at her waist. Stiffening, she pulled away and glanced up.

Damon's face was hard as granite. "You didn't always pull away from me," he said softly but with underlying steel.

"That was in another lifetime." Zen backed up a step and turned to face him. "I'm not some moonstruck girl you can manipulate like a puppet on a string." His angry expression made her take another involuntary step backward.

"You—" He stopped, then gestured to a servant to help Yanos take the baggage upstairs.

Released from the gaze of Damon's impenetrable black eyes, Zen hastened toward the sound of the boys' voices in the living room.

Tea had been served, but, ignoring it, the boys stood facing each other on a Persian carpet. David was tossing a hard roll from hand to hand, and his grandmother was sitting straight-backed on a settee in front of the tea trolley, watching him.

Mouth agape, Zen stared immobilized as David threw the roll into the air and butted it with his head like a soccer ball.

"Now you try it," he instructed his twin.

Daniel sailed his hard roll into the air and dived toward it, head first. He missed it by a wide margin and reeled into a Sheraton table, knocking over an Ainsley lamp.

Zen leaped forward, reaching out to save the lamp just as Damon stepped in front of her. Her hand grazed his cheek moments before he deftly righted the lamp.

"Zen!" he thundered, his right hand coming up to cover the scratched cheek at the same time that her forward momentum thrust her against his rock-hard chest. They staggered, his body absorbing the full impact of hers, then stumbled into a chair. Zen landed sprawled in Damon's lap. His arms tightened immediately around her as they gasped for breath.

"Crikey, Aunt Zeno, look what you did to Uncle Damon's face." David's loud voice echoed in the suddenly quiet room. "She doesn't do things like this at home," he informed his open-mouthed twin. Then he smiled at his grandmother. "Sometimes Aunt Zeno plays soccer with me, though."

"I see." Sophie Aristides had risen to her feet and was regarding with disapproval the tangle of legs and arms on her high-backed silk chair. "Damon, do get up. Xenobia, you will cover your legs." The boys giggled, and Damon muttered darkly.

"Mother," he began, trying to set Zen on her feet, "I think you should pour the boys something to drink." His face was flushed with anger when he stood at last and met his mother's enigmatic expression.

"I do not believe that tea or chocolate would have enticed the boys away from the intriguing sight of their aunt and uncle behaving like children in the living room." Ignoring her son's flaring nostrils and clenched teeth, Sophie put a hand on the shoulder of each boy and urged them toward the tea trolley. "There are homemade biscuits and cookies." She hesitated when she saw David mask a yawn with his hand. "After tea, I will rest before dinner. You may come up and talk with me, David. Daniel might like to speak to Aunt Zeno."

Daniel smiled hesitantly at Zen, melting her anger and making her heart twist with love. In that instant, he looked so like Eleni.

Zen took a chair across from Sophie and close to David, who sat cross-legged on a cushion and began eating a biscuit covered with strawberry jam.

When Damon sat down, both boys stared at the scratch on his cheek. Sophie regarded it also, but said nothing. Embarrassed by what she'd done, but feeling angry and resentful toward Damon, who she didn't trust for one moment, Zen studied the pattern in her damask napkin.

A few minutes later a plump woman in her fifties with black hair streaked with gray entered the room. She bestowed a warm smile on the boys and told them to come with her. Zen recognized the housekeeper who had been with the Aristides family for as long as she had known them.

David hesitated and glanced at Zen.

"You needn't mind, young mister," the woman said. "I'm Lona, and I'm going to show you which room is yours, and then you may go along to your grandmother's room, or wherever you like."

"All right, but I want to sleep near Aunt Zeno. Some-

times she gets nightmares . . . and I take care of her,"
David said.

Zen's stomach seemed to drop to her toes. She knew
David was trying to hide his own nervousness, but she
dreaded Damon's reaction to his revelation.

Lona inclined her head and assured him he would be
close to his Aunt Zeno. The boys left side by side, Lona
leading the way.

Silence fell over the room like a shroud.

Sophie cleared her throat, the sound loud in the abrupt
stillness. "So . . . you have nightmares, Xenobia?"

Zen coughed nervously. "I did . . . a few times." She
had no wish to discuss the bad dreams that had caused
her many restless nights.

"No doubt from losing your sister so tragically," Sophie mused.

Zen nodded, determined never to tell anyone what
had caused her nightmares . . . never to describe the long
struggle to overcome them.

"More coffee, Damon?" Sophie's voice was calm,
unruffled.

Damon held out his cup, his expression unreadable.

"Tell me about your work, Xenobia." Mrs. Aristides
poured more tea for Zen.

"I'm an assistant designer with Deirdre Cable, of Cable Knits Limited, Dublin. Occasionally I design suits
or dresses, but mostly I design fabric. I work closely
with the weavers. I love my job, and I make a good
living for David and myself." She took a deep breath.
"I'm on leave for three months."

"You haven't married."

"No."

"Damon is getting married, next year perhaps, to a
Melissa Harewell."

"That name doesn't sound Greek," Zen snapped, then
bit her lip.

Damon glared at her. "Lissa's bloodlines do not concern me, or should they you," he said. "Her family has
been in this country since the Pilgrims."

"Ah...you mean she's descended from the thieves and reprobates who first settled this country."

Damon rounded on her. "You're twisting my words, Zen."

"It's strange that I didn't see her picture in the *New York Times*," Zen went on, seemingly unperturbed. "I get it in Dublin." She took a sip of tea.

"We haven't formally announced it yet." Damon grimaced at his mother, who placidly dropped two lumps of sugar into his coffee. "Mother, I never take sugar."

"Perhaps she thinks you need to add something sweet to your system," Zen shot at him.

"You haven't changed, Zen," he accused her. "Still the same sharp tongue you've always had." He took a sip of coffee and choked. "Mother, I'd like another cup."

"Of course."

Zen set down her tea. "I think I'll go up and see how David is."

"No need," Sophie said swiftly. "Do tell me about the man you intend to marry."

"Mother, Zen never said she was marrying," Damon said coldly.

"I think it would be good for her to marry. It's difficult to raise a boy alone. Of course once *you* are married, you will be in a position to take both boys."

"Never!" Zen surged to her feet. "If you think I would let you take David from me—"

"I've never said anything like—" Damon protested.

"Then why did your mother—"

Damon jumped to his feet as well. "My mother and I have never discussed taking David from you."

"You can't. Don't forget that. That was all thrashed out in court three years ago when I obtained permission to take him to Ireland." Zen faced him, arms akimbo, her eyes snapping fire at him.

"Why do you keep reading things into what I say?" Damon demanded.

"Because I know you, and I'm going to be watching you all the time. Seamus—"

"Don't bring his name into it!"

"Stop shouting! You sound like a dockworker." Zen shook her fist in his face as his mother's hand hovered delicately over the cookie tray.

"And you sound like an Irish washerwoman."

"Don't you make fun of the Irish," Zen shouted, furious.

"I wasn't making fun of the Irish; I was drawing an analogy," Damon explained in a low roar as his mother dabbed calmly at her lips with a napkin.

"Bushwaugh!" Zen riposted.

Sophie looked up with mild curiosity. "Is that an Irish curseword?" she asked.

"No!" Damon and Zen shouted together, looking at her, then back at each other.

"Oh," said Sophie.

Damon took a deep breath, drawing Zen's eyes to his breadth of shoulder. "We invited you here so that the boys would have a chance to get acquainted. Isn't that right, Mother?"

"Hmm? Oh, yes. I think it would be a fine idea for Xenobia to see how well the two boys would fit into the life you and Melissa are planning." She finished on a sigh, putting a tiny, cherry-filled crepe into her mouth and closing her eyes in enjoyment.

"Mother!" Damon stared at her.

"I am not letting you have David! I would not have come here if I'd known I would be subjected to this kind of aggravation." Zen took a deep breath to continue, but Damon interrupted.

"Aggravation!" he stormed. "What do you call what you did to me at the airport today?"

"Oh? What was that?" Sophie asked, stirring her Turkish coffee in small, precise circles.

"She struck me . . . in the stomach," Damon muttered, not taking his eyes from Zen.

"Really?" Sophie's narrow mouth twitched once, as though she were stifling a smile.

"It was a little lower than that, I think. In the groin, perhaps?" Zen clarified with great relish, glancing at his mother. "Anyway, it was an accident." She looked back at Damon. "I told you that." She lifted her chin defiantly.

"Accident? Bull! I see now that you deliberately tried to incapacitate me."

"Only in the bedroom," Zen riposted, then felt her face flush with embarrassment as she remembered his mother's presence.

But Sophie was busy studying the cookie tray and seemed not to have heard.

"It will be a cold day in hell when you can put me out of commission in bed," Damon said. His eyes had a coal-hard sheen that seemed to pierce to her inner core and spark an inexplicable emotion.

"Who cares what you do in . . . anywhere!" Zen cried.

They stood staring at each other, the strength of their antipathy . . . and some other feeling . . . making them oblivious to everything but each other.

"You are a guest in my house, and as such you will be treated with respect and courtesy."

"Just as you would treat the family goat on the island of Keros?" Zen shot back.

"Stop acting as though we were born in Greece. You were born here, just as I was." Damon struggled visibly to control his temper.

"I was born in Selkirk, New York, not on Long Island," Zen pointed out childishly.

"Oh, I don't think you've changed much," Sophie said into the sudden silence. "Xenobia still has that turned-up nose, which is so un-Greek."

"Many people prefer a turned-up nose," Damon said.

"Not Greeks." His mother shrugged.

"You do not speak for all Greeks," her son thundered. "Besides, this is the United States."

"I am pleased, my son, that your geography lessons were not wasted on you."

Damon's teeth snapped together as he studied his mother, baffled anger twisting his classic features.

"And, of course, Xenobia's endearing habit of attacking you at every turn—"

"She doesn't do that."

"I don't do that."

Damon and Zen spoke at the same time.

Sophie shrugged. "Well, how would you describe that little scene when she scratched your cheek, then fell into your lap with her skirt riding up to her thighs? I cannot say I approve." She selected another sweet.

"It was an accident," Damon growled.

Suddenly Zen had had enough. "Excuse me. I think I'll go to my room," she said through clenched teeth. "I assume it's the same one I had before." She stalked out of the living room before either Damon or Sophie could answer.

Chapter 2

IT WOULD HAVE been an exaggeration to say that the Aristides' home was in a state of siege, but in the days that followed Zen found the atmosphere distinctly unfriendly—except where the two boys were concerned.

Not only had they become friends but David, who had never been interested in anything but games, was trying hard to learn Greek; and Daniel, who, as he told Zen, had never cared for sports, was discovering he had a natural ability at soccer.

The next afternoon, Zen was playing goalie as the boys brought the soccer ball down the field toward the net that Yanos had constructed for them. The ground was damp from a morning drizzle, and the grass was slippery. As the ball sped toward Zen, she dived to repel it, but suddenly she lost her footing and crashed against the uprights holding the net.

She stood up slowly, feeling a little shaken and cradling her left arm, where she knew a bruise would show the next day. Suddenly she was swung up into powerful arms.

Her senses reeled. Her head bounced against a hard shoulder as her rescuer began running for the house. "Damon! Damon, stop it. Put me down. I'm not hurt."

He slowed to a stop, the boys puffing up behind him, but he didn't release her. His eyes swept intently over her, seeming to check every pore.

"Is Aunt Zeno hurt, Uncle Damon?" Daniel asked anxiously.

"Naw," David answered. "Aunt Zeno doesn't get hurt, do you?" David looked up at his aunt as she lay cradled in Damon's arms.

"No, of course I don't. Damon, you can put me down now." She pushed against his steellike body.

"Do you like being carried, Aunt Zeno?" David frowned up at her. "When I grow up, I can carry you, too."

"I wouldn't want you to, dear." She smiled down at the boy, then looked up at Damon. "Will you put me down?" she insisted. She glanced toward the house and groaned as Sophie stepped onto the terrace, watching them.

"Nonna," Daniel called, "Aunt Zeno fell."

"She's always falling...or something," Sophie agreed calmly.

"Ohh!" Zen pushed against Damon with all her strength. "I can walk, you big oaf," she snapped. His eyes riveted on hers, he let her legs drop to the ground, but he continued to hold her close with one arm.

"You were shaken in the fall. I saw it," Damon insisted, staring tenderly down at her. "I was coming up the drive in my car."

Sophie who was strolling toward them, heard his comment. "And you drove your car over my best rambling roses, too." She pointed disdainfully toward the Ferrari, which was parked in the middle of the rose bed. "Usually she manages to get you, Damon, my son, but this time she got my roses." Sophie glanced placidly at the boys, who were watching the adults. "You must be hungry, boys. Come inside. Lona has cool drinks for you." She shepherded them in front of her, not looking back.

"Your mother has a way of twisting reality to suit her own purposes," Zen observed.

Damon shrugged. "She may not be tactful, but she is kind."

"Kind of what? Kind of nasty? Kind of spiteful? She never stops making remarks about... about my..."

"Clumsiness?" Damon suggested.

Zen lifted her chin defiantly. "Now, listen here, Damon Aristides. I'll have you know that I never had the least trouble when I was living in Ireland."

"I wonder why that is," he mused, his eyes making an intent study of her hair. "Do you know your hair is fiery in the sunlight?"

"I never had the least problem hitting people, falling on... My hair?" She lifted a hand to her head, feeling how the waves had tightened into ringlets. "I'm a mess. I'd better take a shower." The quaver in her voice annoyed her.

"You should," Damon agreed, taking her arm and holding it close to him. "I'll go with you. I want to shower and change, too."

As they entered the door at the back of the house Damon curved his arm around her waist and kept it there as he led her through the kitchen, where he spoke to Lona and a heavy woman he called Maria. "Here." He opened a door, showing Zen a back stairway.

She could feel him behind her as they climbed the stairs, almost as though his arm were still around her. All at once, with blinding clarity, she remembered herself as the young woman who had sought the touch of Damon Aristides, who wasn't happy unless his strong hands were caressing and arousing her to fierce intensity. Sucking in her breath, she began taking the stairs two at a time.

"Easy... take it easy, Zen." His warm breath tickled her neck as a strong arm clasped around her middle.

"I don't need help." She tugged at his fingers, finally freeing herself as they reached the upstairs hall that led to the wing where the boys' rooms and hers were located.

Damon's apartment was reached through double doors that led to his private corridor. His was the largest section, of the house and totally separate from the sleeping quarters of the rest of the family and guests.

"What's wrong with you now?" He rubbed the back of his hand, his eyes narrowing on her. "You're like an emotional chameleon. I never know what mood you'll be in next."

"Then ignore me." She whirled away from him, her emotions in chaos. But an iron hand reached out, and Damon pulled her back against him, his two hands coming up and around to cup her breasts, his mouth lowering to her neck and nibbling there.

"Damn you, Zen," he muttered, his right hand leaving her breast to raise her chin. He found her mouth, and his tongue penetrated to tease hers and touch the inside of her lips before he took full, demanding possession. His other hand slid, palm flat, fingers spread, to the small of her back and pressed her intimately against him. "Damn you, Zen," he repeated.

He released her abruptly, and she staggered, disoriented. Then he was striding toward the double doors, calling over his shoulder, "Melissa is coming to dinner tonight. She wants to meet David." The doors slammed behind him, the sound echoing down the oak-paneled hall, freezing Zen in place.

"That . . . that . . . lecher!" She stood immobilized, rubbing her mouth, not able to still the tremors that wracked her body. "If he touches me again, I'll . . ." Drawing in a shaky breath, she turned blindly toward her room.

Her movements were stiff as she took off her clothes and selected fresh underthings to bring into the bathroom. As she stood under the shower spray, lathering her body and shampooing her hair, she considered ingenious ways of taking care of Damon Aristides.

She was sitting in front of her mirror putting on her makeup when she decided to weight him with granite and drop him in Long Island Sound.

"Why are you smiling, Aunt Zeno?" David asked from the doorway. She looked up to see Daniel at his side.

Zen turned on the vanity bench, her head still wrapped in a towel, and smiled at the two boys who were so alike yet so different. "I must have been thinking of you two if I was smiling. How did Lona manage to get you both dressed so fine?" Zen felt a twinge of annoyance at the worsted fabric of the boys' identical suits, but she pushed the emotion away. The pale blue tweed set off their bronzed skin and dark eyes. And if it gave Sophie pleasure to shop for them, Zen didn't have the heart to criticize her extravagance.

David looked down at himself, then grimaced at his aunt. "Lona promised Dan and me two of the éclairs that Maria's making for dessert tonight." Zen laughed, and David looked puzzled. Then he frowned. "Uncle Damon says we're not to play rough with you. Did we hurt you, Aunt Zeno?"

At the mention of Damon, Zen's body tensed. The man was diabolical! Even here in her own room he managed to assert himself.

"You didn't hurt me," she assured David. "I enjoy playing soccer with you. I've told you that many times. Now come over here, the two of you." She held out her arms.

David galloped over, but Daniel held back shyly, his tentative smile making Zen's eyes sting with the memory of her sister. She hugged both boys to her, then told them they could play on her bed while she got dressed.

She watched them for a moment as Daniel pulled out cards and shuffled them dexterously, then dealt the deck for crazy eights, which he had taught David. Soon they were completely absorbed in the game.

In her dressing room, Zen put on the straight, long, cream-colored skirt she had selected. With it she wore a lightweight sea-green wool sweater and medium-heeled pumps of sea-green kid. She chose a seed-pearl anklet, pearl drop earrings, and the pearl pinkie ring that had belonged to her mother.

"I'm almost ready," Zen called to the boys as she entered the bedroom, checking to see that the posts on her earrings were tight.

She stopped in midstream when she saw Damon seated on her chaise longue, his shoeless feet propped up on the ottoman, her jewelry box in his lap. "Where are your shoes? Where are the boys? And what are you doing with my jewel case?" she demanded, wishing her voice were stronger.

Damon pointed to the door. "My shoes are there. The boys have joined their grandmother downstairs, and I wanted to see if you had any of Eleni's jewelry."

Zen stalked across the room and removed her case from his lap, her anger rising close to the boiling point. "What I have or don't have is none of your—"

"I was thinking about you walking barefoot on this fluffy carpet...nice, very nice." Damon crossed his arms on his chest and appraised her thoroughly.

"Stop interrupting. What's nice?" Zen snapped.

"Thinking about you walking barefoot...thinking about your naked body spread out on this carpet."

Zen gasped at his audacity. "Isn't your fiancée waiting downstairs?"

"Melissa and I are not formally engaged. I told you that." Damon settled himself more comfortably in the chair.

"Leave my room." Zen pointed haughtily toward the door, but the gesture had little impact on Damon.

"Do you have the pink sapphires that belonged to Eleni?" Damon asked, ignoring her demand.

"I don't have any of Eleni's jewels." Zen spun around and replaced the jewel case on the dresser. At once, she sensed that Damon had left the chaise and come up behind her.

"What do you mean?" he asked close to her ear. "All Eleni's gems belong to you. She had no daughter. Are you saying that her jewelry was never sent to you?"

"Nothing."

"Hmm. I'll ask my mother."

"I'm sure much of what Eleni had belonged to the Aristides family, and your mother would want it to stay in the family."

Damon's dark brows met over his nose, and his expression tightened. "I'm the executor of the estate. I will say who gets what."

Zen was about to respond when the muscle jumping at the corner of his mouth warned her to say nothing. She didn't want to encourage an argument so close to dinnertime.

"Come along. If we're going to join the others for a drink, we should go down now." He took Zen's arm under his, threading his fingers through hers with an intimacy that surprised her. When she tried to pull free, he tightened his hold and urged her toward the door.

"Who?" Zen cleared her throat and tried again. "Who's coming to dinner besides your fiancée?"

"I told you that Melissa and I are not formally engaged." He shot the words at her, making her blink.

"So you did." Damn the man! Again Zen tried to free herself. Again Damon tightened his hold.

"Pythagoras Telos, my mother's old friend from Greece, has been staying in this country for some time now, checking into his widespread business interests here. He will be staying with us for a while, and of course he will be at dinner." Damon paused at the head of the stairs. "According to my mother, Thag, as he prefers to be called, was once a suitor for your mother's hand. He's a rich man with homes in California as well as in Greece and London."

Zen stared at him in surprise. "What are you saying? That this man whom I never heard of was once my mother's boyfriend? How is it I've never heard his name mentioned?" Zen tried to picture a burly, tall Greek standing next to her statuesque mother.

Damon urged her down the stairs without answering her question. "Melissa's aunt, Brenda Waite, will be joining us, as will another of my mother's friends from her school days in England, Maud Wills."

"Delightful gathering," Zen murmured as they reached the last steps, "but shouldn't we hurry just a bit?"

"Hurrying is very bad for the digestion," Damon said, looking down at her with a smile that seemed to illuminate the dim room.

Zen felt as though her insides had turned to custard. She struggled to find something cool and sophisticated to say. "Really?" she managed.

"Yes." He stepped onto the marble foyer, then turned to face her, not letting her take the last step down. They were almost eye to eye, but still Damon was taller. "It's ridiculous for a tall man to be involved with a small woman," he said as if to himself.

"Yes, isn't it?" Zen agreed sarcastically.

"Did I tell you that you look glorious in that outfit?" He bent toward her, his nostrils flaring as he took in her perfume. "Even though you're small, you have the loveliest breasts." His hand wandered around her waist and down her backside. "Not to mention the loveliest derriere I've ever seen."

"Do . . . do you realize that someone could come out of the living room and see us?" Zen's voice was husky.

Damon leaned away from her, his eyes dark and shining. "Why did you leave me?"

Astounded, she stared mutely at him.

"Ah, there you are, Damon," said Sophie, bustling over to them. "I see you've brought Xenobia with you." She hesitated as Damon stepped aside and she caught full view of Zen. "Ah . . . did you design that outfit, Xenobia?"

"I designed the skirt, not the top," she answered, licking suddenly dry lips.

"I see." Sophie looked from her son to Zen. "Well, come along. We mustn't keep dear Lissa waiting."

Zen glanced suspiciously at Sophie but could read nothing in her expression. She nodded and came down the last step, trying to move away from Damon. But he stayed close to her, so that they entered the living room side by side.

Zen paused on the threshold and said a silent prayer of thanks because for once the boys were quiet. They were playing cards on the coffee table.

From the settee rose one of the most perfectly groomed women Zen had ever seen. Her black hair was caught in a bun, and a small smile was fixed on her patrician features. She and Damon were the tallest people in the room, making Zen wonder for a moment who the short, dapper man with black hair was.

"Pythagoras Telos," Damon whispered at her side.

"It can't be," Zen whispered back, trying to keep her smile in place as she moved forward. "You said he was once a boyfriend of my mother's. Mother must have been a foot taller than this man."

Damon chuckled. "Thag Telos is a man of great personality."

"Indeed," Zen managed.

Damon moved from Zen's side toward the brunette vision. "Lissa, this is Xenobia Driscoll, Daniel and David's aunt. Zen, this is Melissa Harewell."

"How do you do, Miss Harewell." Zen held out her hand and felt the cool smoothness of Lissa's soft grip.

"How do you do, Xenobia," Lissa replied in carefully modulated tones. "Dear Mrs. Aristides has told me so much about you that I feel I know you already."

"And you haven't armed yourself?" Zen smiled to soften her words and reached for a glass of champagne from a nearby tray.

"Pardon me?" Lissa's deep blue eyes widened in perplexity.

Sophie didn't look up from her position behind the silver tray of canapés where she was alternately feeding the boys and asking them questions about the card game.

"Zen," Damon warned. He walked to Lissa's side and kissed the cheek she proffered. "Zen loves to joke," he explained.

"Yes, she does," David surprised everyone by interjecting. "Once Seamus had a party where everyone had to dress like people from books." He paused to beam at his interested grandmother, his uncle, and the other adults. Knowing what was coming, Zen wanted to drop through the floor. "I was Grumpy," David explained, "one of the Seven Dwarfs. Aunt Zeno was Lady Godawful."

"Does he mean Lady Godiva?" Lissa inquired politely.

"I believe he does," Sophie replied smiling. "Ah... it's good for a child to be grounded in the classics."

"Mother," Damon snarled, staring at Zen, a gray cast to his features making them look as though they'd been sculpted in concrete. Anger radiated from every line of his taut body.

"I wore a body stocking," Zen mumbled, not looking at Damon, though she could feel his eyes burning into her.

"Are you ill, Damon?" Lissa asked kindly.

"Sick, yes." His eyes were still riveted on Zen. "You went to a party like that?" He seemed to be grinding out each syllable.

"Isn't it diverting?" Lissa said with pleasure. "Where did you get the horse?"

"Aunt Zeno whitewashed the donkey that Mr. Morphy uses to pull his knife-grinder's cart," David announced clearly.

"How fitting!" Damon growled. "An ass on an ass."

Lissa tittered. "Oh, Damon, you have such a sense of humor."

Zen's hand closed tightly around her glass. "Yes, doesn't he?"

"I do feel, Xenobia, that there is much you could learn about mothering a child," Lissa said. "How to set a good example, to begin with." She smiled.

Zen ground her teeth.

"And," the redoubtable Lissa continued, "I highly disapprove of cardplaying. Cards teach children to gamble."

Zen drew herself up to her full five feet two inches, prepared to do battle for her twins. "Cardplaying is an excellent way to teach a youngster mathematics."

"How droll." Lissa sighed, her doelike eyes shifting to Damon. "No one denies that the Irish are droll, but poor David needs help with pronunciation. I'm sure I can help with that, and with his arithmetic."

"I'll have you know that people in some sections of Ireland are said to make the most perfect use of the English language." Zen took a deep breath. "And you know what you can do with—"

"I think dinner is being served." Damon stepped forward and took Lissa's arm, turning her toward the door.

"Come, boys," Sophie said. She sailed serenely out of the room, the boys and other guests trailing after her, leaving a seething Zen standing furious and alone.

Chapter 3

DINNER DID NOT go well for Zen. If the boys hadn't been there, she would have left the table. She found it most difficult to listen as Lissa continued to explain how to raise two boys who, unfortunately, happened to be twins.

"Of course, everyone knows that one twin is always dominant." Lissa sighed as she looked at David and Daniel, who smiled back at her, then continued eating. "It would be a happier situation if Daniel were the dominant one, even though neither boy seems to have the superior intelligence of my nephew Leonard."

"Now just a minute . . ." Zen struggled to control her temper.

"The boys do as well as their father and uncle did at this age, perhaps a little better." Sophie hastened to interject, smiling at Lissa.

Zen took a forkful of moussaka and gasped as the hot food burned her mouth. She grabbed her water glass and took long swallows.

"They seem to have strange eating habits in Ireland, too," Lissa mused.

"I like Ireland." David scowled. "Robbie lives there."

"Of course, dear. We all like primitive places until we are older."

"We do?" David looked puzzled, then glanced at his aunt. "Why is your face so red, Aunt Zeno? Is the food burning your mouth again?"

"Something is burning me." Zen glared.

When Lona came for the boys a few minutes later, Zen excused herself. "I always tell David and Daniel a story before bedtime," she explained.

"That's a good practice when they are very young," Lissa pronounced brightly, but she held up a cautioning finger. "I do think, however, that at this age, when they are almost ready for boarding school—"

"They are seven years old!" Zen expostulated.

"Ah...true...but the sooner they have a strong scholastic environment—"

"I'll see you in—"

"I think it well for you to see to the boys," Pythagoras Telos interrupted. He had been silent during most of dinner, but now he took Zen's arm in a surprisingly strong clasp and led her into the hall, where he gave her a courtly bow, his eyes following after the twins as they and Lona went up the stairs. "How my Maria would have loved those boys," he said softly.

"My mother?" Zen whispered, feeling much subdued.

"Yes, your mother. I loved her dearly, even after she married Patrick Driscoll." He sighed wistfully.

Zen began to see the older man with new eyes. "My mother was a lucky woman to have two such fine men love her."

Pythagoras Telos regarded her thoughtfully. "You are her child. Oh, not outwardly, but in many ways I see my Maria." He turned on one well-shod foot and returned to the dining room.

Zen went upstairs and changed into jeans and a cotton shirt. Bathing the twins was like an Olympic competition to see who would get wetter—the boys, Lona, or herself. But Zen delighted in the boys' antics.

By the time they were in their beds waiting for their uncle and grandmother to come and say good night, Zen was glad to escape to her room and change again, into dry clothes. Feeling restless, she chose dove gray sweat pants and a sweat shirt. She would jog around the yard before going to bed.

When she stepped outside, she saw that Damon's car was missing. She guessed that he had taken Melissa Harewell home.

The night was so beautiful with the moon rising over the water. Zen paused to admire the scene, then climbed the rickety steps of a gazebo built on a point of land near the water.

Weeds and bracken surrounded the building, whose disrepair contrasted sharply with the well-tended main house and grounds.

Zen welcomed the feeling of solitude and neglect. She was reminded of her untenable position in the Aristides household. She would never give the twins over to the manicured, repressive hands of Melissa Harewell. Boarding school for David and Daniel? Never! She would see Damon in hell first!

"So this is where you are." The deep voice of the man she'd been thinking about, coming out of the pitch darkness, shocked her out of her reverie and made her jump in surprise.

She whirled to face him and stumbled into a network of cobwebs. "Aaagh! Oh, I hate this stuff. It's in my mouth, my eyebrows. Damn you, Damon, must you move like a fox?" She flailed her hands in a futile attempt to escape the sticky webs.

"Here, let me help you." Damon vaulted over the railing with ease and pulled Zen into his arms. He wiped the sticky silk from her face and form with a handkerchief he pulled from his pocket. "There, is that better?"

She nodded. "Yes, thank you, most of it's gone. That's one of the things I hated most about camping—cobwebs . . . and burdocks. I always had them on my clothes.

The more I picked them off, the more they got stuck on me."

"I hated the mosquitoes and the blackflies," Damon said.

"Blackflies!" Zen exclaimed, closing her eyes. "I'd forgotten about them. Daddy used to take us to his cabin on Tupper Lake in the Adirondacks, and he would paint, not seeming to notice when the blackflies started to swarm around him. How they stung!"

"And the deerflies," Damon added.

"Yes! Oh, those horrid flies that would follow when you went to the farm for milk and eggs. Eleni would scream bloody murder. She always hated them worst of all." Zen started to laugh, not even noticing when her laughter turned to sobs. Her return to Long Island had forced her to recall painful memories she'd gone to Ireland to forget.

Damon drew her gently into his arms, caressing her hair and back. "You still miss her, don't you?" he said softly.

Zen gulped and nodded, hardly realizing that her face was pressed against his chest. "It was so awful losing her so soon after my mother and father. If it hadn't been for David, I . . . I don't know what I would have done."

"But why couldn't you turn to me?" Damon whispered in an anguished voice, running his hands up and down her arms in a tender message.

Zen looked up, aware all at once of how her blood seemed to be pounding out of rhythm. She tried to push away from him. "No, I couldn't do that." She gasped for air, feeling as though she had just climbed a mountain, trying to ignore the warmth of his closeness.

"Zen, listen to me. I know you hated what Lissa said tonight about sending the boys to boarding school."

"Never."

"Will you listen?" Damon's voice, harsh all at once, caught Zen's full attention. "You don't have to do anything you don't want to do with either David or Daniel.

You can decide how the boys are raised. You can be
their mother."

She looked at him without understanding.

"Marry me . . . and you'll have both boys," Damon
said in a choked whisper.

Be Damon's wife? Be with him always?

For another moment Zen didn't move—hope, fear,
delight, and desire all whirling inside her. Then fury
erupted. "And what will you do with your other wife,
Melissa? Put her on hold? Or will you put me on hold
and tend her? No, damn you, no!"

Finding strength she didn't know she possessed, Zen
pushed Damon, catching him off guard. He staggered
backward, trying to maintain his balance. When he hit
the railing, it looked as if he would regain his footing.
But the rotted wood of the gazebo gave way with a tearing
crash, sending Damon and the railing down into the
shrubbery.

Zen stood aghast as he began thrashing in the bushes,
trying to stand up. "Oh, my God! How did that happen?
I'm sorry, Damon. What have I done!"

Pain and love raging within her, Zen knew she couldn't
face Damon's wrath. Feeling like the greatest coward
who had ever lived, she turned and ran from him. He
called her name over and over again, but she kept running.

She didn't stop until she was in her room. She tore
off her clothes and stepped under the shower, lathering
her body with vicious strokes that reddened her skin.
"What the blazes does he think he's doing?" she demanded out loud as she stood at the mirror minutes later,
pulling a comb through her hair. "Setting up an At Home
Concubine Bureau, is he? Damn him to hell! He won't
use me."

Furious, she stalked naked into her bedroom, still
mumbling to herself, her body slippery with the lotion
she had just rubbed over it.

A knock sounded, and the door swung open. Damon
entered. "Zen, if you would just listen to me, calm

down—" He saw her and stopped short, one hand raised defensively, bracken still clinging to his clothes. The angry look on his face softened to one of sensual shock as his eyes assessed her.

Zen's temper flared anew. "Get out of here!" Making no move to cover herself, she reached for a figurine on a side table and threw it against the wall with all her might.

The statue grazed the side of Damon's head, making him blink, but he didn't take his eyes off her body. "I'm going," he mumbled, "but this isn't the end of it."

"It damn well better be!" Zen watched the door close, her chin trembling with suppressed emotion. "And what's more, I never used to swear like this in Dublin," she added quietly, sniffing.

Feeling thoroughly dispirited, she pulled on a silk wraparound, slipped on soft silk scuffs, and bent to pick up the pieces of the broken figurine.

A knock on the door sent Zen scrambling for another weapon. But at the sound of the voice coming through the door she sighed with relief. "It is I, Lona, Miss Driscoll. Kyrie Damon sent me to clean up the broken china. He said he broke it by accident."

"He did no such thing." Zen rose from her knees and opened the door, facing Lona with arms akimbo. "I broke it. I threw it at him."

Lona nodded, stonefaced.

"He's an aggravator and an instigator," Zen declared hotly.

"As a boy he was always full of mischief," Lona concurred, sweeping up the broken china.

"Mischief! The man is a ... a revolutionary!"

Lona turned on the vacuum cleaner, effectively silencing Zen. Once the rug was clean, she turned off the machine and picked up the plastic bag filled with shards. "Good night, Miss Driscoll," she murmured.

"Good night, Lona."

* * *

Zen didn't sleep well that night. Not even the sweet-smelling sheets soothed her. She tossed and turned until the eastern sky began to lighten.

She rose late in the morning, still disgruntled, feeling lethargic and out of sorts.

She was wrapping a robe around her when her bedroom door crashed open and the boys tumbled in, grinning exuberantly.

"Breakfast time!" David sang out, flinging himself at her. Daniel hung back shyly until Zen pulled him forward. She hugged him fiercely, suddenly overwhelmed with love for them.

Daniel looked up at her, his eyes glinting with mirth. "Lona said we're having pancakes today."

"Are they like the oatcakes Bridie used to make me, Aunt Zeno?" David asked, referring to the woman who had been their housekeeper in the Dublin apartment.

"A little like that, yes," Zen answered. "Why don't you two go downstairs and wait for me in the morning room? Then the three of us can eat together."

"Uncle Damon will be there, too," David told her. "He's staying home today. He's sick . . . but he's eating with us anyway."

Zen paused at the bathroom doorway. "Sick? What's wrong with him?" Her throat tightened.

"He isn't sick, Aunt Zeno. He itches," Daniel explained. Both boys galloped out of the room, leaving Zen with her mouth open, poised to ask another question.

Dismissing her concern, she showered, brushed her teeth, and put on turquoise slacks and a cotton shirt. The slacks were made of a stretchable wool she had designed herself. The shirt was a madras cotton in cream and turquoise. She wore turquoise hand-tooled Turkish slippers.

She went down the stairs wondering if Melissa was coming to breakfast. Was that why Damon was staying home from work? The boys might have assumed he was sick. She geared herself to face the honey-voiced Melissa. Sophie, she was sure, would still be in bed. Mrs.

Aristides rarely rose before eleven o'clock.

As she approached the morning room, Zen heard David's boisterous voice and the quieter responses of his twin.

"Good morning." Expecting to see Lissa, she stretched her mouth into its widest smile. Instead, she saw only Damon. At least he resembled Damon. Zen stared aghast at his red and swollen face. "What happened to you? You look like the Pillsbury Dough Boy."

"Very funny." Damon's mouth was almost lost in his swollen cheeks. "There was poison ivy around the gazebo," he explained.

"Good Lord!" Zen breathed, torn between contrition and amusement.

Damon shot her a warning look. "If you laugh, Xenobia," he said with a calm menace, "I'll toss you in the poison ivy, too."

"Well, you needn't get huffy," she retorted. "It *was* an accident."

He held up one hand. "Don't say that. Ever since you arrived, you've caused one *accident* after another. I'm beginning to wonder if there's something more than that behind the incidents."

Zen put her hands on her hips. "You're not going to sit there and tell me you think I *knew* there was poison ivy..." Catching the boys' solemn gazes, she fell silent. "What I mean is, I'm very sorry you're experiencing...er...such discomfort."

"Thank you," Damon said politely, then winced and began rubbing his back against his chair.

"I don't think you should scratch," Zen said.

"I can't help it," he snapped.

"What's that funny white stuff on your arms, Uncle Damon?" David asked.

"Poison ivy cream," Damon answered tersely.

"Oh." David considered for a moment before adding, "Daniel said that Lona says it will last two weeks. Will it?"

"Maybe." Damon stared at Zen as she struggled to

stifle a giggle. She coughed into her napkin and took a sip of orange juice.

"Aunt Zeno had a very bad rash once," David said thoughtfully.

Oh, no, not that story! "David, I don't think your uncle is interested in hearing about that," Zen suggested nervously.

Damon regarded her with new interest. "Actually, I'd love to hear about it," he assured the boy.

"Well, the doctor told Aunt Zen that if her tests didn't come out right she would have to go to the health place . . . I think. But she didn't, did you, Aunt Zeno?"

"No, dear." Zen smiled with effort as she remembered the awful rash she had picked up . . . and how the doctor had suggested she might have contracted a recurrent illness from recent sexual contact. The doctor had made her so angry by suggesting such a thing that she had shouted imprecations and left in a huff. The doctor had called back two days later with the results of the test—and to apologize. The rash had been caused by an allergic reaction to some untreated fabric.

Damon waited until the boys were playing games with their alphabet cereal before he leaned forward and whispered, "And did the rash come back, Zen?"

"You have a low-class mind," she accused him.

"How much did you pay the medical people to falsify the results of the test?"

She glared at him, furious at his insinuations. It was on the tip of her tongue to say that, if she had contracted such a disease, she must have picked it up from him, the only man with whom she had ever been intimate in her life. But she bit her lip, knowing he wouldn't believe her.

She considered his present mood. Damon was apt to use any excuse to cross swords with her, but he rarely resorted to such crass badinage. The poison ivy must be driving him wild.

Tamping down her temper, she poured herself a cup of coffee.

Later that day she took the boys down to the Sound. Though it was warm for late April, the water was icy cold. David and Daniel skipped stones, trying hard to outshoot Zen and crowing with delight when they succeeded.

"Is that a dog swimming out there, Aunt Zeno?" Daniel pointed to a dark object bobbing on the cold waves.

Zen held up a hand to shade her eyes and stared, then nodded slowly. "Yes...and he looks tired. What could he be doing out there in such cold water?"

"Maybe he fell off a ship, Aunt Zeno." David said in awed tones. "C'mon, doggy, c'mon," he shouted. Daniel immediately joined in.

"Boys, we don't know who this dog belongs to. Perhaps a neighbor..." Zen's voice trailed off as she watched the animal struggle valiantly against the current. "C'mon, dog, c'mon. You can do it." She looked around for a boat or something with which to help the animal.

"Aunt Zeno, there's a life ring in the boat house that Uncle Damon hangs—"

"Good boy," Zen interrupted Daniel. She hurried to the boat house, calling to the boys to stay where they were.

It took mere minutes for Zen to find the ring hanging on the wall, precious seconds to run back to where David was calling to the dog through his cupped hands, urging it to shore.

Praying she could remember how her father had taught her to throw a ring, Zen began to whirl it over her head in slow circles. She twirled it in wider arcs, then let go. The ring sailed out over the water but fell far short of the dog.

Both boys groaned.

"Try again, Aunt Zeno," David urged anxiously.

"What the hell's going on here?" Damon demanded, coming up behind them. They turned gratefully to him.

Zen vaguely noticed that his poison ivy seemed to be getting worse. "The dog," she panted, pointing out over the water.

Damon followed the direction of her gesture, squinting against the sun. "Poor devil's flagging," he muttered. He grabbed the ring from Zen, coiled the rope, and flung it in a high arc. The ring landed directly in front of the dog. "Damn smart animal," he muttered as the dog lunged at the ring and grasped it with strong jaws. Damon began pulling slowly and steadily, being careful not to swamp the dog and force him to release his hold.

When the dog reached shallow water, Zen rushed forward, but Damon stopped her, pushing the rope into her hands and entering the water himself. He grimaced at the frigid cold.

"He could be dangerous," Damon explained, "even though he looks too tired to be a threat to anyone." As if sensing imminent rescue, the animal fixed hope-filled eyes on him.

The water reached Damon's chest when he was finally able to grab the dog by the neck and pull him close. Moments later, both man and dog reached land safely.

"Will he die, Uncle Damon?" David asked anxiously as the exhausted animal lay on his side, his body heaving.

Zen saw Damon shiver, and her concern deepened. "Damon, you mustn't stay here. You're soaked. I'll take care of the dog. You go inside and change." She gave him a slight push.

"We'll all go back to the house. Leave the ring there, Zen. I'll have Yanos see to it." Damon lifted the dog into his arms and carried him, the boys asking questions and racing around him. Zen trailed behind, muttering to herself. "See if I care if you get pneumonia on top of poison ivy. I suppose you'll blame this on me, too."

"Hurry up, Aunt Zeno. Uncle Damon says we have to get the dog warm." Daniel glanced back at her with a worried frown.

They took the dog to the barnlike building in back of the house where the Aristides automobiles and bicycles were kept. The taciturn Yanos and his wife Maria lived in an apartment on the second floor.

Damon carried the dog to the workroom in the back of the carriage house, where tools of every description hung on the walls. It was a good-sized rectangular room with a potbellied stove set on a brick foundation in the center. "Zen, there are clean drop cloths in that cupboard." Damon nodded toward ceiling-to-floor doors against one wall.

Zen rushed to get the cloths and spread them on the cement floor near the stove, where Damon placed the dog. She began drying the animal with other cloths she found on the shelves. "Damon, go get dressed," she urged.

He nodded. "I'll go take a shower."

The boys helped Zen rub the heavy dog dry.

"Why are his eyes closed?" Daniel asked in hushed tones.

"He's so tired, dear." Zen tried to sound reassuring, but she sensed the dog was in poor shape.

"What's all this?" Yanos asked entering the carriage house. "Kyrie Damon tells me that this creature has come a long way. I will give him some of my herbs, and they will give him strength."

"You will?" both boys chorused, looking at Yanos, their eyes brimming with hope.

"Yes, I will do that. In fact, I will take him to the stable where I keep the tonics for the horses. Soon he will be fine."

It was hours later before Zen was able to convince the boys to return to the house with her. "After all, you've missed your lunch. You must be hungry. Dinner will be in an hour or so. Perhaps we can have some snacks first."

David thrust his jaw out. "I want to take care of the dog. I'll eat down here."

"Me, too," Daniel agreed.

"If you interfere with what Yanos is doing with the dog, he won't have as good a chance of getting well," Zen told them.

Yanos nodded in agreement and assured the boys that they could come down to the barn and visit the dog when they had eaten. Finally they took Zen's hand and went with her to the house.

"He's big, isn't he, Aunt Zeno," Daniel said. "I've

never seen a dog with curly brown hair before."

"I'm not sure, but I think he might be a Chesapeake Bay retriever." Zen paused. "When I was in college I worked for a vet, and he had big charts on the wall with pictures of dogs. This one looks like one of the retrievers."

"I'll call him Curly," David decided.

"I'll call him Curly, too," Daniel echoed.

"The dog may have an owner," Zen warned them, even though she had seen no collar.

Dinner that evening was a noisy affair. The boys related the story of Curly's rescue over and over again, from the salad through the dessert. Since they had already told Sophie and Pythagoras most of the story during the cocktail hour, as they devoured apples and oranges to appease their hunger, Zen was sure Sophie must be growing irritated.

But she replied patiently to all their observations. "I see," she said when the boys told her the dog had no collar.

"He could sleep in the house...maybe," David offered.

"David," Zen remonstrated.

"In our bedroom," Daniel suggested, beaming.

Damon had the last word. "Let's see if Yanos can make him well first. And then we'll see if he's a good dog, and not a rogue."

"He is a good dog." David scowled.

"Yes, he is," parroted his twin.

"Yanos knows all about animals," Thag commented. "I'm sure he will be able to tell us much about the dog." He smiled at the boys. "Every dog needs a boy, I think."

"No, my friend, every boy needs a dog," Sophie amended.

"Either way is good," David assured his grandmother, making her smile.

Zen looked at Sophie Aristides, stunned by the doting expression on her face as she regarded the twins. Zen

cleared her throat to reprimand David for assuming that
he could bring the dog into the house, when Sophie
surprised her further by saying, "When the dog is well,
we will see where in the house he can sleep." She smiled
serenely as the boys whooped with glee.

After dinner, Thag and Sophie accompanied the boys
to the stable to check on the progress of their patient.

Zen was pleasantly surprised when the huge brown
head rose from the bed of cloths and the thick tail wagged
once. "He does look better," she whispered to Damon,
who was standing next to her.

He nodded. "But I don't think we'll say too much to
the boys about keeping him until I run an ad to see if he
belongs to someone."

Zen nodded, watching Daniel and David. "No, wait,"
she admonished them when they tried to mover closer,
concerned for their safety.

Yanos appeared with a bottle of dark liquid and a
chamois cloth. "I'm going to rub him down with lini-
ment. His muscles must be sore."

The two boys watched with absorbed concentration
as Yanos brought the wet cloth down the dog's legs.

"He's a good one, Kyrie." Yanos looked up at Damon.
"He knows that I try to help him, and he is still. Even
when I give him his food, he lets me touch his dish while
he eats. I think the boys can touch him."

"Damon." Zen gripped his arm.

"It's all right, Zen. I'll watch them. Come here, you
two." Damon squatted down near the dog's head, talking
quietly to the animal, who watched him soulfully, then
gazed at David and Daniel as they moved to touch him.
The dog's eyes closed once; then he pushed his head at
the boys' hands, startling them, making them laugh
breathlessly.

"Look at me, Aunt Zen," Daniel called. "Do you want
to pet him, too?"

The boys weren't satisfied until both Thag and Sophie
had also bent to stroke the dog.

Finally Zen was able to urge them back to the house,

the two of them chattering all the way through the kitchen and up the back stairs to their room.

It was past ten o'clock by the time Zen had returned to her own room and prepared for bed. She intended to read before going to sleep.

A noise out in the hall caught her attention. Thinking the boys might be sneaking outside to see the dog, she opened the door quietly. Seeing nothing, she checked on the boys and found them sleeping. She was on her way back to her room when she noticed that the double doors leading to Damon's suite were open. A light shone from the interior.

She hesitated, but finally decided to go to bed. Then she heard a bump and a muttered imprecation. She paused, peering down the corridor. She knocked and waited. When no one replied, she knocked again, then tiptoed down the hallway and entered a spacious foyer. The living room was on her left and a small office or library on her right. Directly in front of her was a stairway leading to a balcony that overlooked the living room and foyer. She stopped there when she heard more bumping sounds and then a curse. The noise was coming from upstairs.

"Damon? Damon, are you all right?" She stopped at the foot of the stairs, looking up, her hand on the banister.

"Who is it?" he demanded striding from the room onto the balcony, naked except for a towel wrapped around his middle. He scratched with both hands at the reddened welts on his chest.

"Don't itch," Zen said, going up the steps, her eyes riveted on his male form, his breadth of shoulder, the silken ripple of muscle across his chest, the narrow black hair that . . . She shook her head and repeated, "Don't itch."

"I damn well can't help it," Damon barked down at her, scowling fiercely.

"Here," Zen gathered her silk robe in one hand and hurried up the rest of the stairs. She followed him into his room, unable to take her eyes from his back. "Let me put some lotion on you," she offered.

"Not yet. I'm going to take a baking soda bath first.
Dammit, this itching is driving me mad." He scratched
his shoulders, grimacing at Zen, then disappeared into
the bathroom. "The tub will run over," he mumbled.

Zen heard a splash and a groan, then more cursing.
She took a deep breath. "Damon, can I help?" Taking
her courage in both hands, she walked into the room.

For a moment she was struck mute by the dimly lit
interior. "Glory," she breathed. "Trust you to have a real
Roman bath. This is the biggest bathroom I've ever seen.
Lord, a sauna . . . hot tub . . . whirlpool bath . . . and all in
peach-colored tile." Zen stared up at the mirrored ceiling,
which hadn't clouded over in the steamy room.

"Salmon color." Damon, lying up to his chest in hot
water, opened one eye to glare at her. "Not peach, salmon.
Are you color-blind?"

"I'm not color-blind. Are you? God, what a testi-
monial to old movies." Zen chuckled, then sobered immediately when her eyes fell on Damon. She could see
very little of him in the dim light, but just the thought
that he was naked left her feeling weak in the knees.

"If you came in my bath just to insult my color
scheme . . . owww!" He closed his eyes and began rubbing his back against the smooth tub. "This is torture,"
he moaned.

As if in a dream, Zen walked forward, pulled up her
silk robe, and knelt down on the carpet. She leaned over
the rim of the circular tub, which was recessed into the
floor. "Turn around and I'll scratch your back for
you . . . even though I don't believe—wait! What are you
doing? I'll get wet. Ohhh, damn you!"

Damon had caught her under the arms and pulled her,
robe and all, into the tub. "Give me poison ivy, will
you?" he said. "Then you come up here and laugh at my
apartment! Well, how do you like this, my girl?"

"You fool," Zen sputtered. Water tasting of baking
soda splashed into her mouth. Her arms and legs became
tangled in her robe. "This is silk, Damon. It will be

ruined." She flailed wildly at him, but the sodden material hampered her movements.

"Relax and enjoy it, darling," Damon soothed, laughing. "Baking soda is good for your skin."

"I do not have poison ivy." She pushed a clump of wet hair off her face. "I just showered." She spat water from her mouth and sneezed.

"Don't worry." Damon reached up to a shelf near his head and brought down several plastic containers. "All the soap you could need or want... any kind." He grinned at her, seeming to have forgotten his discomfort. "Gotcha," he mumbled, her arms tightening around her and his eyes roving possessively over her.

"What do you mean?" Suspicion warred with reason, and won. "You aren't in pain," she exclaimed. "This was a ruse to get me in here!"

"Well, I was in discomfort—at first anyway."

"You lured me in here," she sputtered, splashing more water into her mouth in an effort to free herself from his iron grip.

"You're so dramatic." Damon chuckled and clamped her to his body.

"You're taking a terrible revenge on me, is that it? Infecting me with your poison ivy?" Zen was furious.

"My physician tells me that, unless people are hyperallergic, they're highly unlikely to get poison ivy except from direct exposure to the plant." Damon bent forward, his tongue coming out to tease the corner of her mouth.

"Your doctor is a quack. Besides, how do you know I'm not one of those hyperallergic people?" Zen arched her neck, trying to get away from him.

Damon lifted her slightly away from him, his eyes burning into hers. "Are you?"

"I...I guess not," she answered.

Damon stared at her for a longer moment, then released her abruptly, pushing her to her feet in the tub but staying seated himself. "I've just decided that I can't take the chance with you." He studied her wet body. The silk robe clung like a second skin. She stared back, baffled, swamped by an illogical disappointment with her sudden freedom. "The thought of all that pinky whiteness becoming red and covered with welts is repellent to me," Damon went on. He closed his eyes. "I think I've finally gone around the bend," he added as though to himself. "Having a lovely woman almost naked beside me and not making love to her! I must be crazy!"

Zen's temper burst. How many women had taken baths with Damon. She wouldn't stay with him a moment longer. Rising to her full height, she lifted the hem of her robe and squeezed it over his head. "How dare you try to give me poison ivy?" she lashed out producing the first argument that came to mind. Then she lifted three bottles of shampoo from the shelf, uncorked them, and dumped the contents on Damon. She threw down the empty containers, grabbed a bath sheet, and stormed out of the room.

"Zen . . . what the hell did you do that for? Damn, the bubbles. What's the matter with you? Come back here. We have to talk. We're getting married."

"I'll see you in hell first," Zen called over her shoulder as she dripped down the stairs to the foyer, the oversized towel trailing after her like a train. "Womanizer. Charlatan." She stomped down the hall. "Svengali." She struggled to suppress the feelings that urged her to rush back to him and throw herself into his arms. Part of her longed to be held by him, yearned to forget the rest of the world. "No . . . no, I won't be part of his harem," she mumbled.

Back in her own bathroom Zen dried herself, and climbed into bed. She tried to sleep, but images of her and Damon making love in the tub kept surfacing in her mind.

Chapter 4

ZEN KEPT A wary eye on Damon for the next two weeks as his poison ivy slowly healed. He stayed home for much of that time but kept in close contact with his New York office. Sometimes Zen took his calls. There was an emergency with Venus Airlines, another with one of his shipping interests. Meetings were called that he must attend. She began to see that Damon Aristides was, indeed, an important industrialist and a shrewd businessman.

One day a man named Desmond came to see Damon. He explained that he was sure the dog they were calling Curly had belonged to a friend whose fishing boat had sunk in the Sound. The man's body had been washed ashore a few days previously.

"That's why I came over today, Mr. Aristides. I thought this might be Jocko, old Jim's dog. The sheriff said Jim had teeth marks in his shoulder, as though the dog had tried to tow him for a while after the boat capsized. Then they surmise the current took them farther out. Old Jim died, and the dog tried to save himself." Mr. Desmond knocked his pipe against the bottom of his shoe, nodding to Zen as she stood listening. He turned to watch Curly cavort with the two boys, fetching the ball they threw for him.

"Jim Enright had no family," he went on, "but kids were always coming around to play with Jocko and get fishing lessons from Jim." He shook his head. "My wife and I will miss him, but you're welcome to keep the dog. We can't take him, and I'd hate to see him put down."

"Thank you, Mr. Desmond." Damon accompanied the man to his car.

Zen saw the man shake his head, but Damon insisted that he take the bills he pressed into his hand.

"You did us a favor by coming, Mr. Desmond, and you and your wife are welcome to come by and visit the dog any time."

Zen waited until the car had disappeared from sight before joining Damon on the lawn. "It was kind of him to come," she said.

Damon turned, regarding her through narrowed lids. "Are you speaking to me again?" His eyes made a lazy survey of her, from her breasts to her ankles.

"Stop doing that... and I never stopped speaking to you," Zen said angrily.

"Ah, yes, those poignant phrases like, 'No, I don't care for a roll, thank you,' and 'Yes, the weather is fine,'" Damon touched a finger to her lips. "We're getting married."

"What about Melissa?" Zen's mouth felt dry as hope and despair warred within her. Tell me you love me, damn you, she pleaded silently.

"Melissa and I have had a long talk. We've decided we don't suit. She has interests elsewhere."

Suddenly Zen felt as light as air. Happiness bubbled up inside her, followed swiftly by horror. Had she lost complete control of her emotions? She glanced at Damon briefly, then away. "Will that happen to me after a while? Will we talk, then decide we don't suit?" She swallowed past the lump in her throat, fearing she had exposed too much of her feelings to him.

"No," Damon answered tersely.

She tried to find words to prove that she was as cool as he was. "The boys want me to see Curly's new trick," she said, heading across the lawn. But, to her dismay, Damon's long strides kept easy pace with hers.

Daniel ran to meet them. "Aunt Zeno, Curly can catch the ball and bring it back to us." His bright smile made Zen's heart turn over with love.

"Is that the trick you were going to show me?" she asked.

"Not exactly," David said, coming up to them, a panting Curly at his side. The dog dwarfed both boys, yet he was so gentle and playful that Zen's initial worry had all but vanished. "C'mon, Uncle Damon, you come, too. We want to show you something." David looked up at his uncle. "I know it hurt to have poison ivy, but I liked it when you were home all the time, not just on Saturday." Running after his twin and the dog toward the stable, David didn't see his uncle's face flush with embarrassed pleasure.

Zen knew Damon was deeply touched by what David had said. He'd spent his first days at home constantly on the phone discussing his fishing boats on the West Coast, his computer stores in the Chicago area, his consulting firms in New York, and the airline based in Athens. But the boys had vied for his attention at every turn. More and more, Damon had given in to them. Zen sensed that he felt very close to the twins.

He opened his mouth to say something, then changed his mind, and instead took Zen's arm and followed the boys to the stable in silence.

The sudden darkness of the interior momentarily blinded them. They called out to David.

"Up here, Uncle Damon," he shouted. "Up in the loft."

"I thought I told you not to climb up there unless Yanos was with you," Zen scolded. She stepped purposefully over the ladder and began to climb, stopping when she was able to rest both arms on the floor of the loft and see where the boys were huddled in a corner. Pushing away a little, she shook her finger at them and took a deep breath to berate them—then unexpectedly lost her balance. She grabbed frantically for a handhold, knocking some loose hay off the shelf.

"Zen, for God's sake! Are you trying to bury me in hay?"

She looked over her shoulder down at Damon, who was picking pieces of straw off himself and shaking his head ruefully. "I didn't drop much hay," she replied.

"No? I'm just glad the pitchfork was down here."

"Very funny."

"Aunt Zeno, will you come over here?" Daniel called impatiently. "Look."

Zen hesitated. She wasn't fond of heights and she didn't relish climbing back down once she was up there. But both boys were calling for her. "Oh, all right. I'll be right down, Damon." She climbed the rest of the way into the loft and went over to the boys.

David pointed to a patient mama cat suckling four kittens. "Aren't they nice? Yanos said we're not to touch them for a few days yet." His voice dropped to a whisper. "Aren't they small?"

"Yes, they are." Zen sat cross-legged in the hay and listened to the faint mewing of the tiny creatures.

"I hope Curly doesn't try to come up here," David said.

"I'm sure he's smarter than that," Damon answered as he dropped down next to Zen and smiled at the boys. "So, you're a mother, are you, Zaza?" He reached out and petted the silver tabby. She pushed her head against his hand. "She's a very good mother, too."

As the boys sat entranced, Damon told them stories about other animals on the estate. Zen leaned comfortably against a bale of hay, unable to take her eyes off Damon. Her heart thudded as she studied his dark head and broad shoulders. When he reached out to tousle David's head with a large hand, her face flushed with warmth. He seemed to radiate a sense of care and protection, and deep inside she yearned to have him touch her in the same familiar way. But in her imagination his touch soon turned hot and possessive . . . She shifted restlessly and lowered her eyes.

When they climbed down from the loft some time later, Damon went first, Daniel and David following. Zen took a deep breath, slid over the edge on her stomach, and felt for a rung. An iron hand grasped her ankle and positioned her foot on it.

"There, you're set now, darling. Just come ahead. I'm here." Damon's voice seemed to vibrate through her. She felt his body behind hers as they descended the rest of the way together.

Once on the ground, she brushed the straw from her clothes and watched the boys as they talked to Yanos, the horses, and the dog. She looked up at Damon. "How did you know I was leery about coming down the ladder?"

"I saw the expression in your eyes when you looked down at me." He put an arm around her. "When are you going to admit that it would be better all around if we got married?"

"Better for whom?"

"Better for us. Better for the boys. They need a home with a mother and a father."

"Yes, they do," Zen agreed.

Damon turned her to face him. "Then you'll marry me?"

"Or marry someone else . . . Ouch, you're squeezing me!" Zen bit her lip at the fire in his eyes.

"Don't tease me, love." Damon kissed the tip of her nose. "I don't like it. And you'd damn well better know that to get those two boys you'll have to have me, too."

"I want the boys, but I think we should have a . . . a trial engagement. No, wait; don't interrupt. I mean that we should have a time when we try to get along with each other, to see if we're compatible."

Damon halted in front of her, his mouth twisting wryly. "What the hell—"

"If we fight on every issue, argue all points, disagree—"

"Be quiet, Zen. I get the picture. But don't you think you're approaching marriage in a very unrealistic way? Married people disagree on many things, but they stay together."

"Not today they don't," Zen shot back. "If it doesn't feel good, get rid of it. If the glow isn't there every day, toss it out the window." She shook her head, making her red-gold curls swing around her face. "No, I want a stable home for the boys... or we go back to the status quo."

"Damn you. You would separate those boys again, knowing how much they mean to each other?"

Guilt flooded Zen. What he said was true. The boys would suffer greatly if they were separated again. But they would also suffer if they lived in a home where the husband didn't love the wife, where the husband might choose a different partner after a time...

"Stop daydreaming." Damon gave her a little shake, scattering her thoughts. "You're building straw barriers in that damned convoluted mind of yours." His touch softened. "All right, we'll try it your way... for a while."

Zen stiffened as his arm went around her waist again. "There's no need—"

"Drop it, Zen." His arm tightened around her as they neared the boys and the romping dog.

"He's a magnificent-looking animal, isn't he?" Zen said, forgetting for a moment that she was angry with Damon.

"Gentle and intelligent, too. The first day he was able to walk, I saw him down at the water's edge, looking out over the Sound. To me it seemed as though he was paying his respects to Jim, the man who owned him. When I spoke to him, he looked at me with the saddest eyes, then followed me back to the house."

"The house," Zen mused, looking up at him. "I feel guilty that the boys coerced your mother into letting them keep the dog inside."

Damon shrugged. "Don't worry. Mother doesn't seem to mind. And the staff likes him."

* * *

That evening everyone gathered in the living room for cocktails, the boys regaling their grandmother with descriptions of Curly's newest trick. Zen was surprised when Damon stood up and called for everyone's attention.

"I have had Maria bring champagne to us this evening because I have an announcement to make." Zen's face flamed as she anticipated what he was about to say. Damon lifted the bottle from the ice bucket and opened it, pouring the sparkling wine into tulip-shaped glasses and nodding to Maria and Lona to pass them around. "As you know, it is the custom among Greek people for engaged couples to feed each other." Damon now had the full attention of everyone in the room. He turned to a slack-jawed Zen and held his glass to her lips. "Taste, darling. It's Dom Perignon." He laughed when she sipped without thinking. "Xenobia and I will be getting married soon," he added casually.

As everyone applauded and wished them happy, Zen whispered furiously to Damon, "You should have told me you were planning this." She gulped and coughed as bubbles went up her nose.

"And you would have gone along with me? I thought not," Damon answered with a chuckle. He bent to kiss her on the mouth as though they were alone in the room.

"And what of Melissa?" Sophie asked sternly, her hands folded in front of her, refusing to take a glass from Maria until she had heard Damon's answer.

"I've spoken to Melissa," her son said in frosty tones.

"And what of the two families? Was there not an understanding?" his mother persisted.

"I have talked to her father and to her uncles. Melissa seems to be quite interested in one of the Rivaldos," Damon said flatly.

"You mean the winery people?" Sophie inquired.

"They are fine people," Thag interjected. "Dominic Rivaldo has been my friend since we fought in the British commandos together."

"Isn't Rivaldo an Italian name?" Zen asked, hoping to change the subject.

"Yes. We both left our own countries and went to Britain, where we were trained in guerrilla warfare." Thag smiled in rememberance. "We blew up a few bridges in our time."

"How fascinating," Zen said.

"I want to know more of this," Sophie pursued, reluctantly accepting a glass from the hovering Lona, watching like a hawk as the woman poured white grape juice for the boys.

"Zen and I think the boys will be happier if we marry and keep them together," Damon added.

Zen shifted restlessly at the sight of Sophie's unreadable expression. "We haven't ironed out all the details yet," she said nervously, "but the alternative is to split the boys."

"No," David and Daniel chorused.

Daniel came up to Zen and caught her around the leg. "I want to be with you all the time, Aunt Zeno."

She bent over him, holding him. "I want that, too."

"Then it's settled, I suppose," Sophie said, surprising Zen once again. The older woman lifted her glass. "To my son and his bride-to-be." She sipped the champagne, her face inscrutable.

"To Xenobia," Thag toasted, tapping his glass against the boy's juice glasses, delighting them.

Zen's smile was tight as she edged closer to Sophie and whispered, "We aren't planning to marry right away."

"Really? That does surprise me. My son is a very virile man." Zen choked on her champagne and Sophie patted her on the back, then rose and announced dinner. "Come, boys. You will sit next to me this evening. Aunt Xenobia will want to sit next to Uncle Damon." She stared at her son. "And why does she not have a ring?" she demanded.

"Mother," Damon said, irritated, "as it happens, I was going to give Zen a ring this evening."

"You were?" Zen said, stupefied. "When did you get a ring?"

"Don't you want a ring, Aunt Zeno?" David asked.

"No . . . yes, of course." She clenched her fists and followed the boys into the dining room.

Once David and Daniel had wriggled into their chairs, sitting atop pillows that raised them to a comfortable height, David beamed at her. "Uncle Damon is going to show us how to play lacrosse after dinner. Would you like to come, Aunt Zeno?"

"Yes, dear," she said, then frowned, catching Damon's eye. "Isn't that a dangerous sport?"

"All sports can be dangerous. Do you want to coddle the boys?"

"No, but—"

"There you are, then."

Damon was at his most scintillating during dinner, but Zen's temper rose as he constantly turned aside all her efforts to explain that theirs was a trial engagement.

Nevertheless, she was flabbergasted at the tender attention he showed her. When he reached out to grasp her wrist, intercepting a forkful of food on its way to her mouth and indicating that she was to feed it to him, she thought he was joking.

"Feed him, Zen," Thag urged. "It is an old Greek custom among sweethearts that they feed each other at the table."

"Oh." Her eyes met Damon's as he moved her hand up to his mouth, holding the fork there for long seconds—in what Zen thought was a very suggestive way and inappropriate in front of the boys. What would Sophie say?

But when she risked a glance, the older woman looked utterly serene.

"I think I will have a reception so that the rest of the family can meet Xenobia," she announced, after swallowing a bit of fish.

"Like the one you had for Eleni?" Zen asked, remembering the hordes of people who had milled around the house and grounds, bringing expensive gifts. "I don't think—" Zen began.

"That's a good idea, Mother," Damon interrupted, leaning over and kissing Zen's mouth. "You had a bit of parsley there."

"Did not." Zen glanced at the boys, who smiled back at her.

After dinner she accompanied them out to the darkened lawn, where a cool breeze was blowing off the Sound. Yanos threw a switch, and the front lawn was illuminated.

Zen knew little about lacrosse. She didn't understand the scoring, and the object of throwing the ball from nets affixed to poles completely eluded her.

"You do it, Aunt Zeno," David urged, dragging a stick that was far too big for him over to his aunt.

Zen accepted the long pole with the net at the end. When Daniel pitched the ball to her, she swung the pole like a baseball bat.

"No, not that way. Let me show you." Damon approached her as Daniel threw the ball again. Zen swung. "Oww! Dammit, Zen, my face. What are you trying to do, kill me?" Damon held his right cheek, glaring at Zen out of one eye.

"You know," David mused, "Aunt Zeno used to play games better when we lived in Dublin."

"Oh?" Daniel looked from his aunt to his uncle, his lips pursed in thoughtful concentration. "Nonna says that when she travels she never drinks the water. Maybe Aunt Zeno shouldn't drink the water."

Despite his discomfort, Damon laughed and called to Yanos to collect the sticks before he led the boys and Zen back into the house.

"What did Xenobia do now?" Sophie quizzed, earning a glare from Zen.

"How did you know, Nonna?" David climbed up on the settee next to her. Daniel sat cross-legged on the floor.

"She just guessed," Damon answered, even as his mother was opening her mouth to speak.

Conversation centered on lacrosse until the boys went

to bed. Then talk became general. Zen tried to get Damon alone to discuss breaking their trial engagement before things went too far, but he avoided her.

That night Zen sat at her vanity table brushing her hair for a long time. "I can't marry him. He makes me clumsy," she murmured. "I'd kill him in six months."

For some reason she suddenly remembered one of her favorite poems: "The Rime of the Ancient Mariner." She quoted it aloud:

> "God save thee, ancient Mariner!
> From the fiends, that plague thee thus!—
> Why look'st thou so?"—With my crossbow
> I shot the ALBATROSS.

Damn the man, Zen thought, he is my albatross. Not a good omen but a bad omen..."Ohh!" Zen held her head. "I'm totally nuts around that man."

She raised her head and stared at herself in the mirror. I have to get away for a while. Daddy's place at Tupper Lake would be good, just to get things in perspective. I'm afraid to accept Damon into my life. It frightens me to think that he may be the key to all my happiness, to fulfilling all my needs, to helping me appreciate all that's beautiful on this planet. She scowled into the mirror.

All night she tossed and turned, thinking of Damon and her father's cabin in the Adirondack Mountains.

The next day Damon went to his office in Manhattan. There was a bruise on his cheek, but no one mentioned it at the breakfast table. Afterward, David and Daniel took Curly out for his morning run. Thag sauntered after them, leaving Zen and Sophie alone.

"Mrs. Aristides," Zen began, "I've been thinking of taking the boys on an outing, perhaps a trip."

Sophie's eyes narrowed. "To Ireland?"

"Oh, no, not so far. I thought somewhere not far from here...for just a few days. My father had a cottage in the Adirondacks in a remote section on Tupper Lake. I'd like to take them there for just two days. I wouldn't keep them from you. I give you my word."

Sophie scrutinized her for long moments. "You will need at least a week to sort out your feelings for Damon, but whatever you decide, Xenobia, I must tell you that I have been happy with my grandsons and do not want to give one of them up or separate them."

"I understand." Zen swallowed. "Do you mind if I leave this morning? With Damon leaving for California this afternoon—"

"And he won't be back for several days," Sophie finished, her eyes shining. "My son can be overwhelming at times. I understand your need to be alone with the boys to think."

Zen smiled with relief. "We could take the dog. He'd be good protection."

"And will this place be in adequate condition for you?" Sophie inquired.

Zen considered. "I'll call Terry Watts. He was my father's lawyer, and he'll know if the place is still standing."

Sophie nodded, then lifted a hand to keep her from leaving. "Remember, my son is very aggressive, and I am sure he will find out where you've gone. You will have some days to yourself, though."

Zen's eyes filled with tears of gratitude. "Thank you for trusting and supporting me."

"Hurry along, child. I will have Lona help you."

Their preparations proceeded swiftly. The boys were delighted to be making a trip with Curly.

Yanos checked the Cherokee van and filled the gas tank. Then he gave Zen a few quick instructions on how to drive the cumbersome vehicle. She felt confident that she could handle it.

She was relieved to hear from Terry Watts that the taxes had been paid on the cabin in her name with money remaining from her father's estate, and that as far as he knew the pump, pipes, and appliances had passed their annual inspection by a man hired to check on several pieces of property in the area.

Yanos packed sleeping bags, warm clothing, bug repellent, a first-aid kit, a tent, and all the other sundries he considered necessary into a carrier on top of the Cherokee. Zen belted the boys into the back seat and allowed Curly to run free in the roomy compartment far in the back that could double as sleeping quarters in a pinch.

Calling on all the patience she could muster, Zen drove through heavy traffic to the thruway heading northwest. Once they were speeding away from New York City, she was able to relax somewhat. Riding high in the cab of the Cherokee, she felt as if she were driving a truck.

The boys played endless games of crazy eights while Curly watched them over the back of the seat.

Several hours later, near Albany, she swung onto the Northway, Highway 87, which would take them to the Adirondack region, the mountainous area that covered hundreds of square miles in the northeastern section of the state.

They stopped for lunch at a rest area. Both the boys and Curly loved their double hamburgers with ketchup, onions, and relish.

"I don't think a dog should eat condiments," Zen mumbled.

"Curly likes it, Aunt Zeno," Daniel assured her as he very carefully fed the dog a chocolate milk shake. "Curly isn't fussy."

"Hum," Zen said skeptically.

After they'd finished, the boys disappeared into the men's room while Zen walked Curly on his new leash until he did what he was supposed to, and she cleaned up after him.

Back on the road, the boys' incessant chatter gradually ceased. Zen glanced in the rearview mirror to see that they were both asleep. Curly, too, had his eyes closed, his chin resting on the back of the seat. Zen pushed in a stereo cartridge and played soft music. The traffic thinned out and stretches between towns lengthened after she left the Northway and headed northwest toward Tupper Lake. Soon the road began to twist and turn as they climbed into the mountains.

Zen breathed in the heady spring fragrances of wet evergreens, mossy earth, and sweet wild flowers.

About an hour later the boys woke up as Zen pulled in to a gas station. The attendant, a grizzled man chewing on the stem of his pipe, sauntered over to them. "Fill it, please, but don't top the tank," Zen instructed. "Check the oil too, please."

"Yep . . . and I'll wash the windshield, too." The man grinned at her around the pipe.

Memory washed over Zen as she recalled other days in the north country and the friendly interest of the people there. "Thank you." She smiled at the man, looking past him to the station.

"Name's Harley." He pointed to the sign on the glass window that said HARLEY'S GARAGE. "Ever'body just calls me Harley."

Zen paid Harley and thanked him.

"Where ya headed?" he inquired, leaning on the door of the Cherokee.

"Our camp on Tupper Lake, called Driscoll's Pineview. Do you know it? It's near Mission."

"Yep, I know Mission. One church, a store, two houses, and a gas station. Your place must be on the side of the hill back in the woody section. Kinda lonely up there. Good to have a dog. Get your food at Dina Lipp's place. Fresh stuff." He nodded and saluted them with two fingers as they pulled away.

The boys were growing tired and restless now. They squirmed in their seats and demanded that they be allowed to unbuckle their seat belts.

"No," Zen told them. "We'll be there soon, but the road to the camp is very bumpy . . . at least it used to be . . . and I don't want you bouncing around inside the car. Besides, it's against the law for young children to ride in a car without seat belts. Do you want me to break the law?"

"No, Aunt Zeno." David sighed. "But my bottom hurts."

On the last leg of the trip the boys tried Zen's patience to the limits as she struggled to maneuver the large vehicle down the circuitous road that led from the highway past Tupper Lake.

They entered the hamlet of Mission and turned onto a side road filled with mud and deep ruts. The spring thaw must be worse than usual, Zen surmised, her hands locked on the wheel as the van bucked and skidded down the road. She said a silent prayer of thanks for the four-wheel drive.

They rounded a curve in the muddy road and the lake came into view. A sign read: Driscoll's Pineview Lodge. Heaving a big sigh, she pulled the van to a stop. "We're here, boys. Now, be still. I'm not sure I can make it up the driveway to the cottage."

Zen opened the door of the van and stepped down, studying the winding track that led uphill to a log cabin nestled among the pines. For some reason it looked smaller than Zen remembered. She walked up the rutted track, her heart sinking as she saw the sagging shutters and the holes in the porch screens. It was obvious that no extra care had been given to Pineview Lodge in many years. "Only the taxes have been paid," she said ruefully, deciding to chance the upgrade with the four-wheel-drive vehicle.

She returned to the Cherokee, got behind the wheel, and backed it up to give herself a better start. She drove carefully, and they made it to the top of the incline without incident.

The boys clamored to get out. Curly jumped over the seat and galloped after them. They turned to look at Zen, the boys' faces alight with glee, the dog wagging his tail, his tongue hanging out. Neither of the boys seemed to notice the shabby exterior of the cabin, but Zen dreaded what she would find inside.

"Boys, we may sleep in the van tonight. There will be so much cleaning to do in the—"

"We'll help, Aunt Zeno," David assured her.

Daniel nodded, his eyes bright with enthusiasm.

Smiling, Zen put her apprehension aside as she reached above the door frame for the key that they'd always kept there. "Ah . . . here it is. A little dirty but . . ." She pushed the key into the lock. The door squeaked as it opened. "It ain't much, Ma, but it's home," she said as the musty, dusty interior met her eyes. She reached out to wipe away a cobweb.

"Is it spooky, Aunt Zeno?" David whispered.

"No, but it *is* filthy. Tomorrow we'll have to work hard to get it in shape. Tonight I'll see if we can get the water working. Then I'll clean the bathroom, and you boys can have a shower. We'll eat in the van, from the ice chest."

"That will be fun," Daniel said, looking up the narrow stairway. "What's up there, Aunt Zeno?" he asked, pointing to the spacious loft.

"The bedroom I shared with your mother. There's also a bathroom with a sink and toilet. But the only shower is down here."

Zen went to the power box and threw the switches, praying that the circuit breakers were in good working order. Lights came on, and she sighed with relief, then went to inspect the old refrigerator. "It works," she shouted to the boys, more relieved than she cared to admit when she heard the pump kick in, telling her that water was being pumped from the deep well her father had had dug when he'd built the cabin. She checked the water heater and discovered that it worked too.

"So far everything is on, boys."

To her delight, the boys insisted on helping her scrub the shower stall and tiles. Then they wiped out the small sink and around the toilet. Zen finished by washing the floor and bringing in fresh towels from the camper while the boys took a shower together, she listened to their laughter with pleasure and plugged in the electric heaters. Tomorrow she would check the fireplace flue.

When the boys were finished, Zen took a shower and put on fresh jeans and a shirt.

They ate sandwiches and drank hot tea from one thermos, milk from another. Zen was glad there were few dishes. She was so tired she just rinsed them and left them in the sink.

She released the back seat of the Cherokee to make

a larger area in which to spread the sleeping bags and air mattresses. Curly opted to sleep on the ground outside, his presence giving Zen a feeling of well-being as total darkness descended.

Zen slept restlessly. Damon intruded into her thoughts and dreams. She muttered to herself, punching the pillow, then gazing out the window at the stars. She remembered the young woman who had given herself to Damon Aristides without reserve and knew that she could no longer ignore her still burning feelings for him.

She wanted him. She needed him to complete her life.

She rolled over, sleep claiming her at last.

The next morning was frosty cold, and they shivered in the van.

"You two stay here while I get the cabin warm. Then I'll call you for breakfast."

"Can't, Aunt Zeno. I have to go to the bathroom," Daniel said solemnly.

"Me, too," David agreed.

"All right." Zen laughed at them. "I'll turn on the electric heater in the bathroom. That will warm you up."

The boys scampered out of the camper in robes and slippers, followed by Curly, who didn't seem to notice the cold.

They laughed and joked over breakfast as cereal and eggs disappeared from plates, along with the toast, jam, and milk. Curly devoured two giant dog biscuits in seconds.

The boys surprised Zen by offering to help clean up the cabin. She laughed sometime later when she heard them yelling at Curly to get off the tile floor they had just washed.

Later, Zen found two small braided rugs stored in a closet. After she and the boys had hung them outside on a clothesline and beaten them clean, she arranged them in front of the stone fireplace.

That afternoon they explored the lakeshore. Though Zen warned the boys not to venture onto the wooden dock, which was missing several slats, she felt sure the structure was essentially sound.

"Aunt Zeno, look at Curly." David pointed excitedly as the retriever hurled himself into the water to retrieve a stick. "He's not afraid of the water."

"He was bred to the water, darling. Not even his awful experience would dim his natural inclination to it." The three of them took turns tossing the stick to the dog, who seemed never to tire of the game.

"He gets dry right away, I think." Daniel watched as his pet shook himself.

"Retrievers have an undercoat that protects them from the water so that they can resist both the wet and the cold," Zen told them.

That night, after driving to Dina Lipp's store for supplies, Zen cooked fresh fish and vegetables on the grill. Steamed in foil and seasoned with black pepper and butter, the vegetables were delicious. The fish, broiled with fresh lemon slices and butter, tasted moist and succulent. Both boys ate heartily, then sat in front of the fire watching the flames flicker over the logs.

Zen glanced around the cozy cabin, admiring the results of their hard work. Tonight they would sleep in the front room on air mattresses. Tomorrow they would clean the downstairs bedroom and perhaps start on the loft.

Zen barely had time to make up their beds before both boys fell asleep. Curly lay down next to the front door.

Zen checked the doors, placed a screen in front of the banked fire, turned off the lights, and bedded down next to the boys. But when she closed her eyes, she saw Damon gazing at her, coming toward her, overwhelming her, seeming to swallow her up.

Chapter 5

THREE DAYS PASSED. A bright sun made it warm enough to wear only short-sleeved shirts and slacks during the day, but the nights were cool and they huddled in their sleeping bags dressed in flannel pajamas.

The boys enjoyed working and happily scrubbed floors while Zen washed walls and ceilings.

On the fourth morning Zen was lying in the downstairs bedroom watching the play of sunlight on the pines outside her window, listening to the boys giggling upstairs in the loft. Suddenly Curly began barking and bounded down the stairs. He stood in front of the door, growling.

Just then Zen heard the squeal of brakes, followed by heavy footsteps. Someone knocked loudly on the front door. Her heart pounding, she swung her legs out of bed, snatched up her woolly robe, and stood swaying with surprise as Damon shouted through the door.

"Damn it, Curly, stop that growling. Zen, open this door."

"It's Uncle Damon, it's Uncle Damon," both boys

yelled, half tumbling down the stairs.

"Be careful," Zen called to them. "Isn't that just like him?" she muttered. "Coming on like gang busters, scaring people out of bed. I should tell Curly to bite him." She struggled to pull back the bolt on the front door.

Even as she was turning the handle, Damon burst into the room and lifted her into his arms, leaving her feet dangling above the floor.

"Damn your soul, Xenobia, don't you ever do that to me again." His mouth bore down on hers, his tongue immediately parting her lips. The kiss deepened, his arms tightening as though he would never release her.

"Does this mean you're not really mad at Aunt Zeno, Uncle Damon?" David asked, his eyes wide with curiosity.

Zen was able to separate their mouths by mere centimeters, but she could feel Damon's eyes on her, and his hold didn't ease. "Uncle Damon... is just... concerned," she gasped, pressing her hands against his shoulders. "Damon..."

"That's good. Wanna go fishin'?" David smiled up at them.

"Damon..." Zen repeated, digging her nails into his neck.

"Huh? Fishing? Fine... but I'm hungry."

"I'll make breakfast," Zen offered. When he didn't move, she whispered. "Put me down."

"What? Oh... all right." He let her slide down his body, but a steely arm kept her clamped to his side. Ruefully he rubbed his stubbled chin, noticing the red marks left on Zen's face. "Didn't have time to shave," he muttered. "Drove most of the night, once my mother told me where you were. I had trouble finding the place. I must have driven over most of the Adirondacks before I happened on a gas station that was opening up at five in the morning."

"Harley's?" Daniel asked.

"What? Yes... that's the name." Damon yawned.

"Why don't you go to bed?" Zen suggested. "I'll call you when—"

"Aw, we want Uncle Damon to go fishing." David scowled darkly.

Zen was about to respond, but Damon squeezed her waist, stifling another yawn.

"I'll shave, then take the boys fishing. After that I'll go to bed."

Zen nodded, stunned by the burning look in his eyes. She turned to tell the boys, who were already crashing up the stairs, to get dressed and wear boots.

Damon put his hand on her shoulder. "After that, you and I will talk," he said, giving her a lopsided grin.

Once Damon and the boys left to go down to the lake, Zen quickly changed the sheets on her bed so that Damon could sleep there when he came in from fishing.

She couldn't help the happy feeling welling up inside her as she listened to the boys' faint laughter and Curly's exuberant barks. "How are they managing to keep that dog out of the water while they fish?" Zen mused, sure that no fish would come anywhere near all that commotion.

Her mouth began to water as she pan-fried raw potatoes in a large skillet, then, when they were crisp, added thin wedges of tomato. She grated fresh black pepper over the pan and left it to simmer. In another skillet she cooked bacon and fried eggs over easy. She oven-toasted thick slices of Maria's homemade raisin bread. As coffee perked in the huge enamel pot, she added eggshells to clarify it, in the Swedish way. Then she went to the old chiffonier in the living room and took out one of her mother's embroidered cotton tablecloths, which had been wrapped in foil with mint leaves. She shook it outside and spread it on the oaken table that had been her grandmother's, then ran outside and gathered pussy willows, which she arranged in a vase in the center of the table. Finally she rang the old bell hanging on the porch. The loud clang echoed in the clear mountain air.

A lump formed in her throat as she watched Damon stride up the incline, a boy on either side of him, Curly gamboling behind.

"Umm, whatever that is I smell, I could eat a ton." Damon grinned, then bent down to give her a hard kiss on the mouth. When he pulled away, his expression was serious. "Don't ever leave me again."

Zen stared after him wide eyed as he released her and urged the boys upstairs to wash. Damon himself disappeared into the downstairs bathroom, emerging minutes later, before the boys were finished upstairs.

He surveyed the cabin with approval. "Nice. How did you manage to get it clean so fast?"

"The boys helped me." Zen felt all thumbs under his dark, watchful gaze. "Of course," she hurried to add, "there's much more to do. The screen on the porch is a wreck. The door is hanging off its hinges. The windows need washing." She rattled on. "I intend to—"

"I'll take care of the repairs," Damon said.

"You?" Zen's mouth dropped open. "Is Yanos coming?"

Damon looked haughtily down his nose, the bump at the bridge where he'd once smashed it playing football adding a sinister element to his good looks. "I'll do them. I'll be staying here for a while."

"The couch is too short for you," Zen said without thinking.

"We'll share the bed."

"Not a chance."

"Then you sleep on the couch," Damon replied, looking bored.

Zen stood tall and faced him squarely. "Now listen here, Damon—"

"We'll discuss it later. I'm hungry." He looked up the stairs as the two boys descended side by side. "Shall I pour the coffee?" he inquired of Zen.

"Youuu!" She whirled toward the stove, lifting the huge coffeepot with both hands.

"Put that down. I'll carry it," Damon ordered softly. He took the pot and placed it on the tripod near the open fire where it would stay warm and be within easy reach. Damon and the boys sat down while Zen brought iron skillets filled with food to the table and set them on metal trivets. Over the toast she placed a quilted warmer her mother had made.

For several moments there was silence as the four of them filled their plates and ate heartily.

"Zen, that was delicious," Damon said, rising to pour fresh coffee for her. The boys drank more milk, then decided to go out and play with Curly.

"Are your beds made?" their uncle asked. When they shook their heads, he pointed up the stairs. "Wait. Take your dishes to the sink first and scrape them."

Damon supervised them, then yawned and said that he would lie down for a while. He disappeared into the bedroom.

Zen checked on the boys, admonishing them to stay away from the water when she wasn't with them, and went back to cleaning the cabin. Today she intended to clean the storage cupboard on the back porch. It was a dirty, tedious job. By the time she was finished even her teeth felt dirty.

Before she could shower, the boys came in hungry and tired. She fed them, and then watched them go upstairs to play cards. When she checked a short time later, they were both asleep, the cards scattered between them, Curly sleeping on the braided rug between their beds.

With a sigh of relief, Zen stepped under the shower, lathering herself well. It felt so relaxing to let the warm water course over her body.

She was drying herself with a towel, when she realized she hadn't brought fresh clothing into the bathroom with her. Wrapping a bath sheet around herself, she tiptoed through the door that connected the bathroom to the bedroom, determined not to wake Damon, wincing as she imagined the remarks he would make.

It took several seconds to open the oak drawers on the old dresser where she'd stored her underthings. Mouth agape, she stared down at the neat pile of men's shirts she found there.

"I moved your things to the next drawer," Damon said from the bed. "Since you're so tiny, I didn't think you'd mind taking the three lower drawers while I take the upper three."

She turned to see him lying in bed propped up on one elbow, watching her. She moved back to her task, furious at his high-handedness. "You thought wrong," she declared. "When did you bring in your luggage? I didn't see you."

"While you were doing the dishes." His bare shoulder rose in a shrug. "I was sure you wouldn't mind."

"Well, I *do* mind." She took a step toward the bed. "This is my place, not one of the many Aristides holdings."

"I know that." He stretched slowly. Her eyes became riveted to his chest as the sheet slipped to his waist. "Comfortable bed. I didn't expect that. A little short though."

"It isn't your bed." She took another step toward him, wanting to tip him, bed and all, into the lake. "How dare you," she began, then gave an alarmed gasp and tried to leap back as Damon lunged for her.

But her timing was a tad off the mark. Damon gripped her forearm, a smile twisting his lips. He gave one short pull, and she tripped over the bath sheet and fell forward into his arms. "This is where you belong," he said softly, looking down at her, one leg draped across her middle, his hand loosening the towel from her upper body.

"The boys," Zen warned, feeling as though she was coming down with a fever.

"Are asleep," Damon stated. "I heard you tiptoe down the stairs." The triumphant heat in his eyes both angered and weakened her. "You're so beautiful . . . so mighty, but so tiny." He chuckled when she poked her tongue at him. "Eleni was twice your size, but she was a bit of fluff compared to you. You're not a Greek lady, Xenobia Driscoll Aristides."

"That's not my name," Zen croaked. "Besides, Greek women run their own households. I've seen them." She tried not to react when he inched the bath sheet from her breasts.

"Yes, but they're more subtle, more diplomatic." Damon chuckled again as his mouth nuzzled her throat. "I have the feeling that, if I displease you after we're married, you'll back my car over me."

"Yes, I will. But we're not getting married. It's just a trial engagement." Zen's temperature soared as his mouth explored her breasts.

"You have a tiny beauty spot on your left nipple...here. I've been thinking of it for three years," Damon mused, his mouth closing over the spot. "Your skin is perfect, pink and white." Damon's mouth trailed down her body, making Zen tremble with pleasure.

He pulled the bath sheet away from her, leaving her naked and vulnerable to his gaze. His bold eyes sent fire scorching through her veins. Then he pulled back his own sheet, and she saw that he was naked, too. Their bodies came together as if drawn by a force outside of their control. Zen gasped as Damon's full length pressed against her.

"Damon, the boys..." She said weakly, trying to rally her resistance.

"The door to the hall is locked."

"When did you do that?" she quizzed, hope fading fast.

"When you were showering," Damon muttered, his breathing rapid and uneven.

"Oh." As he began to kiss her instep, holding her foot like a precious jewel, Zen felt as if she were falling off the edge of the world.

"You're my wife," he murmured, suckling her toe, tickling her unbearably. He laughed deep in his throat.

"No." Zen clutched him wildly as she fell into the heady vortex Damon was creating.

"Yes, my darling..." He turned her over and caressed the backs of her knees with his mouth, making her pulse jump in response.

"I won't be controlled." Zen's voice was muffled as she writhed beneath him, her face pressed into the pillow.

"Then control me," Damon invited, sliding his hand up the back of her thigh before following with his mouth.

"That'll be the day," she replied breathlessly as she turned her face away, gasping for air.

When Damon nipped her buttocks, she squealed. "Do your worst with me, Xenobia," he challenged. "I won't fight back. I just won't let you leave me." He flipped her over again and buried his face in her abdomen. "Not ever."

"Crazy man," she whispered, taking hold of his thick hair and pulling him up to face her. "We're so different."

"We're one," he said with a growl. "I'm yours, and you'll never get rid of me."

Zen moved restlessly against the sheets. "Damon!"

"Yes, Xenobia, yes!" He caressed her parted thighs with gentle fingers, then with moist lips. Zen arched her back in astonished delight as measure upon measure of emotion twisted and burned inside her, building into white heat.

Her own hands laid claim to his body as he possessed hers. Memories of their previous lovemaking flooded back, guiding her hands as she touched him, making him groan and shudder. With growing urgency she sought to please him, her exploration of his virile form an erotic impetus to her own delight. She nibbled at his neck, then slid her mouth down his chest until she was tasting his nipples as he had tasted hers.

"Zen...Zen, darling..." Damon folded her closer, his chest heaving against her. All at once his control had broken.

He entered her, her body moist and ready for him, welcoming him, demanding him, embracing him. She held him in deep and loving incarceration; he became her slave just as she was his.

For long minutes they climbed the heavens together, gasping at the peak with pleasure that was theirs alone. The stars were laid bare before them as they gloried in sensual fulfillment.

"Damon, Damon," Zen moaned, long moments later, knowing that he had taken more than her body, that she had given more than her flesh.

"Yes, my darling wife?"

"Engaged," Zen gasped.

"Married," Damon insisted against her mouth.

Under his soothing hands her racing heart calmed, her heated skin cooled. She snuggled closer, reveling in his strength and warmth after being so very long apart.

They heard the clatter in the loft at the same time.

Zen leaped from the bed and sped across the room to the tall dresser, pulling out clothes helter-skelter, then running for the bathroom.

Damon leaned against the headboard of the bed, watching her. "Have I told you how much I love your breasts?"

"Stop it," Zen scolded, slamming the bathroom door on his laugh.

She unlocked the other door to the bathroom, which led to the hall, and called out to the boys that she was just changing her clothes and would join them in a moment. She gritted her teeth when she heard Damon chortle in the bedroom.

Before he was dressed, Zen hurried out to the boys and asked if they would like to go on a hike.

"Sure, Aunt Zeno," David agreed, delighted with the idea of putting a pack on his back with a box of graham crackers inside it.

Zen was relieved that the old canvas backpacks that had belonged to her and Eleni were still usable. She strapped a second pack on Daniel and added two cans of fruit juice.

Curly was only too glad to lead the way into the piney woods surrounding the cabin, and, although Zen was fairly certain of her direction, she marked the trees with a jackknife as her father had taught her. She explained what she was doing to the boys.

"It's very important that you guard against getting lost in an area as large as the Adirondacks," she said. "So you two must promise never to go out into the woods alone, okay?"

"Yes, Aunt Zeno," they chorused, round-eyed with excitement.

"Didn't you think I would want to come, Aunt Zeno?" Damon quizzed behind them, making Zen jump and the boys squeal. She turned to see him leaning against a maple tree.

"It's Uncle Damon," David pointed, grinning.

Daniel nodded, his smile wide.

"I–I thought you needed your sleep," Zen said stiffly, pausing at the top of a gully.

The boys followed Curly, heeding Zen's warning to stay close.

"Don't get too tired, darling," Damon whispered close behind her. "I don't want you to be worn out tonight." His chuckle sent tingles along her skin.

"Balloon-head." Zen pushed hard against his chest.

To her surprise, Damon staggered. He struggled to regain his balance, but his feet slipped on the wet mat of old leaves and pine needles, and he tumbled down the side of the gully, gathering momentum until he crashed against a tree. His leg was bent under him at a crazy angle.

Zen heard his grunt of pain even as she leaped after him. "Damon, are you all right?" she cried, aghast. She reached him in seconds, and, hearing the boys run back, she called up to them, "Stay where you are. Uncle Damon fell."

"You pushed me," he accused, regarding her with exasperated amusement. "And if you say it was an accident, I'll strangle you."

"Does anything hurt?" Zen asked anxiously as he grasped the tree trunk and rose slowly to his feet. He seemed to be favoring one foot. "You didn't break it, did you?"

"Wrenched it." Damon winced, then glanced at her with one eyebrow arched.

"You aren't faking, are you?" Zen watched him closely, suspicion and concern warring within her.

"Xenobia, that's unkind." Damon flinched and laughed as he inched back up the gully, one arm curled tightly around Zen's shoulders.

"I know you," Zen mumbled, breathing heavily as

she made the short ascent to where the boys were watching, wide-eyed.

"Will Uncle Damon have to have his dinner in bed?" Daniel asked as David ran off to get a long stick he'd seen.

"No, of course not, dear," Zen began.

"Maybe." Damon gave a woeful sigh.

"Not likely, you malingerer," Zen retorted as they began hobbling back to the cabin. "Must you put all your weight on me?" she complained, trying to mask her delight at holding him.

"I hate to be a burden." Damon's eyes glinted with deviltry as her face grew warm. "You're so cute when you blush," he cooed.

"I'm going to kick you in the other leg." Zen fumed, manipulating them past some low-hanging branches.

By the time they had covered the short distance back to the cabin, Zen was red-faced and sweaty, out of breath and out of sorts. Though he was still limping, Damon seemed in high spirits.

"Do you want to get into bed?" Zen asked as she helped him through the door and into the main room.

"No, I'll rest on the couch, maybe play crazy eights with the boys."

"Goody," Zen responded sarcastically, but her heart flip-flopped when he smiled at her.

As she chopped the vegetables for poor-man's stew, she couldn't help noticing how well Damon got along with the boys. Only a fool would fail to see the growing rapport among them, or the unfeigned affection the boys expressed for each other and for their uncle. Zen knew that she, too, shared their love. "I'll end up marrying him...and then that chauvinistic Greek will put me in my place," she muttered.

"Not Greek, darling, American, like you." Damon kissed her neck.

Startled, Zen lost her grip on the knife. It slipped and she cut her finger. "Look what you made me do! Are you going to call that an accident?" She swallowed hard, trying to slow her pulse.

Damon nodded and took her bleeding thumb into his mouth, sucking gently.

"Don't do that," Zen said, trying to free her hand.

"I'm fighting infection." The lazy heat in Damon's eyes sent languid warmth through her limbs.

"Indeed," Zen replied. "I have to finish cooking." She jerked away from him and sprinted for the back porch, where the barbecue utensils were stored. After filling the outdoor brick broiler with enough hardwood to cook the foil-wrapped dinner of meat, potatoes, and carrots with herbs, and spices, she lit the fire.

"Don't run away from me, darling." Damon stood behind her as she fanned the flames.

"Aaaah!" Zen jumped again. "Stop doing that. You're supposed to be resting. You can't walk."

"Yes, I can. I found a polished maple root that looks like a long shillelagh."

Zen smiled. "Daddy bought me that shillelagh at the Cooperstown Farmers Museum when I was a little girl."

"Very handy when you've sprained an ankle." Damon leaned around her to peer at the fire.

"I still think you should be resting your foot," she said.

"It's all right: I've done worse on the ski slopes."

"In Lausanne, I suppose," Zen snapped, thinking of all the beautiful women who frequented the resort.

"Gstaad, actually. We have a house there. Had you forgotten?"

"Yes." Zen turned away from him. "I'm going to slice some fruit while the fire burns down to coals."

Damon remained nearby, chatting with the boys as they played cards, then sitting on the step stool in the kitchen from where he could watch them in the main room.

By the time Zen had cut up apples, pineapples, oranges, and grapes and tossed them with a mixture of plain yogurt and honey, the fire was ready.

Dinner was a success, the fresh mountain air ensuring their good appetites.

The boys helped clean up, then joined Damon in the

living room. He fingered a book on his lap. "Would you like me to read the story of the Ancient Mariner?" he asked. "It's a poem I used to like when I was a boy."

Zen's eyes widened in surprise at his selection. How strange that they should share a special fondness for that poem. "You're my albatross," she muttered, polishing the glass in her hand and putting it in the cupboard. "If I hurt you, all bad things will happen to me. If I keep you, all bad things will happen to me." She sighed, feeling sorry for herself.

"What did you say about the albatross, Zen? Do you like Coleridge?"

"Sometimes," Zen admitted grudgingly, shaking out the towel after drying the last dish and draping it over the counter, joining Damon and the boys.

Damon began reading, and though much of the poem was lost on the boys, they seemed to enjoy it. Then he closed the book and began to explain.

"The Ancient Mariner is about a sailor who, many years ago, killed a bird that had been flying around his ship. The bird was an albatross, and after its death, the ship and the sailors on it began to have bad luck. The wind didn't fill the sails, people became ill." Damon spoke in slow, measured tones, holding the boys in thrall even as their eyes dropped with fatigue. "Many people refer to a person who has troubles as one who has an albatross around his neck. But I think the story tries to tell us to take care of the world around us—the earth, the animals, and the people."

"Like we take care of Curly?" Daniel asked yawning.

"Yes." Damon watched Zen lead the boys from the room, his face expressionless. He said good night before they climbed up the stairs, but Zen accompanied them to make sure they brushed their teeth and to listen to the prayers their grandmother had taught them to say each night.

When Zen came down from the loft, Damon was not in the living room. Assuming he was in the bathroom, she went to get fresh bedding for the couch. She was tucking in the sheets when Damon said behind her, "Forget it. We're sleeping together."

Startled, she whirled around. His dark scowl made him look like Lucifer. She drew herself up. "Now, you listen to—"

"Xenobia, please don't argue with me. Not after this afternoon."

"I'm a restless sleeper," she said, voicing the first excuse that came to mind.

"We won't be sleeping much anyway," he countered.

"Damon—"

"I am not letting you sleep without me. Even if you don't want to make love, I will not sleep without you . . . and that's the way it's going to be for the rest of our lives."

"Just like that."

"Exactly like that."

"We'll argue," she warned, taking a different tack.

"Don't underestimate us, Xenobia. We will no doubt argue every day. But that won't change anything. We'll still be in each other's arms at night."

She stared mutely up at him, unable to muster a rebuttal, her mind blank. Her sharp repartee had deserted her.

"Shall we go to bed, darling?" Damon urged softly, watching her from the bedroom doorway.

"But, your leg . . . ankle, that is. We don't want to do any damage—"

"Xenobia . . ." Damon's voice rose almost imperceptibly.

"What is it, Aunt Zeno?" David's sleepy voice drifted down the staircase.

"Nothing, dear," Zen answered, trying to keep her voice light. She glared at Damon.

"We're just going to bed, son," he called to the boy.

"'Kay. 'Night." David's voice faded.

"You said—" Zen cleared her throat. "You said that if I didn't want to . . . to make love . . . we wouldn't."

"Right." Damon leaned nonchalantly against the door frame.

"All right, then. I'm tired," Zen announced.

"So am I." Damon straightened and went into the bathroom.

Zen rummaged through an old chest of her mother's, looking for a flannel nightie. She found one packed in mint leaves and potpourri and held it up, frowning. She hated to give up the delicious sensation of sleeping naked, but she wasn't willing to risk accidentally touching Damon. One brush of his skin against hers and she would go up in flames.

She collected her soaps and the other paraphernalia she would need and when Damon opened the door, she slipped past him into the bathroom.

"Are you in such a hurry, honey lamb?" he crooned, sending shivers down her spine.

"I'm tired. Remember, I told you I was tired." Zen slammed the door on his grinning face.

She had intended to take her time preparing for bed, but when she washed her face and her body, her trembling hand slowed her even more.

When she returned to the bedroom, all was in darkness.

Taking a deep breath and fixing her eyes on the bed, she shut off the bathroom light. It was like stepping into a deep well.

She stubbed her toe against the foot of the bed. Muttering imprecations, she grabbed hold of the offended limb and hopped around on the other foot.

"For God's sake, Zen..." Damon switched on the light over the bed and scowled at her. "Now can you find your way?"

"Yes, and—"

"Then come to bed. And for God's sake, take off that horse blanket you're wearing. You'll suffocate."

"Not on your life." Zen humphed, then eased under the sheet, clinging to her side of the bed as if it were a life raft.

She closed her eyes and tried to sleep, but the nightgown twisted around her legs and pulled at her neck. She grew unbearably warm. Finally she couldn't stand it anymore. She sat up, pulled the gown over her head, and tossed it to the end of the bed.

"Even that slice of moon gives off enough light for me to see your lovely breasts, sweet," Damon murmured.

"I have a headache," Zen mumbled.

"Of course you have," Damon soothed, lying still.

Zen's head sank down on the pillow, and she stretched out, as straight and stiff as a ramrod.

"Good night, Zen."

"'Night." She swallowed dryly, her eyes wide and staring up at the darkened ceiling, where a bar of light was reflected.

She had no idea when her eyes closed. She was preoccupied with surprise and disappointment because Damon hadn't kissed her good night.

It grew colder in the wee hours of the night. Zen awoke groggy and cold in the predawn, wondering if the boys were warm. Stumbling out of bed, she pulled on a robe and went up the stairs. Curly woke up and wagged his tail, but the boys continued breathing deeply, tucked up warm in their quilted sleeping bags. Zen retraced her steps, shivering, and resolved to keep on her robe when she went back to bed.

But when she crawled under the covers, Damon's strong, warm arms came around her, unwrapping the robe from her and pulling her tight to his hard body.

"Your headache must be gone," Damon said, his lips feathering light kisses across her forehead.

"How do you know?" Zen asked, straining to keep from curving into his warmth. When he rested the flat of his hand on her buttocks, she sighed and gave in, closing her eyes in delight as his heat penetrated to her very core.

"You were cold." Damon's voice was gruff as he folded her even closer, his body sheltering hers.

"Not cold now," she mumbled. "Toasty." Her words ruffled the curling black hair on his chest.

"I'm a little more than toasty, darling," Damon crooned, rhythmically stroking her bottom.

"Living with men can be complicated," Zen observed, cuddling into his warmth.

Damon's body stiffened. "Oh? How many men have you lived with?" he asked with a casualness that failed to hide an underlying tension.

"Huh? Me?" She stretched to look up at him. His dark, brooding gaze startled her. "Purely hypothetical," she murmured and put her head back on his chest.

"Who is Seamus—that man David keeps mentioning in connection with Dublin?"

"Actually, he talks about his friend Robbie—"

"Zen, I want to know about Seamus."

"I told you, Seamus Dare is a co-worker at Deirdre's salon. He's an incredible photographer."

"I don't give a damn what he does," Damon said with a growl, his embrace tightening. "Did you live with him?"

Zen's head snapped up. "You have no right to know what I did with my life when we were apart. Have I asked you about the women you slept with while I was in Ireland?"

"Ask away." Damon's face took a grayish tinge in the pale dawn light.

"Were you celibate while I was in Ireland?"

"No," he snapped.

"My answer is the same," Zen lied without thinking, despair engulfing her. Once again his embrace tightened, crushing her. "Owww, Damon, you'll break my ribs," she cried softly.

"Damn you, Xenobia," he said gently. Then his mouth swooped down onto hers, tearing it open at once, his tongue taking ardent possession.

As his mouth trailed down her body, Zen was sure she could hear him cursing, but soon her senses were focused in another direction. A white-hot heat was coursing through her, twisting and turning, building in an intense, overwhelming crescendo.

Damon was every bit as tender as before, but this time Zen sensed a new urgency in him, a purpose, a determination that had been missing the first time. It fired them both to greater heights of passion.

Zen felt as if she were falling into a whirlpool. Part of her struggled to resist the pull. Another part of her knew it was no use. Damon held her in silken fetters. Their three years apart had not broken the bonds that united them. Three thousand miles had not separated their spirits. Something that defied time and distance and their own willful hearts held them enthralled, one to the other, for all time.

Zen reached out for him. "Damon, Damon."

"Yes...my own. I'm here. Let me love you." His mouth moved over her, sending heat through every part of her, making her gasp with pleasure, so that when he lifted his body over her, she was ready and welcoming.

All thought ceased in the onrush of sensation upon sensation that grew and grew until they tumbled together into the wild whirlpool of love, clinging to each other fiercely as shudders of release swept over them.

Zen whispered into his chest so that he couldn't hear. "Damon, I love you. I love you far, far too much to share you with anyone."

Chapter 6

AFTER THREE DAYS in Damon's company, Zen was feeling the strain. She felt as though she were walking across quicksand on stepping stones, with no firm ground anywhere. Every time she thought her feelings for him were under control, he did something to throw her off balance. Sometimes she wondered if he could read her mind, so effectively did he anticipate her moves and counteract them.

One afternoon, when the boys were napping in the loft, and Damon was resting his leg in bed, Zen decided to go down to the old dock and see if she could repair the broken slats. The day was very warm for May, so she decided to wear faded cutoff jeans and a short-sleeved cotton shirt that had been washed so many times it was almost transparent. She shrugged at her image in the mirror, aware that her breasts were barely covered, and started to pull up the zipper on her pants.

A sound stilled her hand. She turned to see Damon leaning against the doorjamb, his arms crossed on his chest. "I thought you were resting your ankle," she said.

454

"I was. It's rested."

"You're better, and you know it," she accused him, feeling her body tingle under his scrutiny.

"I'm returning to good health . . . under your care."

His sardonic look made her sputter. "I have things to do. I don't have time to chat."

"What are you going to do?" Damon blocked her exit from the room. "I wasn't asleep when you were creeping around gathering your clothes."

"No? Well, now you can rest." She shifted from one foot to the other in front of him. "I'm going to see if I can repair the dock."

"I'll help." He straightened from the doorjamb, looking down at her from his six-foot-plus height. "That's the sexiest set of work clothes I've ever seen." Before she could move, he hooked one arm around her and lifted her toward him to press his face to the opening of the blouse.

"I'm in a hurry," Zen protested. She swayed unsteadily when he freed her abruptly.

"You lead. I'll follow," he said.

Zen stomped past him down the hall and out the kitchen door to the enclosed back porch. She unlocked the tool cupboard and flung open the doors to reveal fairly well-stocked shelves. Some of the tools were beginning to rust but others were still shiny new.

Damon reached around her and hefted some of them. "Good ones. I'll have to clean some with oil. I think we'll be using this place a great deal once we're married. The boys like it, and so do I." He was studying the rust on a pair of pliers and didn't see Zen's stunned expression.

Damon Aristides liked a rustic cottage on a mountain lake? Remembering the pictures she'd seen of him in the gossip papers on the newsstands in Dublin, she couldn't believe it. Damon Aristides had squired beautiful women to the Riviera, to Nice, to Rome, to the Greek islands.

"Twaddle," Zen muttered, reaching for tools, nails, and a measuring tape.

"What?" Damon followed her off the porch, carrying clamps and wrenches. "What did you say?"

"Nothing." Zen flounced ahead of him down the incline, then paused. "I'd better check on the boys before I go down to the lake."

"Don't worry. I checked on them before I went to find you. Curly is up there with them, as usual." He paused, but continued to follow Zen. "You have the sweetest rear end, darling. Ummm, so nice."

"You are a crass low-life, Mr. Aristides," she retorted, angry at the secret pleasure his compliments gave her.

"Sweet buns, how you talk to your husband." Damon laughed, coming up to her side and putting his arm around her.

"Don't call me 'sweet buns'!" Zen fumed, trying to pry his arm from her middle. "And I am not your wife."

"I like it." Damon tightened his hold. "And you *are* my wife."

When they reached the narrow strip of shore near the dock, Damon released her and walked out onto the wooden structure.

"Damon, be careful. It hasn't been looked at in years," Zen called.

"I can see that." He squatted down to study the extent of disrepair. "Still, a great deal of it can be mended. It was well built."

Zen began to follow him out onto the dock, but he gestured for her to stay back. "Why can't I?" she demanded angrily.

"That temper of yours erupts at the snap of a finger, doesn't it?" He laughed at her glowering look. "Why don't you put some oil on the bolts? I'll start replacing the boards."

Zen agreed, though she was still irritated. She grimaced at the smell of the oil. "It smells like soiled kitty litter." Zen grimaced when Damon laughed at her. "Why do I put up with that man?" she muttered to herself as she coated the bolts and nuts of the supports, keeping her head averted to avoid as much of the odor as possible.

They worked on into the afternoon, Zen feeling safe and happy laboring beside Damon, delighted when she could see that the new pieces he had sawed and mitered by hand were beginning to transform the shabby pier.

"Aunt Zenooo!" David's voice called. "We want to come down with you."

"All right, dear. You and Daniel get some fruit for yourselves and a biscuit for Curly, then join us," Zen called back. She rose to her feet. She asked Damon, "Why don't I get us a cold drink? Are you thirsty?"

"I'd love some of that well water."

"Not Dom Perignon?"

"That's for later, love, when I'm peeling your clothes from your lovely body, a piece at a—"

"Stop it." Zen threw down the capped oil can and wiped her hands on her cutoffs. "I'll bring you a beer."

"That or the well water." Damon went back to sawing. He'd taken his shirt off, and his back glistened bronze in the sun.

Zen paused, watching the smooth motion of his shoulder and arm as he pushed and pulled the saw in rhythmic strokes. "I suppose you never get sunburned."

"Never. I have tough skin," Damon replied, cocking an amused eyebrow at her.

"Do you like to sunbathe?"

"Sometimes. But only after I've worked out in the water, or on it . . . and I never wear a suit, love."

"You must be arrested regularly."

"Darling, many of the beaches around the world allow nude sunbathing."

"Trust you to find them," Zen snapped, turning away when he chuckled.

"Yes, I think I have been to most of them."

"Viper," she whispered. She forced a smile to her face when she reached the boys, who were cavorting down the incline.

"We brung you an apple, Aunt Zeno. One for Uncle Damon, too."

"Thank you, Daniel, but say, 'We brought you an

apple,' not 'brung.' Take them down to the lake, and I'll bring some fruit juice and crackers."

David thought it over. "And cheese. And maybe another biscuit for Curly, and—"

"I'll try to bring everything," Zen interrupted, hoping to cut short his lengthening list.

Zen washed her hands and face. Then, loaded down with the food David had requested, she returned to the lakeshore.

The boys were sitting on the end of the dock talking to Damon, and tossing a stick to Curly, who never seemed to tire of leaping into the cold water and retrieving it.

Damon took the cold beer she handed him and held the icy can to his forehead. "Any moment now I may join Curly in the water."

"Don't be foolish. You'd freeze," Zen admonished.

"Will we come up here later, when the water is warm, Uncle Damon?" David asked.

"Sure. We'll come up on weekends. We'll get a boat, too."

Zen opened her mouth to say that she wasn't sure she would be doing that, but one look at the joyful expression on the boys' faces stilled her retort.

Zen spread a cloth on the deck and unpacked the things she had brought.

"I like it here," Daniel said. "I like being with you, Aunt Zeno."

Zen blinked back a sudden moistness in her eyes. "And I like being with you, too, love."

Damon leaned down into the water and washed his hands, then joined them. He startled Zen by lying down with his head in her lap. "Yes, I like it here. We'll come often," he agreed softly.

The days continued to grow warmer, but the evenings were often chilly.

Each night Zen slept in Damon's arms. She had stopped protesting when he reached for her in the dark, but each time they made love, she felt a sense of defeat. She would have to give him up someday. She would never be able to hold him. But it would be so hard, now that she had belonged to him so completely. For him the feeling would pass. He would go on to someone else. But for her there would be no one else—just Damon.

He seemed in no hurry to end their holiday, although Zen knew he had important responsibilities as director of the Aristides businesses.

One morning when the boys had gone out to play after eating breakfast, Zen approached Damon on the front porch, where he was repairing some screens. "I think we should go back now," she said.

"Do you, darling?" He put down the tack hammer and hooked his arm around her waist. "All right, we'll go home. I've missed two important meetings that I remember . . . But we'll be coming back here. The boys thrive on the mountain air. I feel good myself. How do you feel? With that honey glow to your skin, why should I ask, right?"

"Right," she agreed out loud. But in her mind she shouted, I feel as if I've been emotionally drawn and quartered.

The boys didn't make a fuss about leaving, since their uncle assured them they would be coming back to the cottage during the summer.

The day before they were to leave, the weather turned cold, and work on the dock, although almost finished, stopped.

Damon bundled the boys up in winter coats and boots, and took them for a walk, Curly at their side. Zen stayed in the cabin and made chicken soup from scratch. She chopped every vegetable available, except the fresh cooked beets, which she intended to slice and marinate in oil and vinegar with onions and chives.

While the stock and vegetables were simmering, she packed some of the boys' things, to save time in the morning.

She was back in the kitchen stirring the soup, then lifting a wooden spoon to taste it, when Damon crooned in her ear, "Feed me." Startled, Zen jerked her hand and spilled some of the soup.

"Damon! We both could have been burned." She

frowned at him as she lifted the spoon to his mouth. "Where are the boys?"

"Mmmm, good. Ahh...hot! The boys are lying in front of the fire with Curly." Damon sipped the rest of the soup off the spoon, then kissed her, his mouth opening on hers. "Thank you...for the soup."

"Yes." Zen swung around to gaze down at the bubbling kettle, not seeing the vegetables floating there. Damon's face filled her mind.

That evening, Zen served dinner from a blanket spread out in front of the fire. Damon and the twins helped bring out the food, but with a great deal of teasing and giggling.

"Curly can eat with us," David decided. Daniel nodded.

"Curly will eat outside," Damon corrected. "Then, when we've cleaned up our dishes and taken our walk, Curly can join us by the fire."

David frowned at his uncle, but, seeming to decide that arguing wouldn't change Damon's mind, he nodded.

The soup and hard rolls disappeared like magic, and, to Zen's surprise, so did the beet salad. For dessert there were apples, grapes, and cheese, which they ate after Damon and the boys had cleared away and washed most of the dishes, as Zen watched from the doorway.

"Stop looking so surprised, Zen," Damon chided her. "I know how to wash dishes. I lived in Alaska for a time, up near Barrow. I learned how to cook and take care of myself. I also backpacked to Alice Springs in Australia with a friend. Dug for opals, studied the aborigines..." He shrugged.

"I never knew that." Zen took a chair in the kitchen and watched the boys dry the plates.

"Was it scary?" Daniel asked.

Damon shook his head. "Australia is awesome, not scary. I loved it...and I'm going to take Aunt Zeno there on a trip someday."

Zen felt her neck redden as Damon chuckled and both boys cried, "Take me, too."

After they went for a walk, the boys stretched out in

front of the fireplace, and Damon held up a guitar he'd found in a cupboard. He raised his eyebrows at Zen.

"My father's," she explained, reaching for it. She twisted the string screws to see if it could be tuned after such a long time and after having experienced such extremes of temperature in the cabin. Several minutes passed before she decided it might be playable. She strummed a few chords and found it in fairly good tune. When she sang the mountain song "Shenandoah," the poignant words and melody carried her away. She was taken aback when Damon's rich baritone joined her lilting soprano.

It took all her courage to continue playing. His voice seemed to reach out to her and pull her into himself, as though now her blood ran with his.

The boys applauded and sang a song Daniel had learned in school and taught to David.

When the boys could no longer keep their eyes open, Damon carried them up stairs, Curly at his heels, Zen following behind them.

In no time the twins were asleep, the dog curled up on the floor between the beds.

"Let's have some wine." Damon went out to his car and returned with a bottle of French champagne. "A friend of mine, Marcel Daubert, has vineyards in Provence," he explained. "This is his family's wine."

"Did you meet him when you were at Oxford?"

Damon paused in opening the bottle. "How did you know I went there?"

"Eleni told me you were a Rhodes scholar." Zen was tickled that Damon seemed discomfited. "She said you were the brainy one of the family," Zen added, deliberately provoking him.

"And no doubt she told you I don't like to talk about it," Damon said dryly, watching her.

"She might have." Zen smiled. "But why wouldn't you want to talk about something as prestigious as being a Rhodes scholar?"

"My mother and grandmother and uncles all talked of nothing else whenever they were in my company. Finally

I convinced my mother to spread the word that I didn't
want to talk about it anymore."

"Poor baby," Zen soothed.

"Little demon." Damon reached and grabbed her before she could get away. He sat down with her in his
lap, holding her with one arm while his other hand touched
the pleasure points of her body. "Tease me, will you?"

Zen laughed, then gasped. "Stop it, Damon. The
boys . . ."

He glanced up the stairs, then back at her. "All right.
For the moment." He reached behind him and hefted the
guitar. "Play a song for me."

Zen played and sang, and Damon sang with her. For
a short time the real world seemed to fade away, and
they escaped to another realm that contained them alone.

When at last they prepared for bed, Damon's arm
curled around her waist; hers rested across his broad
back. The champagne was gone, and the evening had
taken on a luster that had nothing to do with wine.

"You may have dark circles under your eyes in the
morning," Damon said as he began to undress her, keeping her standing in front of him. "No, don't cover your
breasts . . . please." He leaned down to take her nipple
into his mouth.

His touch made her body tremble. She closed her eyes
as he released her breast and knelt in front of her to slide
her jeans, then the bikini panties, down her legs.

"Naked or dressed, *agape mou,*" Damon said in gut-
tural Greek. "You are Venus to me." He pressed a kiss
to her abdomen, then stood and flung off his own clothes
and caught her to him again, leading her to the bed and
sinking with her down into its comfort.

The night was long and beautiful. Zen could deny him
nothing. But each time their bodies separated, she felt
an overwhelming sense of loss that filled her with despair.

The next morning was sunny, crisp, and cold. The
lake sparkled like a sapphire.

Zen packed quickly and easily. Though she tried, she couldn't smother the sadness that engulfed her at the thought of leaving. These days with Damon and the boys had been some of the happiest she had ever known. She might return to the cottage with David and Daniel, but surely she would never return with Damon.

"Now remember, Zen, I'll be right behind you," he said, pointing to the map. "This is the first leg of the trip. We'll stop there." He punched a point with his index finger.

She nodded, then looked up at him, trying to keep her face expressionless. "Fine. We'll see you at the restaurant near Johnsburg."

He smiled down at her, studying her intently. "You'll never be free of me, Xenobia. You're tied to me." He turned to call the boys and the dog, then checked once more to ensure that the doors and windows were locked and the pump shut off.

Zen stood frozen to the spot, watching him, wanting both to strike him and to cling to him. She hated their hot–cold relationship, the ambivalence that kept her emotions seesawing from high to low.

When both boys and the dog were settled in the Cherokee, she began to climb into the car. Then she felt herself being lifted into the seat.

"Are you sure this isn't too tough for you to maneuver? Wouldn't you rather drive the Ferrari?"

God, no, she thought, shaking her head. She needed the distraction of the boys—their laughter, bickering, and interminable questions.

Reluctantly Damon let her go and climbed into his own car.

The drive to the secondary road was uneventful, but, though the highway wasn't as busy as it would be on the weekends, there were still enough cars to demand Zen's full attention.

When they arrived at Harley's Garage, she turned in to fill up on gas.

"Hi, there. Nice to see you folks again." Harley

squinted up the road as the Ferrari pulled in after them. "I see your husband found you all right."

"Ah, yes." Zen smiled weakly, letting the boys out of the car and snapping a leash on Curly.

"What's that for?" Damon asked, nodding toward the dog scooper and taking the lead from her.

"I use it to clean up after Curly when we're traveling," Zen explained. She stifled a giggle as Damon grimaced, shook his head, and walked away. The thought of the great Damon Aristides cleaning up after a dog threatened to send her into peals of laughter.

Damon glared back at her. "There's always tonight, Xenobia, when we're in bed," he warned.

"We'll be at your mother's house, in our own rooms," she retorted.

He shook his head. "The house is mine, and you *will* be sleeping with me—either in my suite or yours."

Zen made a face at his back. "Go suck an egg," she muttered, then sprinted for the bathroom where the boys were, sensing that Damon had heard her.

The boys had decided that they didn't want to be encumbered by their seat belts, and they were arguing the point with Zen when Damon returned with Curly.

"Don't let me hear you talk that way again," he said more sternly than he had ever spoken to them. "When it comes to safety, there is no arguing. Understood?"

"Yes, Uncle Damon," the boys murmured, chastened.

During the rest of the trip, they stopped at intervals to stretch their legs and feed the boys. Still, David and Daniel became cranky and rambunctious as the trip lengthened. They took only a short nap. Then they began arguing. Several miles farther on, Damon passed Zen and signaled for her to pull over.

"I'm taking over the Cherokee, Zen. You drive the Ferrari."

She gulped. "I've never driven such a sophisticated machine."

"Don't worry. You know how to operate a standard shift, so I'll just adjust the seat for you, explain a few of the features, and you'll be on your way. We have only about a hundred miles to go, and I can see that the boys are beginning to act up."

Zen listened to his instructions with half an ear, feeling more inclined to watch his bent head and the way the sun glistened on his hair.

At last she was alone in the car, watching Damon signal and pull onto the highway. She did the same, keeping a safe distance behind the Cherokee.

When they had traveled several miles, a Camaro passed her carrying two young men who whistled and called out to her. Zen ignored them, but they pulled in between her and the Cherokee and began making gestures out the window, signaling for her to pull over. When she had the chance, she pulled out in front of them and floored the Ferrari, letting it leap ahead. The Camaro began to speed up.

Zen glanced at Damon as she pulled up alongside the Cherokee. He, too, motioned for her to pull over to the side of the road.

When she pulled to a stop, the Camaro pulled over as well. Apparently the young men didn't notice that Damon had stopped, too.

Even as he was stepping from the Cherokee, a State Trooper arrived. Zen wondered if Damon had called him on the CB. The men in the Camaro made as though to return to their car, but Damon collared them and told the officer that the men had tried to intimidate his wife.

"Hey, Mac, we didn't know she was yours," said one of the young men.

"You sure knew she wasn't yours...and that it's against the law to play games like that on the highway," Damon retorted angrily, the words coming from his mouth like bullets, his hands clenching and unclenching at his sides. "Officer, I'd like to charge these men with harassment."

Both men shifted restlessly on their feet, their faces flushed with anger.

The policeman wrote busily on his pad. Damon assured him that his lawyer would visit the State Police headquarters to see that the men were charged as he felt they should be.

Zen wasn't sure, but she thought she saw the trooper's lips twitch as he read the men their rights. Was he enjoying this?

When they finally turned into the long circular drive leading to the Aristides estate, Zen could see Sophie standing in the drive, her hands clasped in front of her. Thag was there, too, as usual, but this time he seemed filled with anticipation as he shifted restlessly from one foot to the other. Zen was glad he'd stayed. She hoped to get to know him better. Yanos was leaning on his rake, and Maria and Lona stood farther up the steps.

The Ferrari and the Cherokee pulled to a stop, and the twins tumbled out.

"We had fun!" David exclaimed as he hugged his grandmother.

Daniel hugged her, too. "David and me slept in the loft. Aunt Zeno and Uncle Damon slept downstairs."

Zen's cheeks burned with embarrassment as Sophie's eyes turned to hers, one eyebrow arching just the way Damon's did. Pythagoras was grinning.

Curly jumped down from the van and immediately watered the rose bed.

"Damn you," Damon said mildly, looking amused. "If you kill those roses, Yanos will have your ears." His eyes caught Zen's, where she was still standing beside the Ferrari. "Come over here, darling, and tell Mother what a good time we had."

"We did, we did," Daniel answered for her. "And Uncle Damon says we can go back when the weather is warmer." He looked around him. "It's warmer here, isn't it?"

"That's because you were in the mountains where the air is cool," Thag told him.

"Curly likes the lake, too, Nonna. Can you come with us next time?" David asked as his grandmother turned to lead both boys into the house.

"Yes, indeed, that would be very nice," she replied.

David paused on the top step, frowning. "You'll have to sleep with Aunt Zeno and Uncle Damon. They have the biggest bed."

"David," Zen said, "it's time to get washed for dinner." She wanted to die from embarrassment.

"I'm hungry," he announced plaintively.

"Come along with me," Lona offered. "I have nice shiny apples up in your room with wedges of cheese."

"Oh, goody." Daniel smiled at his old nurse, trying to smother a yawn.

"Come on, darling. We'll take a shower before we have a cocktail," Damon said, placing a strong arm around Zen's shoulders. He guided her into the foyer and up the stairs.

"Stop it," she stage-whispered, trying to dig in her heels. "I haven't even spoken to your mother or—"

"That's all right, Xenobia. We'll talk when you come down again," Sophie called.

Zen tried to look over her shoulder at the older woman, but Damon was taking her up the steps so fast she caught only a fleeting glance of the enigmatic face. "This is very embarrassing. Did you hear what David said?" Zen whispered as they went down the corridor leading them to their room. "I am not staying in your apartment, Damon. Surely you can see—"

"Then I'll stay in yours. Even though the bed may be too short."

"Don't be ridiculous. The bed is monstrous...What? You are *not* staying in my room!"

"We're sleeping together."

"No!" She shook her head until she thought her neck would snap. "I can't do it. I'll move out first."

Damon's expression grew as dark as midnight. "Why is it so bad to sleep with me now when we slept together at the cottage?"

"Your mother wasn't at the cottage, Damon. And don't look at me like that. I won't change my mind. So, which shall it be? Do I get a hotel room or do I sleep alone?"

His mouth tightened with anger and frustration. "I

don't like being pushed around, Zen. That's the one thing I will not tolerate." He spun on his heel and strode down the hall that led to double doors and beyond to his quarters.

"I don't like it either. You remember that," Zen called after him, watching his broad shoulders stiffen as he paused. He pushed open the double doors with a crash that made her flinch.

Zen stumbled into the shower, letting the steamy water pour down on her, feeling bruised in every muscle.

When she emerged a long time later, she felt a little more relaxed and in control.

Maria had already put most of her things away. "I thought you would want me to press this dress, Kyria." She gestured at the shoes and underthings she'd laid out on the bed.

"Isn't that a little too formal for dinner with the family?" Zen pointed to the grape-colored silk dress Maria was holding.

"There are guests this evening, Kyria." Maria left before Zen could question her further.

Yawning, she shrugged and flopped face down on the bed. Her body felt as flaccid as well-done spaghetti.

Damon's face appeared in her mind as she closed her eyes. Every pore, every laugh line, was familiar to her.

The phantom Damon laughed with her; then his face turned to sculpted stone. His eyes lost their gleam.

"You've run away from me once too often, Xenobia," he said. "Now I don't want you."

"You can't go away," Zen pleaded with him in her dream. "You're my albatross. I left you three years ago and, deep inside, I've been unhappy ever since. If you leave me again, I won't be able to bear it. Come back, Damon." Zen called to him and called to him. "I don't mean you're my good luck. You're my bad," she wailed in her dream. She saw the majestic albatross and whimpered in her sleep.

Suddenly, she sat up in bed, aware that the dream was true. If Damon left her, life would have no meaning.

She shook herself fully awake and straightened the covers on the bed, then reached for a robe to wear while she put on her makeup. Her eye caught the grape-colored dress hanging on the clothes tree, its silky flounces moving at the least breath of air.

The dress was street length but designed for evening wear. The off-the-shoulder ruffle was repeated in a diagonal sweep around her body from one shoulder to the hem. Zen slipped the dress over her head. It clung to her form like a gentle caress. With it she wore the pink sapphire earrings which had belonged to her sister and which Damon had given to her. She twisted her hair into a coil at the back of her head.

Taking a deep breath, she stepped into the hallway. Would she have time to visit the boys? She saw Lona coming from their room. "Are they sleeping?" she asked.

"Yes. I fed them some soup after they ate their apples and cheese. They are so tired . . . but it's a good kind of tired. I have never seen Daniel look so bright and healthy. They need each other, don't they, miss?"

"Yes, they do," Zen replied softly, a wrenching sadness welling up inside her. It was true. The boys did need each other. They needed to grow together, to go to school, to play, to discover each other. The words echoed in her head as she descended the stairs.

Blindly, her thoughts like smoke clouding her mind, Zen pushed open the double doors of the living room and was assailed by voices and strange faces. Surprised, she hesitated on the threshold. Where had all these people come from?

"There you are, darling," Damon said, stepping toward her and pulling her close to his side in a powerful embrace.

"Who are these people?" Zen asked through suddenly dry lips.

"Our guests. They've come to help us celebrate."

"That's nice." Zen glanced around her and realized that she recognized only about three people in the room. She turned back to Damon. "Celebrate what?"

"Our forthcoming marriage. Darling, I want you to meet a colleague of mine. Vince, this is Xenobia Driscoll, my fiancée. Zen, my love, this is Vince Dante, my partner in the Olympus Fishery."

"Fish?" Zen repeated stupidly, her head whirling. The room and the smiling faces in it seemed to be distorted, as if seen through a fun house mirror. She swayed and felt Damon's arm tighten around her.

"Yes. And this is Terry Riedle, vice-president of Venus Airlines."

"Planes?" Zen felt as though she had no control over her facial muscles. Her smile seemed to be slipping sideways, her eyes were heavy, and her lips felt like plastic.

"Must you keep repeating what I say?" Damon whispered in her ear.

"What?" Zen looked up at him, trying to focus. When someone held out a drink, she took it without thinking and tipped the iced liquid down her throat. She started to choke, and Damon patted her back and took the empty glass from her hand.

"I never knew you were a drinker," he commented, when she took another glass from a passing tray. "No one should toss off martinis on the rocks as though they were water."

"I don't expect you to believe me, but I thought it *was* water until I'd already taken a swallow." Zen lifted the full glass to her mouth, but paused when she saw the twist of lemon floating in it. She shrugged and sipped the bitter brew of gin and vermouth.

"Why would I not believe you, love?" Damon leaned over and took her lips, his tongue invading her mouth at once.

"Come, come, Damon...Xenobia. Not now," Pythagoras admonished gently. "Sophie is about to make the announcement." He smiled at Zen when she swayed in Damon's arms.

"Right. We're coming." He urged her into the center of the throng, where Sophie stood instructing everyone to take a glass of champagne.

"I am delighted to invite you all to my son's wedding, which will take place in two weeks," she announced.

Zen glared at them all. "Not a chance," she murmured. But her voice failed to carry over the chorus of congratulations and best wishes.

Chapter 7

"AND WHEN IS the shower? I suppose you'll expect me to have it," Damon's Aunt Dalia said sourly to Zen. She turned to Sophie. "She doesn't even look Greek."

Zen swallowed more of her martini, squinted to get her bearings on Aunt Dalia's position and started for the woman, fists clenched. "You know what you can do with—" Zen was jerked back into familiar arms and pressed against a hard chest, her words smothered in a silk dinner jacket.

"What did she say?" Aunt Dalia lifted her classic chin and looked down her patrician nose.

"She said there isn't much time if we're to have the shower before the wedding, and if you feel it's too much..." Damon held tightly to Zen, lovingly pressing his finger over her lips.

"Me? Not be able to hold the traditional couple's party for the bride and groom? Ridiculous! We'll have it on next Tuesday. My secretary will call everyone." Aunt Dalia gave a satisfied sniff. "Is Friday the day you're to be married?"

472

"Yes. In the evening by a judge who's a friend of mine. Here at the house," Damon told her.

"Of course you will have a religious ceremony at some later date." Aunt Dalia gazed at them with disapproval.

Zen freed her mouth. "You can go—"

Damon bent to kiss her, wincing only slightly when Zen bit his lip. He lifted his head and smiled at his aunt. "She said it's getting stuffy in here. Perhaps we'd better get some air."

"Your lip is bleeding." Aunt Dalia looked askance at her nephew. "In my day we saved such things for the bedroom."

"Xenobia is very earthy," Damon observed, only blinking when Zen kicked him in the shin.

"Loose. That's what the world is today, loose." Aunt Dalia humphed and turned away to speak to her nephew Sandor, who was proffering a drink to his aunt and ogling Zen at the same time.

Zen had never liked the oily Sandor, but now she beamed at him and beckoned him to her side.

Sandor waved his lighter close to Aunt Dalia's hair, nearly setting her on fire, then hurried over to Zen and Damon. "If you have guests to speak to, Damon, I will keep Zen company."

"No," Damon barked.

"Lovely idea," Zen said at the same time, moving forward as much as Damon's arm would allow. "Let me go, Damon dear. I would like to talk to your cousin."

"Sandor," Damon said casually, releasing her, his teeth coming together with a snap, "if you keep looking at Xenobia that way, I will blacken both your eyes . . . here . . . now . . . in this room."

Sandor looked at his tall, well-built cousin and would have moved away, but Zen clutched his arm just as another guest demanded Damon's attention and pulled him aside.

Zen needed to clutch something. The unaccustomed gin made her feel as though she were crossing the deck of a ship at sea.

"You have lovely breasts, Xenobia," Sandor murmured boldly in her ear.

Zen's eyes widened in shock at his audacity. "Are you adopted, Sandor?" she asked casually. "No one in this family talks in such a fashion. And incidentally, if Damon hears you speak that way, he's liable to beat your brains in."

She whirled away from Sandor—right into Sophie. "Oh! Excuse me. Ah... about that announcement."

"I know you said you would play the piano for us after dinner," Sophie gushed, "but so many of the family are dying to hear you play now."

Sophie urged her toward the mammoth Steinway. "Eleni played, not me," Zen whispered. "I play the guitar... and not very well."

Sophie ignored her and clapped her hands for attention. "Xenobia has consented to play for us," she announced loudly.

"She doesn't play very well, as I remember," Aunt Dalia warned the assembled guests, earning a glare from Zen.

"I'll play... and Zen will sing," Damon said unexpectedly. "Come, darling. Would you like to sit next to me or stand at the side of the piano?"

"I'd like to get a bus to Cleveland," Zen muttered.

"Why is she talking to herself, Sandor?" Aunt Dalia trumpeted. "She was never too bright as a child, as I recall."

Damon seemed amused by the dark look Zen shot his aunt. "Your family is the most irritating group of cretins," she mumbled between clenched teeth.

"Ignore her," Damon said. "I do. Now tell me, is there anything in this mountain of sheet music you would like me to play?"

Zen was about to tell him she didn't care what he played when her eye caught the title *Songs of Ireland* on a thick book. She took it from the stack and began leafing through it. She pointed to a song and swallowed to moisten her throat.

"Are you sure you wouldn't like to sing something Greek?" Damon laughed when she curled her lip.

"I'll leave that to you," she said, then listened to the introduction, remembering the night when Seamus and several other Irish friends of hers had gathered at her apartment and sung around the piano for much of the evening, even allowing David to sing with them. The words of the ballad had remained in her memory, and her untrained but pure soprano filled the room with the poignant melody.

Zen was so lost in the words that at first she didn't notice when Damon's baritone joined her. The sweet tune came as natural as breathing as he sang the words to "The Isle of Innisfree."

They sang other songs from the book, and Zen felt such a pull between them that she forgot for a moment that she was angry with Damon and his family. She even forgot that there were other people in the room.

When she signaled to Damon that she could sing no more, he rose from the piano and turned her to face the applause.

Sophie came forward to take her hands. "And did you learn those lovely songs from your friends in Dublin?" she asked.

"Yes." Zen smiled in remembrance. "Seamus Dare and some others used to gather at least once a week, and we would sing the old songs, some in Irish. David knows a few Irish songs."

"You saw Seamus Dare once a week?" Damon asked, his voice like velvet-covered steel.

"More frequently than that." Zen laughed. "I worked with him. He would often come home with me to visit David. They were great friends."

"Were they?" Damon's angry words made Zen and Sophie regard him in surprise.

Zen opened her mouth to speak, but Sophie interrupted. "Dinner, everyone." She cleared her throat. "It's time for dinner." She hooked her arm through Zen's and pulled her away, calling to Damon over her shoulder,

"My son, you will kindly escort your Aunt Dalia and your Aunt Sophronia. Zen will sit between Vincent and Terence."

"You needn't lead me away from him," Zen protested. "I know his damn temper is firing up again. I don't know why, and I don't give a damn. Your son is the most capricious, volatile, unstable..." Zen accompanied Sophie to the dining room, still listing Damon's many faults.

"He's jealous," his mother said.

"Bull chips!" Zen expostulated, then clapped her hand over her mouth in chagrin.

In all her years, she had never dreamed of using that particular expression. "You use such colorful language, Xenobia," Sophie said calmly, taking her place at the head of the table.

Zen felt her face burn with embarrassment. "Forgive me. I didn't mean—"

"Tut, tut, child, I meant no censure." Sophie caught and held Zen's gaze. "I'm glad you're with us, Xenobia. You have brought life and laughter to this house. Even my friend Pythagoras says he can't remember when Daniel ever laughed as he has laughed since David arrived. It is good." Sophie patted Zen's hand on the snowy damask tablecloth, then gestured to the maid to begin serving.

They had moussaka and a rack of lamb with rosemary and lemon, but most of the other dishes were either American or Continental. As was the custom in the Aristides home, there were several courses consisting of fish, vegetables, and fruit as well as meat.

Zen fully appreciated the food after having cooked for herself at the cabin. She complimented both Maria and Sophie.

"Soon you will be directing us, Kyria Xenobia," Maria said with the ease of a life-long retainer. She had helped to raise both Damon and Davos.

Zen coughed and reached for her water glass. She shook her head.

"Of course you will, Xenobia." Sophie patted her back

and gestured to Yanos, who was acting as butler for the evening, to refill her wine and water glasses. "It is time I retired from running this house and traveled. I want to turn it over to you, just as I turned my business interests over to my son."

There were choruses of "Good idea" and "Just the thing to do" from various guests.

"I don't think you should retire," Zen protested, her eyes watering from her coughing. "Do you, Damon?"

"I think it would be good for Mother to travel," he said. "She will still have her apartment in the house and can come back any time to visit us and the boys."

"I think it is a good idea," Pythagoras agreed. He looked startled when Zen glared at him.

Tiny Aunt Sophronia, who was said to have Albanian blood, leaned forward in her chair and fixed Zen with her eyes. "It is well past time that you tended to your duties, young woman."

"Well, of all the—"

"Darling, you're going to love the dessert," Damon interrupted, rising from his chair to come around in back of hers. "In fact, I want you to be surprised, so I'm going to cover your eyes."

"Youuu, you're covering ma mouf . . ." Zen glowered up at him, pulling at his hands.

"Ah, here's Maria. Just in time," Damon announced.

Zen freed her mouth at last and took a deep breath to tell Damon what she thought of him and his family, but he reached for the tray Maria was carrying and pushed a honey cake into her mouth. "There! I knew you'd love it." He looked up at Maria. "She loves them."

Zen was aware that all eyes were on her as she pulled the sticky cake out of her mouth. She licked the honey from her lips, camouflaging her awkwardness behind a napkin.

"What's she doing now, Sandor?" Aunt Dalia bellowed. "She's a strange creature. Don't know what Damon sees in her."

"I do." Sandor smacked his lips. Damon's onyx eyes

bore down on him like twin mortars on a target. Sandor laughed nervously. Damon ground his teeth.

"Damon, do take your seat," his mother said, frowning.

"Mother, I think it would be nice if we all had coffee and liqueur in the living room," he suggested.

Maria brought Zen a finger bowl while Yanos distributed them to the other guests. "Let me help you, Kyria Xenobia," Maria said.

"Ah . . . thank you. I can manage." Zen glanced over her shoulder at Damon. "I intend to have a mail bomb put into the In-box in your office," she said in dulcet tones.

"Darling, how sweet! Of course you can buy me a betrothal gift. I think that's very nice."

Zen rose with the others to leave the dining room. Damon kept hold of her elbow. "Release me, you savage," she demanded.

"Love, I thought you liked it when I touched you," Damon baited her.

"Stop that!" Zen caught the narrow-eyed glances of Damon's two aunts. "Your family despises me."

He was unperturbed. "I don't give a damn what they think."

"They own stock in Olympus Limited," Zen said, holding back as they approached the living room.

"If you're worried that I can't support you and the boys, my love, forget it." Damon's thick eyebrows came together over his nose; white lines bracketed his mouth.

"Don't be an ass," she retorted. "I just don't see why you want to be tied to someone who will be stared at by the family at every get-together." She fell silent.

Damon shrugged. "If they annoy you, we'll avoid my family. Of course, I'll have to arrange to see my mother with the boys now and then."

"Damon." Zen's throat tightened. "I . . . I would never try to separate the boys from your mother. I'm not like that."

He halted in front of the double doors to the living room, in full view of the occupants, who were turning slowly to observe them. "I know you hold the best interests of both boys as your primary concern. I never thought otherwise of you." He kissed her full on the mouth, his tongue chasing hers lazily.

Zen felt as though someone had set fire to her inside. Her blood seemed to be burning up.

"Was Damon always so . . . so loose, Sophie?" Aunt Dalia asked disdainfully.

"Do you not remember how it was when we were in love, Sister?" Sophie asked, raising her chin.

"Yes . . . yes, but we were not wantons like that . . . that one."

Zen pulled free of Damon. "Now, see here Aunt Dalia." She stalked into the room and stopped directly in front of the stalwart Greek woman. "You've been criticizing Damon and me all night, and I've been very patient." She turned to glare at Damon when he laughed. "But I've had enough."

"I, also, have had enough, Sister," Sophie interrupted. "I want you to come to my son's wedding and give the couple's party, but if you don't want to, someone else can."

Silence, thick, heavy silence, filled the room.

"I will give the couple's party, as I always do." Dalia sat down on the settee.

Sophie gave one curt nod and sat down next to her. "Xenobia will pour the tea," she announced.

"Good Lord," Damon whispered, backing away as if Zen's pouring tea would place him in danger.

Zen spilled some tea in the saucers. Dalia and Sophronia rolled their eyes. The other cousins drew closer and began to chat with Zen. She had no real trouble until she handed Damon his tea. Had she not looked up at him and seen the black heat in his eyes, she might have muddled through, she told herself, but she did look at him. The cup wobbled on the saucer, and she spilled hot tea on his wrist.

"Aaaagh! Damn it, Zen. I knew I shouldn't have taken tea."

"You should have asked for coffee," Aunt Dalia agreed

brusquely, her lips pursed as she presided over the silver coffeepot. "Greeks should drink coffee."

"Thank you." Damon grimaced at his aunt, then frowned down at Zen. "Stop mopping at me."

"You need some lotion." When he tried to pull his arm free, Zen thrust out her jaw. She saw Sandor place his scotch on the table and spied the ice cubes in his drink. "Pardon me, I need that." She reached into the glass and drew out an ice cube. After wrapping it in a napkin, she pressed it on Damon's skin. Part of her was appalled that she could do such a crass thing, but concern for Damon was uppermost in her thoughts.

"Damn it all, I just poured that drink," Sandor complained.

Zen ignored him. She lifted Damon's hand to her mouth and kissed the red spot.

He gasped and leaned over her. "Do that again, please."

"Sophie, I cannot stay in this house if they are going to continue to make love in public," Dalia said in stentorian tones.

"They are like this all the time," Sophie answered serenely.

"You must not be offensive, Xenobia." Aunt Sophronia sniffed. "Ours is a proud family."

"Goat chips, Sophronia," Pythagoras drawled, smiling at Zen and receiving a smile from her in return. "If you intend to stay in this house at any time in the future, you will have to become accustomed to seeing displays of affection. We thrive on it here." He moved closer to Sophie.

"My dear departed brother Dmitri, who was your husband, Sophie, would not approve of such looseness." Sophronia's pursed mouth looked like a prune.

To Zen's surprise, Sophie bit her lips and stepped away from Thag, looking distressed.

"Sophronia Aristides, if you think to upset Sophie, cease," said Pythagoras. "We will be married soon, and I will take it ill if anyone upsets my future wife." He gave each guest a warning look.

"I didn't know they were getting married," Zen whispered to Damon.

"It's about time he forced mother off the fence." Damon smiled down at her. "That's the only way to handle a woman—throw her over your shoulder and cart her away."

Zen raised her chin, prepared to do battle with him, but she paused when she caught him grinning at her. She took a deep breath. "If you're trying to bait me, it won't work."

"It usually does. Let's go to bed."

Zen gasped and glanced nervously around the room, but most of the family was staring at Sophie, whose face had turned brick red. "Not in your mother's house," Zen whispered.

"How many times must I tell you that this is my home, under my name, and in two weeks it will be your home as well."

"What do you mean?" Zen's head snapped back to him.

"It means I've instructed my lawyers to place this home and the apartment in London, plus a twenty percent share in my holdings, in your name on our wedding day."

"No." Zen shook her head, aghast. "I don't want anything. I can earn my own way. I won't be paid—"

"Stop babbling, darling. I know all about your independence, and your lack of interest in material things, but I fully intend to protect you. If anything happened to me, my enemies would try to cut you out of everything. You would win in the end, because my will is solid, but in the meantime a long litigation would be very distressing. This way no matter what happens there will be no discomfort. You will have your own property and money, deeded to you in my lifetime."

"Don't talk this way." Zen wrung her hands, imagining all sorts of catastrophes. "I don't want to hear about you dying. I hate it. I won't listen."

Damon pulled her close to his side, ignoring his clamoring relatives who pushed close to Sophie and Thag, interrogating them. "I am not leaving you," he said, "but you're not practical, my fey darling, and I intend to see to your welfare. Even if I die before we marry, you will still have twenty percent of my holdings."

"Stop, please stop." Zen squeezed her eyes shut, trying to wipe out a suddenly vivid picture of Damon trapped under the wheels of a truck.

"Darling." Damon pushed her a little away from him and stared down at her stricken face. "Darling, I'm sorry. I didn't mean to upset you." He ran his index finger down her nose. "Where has your down-to-earth common sense gone?"

"It drowned in the Irish Sea," she mumbled, letting her arms slip around his waist for a moment before she pushed away from him and turned to watch the others. "Why are they so concerned that your mother is marrying Thag?" she asked. "I should think they would be happy for her. He doesn't want her money."

"I should think not." Damon gave a hard laugh. "He could buy and sell anyone here tonight—except me." His hand settled at her waist, where he stroked her gently.

"Then why do Sandor and Dalia look so sour?"

"Because my mother has been supporting them for years—even though they have money of their own. My dear aunt and cousin do not believe in spending their own capital if they can sponge off my mother. She allows it, though she knows I disapprove. Thag will put a stop to it, and they know that, too."

"Good. I hope she marries him tomorrow," Zen said with conviction.

Damon laughed, then raised his voice. "Mother, my future wife says she wishes you would marry Thag tomorrow."

"Damon, for God's sake!" Zen felt weak with embarrassment as every eye in the room fixed on her.

"Do you, Xenobia?" Sophie sounded like a breathless schoolgirl.

Zen's gaze moved from one guest to the other and finally settled on Thag, who looked unnaturally pale. But despite his obvious unease, he stood protectively close to Sophie, and Zen was struck anew by what a kind and caring man he was. He would make Sophie a faithful husband, a loyal defender, and a charming companion.

"Yes," Zen said, "I would like it very much if you married Thag—soon, so the boys will have a grandfather."

Sophie's eyes widened. "I hadn't thought of that. Yes, the boys do love you, Thag. We will get the license tomorrow."

Pythagoras let out a deep breath and kissed Sophie's cheek. "Tomorrow we will be the first in line at the license bureau."

"Ridiculous!" exclaimed Dalia, trying to take hold of her sister's arm. "Let me talk to you."

"No," Zen said loudly, surprising herself. "You've talked too much already. They'll be married as soon as possible, and the boys will attend the ceremony."

Dalia assessed Zen with deep contempt. "Your sister Eleni was never so bold."

A mutinous look came over Sophie's face. "Many times you caused Davos and Eleni unhappiness, Dalia," she said. "They loved each other so much, yet you hurt my daughter-in-law by saying unkind, spiteful things." Sophie glanced at Zen. "You have been unkind to Xenobia as well."

Zen's instinct to protect her loved ones—whether alive or just remembered—rose to the fore, and she stepped toward Dalia with deadly menace in her step. "If I had known you hurt Eleni—" Suddenly two iron-hard arms came around her chest, knocking the breath out of her.

Damon's warm breath grazed her cheek before his firm lips nuzzled her neck. "Watch out for my tiger, Aunt Dalia," he warned, chuckling. "She bites."

Dalia sniffed disdainfully and stomped away.

Gradually, in desultory fashion, members of the family began to take their leave. Unlike Dalia and Sandor, some smiled and wished the newly engaged couple sincerely well in their new life together.

When Sandor took Zen's hand and lifted it to his mouth, Damon was there to free Zen's hand and glower at his cousin.

"A simple handshake will do, Sandor," he said.

"You were always possessive of your toys."

His words inflamed Zen. "I'm no one's toy, Sandor." She, too, gave him a dark, warning look.

"Good night, Aunt Dalia." Damon smiled at his stern-faced aunt.

"I hope you know what you're getting into, Damon." Without another word she swept past Zen into the huge foyer and out of the house.

"Your family—" Zen began angrily, immediately mollified when Damon's arm circled her waist. His laughter tickled the hair on her neck.

Zen broke away from his embrace and turned to say good night to Sophie and Thag, who were sitting on the settee. They were staring into each other's eyes, awed expressions on their faces. Zen smiled fondly. It was lovely to see two people so much in love.

Feeling somewhat sentimental, and in no mood to confront Damon, Zen hoped to slip upstairs while he was giving Yanos instructions about how to store the remaining bottles of unopened champagne.

She had climbed the stairs and reached the sanctuary of her room when the door opened and closed behind her. She turned to see Damon, a determined look on his face. "Now, Damon, I already said that I would not sleep with you while—"

"Love." He held up both hands, palms out. "I haven't come to coerce you. I just thought you would like your ring. After all, it *was* your engagement party."

"Oh, I forgot."

"Did you?" He smiled lazily, but his eyes burned with a light she had seen all too often.

"What I mean is, I don't need—"

"No, don't say anything. Not about this." In an instant he was at her side, enfolding her in his arms. "I want to give you the world." He reached into his pocket, pulled out a box, and flicked open the lid.

An exquisite marquise diamond lay on apricot-colored velvet. Zen gasped. It was beautiful. But far too precious for her.

She gulped. "I'd be afraid to wear it."

"If you don't, I'll give it away," Damon said, pushing it onto her finger, then lifting her hand to his mouth.

Zen reeled. "Don't talk like that."

"Then don't say you won't wear it." He stared moodily down at her. "Do you like it?"

"Very much. Especially the gold filigree setting. It looks like an heirloom."

"It should. It belonged to my grandmother Aristides."

"It did?" Zen's hand jerked out of his. "But it must be so valuable. Are you sure it's safe to wear it?"

"I asked the jeweler that when he sized it for you. He checked all the points."

"How?"

Damon didn't pretend not to know what she was asking. "How did I get your ring size?" He smiled. "I enlisted Lona's help. I asked her to watch and see if you ever left your school ring on your dresser." He shrugged. "You did. I measured it, and Lona returned it for me."

"Sneaky, aren't you?" Zen held up her hand to the light.

"With you I have to be." He growled into her hair. "Do I get a thank you kiss?"

She hesitated. "I suppose so." She glanced up as his mouth descended to hers, raising her index finger between them. "But I can't sleep with—"

Damon bit her finger. "For God's sake, woman, don't tell me again that you aren't sleeping with me. I don't like hearing it." His mouth took hers with heart-melting tenderness, his tongue a gentle probe between her lips. "I do love to kiss you," he muttered against her mouth. She was lost to him.

"I like it, too," Zen murmured, letting her body mold itself to his.

"Lord, Zen, don't do that. I'll be in the shower all night."

She laughed. She felt as light as a balloon and as

powerful as an Amazon. Her skin tingled. She was going to marry him, the man she had loved since she was twenty years old! It was too good to be true.

Yes, far too good to be real, a cynical side of herself argued. Dreams didn't come true. They died slowly, a lingering death.

Whatever Damon felt for her—and she doubted it was love—was bound to change, probably sooner rather than later.

Damon groaned and stepped away from her, not hiding his arousal. "Zen, I'm not used to this—and I damn well don't like it. Good night!" He pivoted on his heel and left the room.

Zen had felt as if she were floating on a pink cloud, but now she landed with a bump. "Do you mean you're not used to denying yourself sex?" she demanded of the closed door. "How dare you be unfaithful to me!" Her anger grew threefold as she imagined him chuckling with a blond...no, a redhead...no, a stately brunette. "I'll cut him out of my heart before he cuts me out of his life," she decided.

All at once a wave of fatigue assailed her. It had been an exhausting and emotionally draining day.

She washed her face and climbed into bed, cradling her cheek in her left hand and falling almost immediately into the black well of sleep.

The next day Sophie and Thag took the boys with them to the courthouse and obtained a marriage license. They returned to announce that they would marry a few days later. Zen shared their joy. Sophie's obvious happiness made her see her future mother-in-law in a new light.

The wedding was simple and small, attended only by David, Daniel, Zen, and Damon. When they returned to the house, they enjoyed a special dinner prepared by Maria and served by Lona and Yanos, who were all encouraged to join the toast with vintage champagne.

"Are we drinking champagne, Aunt Zeno?" Daniel

quizzed, watching the bubbles in his glass.

"No, dear, you're drinking sparkling grape juice. Do you like it?"

He nodded and edged next to her on the settee. He leaned his head on her arm.

Concerned, Zen raised his chin in her hand and studied his face. "What is it, dear? Aren't you feeling well?"

"Yes ... I mean I'm fine." Daniel's voice faltered.

"Tell me. What's wrong?"

His lip quavered before he bit down on it. "Aunt Dalia said ... she said that you and Nonna won't want me and David when you get married." Daniel's eyes filled with tears.

"My own boy," Zen cried, enfolding him close to her, her face pressed against his head.

"What is it? What's wrong?" David climbed up on Zen's lap, wanting to be hugged, too.

"My babies ..." Zen was so full of feeling that she couldn't say anything else.

The three of them sat locked in a tight embrace for long, emotion-filled moments.

Damon glanced at them from where he stood with Maria, Yanos, and Lona and strode immediately over to them. He sank to his knees in front of them. "All right, what's going on here?" he demanded.

"Your aunt Dalia told Daniel that your mother and I wouldn't want the boys after we were married." Zen reached for a tissue to dry her eyes.

"Such big tears on your cheek, love. Ummm, salty too," Damon crooned. Then he turned to the boys and held their gazes with his own. "Nonna and Thag will be going on a trip soon," he explained, "but they will be back before Zen and I get married. When we go away for our trip, they will stay here with you. When we come back, all of us—David, Daniel, Aunt Zeno, and I—will be going on a trip together. Then the four of us will come back here to live. We're a family now. We'll be together."

"Then Aunt Dalia was wrong?" David asked, sighing.

Damon nodded. "Aunt Dalia was very wrong."

Both boys smiled, then slid from Zen's lap and ran to their grandmother and their new grandfather, talking at full speed. The indulgent adults hovered over them.

"And you," Damon continued, still kneeling in front of Zen, "must stop jumping to conclusions. Come to me if something is wrong. We'll settle it together." He rose, pulling her up with him. "We'll be married in one week— in nine days, to be exact, and then all your ghosts will go away."

Amazed, Zen looked up at him. He could see into her heart of hearts. He had opened the door that no one had ever opened, the door that concealed her most private fears. He seemed able to recognize and fulfill her needs before she recognized them herself.

While Sophie and Thag went on their short wedding trip, Zen was thrust into prewedding chaos. She had expected to shop for a dress; she had not expected a phone call from a designer named Charine, who informed her that her showroom was located on Madison near Sixtieth Street and to ask if Thursday morning would be suitable for the first fittings.

"Fittings?" Zen repeated, waving frantically at Damon, who had entered the room. She held her hand over the phone and explained who was at the other end.

He nodded and took the phone from her. "Charine? Damon Aristides. Yes, fine...Right. I'll bring her in myself. Yes." He replaced the receiver. "I have to get some work done anyway. I'll leave you at the showroom. Then when you're ready you can come to the office. I'll send my driver to pick you up."

"You will?" Zen was amazed. "But you'll be busy."

"Yes. I generally am...and lately I've taken off more time than ever before. But I have a very efficient staff." Damon shrugged and kissed her open mouth. "Don't look so surprised, love. The boss should be able to play hooky now and then."

"Yes," she agreed, bemused.

Damon frowned. "Perhaps you would prefer another designer. I should have remembered your own designing talents. Would you rather design you own dress, love?"

Zen considered for a moment and shook her head. "I'll probably have a few ideas of my own, but I know and admire Charine's work."

"Good." Damon kissed her again. "I just came in to say good-bye. I have a meeting at eleven."

Thursday was a drizzly day with a bite to the misty wind. Zen was content to cuddle close to Damon during the ride into Manhattan, glad that they were being chauffeured.

Damon dropped her at the designer's, after explaining that he wouldn't come in with her. He had piles of work to go through.

Charine was a small, birdlike woman with coal black hair that she wore twisted into a chignon. From her Italian leather shoes to the diamond studs in her ears she gave off an aura of French chic.

To Zen's surprise, the first order of the day was to provide her with nightwear.

"This was Madame Aristides' idea," Charine explained, smiling. "She informed me that you are to have silk in golds and greens that complement your coloring." Charine studied Zen as she stood before her in bra and briefs. "Madame was right. Those colors are good for you." She snapped her fingers, and an iridescent garment was placed in her hands, a pale gold silk kaftan that fell full from the shoulders. The front closed with two tiny hooks.

Zen tried it on, and a tiny smile appeared on Charine's face.

"Ah, good," She turned Zen in front of the three-way mirror in the large fitting room. "See for yourself."

Zen's eyes widened at the sight of the transparent fabric, which rippled on her form like a silken waterfall. "It's beautiful."

"Your husband will lose his mind," Charine predicted, fully satisfied.

Zen lost track of the garments she put on. Her head was filled with silks, woolens, and linens.

Finally Charine brought her the wedding dress. Zen took one look at the ruffles and balked. "No. I look better in tailored clothes," she said. Nothing would dissuade her. "It has too many ruffles for me."

Charine sighed and tapped one finger on her chin, then snapped her fingers. "Bring the special one—the cream satin," she told the assistant.

The pale cream satin had thin straps and no other decoration. The bustline was defined by stitching, but the dress fell to a demi-train that was plain and unadorned.

When Zen put it on, the designer and her assistants inhaled sharply. "You look like a miniature Venus. Though you are tiny of stature, mademoiselle, you have poise. And you are right about the dress. I will add sleeves—long and tight to the wrist," Charine mused. "And the neckline shall be square with the shoulders barely covered and the back falling to a deep V. It shall be stark—your hair, the gold-red color, and pink pearls in the ears shall be your only adornment. Five white flowers will tie back your hair so that it cascades down you back like a veil." Charine's eyes snapped in creative fervor. "You will be a goddess."

"I'll settle for making it down the aisle without falling," Zen said, smiling weakly as Charine buzzed around her like a queen bee, tucking, nipping, straightening, grumbling to herself.

"What? What did you say? Oh...ha, the American joke. How droll."

Not all of Zen's protestations that she really wasn't a clothes horse, despite her work in fashion, convinced Charine that she didn't need all the clothes and lingerie that an assistant jotted down in a loose-leaf notebook.

"Well, it is done, Mademoiselle Driscoll. The dress will be ready in plenty of time. Monsieur Aristides assures me that no expense must be spared." Charine smiled at Zen.

"But I won't wear half of these things," Zen protested.

Charine shrugged. "But it will be such a comfort to know that they are there to discard." Charine herself accompanied Zen to the front entrance of the showroom and bowed her out to the waiting Rolls-Royce.

"That must be the logic that sends such a large number of Americans to bankruptcy proceedings," Zen muttered, sitting back against the plush cushions.

Slowly they made their way through Manhattan traffic. Brakes screeched; horns blasted. Finally they pulled up in front of Olympus Ltd, managing to beat a Mercedes Benz into a parking space.

The chauffeur opened Zen's door, ignoring the fist-shaking driver of the Mercedes.

Zen, too, ignored the man's invective. She was about to identify herself to the security man on duty when he bowed to her and led her to an elevator.

"Mr. Aristides has been calling down every fifteen minutes for the last hour," the man explained in a Brooklyn accent. "I've worked for the boss for a few years and never remember him gettin' in such a whirl over a woman." He smiled at Zen as she entered the elevator. "Just punch the button. Take ya right there."

Zen's stomach and knees met in the tingling, rapid ascent.

When the doors opened, Damon was standing there. He pulled her from the elevator into his arms. His mouth came down over hers.

Immediately her limbs grew weak, and her thoughts whirled away. Damon filled all her senses. "People will see," she managed to gasp, trying to force her eyes open.

"Darling, you're in my private office," Damon explained, pulling her over to his desk and sitting down with her in his lap. I've been thinking about you all day, haven't been able to concentrate on the Rothman Cable problem at all."

"Business first," Zen croaked, clutching at his shoulders, rubbing her head against his chin.

"Tell me what—" A red light blinked on the desk

console. Damon glowered. He punched a button. "Yes?"

"I'm sorry, Mr. Aristides, but Miss Crawford insisted. She says she is only in town for—"

Damon barked into the speaker, then broke the connection.

Zen watched, fascinated, as his face darkened to crimson. She was sure he had forgotten her, even though she was sitting on his lap.

Who was Miss Crawford that the mere mention of her name provoked such an immediate embarrassed response from him? Were they involved? Did Damon love her? Zen shook her head to clear it of the black thoughts that crowded it.

Chapter 8

THE WEDDING DAY dawned gray and drizzly. It perfectly matched Zen's mood. She and Damon had been walking a tightrope for the last three days—ever since she had demanded to know who Miss Crawford was.

At first Damon had hedged. Then finally, infuriated by her needling, he'd told her.

"All right, dammit, she was my mistress. But I haven't seen her in six months." He had stood before Zen, fists clenched.

She took several deep breaths. She felt as though a truck had just rammed her middle. "So, in the meantime you found a substitute—me," she accused. "But now your West Coast sweetie wants you back. Is that it?"

"No, that is not it." Damon's body tensed with anger. "And don't jump to any—"

"Don't you swear at me," Zen retorted, her hands on her hips.

"I'm not swearing at you." Damon ground his teeth.

"Don't you raise your voice either, because I won't

let you push me around." Zen drew herself up to her full five feet two inches and glared at him.

Damon gazed down at her, his chest heaving. "Just damn well remember that we're getting married in three days." He stormed from the room. The door banged shut behind him, the sound reverberating through the house.

"Womanizer!" Zen called after him. "I never cry, I never cry," she murmured to herself, very fast and restlessly pacing the room. "Well, hardly ever," she amended. She held a hand to her mouth as shudders wracked her body.

Now, on her wedding day, Zen stared out the window at a gray Long Island Sound. "I should take the boys and skip town," she said to herself as she gathered sweet-smelling soaps and shampoos for her bath.

As she lathered her body and hair, she imagined herself with the two boys in a giant balloon crossing the United States, then on camels traversing the Sahara Desert, then in a three-man sailboat braving the Pacific. She would just disappear, she thought as she spread lotion on her body, then donned the filmy panties and stockings that would be her only undergarments. The heavy satin gown was lined with the softest cotton.

Sighing, Zen let Lona drop the gown over her head just as Sophie walked into the room. The older woman sighed, too, and folded her hands in front of her as she watched Lona arrange the garland of white roses at the back of Zen's head. "Charine told me you would look like a goddess from Olympus and you do, child," she said. "Eleni was lovely, but you are beautiful."

Zen swallowed. "Thank you, Mrs. Aristides."

"Can you not call me Sophie now?"

"Yes, of course. If you like." Zen felt uncomfortable under Sophie's soft gaze.

Lona turned Zen around so that she was facing the three-way mirror. She sucked in her breath. She had never looked better. The pearl studs in her ears seemed to have the same pink sheen as her skin. Her hair was like golden fire. The skin above her breasts was almost the same creamy color as the dress.

She picked up the one long-stemmed white rose that she would carry and felt something hard in the nylon net hand holder. She pushed aside the ruching. An emerald pin in the shape of a shamrock!

"There's an inscription on the back," Sophie said, smiling.

"My sweet luck. Damon," the inscription read, making Zen's eyes fill.

"Lona, leave us," Sophie said imperiously. "I wish to speak to Xenobia alone."

"But, madame..." Lona frowned, and glanced at the clock.

"It's all right, it's all right. I will not make her late. Father Constantine will wait, regardless, and the judge is a friend of Damon's."

Zen watched as Sophie followed Lona to the door and shut it behind her. She braced herself.

Sophie turned. "Do not be alarmed, child. I have no intention of attacking you. But I do want to apologize." She took a deep breath. "Three years ago, I let my sister chase you away. Because I was afraid, I suppose, but whatever the reason, I regret it. I caused you...and my beloved son...much pain. You see, I saw how much in love with you he was."

Zen was speechless. "That's not possible."

"Yes, child, he was in love with you—so much so that, when you left to live in Ireland, my Damon became someone else, someone hard, cynical, often unkind, often cruel. Although he was never dishonest, he became ruthless. You had been gone two years when I finally came to accept that what he felt for you was great and all-consuming. The feeling had turned inside him like a Judas blade, destroying him."

Sophie's eyes shone with unshed tears. "I recalled how he had been with you in the beginning...how he had laughed, how open and alive he'd been. Because you were gone from him, he had hidden his feelings behind a locked door." She pursed her lips. "His adven-

tures with women were chronicled in too many period-
icals."

"I...I saw some of the write-ups in the American
papers I received in Dublin," Zen admitted.

"Lord, that son of mine. Even in Athens—" Sophie
shook her head and fell silent. "Finally Thag convinced
me that Damon was pining for you."

"No," Zen whispered, though a faint ray of hope was
dawning. She tried to tamp it down.

"Yes. That is when I decided to convince you to come
home again. That and the desire to see my David as well.
I hurt you both, and for that I am most sorry."

"It wasn't your fault. Damon and I are too volatile
together."

"Yes, you are that," Sophie concurred. "But you are
also good for each other. I have heard Damon laugh
again, seen him come alive. He is once more eager to
enjoy all that life has to offer. I have seen you. You love
my son—as you loved him once before."

"No," Zen whispered, "I love him much more now."

"Oh, dear." Sophie smiled. "That could be very dangerous for Damon, couldn't it?"

Zen's face flushed with embarrassment. "I don't know
what's the matter with me. I'm such a klutz when he's
around me."

"The boys told me that Damon read them the story
of the albatross, the bird that brought bad luck when the
mariner killed it. I see a parallel between that story and
your own. Fortune smiled on you and Damon when you
first fell in love. It was only after you denied that love
and separated that you both became so unhappy. It's only
when you are fighting that love, instead of accepting it
in your heart, that you have these accidents." Sophie
chuckled. "I am sure that soon you will be handling my
son with ease."

"Never with ease." Zen grimaced ruefully, and Sophie
laughed.

"Come, my child, say that you forgive me. My son
must be growing impatient. He told me you would not

let him near you while I was in the house."

Zen lowered her eyes. "He shouldn't have said that."

"Ah, but it was so good to have Damon come and talk to me about you. Instead of the cold man who would not answer my questions, he is once again a loving son."

"He's still a blabbermouth."

Sophie laughed again, and Zen felt a smile pull at her mouth. She stretched and kissed the older woman's cheek. "I forgive you . . . and I thank you for Daniel. He is a beautiful boy."

Just then someone banged on the door, startling them both.

"Zen, for God's sake, hurry."

Sophie looked at Zen, her eyes brimming with mirth. "I think the bridegroom has lost what little patience he had."

"He won't wait for anything." Zen took a deep breath, wanting to believe what Sophie had told her but not able to heal all her deeply buried wounds in an instant.

"Oh, by the way, Xenobia, there is an Irishman downstairs who says he is a friend of yours."

"Seamus! He came!" Zen clapped her hands in delight as Sophie nodded that that was the name he had given— Seamus Dare.

"Is my mother there with you?" Damon demanded, rattling the doorknob.

"Yes," Sophie answered, opening the door. "But you cannot come in. Go downstairs and watch your bride descend to join you."

"Tell her to hurry. The guests are getting anxious," Damon said.

"Pooh," his mother responded. "You are the one who is growing anxious." Sophie looked back at Zen. "I am glad the priest will marry you."

Zen heard Damon's disgruntled voice fading as he returned to the small gathering who would witness the ceremony. Three times the number would join them for the reception.

Zen checked her appearance in the mirror, feeling a

momentary sadness because her other Irish friends couldn't be there. Still she was glad that Seamus had come all this way to toast her new life.

There was another knock on the door as she was about to leave the room. She was ready to tell Damon that the groom should not see the bride before the ceremony. But when she opened the door, she was enveloped in a huge hug.

"Seamus," she breathed.

"Did you think I would miss this, colleen?" The sound of his Irish brogue brought tears to her eyes. She had such wonderful friends in Dublin. Would she ever see them again?

"I've come to see that rapscallion, David."—Seamus kissed her nose—"Not to see you." He leaned away from her, still clasping her arms. "Not that you aren't passing pretty today." He kissed her again as they both walked to the top of the stairs, where they stood in full sight of the assembled group.

Damon was standing there with the boys, Father Constantine, and the judge.

David caught sight of them. "Seamus!" he called out, then clamped a hand over his mouth as Aunt Dalia shushed him.

"I've decided that I will give the bride away," Seamus told Zen, his eyes twinkling. "That will give that fulminating giant something to think about."

"He may kill you." Zen warned, but she took his proffered arm, feeling the need of his assistance.

They descended the stairs together, as the processional began.

Zen kept her eyes straight ahead, smiling a little when she heard Daniel whisper, "Aunt Zeno sure is pretty."

When she stopped next to Damon, Seamus kissed her on the cheek and stepped to one side.

She looked up at Damon, but his eyes were fixed on Seamus.

Father Constantine cleared his throat several times before he was able to catch Damon's attention. "Join hands, please," he intoned.

Zen felt her hand being taken, felt Damon's life force pumping into her blood.

She made her responses in a low voice. Damon answered strong and sure... the way he did everything.

When he turned her toward him, she felt as light as air and filled with joy. Her hand rested on his cheek as he lifted her off her feet, and his mouth found hers and lingered there.

Then people were crowding around them, congratulating them with exuberant hugs and exclamations. Damon was forced to release Zen. Well-wishers kissed her cheek. Seamus kissed her mouth.

"You're just trying to start something," Zen chided him, then grinned when David tackled him around the knees.

Seamus was about to swing the boy into the air when all at once he paused, staring at someone behind David. "So... and you must be Daniel. And a fine broth of a boy you are with such a name." Seamus kept hold of David's hand as he held out the other to Daniel. "And I'm your Uncle Seamus."

Zen's smile faltered as she looked up at Damon and saw the grim expression on his face. His black eyes were on Seamus. Then, even as she watched, a stunning woman, tall and dark, slipped her hand through Damon's arm, commanding his attention.

"Damon, darling, you must introduce me to your... ah... cute little wife." She turned to Zen. "I'm Cherry Crawford. Damon and I have been close for years."

Zen didn't hear what Damon said to the woman. A roaring in her ears and a red haze in front of her eyes deafened and blinded her.

Then Sophie was at her side. "Xenobia, dear, you must meet the Levinsons. She was Marta Leandros, and we went to school together." She plucked at Zen's sleeve. "She has brought you a set of Haviland china. I know you're so partial to dishes." Soohie's eyes darted nervously from Zen to Damon and back again.

"I am?" Zen stared blankly at her mother-in-law, then patted her arm.

"Sophie." Thag appeared at his wife's side. "Don't worry. Zen is not worried." But his frown conveyed his own concern.

With great effort Zen smiled at her mother-in-law, masking an anger that threatened to overwhelm her. How dare Damon invite his former mistress to the wedding! But out loud she said, "Thag is right. I'm not upset."

Sophie closed her eyes in dismay. "I couldn't believe it when I saw her walk into the room and take a seat. Dalia had pointed her out to me many times before, so I knew her."

Just then Seamus broke away from Damon and Cherry and returned to Zen, who introduced him to Sophie and Thag. "Shall I take the luscious Cherry away while you receive your guests?" he suggested.

"Would you?" Sophie gave him a grateful smile.

"Perhaps she would like to receive with us," Zen whispered sarcastically to Thag.

He bit his lip and agreed, "That would be interesting."

Damon strode toward them, his eyes narrowed on Seamus. "You seem to be everywhere my wife is."

"And you seem to be everywhere Ms. Crawford is," Seamus observed.

Damon seemed to swell with indignation.

"Mr. Dare," Sophie interjected, "has offered to accompany Ms. Crawford through the reception line."

"Fine," Damon snapped.

"Delighted, ma'am," Seamus said at the same time. He grinned at Zen and winked, then reached for Cherry's hand and tucked it into his arm. "C'mon along, my lovely. You just got lucky, as you Yankees say."

"Really?" Cherry drawled, her smile not quite reaching her eyes as she touched Damon's arm. "We'll talk later, darling—when we're alone."

Zen reeled. Stars, wheels, and big dots floated in front of her eyes.

For a moment, as she and Damon moved toward the arch of white orchids that led to the dining room, Zen had to resist the urge to heave the tiered wedding cake at her husband. "How dare you do that?" she demanded.

"What the hell are you talking about?" They stood grim-faced under the arch. Sophie and Thag stood to one side and began to form a receiving line that led into the dining room.

"Don't swear at me, you womanizer," Zen snapped.

"Womanizer!" Damon exclaimed. "Will you kindly explain what you mean by that? And where the hell did that Irish rover come from? Why was he up in your room?"

"Seamus Dare is my friend and a man of honor." Her voice softened as she addressed Daniel. "Yes, dear, you and David come stand with us."

"Friend!" Damon's voice rose. His mother leaned forward and shot him a warning glance.

"Seamus and I—" Zen began hotly, then lowered her voice as Daniel looked up at her. She smiled and leaned closer to Damon, speaking in a harsh whisper.

"Seamus and I have never lived together."

"That's what you're telling me. I saw the way he looked at you as you came down the stairs with him."

"Don't try to weasel out of—oh, yes, Mrs. Dinmont. Damon has spoken of you often. Thank you. Yes, how do you do?" Zen's head began to spin as dozens of guests greeted her. Damon played the charming host at her side, but Zen sensed the lingering tension in him.

Long before everyone had arrived, David grew bored greeting guests. "Aunt Zeno, Curly is thirsty." He leaned around Damon's legs and gazed out the window at the lawn that swept down to the water. "I better go give him a drink. All right?" His hopeful look was mirrored in Daniel's face.

Zen was about to tell them that they could play on the terrace when Damon said, "You may go outside, but you cannot go down to the water or throw sticks for Curly that might go into the water. Is that clear?"

Both boys nodded enthusiastically.

"Stay in sight of this window," Damon cautioned, his voice brooking no disobedience.

"We will, Uncle Damon," they said in unison. They pushed open the French doors and skipped out onto the terrace.

"I should have insisted they change their clothes." Zen winced as David climbed the low concrete balustrade that circled the terrace.

Damon shrugged. "They need the fresh air more than they do a wedding reception. Besides, if I know Yanos, he's out there somewhere watching for them. He won't let them get into too much trouble."

"No." Zen smiled up at Damon, then remembered that she was angry with him. She looked away.

"I want to know more about Seamus Dare," he said, his arm tightening around her. "I thought he was older, not so close to you in age."

"I will be glad to answer any of your questions—if you will tell me why Cherry Crawford was invited to our wedding."

"Cherry wasn't invited—at least not by me."

"Hah! Do you think I'm a fool?"

"You're a fool if you think I would invite my . . . that is . . ."

"Do go on. You were about to say 'my mistress,' I believe."

"Damn you, Zen! You know I wouldn't invite her to our wedding."

"How do I know that? She called you at the office when I was there, and you forgot all about me."

"It would be pretty damn hard to forget you when you argue and fight with me all the time."

Zen felt a sharp pain at his words. "I . . . I . . . we don't fight all the time."

"Most of the time. And I'm sick of it. I don't want any more of it. You know damn well that I would never invite—"

"Damon, dear," Cherry Crawford called, "do tell me what you wanted when you rang me a week ago. I called your office, but someone was with you and you couldn't talk." Cherry glided up to them, her black silk suit clinging to her. She turned to Zen. "I hope I haven't offended you by wearing black to your wedding, dear, but I am in mourning of a sort, you know. I even have black undies on, Damon." She smiled up at him, then back at Zen. "You understand, of course."

Suddenly the situation struck Zen as incredibly funny. She couldn't contain her laughter as she told Cheery, "Yes, I think I do understand. My husband must have had his hands full with you."

"I did." Damon's answering chuckle sent a warm tingle down Zen's spine.

Cherry's doelike eyes narrowed in suspicion.

"I think what my wife is saying is that she knows I didn't invite you to the wedding, Cherry," Damon explained quietly. He reached out to clasp Zen to his side, and his mouth brushed the top of her head in a tender caress.

Seamus ambled over to them. "Come, my lovely. Soon the musicians will begin playing." He shook a finger at Cherry. "I could have told you it would be most foolish to spar with Zenny Driscoll."

"Zen Aristides," Damon corrected, glowering.

"Xenobia Driscoll Aristides," Zen amended firmly, her eyes darting between them.

Damon's hard gaze was locked on Seamus. Then, to Zen's surprise, his expression gradually softened, and he chuckled. A mischievous twinkle crept into Seamus's eyes, and he clapped Damon on the back.

"Women," he exclaimed and let out a boisterous laugh.

"Women," Damon agreed in a spirit of hearty male camaraderie.

He swooped down to give Zen a resounding kiss and walked off with Seamus, talking with him like an old friend.

Zen stared after them in stupefied amazement. Then a family friend claimed her attention.

Much later, after she and Damon had cut the cake, dancing began in the spacious solarium, which offered a sweeping view of the Sound. Potted flowers, all white, had been banked around the five-piece orchestra.

As their guests drifted through the spacious rooms, Damon and Zen found themselves alone for a moment.

Zen fed Damon a piece of cake from her plate. "So you're a pantie collector, are you? And do you like black in particular?"

Damon held her wrist as he nibbled the cake, then nipped at her skin. "I admit to having a bent for sensual things, and I like all colors, especially if you're wearing them. If you should ever want me to chase you around the grounds before removing your underthings, I accept the challenge." Damon leered at her. "In fact, just imagining it is having an effect on me. Shall I send the guests home?"

Zen laughed, feeling both powerfully sexy and deliciously weak. "We can't do—" she whirled toward the French doors. "Where are the boys? I haven't heard or seen them for quite a while." She stepped outside.

Damon followed, frowning. "Are you putting me off again?" he demanded.

"No." She had to smile at his dark expression. "You look just like David and Daniel when you do that."

Damon took hold of her arm, stopping her, then stripped off his silk jacket and draped it over her shoulders. "There's still a nip in the air, and too much of you is showing," he explained, holding the jacket closed in front of her. He leaned down to kiss her. "You're mine, Mrs. Aristides."

"Driscoll Aristides," Zen insisted.

"Is that so important to you?"

"What?" Zen couldn't suppress a grin. Damon chuckled, and kissed her. "Let's go find the boys."

Hand in hand, they crossed the lawn. As she gazed up at Damon and he returned her tender gaze, Zen felt filled to bursting with happiness. But as the minutes went on and the boys didn't answer their calls, she began to worry.

When she caught sight of Yanos heading toward the water, also calling for them, she sucked in a shaky breath.

"Zen, stop it." Damon pulled her around to face him. "Don't start imagining things. I'm sure they're all right."

"Yes, but we have to find them, see them."

Damon hailed Yanos and strode over to him. Zen stumbled after him, impeded by her satin sandals.

Damon turned to face her. "Go back to the house. Yanos and I—"

"No!" Zen shook her head, stubbornly determined to stay and help.

He shook his head but didn't protest further and followed Yanos to the carriage house.

Zen headed instinctively toward the water. Something seemed to be pulling her there.

Suddenly she saw the boys. They were sitting in a raftlike wooden vessel, floating about a hundred yards from shore. Curly was swimming next to them, trying to push them.

Zen didn't hesitate. She threw Damon's jacket to the ground and peeled the satin wedding gown from her body, then kicked off her shoes.

"Damon!" she called once, then began wading out into the icy water, forcing herself to disregard her numb arms and legs.

Curly was making a valiant effort, but Zen could tell that he was tiring. Though the boys weren't far from shore now, if Curly let up on his struggles, the flimsy craft would drift away, pulled by unseen currents.

The water had reached Zen's breastbone when a hand suddenly caught her arm. "Go back, Zenny. I'll get them," Seamus said at her side.

"Oh, Seamus, I'm so glad to see you. It may take two of us to bring them in."

Before Seamus could reply, Damon bellowed from shore, "Damn you, Zen, I could throttle you! Get back here this instant. Are you trying to kill yourself?"

She glanced back to see Damon stripping off his shirt and shoes. In a flash he was plowing through the water in a powerful crawl. She watched, treading water, as he reached the boys and began pulling the raft toward shore.

Without speaking, awash in relief, Zen turned around and headed back, sure that the boys were now safe. She stumbled onto dry land, shivering, and was vaguely aware that blankets were being wrapped around her and Seamus. But her eyes were fixed on Damon and the twins as he lifted them from the raft and into the blankets Maria and Lona held ready.

Zen rushed over to them, oblivious to all else. "Don't you ever do that again," she scolded even as she drew them into a fierce embrace. She sniffed and hurried after them as Damon whisked them across the lawn, into the house, and up the stairs.

Sophie stood in the foyer, wringing her hands and whispering over and over, "Thank God, thank God."

Damon dissuaded Zen from giving the boys their bath. Instead, he left them in the servants' capable care and led Zen to his own apartment, where he ran a tub of hot water.

"But are you sure Lona and Maria will watch them?" Zen asked as she sank to her chin in the soothing water. "Oh, Damon, I blame myself for not watching them."

He stripped the clothes from his own body, his eyes never leaving her. "Yanos blames himself, Lona blames herself. My mother is filled with guilt." He sank down next to her in the spacious tub and folded her close. She closed her eyes in utter bliss, letting the water lap over and calm her. "The boys have lived here together for several weeks and haven't disobeyed," Damon went on. "This time they did disobey and they will be punished for it. They were using the top of the old cistern for a raft. Yanos had put it on a pile of junk to be burned. The boys found it and decided to play Huckleberry Finn. That's it. It's all over."

Damon massaged Zen's warming body, arousing an even deeper heat. "Boys do crazy things," he mused. "It's the part of them that tells them to assert themselves, rebel, accept any challenge. If a boy survives a wild boyhood, he can survive anything."

"Do mothers of boys survive?" Zen mumbled against his throat.

"Only sometimes." Damon chuckled.

"Did you ever use this tub with Cherry?" Zen asked faintly.

"No woman has ever shared these rooms with me — and no one ever will, except you."

"You had an apartment in town?"

"A penthouse in Manhattan, yes," he answered. "I won't lie to you, Zen. When we were apart, there were many women, all sizes, all shapes, all —"

"Twaddle. You only had tall, gorgeous creatures with big breasts and long legs," Zen grumbled, pulling at the hair on his chest.

He laughed. "It's true that none of them was as small as you."

"You love tall women."

"No doubt I thought so once."

"Now you have a short woman. Short women are out of style."

"Good. Then I won't have to beat the men off with a stick."

Zen giggled. "There weren't many men."

"Some, though."

"Oh, yes."

There was a long silence as Damon caressed her, his hands exploring gently. "And you would have married Seamus?" he asked.

Zen realized now that it would have been a mistake to marry Seamus when her feelings for Damon were so strong. "Yes, I was leaning that way. I knew that Seamus would be good with David. He's a man of high principles, which not all his joking and easy manner hide."

"A paragon," Damon agreed ironically.

"You asked me..."

"I know what I asked you." Damon surged to his feet, pulling her with him out of the tub and into the shower stall.

"No...eek! Stop it, Damon! I hate cold showers." Zen pummeled his chest.

"All right." His expression relaxed, and he switched the water to slightly warmer. He stepped out onto the tile floor and held out a heated bath sheet for her.

"Why did you do that?" She demanded, glaring up at him.

"Caprice," he replied, his jaw tight.

"More like meanness." Zen stalked into the bedroom—and stopped dead. She had forgotten she was in Damon's wing of the house. She had no clean clothes with her.

"Your clothes are over there." Damon gestured to a long wall of cabinets in the dressing room.

"When were they moved?"

"Lona did it this morning." He held up her wedding gown. "Do you want to put this back on. Our guests will be waiting for us."

"Yes, I'll wear it." She didn't bother to tell him that she loved the dress, that she enjoyed wearing it.

They put on their clothes in comfortable silence, though several times Zen felt Damon's gaze burning into her, hot with desire. Feeling self-conscious under his probing stare, she fumbled with the tiny buttons on her gown and gratefully accepted his help when he bent to fasten them for her. He straightened in front of her, looking so handsome in his dark silk suit. When he pulled her into his arms and kissed her hard, his tongue filling her mouth, it was all she could do to remain standing. Her blood raced hot in her veins as he took her arm and led her to the top of the stairs.

They descended the grand staircase, the sounds of music, laughter, and the clink of glassware growing louder as they reached the bottom. Damon held Zen close to him. "Did I tell you that we're going to spend the night at my apartment in Manhattan?"

"Since when? I thought we had decided to stay here and take a trip later with the boys." She paused a step above him.

Damon urged her back to his side. "Yes, but we can take one night for ourselves. I've ordered a dinner to be sent there, with champagne..." His voice trailed off, his thoughts wandering as his eyes lingered on her red-gold hair.

"There's enough food here to feed all the starving people in Africa."

"My mother has mentioned that you are horrified by what we've spent on our guests...so I have had my lawyers allocate an equal amount to charity."

Zen stopped again. "What charity? Some big organization in which the money twists and winds through a bureaucratic system and only a small fraction of the original amount gets to the needy?"

Damon chuckled. "Have a little faith, wife. The money is going to build recreational facilities for the hearing-impaired, the blind, and the retarded."

He turned to stand in the foyer, one step below her. Now he was only a little taller than Zen. Her hand came up to touch his cheek.

"Thank you. That's the nicest wedding present you could have given me." Her chin trembled.

Damon sighed. "You are the least acquisitive person I have ever known. Isn't there one material thing I can give you? Please?"

"Well...although I do appreciate how useful the Cherokee is, it would be nice to have—"

"You're joking," Damon interrupted, throwing back his head to laugh and clutching her upper arms.

"It isn't necessary for you..." Zen began, puzzled.

"In the garage, at this very moment, a gold-colored Corvette is waiting for you. I was afraid to give it to you for fear you'd be angry."

Zen stared at him. He was afraid of angering her? Incredible! "A Corvette? That's some runabout. I was thinking more in terms of a VW bug or—"

Damon touched his tongue to the corner of her mouth.

"The guests will see," Zen protested, her hands tingling, her legs weakening.

"That's a very bad habit, Xenobia—always putting me off when I begin to make love to you."

"Then pick a more private place." She gave a small screech as she was swept off her feet into his arms.

Damon headed back up the stairs with powerful strides.

"Where is Uncle Damon taking you now, Aunt Zeno?"

David asked from below them in the hall. Zen twisted to see Daniel by his side, Curly and Yanos behind them. "Are you going to take a nap? I told Lona that Dan and I would like to stay up for a while. Is it all right for Yanos to meet all the people, Aunt Zeno?"

Damon paused halfway up the stairs and then returned to the foyer, letting Zen slide down his body but not releasing her. "Of course Yanos will come with you to meet the people," he said, "and you will stay close to him and Lona." He squatted down in front of the boys while Zen hovered over them, touching them, leaning down to kiss them. "You are never to do anything like that again," Damon admonished them. "Both Nonna and Aunt Zeno were very worried."

Both boys nodded, looking at Zen askance. "We won't do it again, Aunt Zeno," Daniel promised.

She nodded and gestured for them to precede her through the lounge and into the dining room. They stopped here and there to explain to people that the boys were indeed all right. "I'm fine now," she assured Aunt Sophronia, another of Damon's aunts.

"In my day girls didn't swim in cold water," said the tiny old lady. "Of course, I'm glad the boys were rescued. They are Aristides, you know." She waved her hand like Queen Victoria bestowing a blessing and moved toward the canapé tray.

Zen shook her head in exasperation. "Your family is—"

"Doesn't it make you feel good to know how important you are to them?" Damon interrupted, chuckling and hugging her to him.

"Dear Aunt Sophronia would no doubt arrange a French picnic in honor of my hanging," Zen said, watching the birdlike woman pop an entire stuffed mushroom into her mouth, then wrap some in a napkin and stow them in her capacious purse. "Why don't you give her some money, Damon? The poor dear doesn't have enough to eat."

"Aunt Sophronia is worth millions, my love. She has

a house staff of thirty. None of her investments, which are legion, has ever suffered a loss."

"But she's stealing food," Zen whispered, her eyes widening as Aunt Sophronia wended her way past trays of delicacies, selecting liberally from each of them.

"She always takes food. No one is sure what she does with it, but you can be certain it won't be wasted. Aunt Sophronia is very thrifty."

"Amazing."

Damon led Zen out onto the dance floor. As they danced, she continued to watch his aunt and to keep a wary eye on the boys. "Damon, I think she's going to take—my lord, she put a bottle of champagne in her purse!"

"And after she takes it out to her chauffeur to stash in her Rolls, she'll be back for more."

Zen looked up at him and saw no contempt or censure in his face. "You don't mind, do you?"

"Why should I mind? Aunt Sophronia supports a Boys' Club and is active in promoting rehabilitation houses for first offenders. I admire her."

Zen felt ashamed of her previous rude behavior toward the old woman. "I didn't know," she whispered as the tiny creature upended a peanut dish into her purse. As soon as she moved away, Maria refilled the dish.

Damon whirled Zen around the spacious solarium, his mouth tight, his muscles tense.

"What is it?" she asked.

"We're dancing together. We've just been married, but you, the bride, are more fascinated with the guests than with the groom." The cords in Damon's neck stood out as he stared out over her head.

Zen felt a girlish hesitancy as she looked up at him. She remembered the twenty-year-old Zen who had first worshipped Damon Aristides, and the twenty-five-year old Zen who had fled from him, brokenhearted. "I love to dance with you, Damon," she assured him.

"How do you know? We haven't danced together much," he replied sternly. Even when the beat became faster, he held her close to him and twirled sedately round the room.

"Pardon me, may I cut in?" Seamus beamed at a glowering Damon, who showed great reluctance in releasing his wife.

In seconds, Seamus and Zen were gyrating to a hot rhythm. They faced each other, not touching, but their feet and bodies moved in perfect synchronization.

When several of the guests backed away to give them more room, Seamus became more daring, his movements more complex. Zen laughed when Seamus whirled her around him, then caught her back to him in a graceful, shallow dip. Not once did her nimble-footed friend miss a beat.

When the number ended. Seamus caught Zen in his arms and planted a kiss on her mouth as the crowd laughed and applauded.

"It's time to leave." Damon all but lifted Zen free of Seamus's hold.

"So soon?" she asked, a little out of breath.

"Yes," he bit out.

Zen was about to protest, but one look at his black expression made her change her mind. "I'll go up to change my clothes," she said.

Upstairs, Lona helped her take off her gown. Her head was still buried in the depths of material when she heard the door open.

Lona was quick to slip a silken wrapper around her before Zen faced her mother-in-law. "Sophie?"

"I don't know whether to laugh or cry." Damon's mother paced restlessly up and down the spacious dressing room. "That sister of mine is filling Damon's head with foolish stories, and he is filling his mouth with whisky."

"I'll drive, don't worry," Zen assured her.

"That isn't what's worrying me, Xenobia," Sophie said. "Not that Damon will let you drive. No one drives Damon except his chauffeur, or Yanos in a pinch." She pursed her lips. "No, I'm afraid Damon might become violent. It would be most embarrassing."

"Damon is very correct in his behavior. You needn't worry." Zen zipped up the skirt of her blue Irish linen suit. Her leather shoes and bag were of the same pale color. "Did you pack everything already, Lona?" she asked.

"Damon is never civilized where you are concerned, Xenobia," Sophie said. "And it annoys me that you should continue to be so unconcerned when you husband may be downstairs fomenting chaos. Damon is terrible when he feels he is being threatened. He will attack first and ask for the full story later." Sophie raised her eyes in supplication. "I could kill that Dalia. Just because she didn't want me to marry Thag...And, of course, she knows that she cannot control you."

"How does she know that?" Zen checked her makeup for smudges.

"Damon can't control you, so how could Dalia?"

Zen knew Sophie was deeply irritated with her. "What do you want me to do?" she asked.

"Get him out of here—and do not talk to that Irishman again tonight. Not that he isn't a most charming fellow, Xenobia, but..." Sophie glanced at Lona and nodded curtly. When the woman had left the room, she added, "One of my husband's ancestors was from Mani, the region of Greece where the wild people live." Sophie nodded thoughtfully. "Sometime I see the same wildness in Damon."

Zen wanted to laugh, but Sophie's sober look stopped her. Instead, she bent to pick up her overnight case and gestured to Sophie to open the door.

As she descended the stairs again, Zen experienced a sense of déjà vu. How many times had she gone down those stairs that day?

"I don't hear any disturbing noises," she said, smiling at the older woman.

"Let's hope you can get Damon out of the house in a hurry," Sophie replied.

When they entered the living room, the first person

Zen saw was Damon, lifting a glass to his mouth and draining it. "Oh, dear," she whispered as Seamus came towards them both arms outstretched. She patted Sophie's arm. "Don't worry. No doubt Seamus wants to say good-bye. He's returning to Ireland soon."

"Not soon enough," Sophie whispered.

Zen followed the direction of her mother-in-law's gaze, and her mouth dropped open. Damon was striding angrily through the crowd, his face a hard mask. Guests stepped hastily out his way, clearing a narrow path for him.

"Damon." Zen stepped in front of him, but he lifted her like a doll and set her to one side.

Seamus looked up in surprise as Damon bore down on him. Everyone seemed turned to stone.

Zen ducked under her husband's arm and stood up, stopping him short. She reached up and pulled his stiff head down until their lips met. She let her mouth soften and move on his until she felt his response, his tongue moving to touch hers. She massaged his face and neck, and she didn't release him when she moved her mouth back an inch. "Damon, we're married," she murmured.

"I won't have him kissing you," Damon muttered back, though he didn't move away from her.

She stroked his cheek. "Seamus is a friend." She kissed him again. "People kiss their friends."

Damon straightened but kept his hands on her, kneading her shoulders, swaying imperceptibly. "Let's get out of here," he said at last, the words slightly slurred.

"Damon, if I ask for the keys to the car—because you have been drinking more than you should—what will you say? Or would you prefer having the chauffeur drive us into Manhattan?" Zen kept her voice low, for his ears only.

His mouth caressed hers. "I say I don't like it, but it's the smart thing to do." He fumbled in his jacket pocket and handed her the keys, kissed her again, then turned to speak to Sophie and Thag.

With a sigh of relief, Zen turned back to the guests and began bidding them good-bye. Damon, stiff but cordial, remained close to her side.

When it was Seamus's turn he grabbed her around the waist and kissed her full on the mouth with a noisy smack.

"Stop that, you fool," Sophie said. She tapped Seamus imperially on the arm.

Thag shook his head. "You are a wild Irishman," he said, but he, too, was smiling, and Zen couldn't help grinning in return. Seamus would keep the family well entertained during his visit.

Zen was still chuckling over something Seamus had told her as she followed Damon out to the Ferrari. Yanos was just slamming the lid of the trunk shut, having stowed away their luggage.

The old Greek rolled his eyes toward the front seat, where Damon slouched on the passenger side. "He is more in the wine than he should be, Kyria Xenobia."

"More in the Old Bushmill's, I think you mean." Zen smiled wider when the old man's lips pursed at her reference to the Irish whisky Damon had been drinking.

"He is Apollo's son, Kyria. He is much used to being boss and clearing all obstacles."

"And being full of himself, as Apollo was," Zen pointed out, moving toward the driver's side.

Yanos's lips twitched. "That too, Kyria."

Zen leaned over and kissed the grizzled cheek. "Take care of my boys, Yanos."

"That I will do, Kyria. I will not let them out of my sight." He held the car door for her and closed it behind her after she slid behind the wheel.

"So far you've kissed every male in the place but your husband," Damon complained, hitting the dashboard.

"Not true." Zen slipped the car into gear and headed down the driveway. "I kissed most of the men at the wedding, not all." She bit her lip when he growled. "And, as I recall, I kissed you five minutes ago. How could you forget that."

"I recall every kiss and embrace we've ever shared, every moment of our lovemaking. Shall I tell you about the first time? We sailed all day on my schooner, then anchored out from the dock—way out, as I remember."

Zen's palms grew damp. "There's no need to go into it now."

"Oh, but there is, my wife. You were mine then. You wanted me to take you. You asked me to make love to you, said that you wanted me to be your first and only love. Do you remember?"

Damon's words, like velvet-covered steel, seemed to pierce her very core and arouse all her desires once again. He talked on and on, recalling their lovemaking in excruciating detail, making her burn all over for him.

Even as she sought to concentrate every effort on driving, Zen recalled her younger self, as she had been then. She envisioned a twenty-year-old Zen as she followed Damon into the cabin, where they were going to change into dry clothes after having gone swimming. Then they would eat dinner.

Damon had gone to the bow of the boat, leaving the cabin for her.

Zen had removed her bikini top, but instead of taking off the bottom and showering, she had leaned against one of the bunks and looked out the window over the water. She felt like one of the luckiest people in the world because Damon Aristides was paying attention to her, because he looked at her as though he wanted to possess her. She didn't hear him enter the cabin, but when she heard him gasp, she knew he was behind her.

"I'm sorry, little one, I thought you'd changed. I'll be on deck—"

"Don't go, Damon." Zen whirled around to face him, and his eyes riveted at once on her breasts. Instead of hiding herself, she took a deep breath and pushed her shoulders back, wanting him to keep looking at her. She had been repelled by the thought of other men touching her . . . but she ached for Damon's caress.

"Zen . . ." Damon cleared his throat, his voice taut with tension.

"I want you, Damon. Is that so very bad?" she had said in a low voice.

"No, my angel. But you're so young. We'll wait a couple of years."

"Years?" Zen had wailed, catapulting herself across the cabin and against his bare chest. "I don't want to wait. You'll grow tired of me and want someone else."

"Not a chance," Damon had whispered, his body curving protectively over hers, his hands coming up to clutch her bare waist.

His mouth brushed her hair, and she lifted her face for his kiss.

Instead, he had lifted her off the floor and said against her mouth, "Love, are you sure? I can't . . . I won't—"

"I want you to love me, Damon."

"Dear God, you're a child . . . but I must have you," he murmured, his hands pressing her lips tightly against him, still holding her high off the floor.

"I love being so tall." Zen giggled, biting his chin, licking his cheek.

"Do you, darling?" Damon's voice was rough. "And I love it when you taste me."

"Oh, Damon, I want to keep you," she had whispered, moving restlessly in his arms.

"Yes, my little one . . ." He stripped the bikini bottom from her and carried her to the larger forward cabin, where he placed her on the king-sized bed. He stood back, and his eyes roved hotly over her naked body. "Your skin . . . and hair . . . your lovely breasts. I'll be gentle, my little one."

And he had been, loving her with his mouth and hands until she was on fire for him. She hardly felt the moment of discomfort when he penetrated her fully.

"Damon!" she had called out to him, her back arching as wave upon wave of love filled her and overflowed.

"Yes, my little one, I'm here." He had chuckled as he held her close. "My little voluptuary, I'm here with you."

She stayed with him through the night. It had frightened yet exalted her to know that Damon couldn't seem to get enough of her.

That summer they were together every minute...

Zen shook herself from her reverie, blinking at the Manhattan traffic.

"Even at twenty-five you were tricky. When I thought you were mine, you left me. Turn here and go up Park," Damon instructed.

"Me? Tricky? As I recall, you intimated that I would be the only woman in your life. Well, what do you call Cherry Crawford... not to mention other women associated with you in the tabloids?"

"You walked out on me, Xenobia Driscoll Aristides. You'll never do that again."

Zen's temper flared. "Are you threatening me?"

"If that's what it takes to keep you by my side, yes, I'm threatening you."

"You damn well can't threaten me," Zen said, fuming. She turned into the underground garage, anger making her just careless enough to come a hair too close to a cement column and scraping the side of the Ferrari.

"Xenobia..." Damon straightened in his seat and turned to glare at her. "What the hell are you doing to my car?"

"You are a most nerve-wracking man. I was doing fine until you began needling me." Zen bit her lip in remorse as she parked the car.

Damon flung open his door and stood there staring at the scratch. "Do you have any idea what it will cost to repair this?"

"Damon, I'm sorry. I'll pay for it." Zen struggled to unfasten her seat belt and climbed out of the car. "It was an accident."

"It's always an accident with you. I suppose I should be glad that you didn't ram us into a truck." Damon reeled ever so slightly as he reached for her.

Caught between laughter and chagrin, Zen pushed him away and whirled toward the elevator. The doors opened, she stepped in, and the doors closed before Damon reached her.

"Hey, wait—"

Damon's words were cut off as she was whisked upward at heart-stopping speed.

The elevator opened on a small foyer with two doors. One of the doors opened and a man with a mustache glanced out. She went to the other door and pushed her key into the lock. It wouldn't turn. The man stared at her.

"Are you a friend of the Winthrops?" he asked coldly.

"Who?"

"The Winthrops live in that apartment. Who are you?"

"Well, then is that—"

Before Zen could say any more, the elevator doors opened and a grim-faced Damon stepped out.

"There you are," he said, then turned to the man in the doorway. "Hello, Aubrey. She made a mistake and got on the wrong elevator."

"It's okay. As usual, Aristides, your taste in women is quite good." The man shut his door.

Zen glared after him. "Twit," she called. "I'm not one of his live-ins. I'm his wife."

"Will you keep your voice down and get in this elevator before Aubrey reports us both for breaking and entering," Damon said.

"Let him try!" Zen lifted her chin and raised her fist to knock on Aubrey's door, but Damon reached out and pulled her into the elevator.

Not releasing her, he punched the button for the garage. "Don't you ever listen? I called out that it was the wrong one."

"You sound more sober now," Zen commented, then frowned. "How the blazes was I to know that each tenant has his own elevator? That's disgusting."

"It's a good safety feature. When you didn't put your key into the elevator and didn't press the red light, as an invited guest would have done, Aubrey knew you were unauthorized. That's why he met you at the door. He has an alarm button that he could have pressed instead of opening the door. But he has a predilection for beautiful women."

"Do you think so?"

Damon's brow furrowed. "Do I think what?"

"Do you think I'm beautiful?"

"Yes." He led her out of the elevator and across the garage to another one. Inside, he punched the console. "That's been my problem for years. I think you're too damn beautiful."

Chapter 9

ZEN STARED AT him as they stepped into a foyer that led
directly into his apartment. Surprised at this, she forgot
what she had been about to ask him. She walked farther
into the circular foyer, admiring the royal blue Chinese
carpet with a sundial pattern in soft beige. The sunburst
at the center was located directly under a crystal chandelier.
"This is a bit opulent, isn't it?" she asked.

Damon strode past her down two steps to an oblong
room, the floor of which was also scattered with Chinese
carpets, these in mandarin red with geometric details in
jade green. Damon poured himself half a glass of whisky.
"Don't tell me. You want me to sell the carpets and give
the money to indigent actors from the Abbey Players."

"There are no indigent actors at the Abbey Players,"
Zen retorted. "They're so good they always have work."

"Bull. There are always out-of-work actors and writ-
ers." Damon took a long swallow.

"I don't think that will do your headache any good."

He glared at her. "I don't have a headache."

"Early hangover?" she quizzed, earning another glower.

"I'm going to take a shower." He strode across the room, then stopped. "You may use the shower in the master suite. I'll use the other one."

"I never imagined eating my wedding supper with a tipsy bridegroom," Zen called out. His back stiffened but he didn't pause. Zen went into the master suite.

"Why did I provoke him?" she asked herself as she took off her clothes and stepped into the shower stall. "I was baiting him."

She soaped her body then took the time to brush her hair so that it rippled past her shoulders in red-gold curls.

She removed the silk kaftan that had been purchased from Charine and shook it out of the tissue paper.

From the box of jewelry that had been Eleni's and their mother's and that Damon had insisted was now hers, she selected antique earrings of topaz that swung like golden prisms against her cheeks. She stared at herself in the mirror. "Lord, you look as if you belong in a harem." From her dresser she took the vial of French perfume that Thag had ordered made especially for her. It was called Xenobia. She dabbed some on her neck and her wrists, ankles, and behind her knees.

Prepared for seduction, she crossed the short hall that led to the landing over the foyer and descended the curving stairs. Her Turkish slippers made only a whisper of sound as she entered the living room.

Damon was standing in front of the fireplace, a steaming mug in one hand, the other resting on the mantel. A burgundy silk robe was tied around his waist.

With great deliberation Zen stepped sideways until the light of a side lamp outlined her in the dimly lit room. Damon's shape was clearly etched by the flames in the fireplace, which cast odd shadows on his face, making him look like a demon from another world.

As Zen stepped forward, the swish of her kaftan brought his head up. In slow motion he turned, straightened, and looked her over from head to toe. "That's a very sexy outfit," he said at last, tipping the rest of whatever was in the mug down his throat.

"Charine suggested it." Zen coughed to clear her throat of its hoarseness.

"Did she? I must thank her." He moved a fraction of an inch closer. "You have such a tiny body, but so strong, so well made."

Zen's face warmed with embarrassment. "Damon, stop it. I feel as though your eyes might set my kaftan on fire." Her Turkish slippers seemed to be nailed to the floor.

Damon's laugh was harsh as he approached her, like a hunter who had trapped his quarry. "You're mine."

"And by the same token, you're mine," Zen replied boldly.

"Of course." They were face to face. Damon stood looking down at her without touching her. He bent to kiss her, his lips moving over her mouth with gentle insistence. "I have a surprise for you," he murmured.

"Another one? You've been surprising me all day." Zen smiled, then caught her breath as a deep flush darkened his face. "I didn't mean your drinking," she tried to explain.

Damon waved his hand to silence her, then took her hand and pulled her toward the table. "Maria sent us some wedding cake. She will freeze the top layer for our first anniversary, but she arranged to have the second tier brought to us. This is Greek honey cake." Damon opened a bottle of champagne and poured Zen a glass, then poured coffee into his mug.

"I like coffee," Zen said lamely.

"Not Turkish coffee you don't." Damon gave a hard laugh at her grimace. "And I've had more than enough alcohol."

"Damon, I didn't mean what I said—"

"What you said was the truth...and no woman deserves a drunk husband on her wedding night."

Zen accepted the piece of cake he cut for her and lifted

it to his mouth. Damon backed warily away. Zen laughed and shook her head. "I'll be very careful," she promised.

"Just put down the knife before you feed me." Damon grabbed both her wrists to steady her, then opened his mouth and took the piece she offered. "Ummm, good." He swallowed, and his tongue came out to catch a crumb at the corner of his mouth.

Watching him, Zen felt as if her heart had fallen a hundred feet and bounced up again. She couldn't imagine any other man in the world having such beautiful lips, such a lovely nose, such mesmerizing eyes. She loved his chin, and the laugh lines at the corners of his eyes. Had anyone else ever had such cheekbones? Without thinking, she raised her hand to trace his face.

"That gown should be registered with the police as a dangerous weapon," Damon muttered, letting his fingers rest on the light-as-air fabric. "You haven't changed at all since you were twenty."

"Yes, I have." Zen's breath came rapidly, as if she'd just run up a mountain.

"Oh, no, you haven't. I remember. Will you be afraid to spoil it by having children?" Damon bent over her and batted the dangling topaz earrings with his nose.

"I don't consider the changes in a woman's body that are brought about by childbearing to be bad." Zen's eyes fluttered shut as his mouth traveled to her neck.

"Do I take it then that we will have lots of children?"

"But you haven't said that you want them—I mean more of them."

"Having my own child grow in you, Xenobia? Oh, yes, I want that. But only if you're able to give birth safely. That you must discuss with your doctor."

"You want me to ask my doctor if I'm healthy enough to have children?" Zen gave a breathless laugh. "That's silly."

"I'm serious, Zen. We won't start a family unless I know that you're capable of carrying one without possibly harming yourself." Damon's expression was utterly serious. "We already have two boys. If we can't have others, then they will be enough."

"Damon, I..." Zen looked up at him, confused by the strained look on his face.

All at once he crushed her to him. "I don't want to talk about it anymore tonight."

He led her to the large U-shaped couch and sat down with her. "Watch." He pressed buttons on a console and a king-sized bed unfolded from the middle section.

Zen raised a skeptical eyebrow. "I've heard of passion pits. I suppose—"

"You suppose nothing. I had this installed after we announced our engagement. Listen." He pressed another button and music filled the room. "There's also a hidden television, a small bar—"

"All designed for seduction," Zen breathed. She laughed as his face turned dark crimson. "Damon, I don't believe it. There you go getting embarrassed again. You've been doing that all day, as though you were nervous." She stared up at him in sudden understanding. "I don't remember you ever being the least bit off balance about anything, but since the wedding..."

"My life has changed. I'm a husband and a father." He grinned down at her. "And remember, I have to be on my toes every minute. My bride is trying to do me in." He laughed when she poked him in the arm. "Of course, she calls her attempts to murder me accidents."

"They *are* accidents!" she exclaimed, feeling absurdly happy to be laughing with him, held close to his heart. "How do we get onto this humungous bed?"

"Easy." Damon swung her up into his arms, stepped down one step, and walked onto the bed. He sat down in the center, still holding Zen in his arms. "See?" His grin faded as he stared down at her. "You don't have anything on under that, do you, love?"

She shook her head.

"How farsighted of you." Damon relaxed his hold on her so that, although she remained in the V formed by his legs, he could now gaze at her reclining body.

"I don't like to walk on this lovely thing with my

shoes on," Zen said softly, held spellbound by his onyx eyes.

"Don't worry." Damon reached down and removed a slipper. Then he lifted her foot and nibbled on her toes.

"You have a foot fetish," Zen accused him.

"A fetish for your foot, yes." Damon sucked gently on her anklebone. "You have the trimmest body . . . Tastes good, too."

"Are you crazy?" Zen failed at repartee, her thoughts focused on the delicious sensations he was producing.

"Are you planning an accident that will cause brain damage and make me crazy?" Damon asked casually, removing the other slipper and kissing her little toe.

"That's very unkind." Zen clung to his shoulders as he pushed the kaftan up past her waist to her arms. She let go briefly as he lifted the garment over her head.

"Will you be warm enough, Zen?" Damon lowered her to the bedspread and leaned over her as he took off his robe.

"Warm." She nodded, looking up at him, loving the play of firelight on his face.

"I'll be your blanket," Damon growled into her neck.

"How kind of you." Zen felt as though she'd been disembodied and was floating around the room. She didn't seem to be connected to her body, though each separate part was clamoring for Damon's special attention. "Making love is so nice," she said, sighing.

"*Nice?* God, wife, you do have a talent for understatement."

"Thank you." Zen let her fingers furrow through his hair, loving the crisp feel of it. "Damon, will we leave it as a couch when the boys are with us?"

"What? What boys?" Damon seemed to have trouble focusing. "Xenobia, we're making love. We'll talk about the boys later."

"Lovely." Zen pulled the curling hairs on his chest. "I thought men couldn't make love when they had too much to drink." She nibbled on his chin.

"What?" Damon's hair stood on end where she had mussed it.

She couldn't suppress a giggle. Damon stared at her as if she had just popped in from Mars. "Don't you feel like making love?" he demanded sternly.

"Yes, I do." But she burst out laughing. He looked so silly glowering so darkly with his hair sticking up. Suddenly all her happiness bubbled up from inside her and broke forth in peals of laughter.

She sensed his angry withdrawal. "Don't go," she pleaded. "I really do want to make love." She shrugged one bare shoulder. "It's just that we've never been married before. I don't know why, but it's different now." A dark gleam flickered deep in his eyes. "I can't explain it, Damon. Don't be angry."

He pushed her down and leaned over her, his breath coming in harsh pants. "Why should I be angry about making love to Chuckles the Clown?" His body pressed against hers, his flesh touching her everywhere. "It's a new experience for me, too. I can't remember ever making love to a woman when she was laughing. No, don't talk. I don't want to hear any more."

She fell obediently silent as his hands and mouth explored her intimately, from her chin to her toes.

Their lovemaking was as forceful as always, but Zen sensed a restraint in Damon. When she began to speak, he would shush her, and soon the volcano that was between them erupted and spilled them out of themselves into a new dimension.

She fell asleep. When she woke sometime later, he was gone. She sat up in bed and punched the pillow. She wanted to get up and see if he was still in the apartment, but she was too tired. She fell into a restless sleep.

She woke again with a jerk, sitting bolt upright in bed, the sheet wrapped around her body like a shroud. She was still alone in the bed.

She rose with a sigh and went to the bathroom, where she ran the water until it was ice cold. She drank several glasses.

Where was Damon? Had he gone out?

She went into the bedroom and rummaged through her things until she found a light robe. She couldn't bear to look at the kaftan crumpled on the living room floor, where Damon had dropped it.

She wandered through the semidark apartment. A faint, predawn light filtered through floor-to-ceiling sheer curtains over a wall of windows in the living room. She was about to retrace her steps to the bedroom when she heard a muffled mutter that made her freeze in her tracks. Goose bumps covered her arms. Then she saw Damon sprawled face down on a couch on the other side of the living room, far from the king-sized bed.

She edged closer and took the glass from his hand, then lifted an empty bottle from the floor. "I hope you didn't drink all this, husband of mine, or you will have one aching head when you wake up." Zen bent to give him a closer look. Though he was breathing heavily, he seemed in fair shape, so she left him where he was.

She returned to the bed, but she didn't sleep. For hours she considered—and rejected—all sorts of possible explanations for Damon's uncharacteristic behavior. None of them made any sense. Was he so unhappy being married to her that he had to drink himself into a stupor? Had he felt that laughter during their lovemaking had emasculated him in some way? The Damon she knew was made of heartier stuff than that. She just didn't understand him.

At midmorning she gave up her attempt to sleep, and went to the kitchen to make a pot of coffee.

At first she was puzzled when she couldn't find a small percolator. Then she remembered that Damon had used one the night before. Rather than seek it out, and perhaps disturb him, she used a drip coffeemaker to prepare a full twenty-cup pot.

The phone rang as she was scrambling eggs for herself. She lifted it on the first ring.

Sophie answered. "Xenobia? Is that you, dear? I hated to wake you, but Thag and I thought we would take the boys up to Saratoga overnight and perhaps drive to Cooperstown to show them the Baseball Hall of Fame."

"Wouldn't it be better to take two nights, Sophie?"

Zen suggested, then smiled to herself when she heard her mother-in-law's sigh of relief.

"Yes, dear, it would. That's a wonderful idea. We'll take Seamus with us. David is so fond of him, and now so is Daniel. We just can't let him return to Ireland without doing a little sight-seeing now, can we?"

"Of course not. Kiss the boys for me, and we'll see you on Friday."

"Thank you, dear. And how is that son of mine?"

"Still sleeping," Zen said.

"My, my." Sophie was still chuckling when she hung up the phone.

Zen finished scrambling her eggs, then made herself some toast from homemade raisin bread the housekeeper had left.

"Is the coffee for anyone?"

Startled, Zen dropped the toast and whirled around. Damon was standing in the doorway, a towel wrapped around his waist, his feet, legs, and chest bare, his hair glistening wet.

"It's for you, Dracula," Zen said with forced lightness. "But I think you would do better with a transfusion."

"Thank you, bride of Frankenstein." Damon winced when she laughed. "Why is it I never noticed that you have a macabre sense of humor? Maybe because I spent so much time dodging the barbed words you were firing at me, and trying to survive your attempts to kill me."

Zen placed a mug of coffee in front of him. "If you're referring to the few times you had unfortunate accidents—"

"Accidents! How I hate that word! Damn, Zen, did you have to bang that pot on the table?"

"I did not bang it. It's glass. I would never bang glass."

Damon closed his eyes in resignation and sipped his coffee.

"Head hurt?" Zen inquired, munching on toast.

"Yes. Could you kindly stop chewing so loudly?"

"Touchy, touchy." Zen placed some of her scrambled

eggs in front of him. He glared at them, then at her.

"Remove that garbage."

"Damon, I'm sorry that you have a hangover, but it's your own fault and—"

"Don't lecture. May I please have some more coffee?"

Zen poured some, and Damon drank it in silence, then pushed his chair back from the table.

"What shall we do today?" Zen quizzed his retreating back.

He stopped but didn't turn to face her. "I thought we were going back to the house."

"We don't have to. Your mother called and said that she and Thag are taking the boys to Saratoga, I suppose to see the battlefield there, and then perhaps to Cooperstown. Sophie felt that since Seamus—"

"Seamus?" Damon interrupted. "Is he still here?" He rubbed an index finger across his forehead.

"Yes. Your mother didn't want him to return to Ireland without seeing something of the country," Zen explained.

"Dandy."

"So what would you like to do. After all, this *is* our honeymoon."

"I'm not the one who needs to be reminded of that." Damon glared at her.

"If you're referring to my laughing last night—"

"I'd rather not discuss it."

"I just want you to know that I'm sorry you misunderstood—"

"I misunderstood nothing. Excuse me, I'd like to get dressed."

"Hardhead," Zen muttered, taking her cup and plate to the sink. She washed the skillet by hand in a sinkful of suds.

She wandered aimlessly around the apartment, checking each room, deciding that she didn't feel comfortable in such stark surroundings.

"Change it if you wish," Damon said behind her in the study. She dropped the Eskimo whalebone she'd been examining.

"Will you stop doing that? I could have broken this!"

"So? It's yours. Replace it." Damon shrugged and handed her the carving. "You don't like the apartment as a whole, do you?"

"No. It's a bit too modern for me."

"Then redecorate it. You have unlimited funds now, my love." The sardonic twist of his lips disturbed her. What new product of his imagination was plaguing him? "Would you like to take a walk?" he suggested. "We're close to Central Park."

"Are you sure you're feeling—"

"I'm fine."

Zen opened her mouth to protest his rudeness, but the bullish expression on his face silenced her. "Yes, I'd like to take a walk," she said.

They got their coats and rode down in the elevator. As they approached Central Park, Zen saw that the trees were coming into full leaf. The greenery gave the park a fresh, bright look.

They wandered in silence along winding paths near the pond, watching the joggers and strollers who passed. Soon they left the park and headed down Fifth Avenue.

There was a cold bite in the air. Zen was upset to see a stern expression on his face. She took hold of his arm, tucking herself close to his side.

He looked down at her. "If you're cold, we can go back."

"No, I like to walk. In Ireland everyone walks. My hand was cold; that's all."

Damon's mouth softened, and he held her hand warmly. "I haven't walked in Manhattan in a long time. I forgot how beautiful New York is in the springtime."

"It's a wonderful city. I missed it when I was in Ireland."

"Was that all you missed?" His probing gaze told her he meant the question seriously.

"No, that's not all I missed." Zen felt as light as sunshine when he smiled at her.

"The fresh air has cleared my head," he admitted.

"Then it must have strong powers, indeed," Zen said, teasing. She looked up warily to find him chuckling.

"What a tongue you have. I must be masochistic to take you on for life."

"Is it for life?" she asked shyly. "Marriage is a very disposable item these days."

"Not ours." Damon tugged her close to his side so that their bodies bumped together gently.

All at once the spring air seemed ten degrees warmer. Zen felt welcoming heat penetrate to her very core.

Damon lifted his hand and hailed a taxi. They climbed inside.

"Where are we going?" Zen asked as he pulled her into his arms.

"Wait and see," he whispered into her ear. "We might as well enjoy the short time away from our sons. Don't you agree?"

"Yes." She smiled up at him, not caring where the cab was going as long as Damon was with her and he wasn't angry with her.

She glanced around her from the shelter of Damon's arms. "Oh, we're in Greenwich Village, aren't we. Isn't that Washington Square? Where . . . ?" She fell silent as the taxi pulled to the curb, and Damon helped her onto the sidewalk. She looked up at a sign over a store that said Village Deli.

"Do you remember when we came here?" Damon asked behind her.

"Yes." Zen leaned against him. "I had come into Manhattan on the bus from school. You met me and brought me here and fed me. Then you dropped me at your apartment because you had to go back to the office. That night—"

"We went to a show, then to a club to dance." Damon led her into the deli and ordered bagels and lox, coleslaw, and coffee. They sat on soda-fountain chairs at a miniscule table.

"I was very embarrassed because I had to wear a plain blouse and skirt to the show and the club." Zen closed her eyes as she forked coleslaw into her mouth.

"I thought you looked perfect." Damon offered her some salmon and laughed when she smacked her lips.

"I was very impressed by all the people who came up to speak to you and call by name," she said. "I had never seen so many celebrities before."

"I don't remember anyone except you." Damon rested his chin on his folded hands and stared at her. "You were a doll—too young for me but a doll."

"I wasn't too young for you," Zen said indignantly.

"I was twenty-eight and a man. I had finished school and already made my first million."

Zen stared into his dark eyes and forgot what she had intended to say in rebuttal.

"Why did you leave me?" His low words started her heart pounding. Suddenly the tone of the conversation had changed to one of utter seriousness.

"I...I..." Zen didn't have an answer. All at once she didn't know why she had left him—except that fear had chased her across the Atlantic.

"After you went to Ireland, my mother explained my aunt's part in sending you away. I directed all of my anger at you for running away from me, and my feelings toward her changed, too." Damon smiled at her. "How she hated the women in my life! I think that was part of the reason why she insisted on my writing to you." He shook his head. "I didn't want to ask you to come back. My pain had grown numb over the years, and I didn't want to open old wounds."

"I thought I hated you," Zen admitted painfully. "But when I came back and saw you, I knew I'd been lying to myself all that time."

"Let's get out of here."

They paid the bill and left quickly, hailing a cab to take them uptown.

"Have we been fools, Damon?" Zen whispered.

"Fifteen kinds of a fool, my love." He kissed her lingeringly, his mouth insistent, demanding.

"Damon..." Zen loved the feeling of being enveloped

in his arms. "When we were separated, I had nightmares that you would never hold me again, never love me. In my dreams I chased after you, called to you..." She looked up at him, and realized with surprise that there were tears on her cheeks.

"Zen, my darling, we'll never be separated again," Damon vowed, his arms tightening around her.

Chapter 10

THAT NIGHT THEY went to see a show, a rollicking, racy musical that made Zen laugh and tap her feet. After the show she and Damon were slow to leave their seats.

"Relax," Damon said. "It's raining. Everyone will be fighting for cabs. Once the crowd thins the car will be waiting to take us to Dominie's." Damon's eyes ran over Zen. "Not that I care to take you anywhere, dressed as you are. You look like a pink moonbeam." His dark eyes seemed to touch every part of her. "I would never have picked that color to go with your hair, but it looks great." He toyed with the cluster of curls that she'd swept behind her ear and fastened with a comb encrusted with pink crystal.

"I don't often wear rose, but Charine and your mother thought it would be a good color for me." Feeling shy under his intense gaze, Zen tried to smooth down the muted pink ruffles that decorated the knee-length hem of her strapless dress. The simple bodice was cut straight across the top of the bust. She wore medium-heeled silver sling-back shoes and carried a matching purse. She carried a crocheted lace shawl that one of Damon's great aunts had given her.

"You are the most beautiful woman in this theater, and if you weren't my wife already, I would seduce you and make you mine."

Zen's skin blushed as pink as her dress, and her eyes darted left and right to see if anyone had heard what Damon said. "You Greeks say the most outrageous things," she admonished her husband.

"I'm an American, as you are, my lovely wife." Damon caught her bottom lip with his teeth and nipped it gently.

"Stop. People are looking."

"Let them." Damon grinned at her, unrepentent.

A few moments later he rose and pulled her up with him, his hand tucked under her elbow. With great care he draped the shawl around her shoulders. "Will you be warm enough?"

Blue fire was coursing through her veins at his simple touch. Zen nodded. "I think I'll be comfortable."

Damon kissed her bare shoulder where the shawl had slipped. "Tell me if you're not. I'm more than willing to warm you."

"How kind of you," she said lightly, though her heart was pounding out of control.

They made their way past stragglers in the lobby to a cluster of people who were huddled under the marquee to keep dry.

Damon held her in the curve of his arm and peered up and down the street for the limousine. which cruised to a stop at the curb. The driver held the car door open directly under the canopy. They hurried into the warm, dry interior and settled gratefully against the leather seats.

Ensconced in Damon's arms, Zen was content to watch the rain streak down the window. They could drive to hell and back. She didn't care a long as she was with her husband.

Dominie's proved to be a popular club. People standing, sitting, and leaning everywhere. The dance floor, though larger than average, was packed.

"Good evening, Mr. Aristides. How nice to see you and—" The maître d's plastic smile barely faltered as he tried to remember Zen's name.

"Good evening, Leonard. This is my wife, Mrs. Aristides. Darling, meet Leonard." Damon's introduction was cool, almost aloof.

The maître d' led them to a booth screened by a row of plants. "Your table, Mr. Aristides," Leonard said stiffly.

Zen let her shawl fall from her shoulders to her elbows. "He sensed that you're angry with him. Is it because you wanted him to be more discreet, and not act taken aback because you weren't with one of your... er...friends?" She rested her chin in her hands and watched as he stared out at the dancing couples.

"Yes." He turned toward her. "And damn you for realizing that, Xenobia. I don't relish having a wife who reads my mind."

"And I don't like the fact that you've come here before with other women," Zen retorted.

A waiter arrived with mineral water for her and whisky for Damon.

"But I couldn't forget you, Xenobia." Damon stared into his drink, then reached over and took a sip of hers. "Ummm, that's good. After last night, that's probably what I should be drinking." He looked askance at her. "Do you think I'm trying to change the subject?"

Zen laughed. "Yes, but at least we're talking. About how we feel, how we react to each other." She shrugged. "I consider that a move in the right direction."

Damon entwined her fingers with his. "I won't tell you about all the women I had when we were apart. I will tell you, though, that I tried everything, every trick I could think of, to blot you from my mind. I hated not being able to. It made me feel weak. I woke up in the middle of the night with your face filling my mind, your name on my lips."

"And another woman in your bed." Zen finished for him. But her words held no censure. She understood a little better now the demons he had been fighting.

"Yes," Damon admitted. "And another woman in my bed." He lifted his glass and tipped some whisky down his throat. "I wanted those women to mean something to me. I wanted to find a woman, any woman, I could take home to mother and marry. I thought I didn't give a damn who she was...but I couldn't bring myself to do it."

They sat in thoughtful silence. When the waiter returned, Damon ordered a light supper of broiled prawns on a bed of endive. They drank a sharp, crisp Riesling.

After they had eaten, Damon squeezed Zen's hand. "Shall we dance?" he suggested. "Please."

As she followed Damon to the floor, Zen remembered a younger Zen Driscoll going to a club with Damon and dancing all night. How surprised and pleased she had been to discover that he knew all the latest steps.

Now Damon held her close, and they moved together to the slow, sensuous rhythm. When the tempo changed to a tango, Zen shook her head and laughed, "I've never danced the tango," she protested. But Damon led her effortlessly and twirled her dramatically. Zen laughed breathlessly as he swung her away from him then pulled her back.

"Haven't you ever tangoed, my love?" Damon asked, grinning at her. "You do it very well." He guided her with firm but light pressure.

She could feel every muscle in his thighs as he held her. "My goodness," she exclaimed.

"A very sensual dance, isn't it?" Damon laughed down at her, his eyes twinkling.

"Damon Aristides, you should be ashamed of yourself." Despite their recent openness with each other, Zen felt a stab of envy at the thought of the other women who had enjoyed her husband's skillful dancing.

He leaned close to her as the music slowed to a ballad. "I was never quite as aware of a woman's body as I am tonight, my angel," he muttered into her hair. "However much I wanted a woman, I was never in danger of losing control. With you I'm never in control." He paused to maneuver around another couple. "Did you want many men when we were apart?" At her skeptical look, he added, "I'm being masochistic tonight, as Greeks often are." He sighed. "I want to hear—but I don't want to hear."

Zen met his smoldering gaze. "There were several men. I liked their company. I might have married Seamus eventually. He likes David very much, and he would have been kind to me. But I saw marriage to Seamus as something that would happen in the future." Zen wrapped her arms around his neck. "We're married now. We have advantages other married people don't have. We've had our baptism of fire. We won't be quick to part."

"We will never part, Xenobia, no matter what happens." Damon seemed to be all around her, enveloping her in a sense of warmth and protection.

Just then, an all-too-familiar voice carried across the room. "Damon," Cherry Crawford caroled. "How sweet! You brought your bride to Dominie's. Did she want to meet all your former mistresses, darling?"

"Not all of them Cherry," Damon drawled, "just a few."

Zen leaned against his chest, loving the steady beat of his heart under her cheek. She regarded Cherry with indifference, content to let Damon lead where once she would have demanded independence. Where once she would have demanded to be heard, now she was content to wait in silence.

"Carter and I will join you," Cherry said, turning away. "I know where your table is."

Damon's body stiffened under Zen's hand. "Shhh, don't worry," she said. "We won't be staying long anyway." She smiled up at him, feeling lazy and confident.

A look of amazement furrowed Damon's brow. Then his tough-tender smile transformed his face, moving her almost to tears. "You don't give a damn if she joins us, do you?" he said softly.

"I don't care if she invites the whole world to our

door. We'll always be alone if we choose to be, won't we?"

"Yes, my love," Damon's eyes stayed fixed on hers.

"Damon, lean down. You're so tall, you know, and I want to whisper to you." Zen chuckled, then stroked him when she felt him stiffen at the sound. "I love you, Damon—desperately, totally, completely. I've loved you since the first moment we met at Eleni's and Davos's wedding rehearsal." She laughed again, pressing her nail into his chin. "I laughed last night because I was so happy." She paused and glanced around her. Damon had eyes only for her. "I'll tell you more later when we're alone, shall I?" she suggested with an impish grin.

"Please." Damon kissed her forehead.

"We should sit down. People are staring at us." Zen struggled to control an insane desire to laugh out loud.

"Will you believe me if I tell you that I've loved you since before you loved me?" Damon grinned at her open mouth and began to lead her from the floor.

"How can that be?"

"I have something to tell you later, too," he replied, laughing now, too.

"Keep careful watch on me or I might put something in Cherry's drink to get rid of her." Zen muttered just as they reached the table.

"Darling Damon, how nice to hear you laughing like that." Cherry bared her teeth in an insincere smile. "You know Carter Siddons, don't you?"

"Siddons," Damon nodded. "This is my wife, Xenobia Aristides. Darling, you know Cherry, and this is Carter Siddons."

"How do you do." Zen was about to slide into the booth, but Cherry stopped her.

"Do let Damon sit here, Zen. I refuse to call you that horribly ponderous name that Damon calls you. But I'm sure you understand that Damon and I have so much to say to each other."

But Damon's firm hand on Zen's arm, kept her at his side. He gestured to the waiter. "Please bring them whatever they choose and put it on my tab," he instructed.

He reached for Zen's shawl. "So sorry, but Zen and I are tired." Damon smiled at tight-lipped Cherry and affable-looking Carter. "Have a nice evening." The bored look on his face made Zen bite her lip to hold back a grin.

They left hand in hand. Their wide smiles earned a wary glance from the maître d'.

"Leonard thinks we're smashed," Zen said as she and Damon waited for their car to arrive.

"I feel more drunk than I ever have in my life."

On the way home Zen sang a song in Irish.

"What does it mean?" Damon asked, cuddling her.

"Oh, like most Irish songs, it's about life, death, and eternal love. The Irish are so romantic." Zen yawned.

"Are you tired?" Damon's voice held a note of disappointment.

"Not a bit. Just so relaxed that I feel as if my bones have collapsed." She looked up at him. "You've set me free, Damon. How many free people do you know?"

"Do you mean how many people do I know who are in love?" Damon asked her.

"Wise man." Zen rested her head on his chest, feeling so protected, so cared for, yet so strong and unencumbered. "It's really too bad that there are no more dragons to be slain. I could handle two of them tonight, with one hand tied behind my back."

"A lady knight." Damon sounded amused.

When the car pulled up in front of their apartment building, Zen followed Damon out of the vehicle and turned to face the driver. "Thank you for the lovely ride. It was wonderful."

The driver nodded seriously. "Thank *you*, ma'am." He doffed his cap and drove away as Damon and Zen strolled into the foyer.

"He thinks I'm tipsy." Zen clamped a hand over her mouth to smother her laughter.

"He doesn't understand that you've discovered the fountain of all happiness," Damon said, ushering her into the elevator.

"You." Zen twined her arms around his waist.

"Darling, do you know that you make me feel very humble?" The elevator doors opened to their apartment, and they wandered into the living room. "I feel as if I should pay the national debt or do something equally grand. I have so much to pay back. Do you understand what I mean?"

"I know exactly what you mean." Zen threw her arms wide. "Sometimes you feel guilty for having found so much love when you know how rare it is. Yet love is the common denominator of life, the most basic thing there is." She whirled to face Damon. "Are we getting philosophical?" she asked, her eyes wide.

"We are." He answered sagely. He led her to the couch and pressed the button to open it into the mammoth bed. His eyes fused on her body and surveyed her slowly, sending white heat pulsing through her. "You look glorious," he said huskily.

"I should hope so." Zen laughed, then clapped a hand over her mouth again. "I'm trying not to laugh, but love has a weird effect on me. All the tittering, smirking, giggling that I didn't do all those years we were apart is spilling out of me. You see"—she took a deep breath to steady herself—"love is strange. It makes you look glorious. It makes you chortle like a teenager. But"—she held up an index finger—"only if you're loved back." Her bottom lip began to tremble. "Last night I realized that Damon Aristides loves me." She shrugged one bare shoulder, bringing Damon's gaze to it. "I couldn't handle such a momentous realization." She blinked at Damon. "Did you ever laugh at something foolish and keep on laughing, not because your foolishness was funny but because your insides were celebrating? Mine were celebrating the stupendous revelation that you loved me." The words were pouring out of her. "Until that moment, I thought I could live without your loving me. Then I discovered that . . . that you pull the sun up in the morning for me, that the moon is full because you touch me." She took another shaky breath. "Now do you understand why . . . why I was laughing?"

Damon looked at her, unable to speak, a dark red

staining his cheeks. "Will you be my wife?" he asked finally.

Zen chuckled. "I am your wife, silly."

"I'm going to ask you that question every day for the rest of our lives, Xenobia Driscoll Aristides."

He swept her up in his arms and stepped into the middle of the bed, sat down, and held her on his lap. "Now, where were we? Ah, yes. I was just thinking about kissing your knee. Have I told you, my love, that you have sexy knees?"

Zen giggled and cuddled closer to him, closing her eyes in rapture as his tongue touched the back of her leg. "No, but you must tell me that every day, too. Oh, I'm going to love being married to you." Her eyes popped open when he fell still beside her.

He was regarding her intently. "On your birthday— I think it was when you turned twenty-six and you had been gone a year—I was here in my apartment alone, preparing to get drunk, as I did every year on your birthday."

"You did?" Zen grieved for the pain he had suffered. She cradled his head against her. "I won't let you be hurt anymore."

His tongue caressed her shoulders. "There's nothing in this world that can destroy me if you stay with me, my love."

"Me, too." Zen gazed at him with a solemn promise in her eyes. Then her mouth curved in a smile.

"Here comes Chuckles the Clown again," Damon murmured, easing her onto her back in the bed, his grin widening when she began to giggle. "You are my love challenge," he said.

"Do you think you can make me stop laughing?"

Damon's soft smile conveyed a hunger she was eager to satisfy. "I will enjoy the challenge, my darling albatross."

"What?" Zen struggled to a sitting position. "What are you saying? You're *my* albatross, not the other way around, Damon."

"So you told me at the cottage one night in your sleep.

Whether I stay or leave you, you said, I'm your albatross." In one gentle motion, he pulled her bodice down to bare her breasts. "Ummm, so lovely . . . so tasty." He leaned over to suck her nipple.

"Yeeek! Damon Aristides, stop it. We're talking," Zen moaned.

"So talk, darling. I won't stop you." Damon put his arms around her waist as he shifted to the other breast.

"Did I really talk in my sleep?" Zen ran her fingers through his hair.

"Many times. You were often restless, my sweet, so I held you. The night I read "The Rime of the Ancient Mariner" to the boys, you called me your albatross in your sleep."

"I thought about it when I woke up, too—how the bird flew around the ship and the winds filled the sails, then the bird was killed and the winds died and bad luck followed the Mariner." Damon's arms tightened on her. "Without you, nothing went well in my life. Oh, it carried on. David made me happy, my career was satisfying. But there was no luster, no freedom, no deep delight, no joy." Zen grew frustrated as she tried to express her feelings to Damon. "What's the matter with me? I talk constantly these days."

"Go on, my darling." Damon kissed her navel. "I love hearing that I'm important to you."

"Important? What a milksop word! Try intrinsic to my life, indigenous to my being," Zen expostulated, then giggled. "I'm doing it again, philosophizing." She looked up at him. "How many of the women you made love to also expounded on philosophy?"

"Not more than ten." Damon chuckled when she punched his arm.

"Damon," Zen said, "what were you going to tell me about getting drunk on my twenty-sixth birthday?"

Damon rolled over onto his back, placing his head in her lap. "My mother had been nagging me to get you to bring David back to see her. As usual, I told her that I felt it was up to you to make the first move.

Well, that night, as I opened my bottle of whisky and prepared to drown my sorrows, it suddenly hit me that I had no chance of ever having you again as long as you were in Ireland, that you might even marry over there, and then you would be completely lost to me. In that moment I decided I would fight, fair or foul, to get you—and that I would win." He looked up at her and fell silent.

She leaned over him, letting her red-gold hair drape around him. "And what did you mean when you said that you loved me first?"

"I like this," he whispered, "being curtained by your hair. I've never felt so secure. We're good for each other, aren't we, my love."

"Tell me," Zen urged, her fingers caressing his face.

"When Eleni and Davos began dating, you must have been about seventeen or eighteen. I was down at the dock with my boat when they asked to go sailing with me. Eleni was always a good sport about doing whatever Davos wanted. She sailed even though I don't think she liked it."

"She didn't," Zen recalled.

"On this particular day we jibed unexpectedly, and Eleni's purse slid across the deck. Her wallet fell out, open to a picture of a woman in a bikini, and I asked who it was. It was you. Eleni and Davos were so busy gathering her belongings before they blew away that they didn't notice when I pocketed the picture."

"You did?" Zen's nerve endings hummed with joy.

Damon reached for the jacket he had tossed aside. He fumbled through his wallet and drew out a worn snapshot of a younger Zen, smiling directly into the camera. He dumped his wallet upside down, and other pictures of her fell onto the bed, photos of her in her early twenties, then a newspaper picture of her just before she left for Ireland.

"This was all I had of the woman I loved," he said hoarsely. "I was ashamed of loving an eighteen-year-old girl, but I did love you. I saw you at nineteen when you

swam in the state meet in college. I went alone to watch
you. I wanted you even then."

"I wish I'd known that."

"Oh, God," Damon groaned, kissing the inner curve
of her breast. "I didn't want you to know then. No one
ever knew. And when I met you through Davos and
Eleni, I pretended it was the first time I'd seen you."

They fell into a long, thoughtful silence as Zen as-
similated this new knowledge of him.

"Damon, your mother approached me once during the
court battle to take David to Ireland. But I thought it was
to castigate me further. I was young and raw with loving
you. I see now that she might have been trying to mend
fences."

"I forgave her long ago, because I saw how upset she
was about what my Aunt Dalia said to you. But I ignored
all of her pleas to get in touch with you. I don't know
why. I guess I was too stubborn and proud to admit that
I'd been wrong to let you go away. Then, when you
returned from Ireland, I was determined to move heaven
and earth if need be to win you back." He chuckled. "I
must say, working through David was simpler."

"Devious man."

He nodded, his thick hair tickling her bare breasts.
"Angel, your pink dress is getting badly wrinkled. Let
me take it off you. After all, I'll want to see you in this
gown many more times. Of course, only when we're
dining alone."

"Silly," Zen cooed, lifting her arms so that he could
ease the dress over her head. She was wearing a half-
slip of pink silk, pink silk panties, and a pink garter belt
and stockings. Damon's eyes were riveted to her. Her
hand touching his arm recalled him from his contempla-
tion of her.

"Would you hire me as your lady's maid?" he asked.

"Job sharing," Zen said dreamily. "I'll be your valet,
and you can be my maid. What's a fair salary?"

"No salary, just fringe benefits." Damon swallowed
hard as he unhooked each garter and rolled the stockings
down her legs.

"Is this what the well-dressed wife of Damon Aristides should wear? Dangling earrings and nothing else?" Zen giggled as Damon urged her down on the bed and stretched out next to her.

"Yes. Now, about me making you stop laughing . . ." Damon had a devilish leer on his face as his mouth moved closer and smothered the chortle just escaping her lips. His tongue filled her mouth, tangling playfully with hers. His hands skimmed over her, reacquainting themselves with each dip and curve of her body. He sought out each pleasure spot, and she gasped when he touched her, first with his hands, then with his mouth.

"Damon . . ." She heard her voice as if from far away. It seemed to belong to someone else entirely. She opened her eyes to find his black gaze drawing her into a sensual vortex.

Sensation upon sensation built within her in an exquisite crescendo. She was lost in him, one with him, enveloped and overwhelmed by him, body and soul. Again and again he caressed her flesh to throbbing readiness, then calmed his touch and soothed her restless yearning, only to build it to fever pitch once more.

At last, their bodies damp and straining, he moved to take complete possession of her. His thrusts were slow and powerful and made her cry out with every stroke. She clung to his shoulders like a drowning person to a lifeline in a turbulent sea.

As he moved faster and faster within her, she lost all sense of herself.

She was climbing steadily on a still sharper ascent. There, everything stood still, teetering on a splendid brink, pausing in breathless ecstasy. And then she tumbled, tumbled, and was flung high up on a dry beach, still clutching Damon in her arms.

Long moments later, side by side, nose to nose, Damon whispered, "Now I understand why you laughed. I hadn't realized how much joy was bottled up in me, my love." He shook his head. "I'd watched you with the boys and felt such a complete happiness, especially the day you were trying to head the ball in soccer."

"What do you mean, trying?" Zen's eyes flashed.

"You were good," he assured her. "And no wonder, since you were such a tomboy when you were young." Damon rubbed her back.

"And you know all about that because you were there for some of it."

"Yes, I was there. Whenever I could drive upstate, I attended your meets. And no one knew, not even you."

"Maybe I knew deep inside. I used to wish that I had parents who were watching me. Sometimes I would imagine that the cheering was for me. Did you cheer?"

"Oh, yes, my dove, I cheered." Damon pulled her onto his chest. "Shall we take a shower?"

"Together?"

"Of course. You're my wife, and I'm not letting you out of my sight."

"Good plan." She allowed him to pull her up.

He was momentarily distracted by her bouncing breasts. "I like it when they do that," he said.

Zen shook her head. "I do feel sorry for the women that David and Daniel put their eye on, because I think they are just like you."

"Do you?" Damon preened, flexing his muscles, drawing her eyes to his body. "Good. Then I hope they find someone just like you, someone to drive them mad." He swept her into his arms and headed toward the bathroom.

On the way, Zen spied a bronze sculpture on a Sheraton table. "Oh, how beautiful!" She scooped up the bronze as Damon walked past and began to examine its intricate detail. But her movements caused Damon to lose stride and stagger. He jostled Zen in his arms, and her tenuous grip on the sculpture loosened. The statue slipped from her fingers. "Oh!" Zen gasped.

"Aaaaagh! Xenobia, my toe!" yelled her naked husband, putting her down abruptly.

"Oh, darling, are you hurt?" she cried. "Oh, let me see. Oh, dear, your toe is so red." Zen tried to get a

closer look as Damon hopped around on one foot, holding
the other foot in his hand.

"Don't you dare... call it an accident," he warned
her, wincing in pain.

Once Zen was sure Damon was all right, she had a
hard time containing the laughter that was bursting inside
her. She clapped a hand to her mouth.

Damon glared at her as she ran from the room to find
some soothing ointment. "Damn you, Xenobia," he
shouted. "That had better not be laughter I hear. My toe
hurts."

Zen returned moments later, still as naked as her glowering husband. "I don't suppose you'll believe that I love
you more than anything or anybody in the whole wide
world," she said, kneeling in front of him to rub his toe.

"Oh, yes, I believe that. I just don't believe you will
ever get over this propensity to do me harm." Damon
pulled her to her feet. "Forget the toe. It isn't broken,
and the shower will feel good on it." His eyes glinted
with sensual mirth. "Our grandchildren will be horrified
to hear how you tried to murder me on our honeymoon,
strutting around unclothed and sexy."

"Then I'll tell them the terrible effect you have on
me." Zen hesitated, caught by his hot gaze. Her mind
went blank. "I forgot what I was going to say," she
admitted.

They walked into the bathroom side by side, their
arms around each other.

In the shower they began a game of love that continued
in the bedroom.

"Do you want to eat?" Damon asked some time later
as he lay sprawled next to Zen on the bed.

She regarded him lovingly. "I don't need food when
I have you. You nourish me." The smile faded from her
face as he continued to caress her. "You're my vitamins
and minerals," she murmured.

"And you are all things to me, my albatross love,"
Damon muttered into her neck.

"No..." Zen's words were hoarse. "You're *my* albatross love."

All through the night their sensual discussion continued, neither one wanting to end it.